The Secret of

The Lost Island

By

David C. Filax

Also published works:
The Nefarious Mr. X (2012)

This book is dedicated to the two little children, Danica and Hayden, whose birth on the same day inspired my characters.

As for the rest of the story, that comes from the dark rivers of my mind.

- David C. Filax

And to one well read editor, Leanne Hart, who makes my book a better read.

- David C. Filax

"Some things were never meant to be found."
- Carlos Santiago.

All characters appearing in this work are fictitious. Any resemblance to real persons, living or dead, is purely coincidental.

1

March 23rd, 1866

The storm was riding high in the sky, a tempest of gusting winds and torrential rain blending in a violent mix of raging weather and nature's fury. The clouds were as dark as smoke, massive formations of grey fog with long tornado shaped tendrils which reached out and gripped the spring daylight in its shadowy embrace. The air stunk of electricity and ozone, as though having been belched forth from an angry volcano, spewing its hot and venomous billows of dense coughs into the air at not having a fine young virgin tossed into its molten stomach. Streaks of lightening and roars of thunder rode the ripples of condensation in a rollercoaster display of power and madness running along the skyline.

For an early afternoon, the sun was shielded from the world below, surrounding the ocean's horizon with a twilight pall of blue and purple gloom. The dark sky was traced below by a horizon of undulating water as the ocean surged, splashed and fumed in large troughs and bows, pushing powerfully at the ship's wales with its massive walls of thrusting aquatic force.

The rain swept like a blanket across the bow of the ship, covering all it touched, as the wind tore across the deck in long powerful gales, sending shockwaves of energy throughout the sails as the ship rocked and rode the waves seeking purchase and dominion, but most importantly, remaining afloat.

The first mast on the ship pulled and thrust with defiance, fighting an invisible tug of war with Mother Nature. And with the ferocity for which the wooden boards creaked and groaned in pain, this poor man-made vessel had to assume the mistress of the sea had lost her temper and was having a tantrum.

On the deck, salt and sea spraying across his face, the air gusting past his brow, rustling the coarse hairs of his thick and well kept beard, steadfastly refusing to leave the helm, stood the invincible Captain Estefan Rodriguez Rios.

Master and lord of this ship.

He had both hands on the wheel, large meaty paws with thick hairy fingers, gripping the bar with power, held firm but with a loving embrace, as the Captain did not blame the fighting controls on the ship. He blamed it on the ocean. Holding steadfast to his position to which he was committed, he refused to give in. No woman had tamed him before today, and the sea herself would not be the first.

He stood at six two with broad shoulders and chest which seemed could bear the weight of the ship itself if forced to get out and carry his vessel out of these raging waters on his back. His tanned skin, pock-marked from a minor smallpox outbreak in 1856, was ruggedly handsome, bronzed by many days at sunny seas, and icy blue eyes which could make most mutineers dive over the sides in fear to suffer the fate of the deep as opposed to his fury.

At his waist to his right, he wore his 1805 Harper Ferry Flintlock pistol, a gift from a soldier he saved from the seas years before when the man's ship was taken by pirates and he was tossed overboard. It was a .54 caliber gun known for its single shot capacity, and the

Captain only needed one based on his marksmanship. He carried it always with him for luck.

However his weapon of choice was his finely crafted and constantly cleaned sword. A single handed Navy Cutlass with a 27 7/8" blade, leather handle with an iron forged basket hilt for smooth motion, easy gripping and more importantly, resting his hand upon when strapped to his left side, in its sheath, waiting to be drawn, to make the Captain appear intimidating as though it could be pulled and swung in seconds.

His greatest feature, and his favourite, a fully brushed beard and mustache which rode long and heavy over his face, from ear to ear, to the middle of his chest. He kept it cleaned daily, brushed lovingly by himself, curled in many areas, causing him to be known as 'Brown-beard' to his crew.

Rios loved his facial mane, as he felt it gave him sustenance. Many a day he could be found running his fingers through it, slowly, constantly and gracefully. It was his tell during the course of ship inspections. With a quiet revere, when noting ship reviews and orders, the crew knew they would find his left hand pulling through it when he was pleased and his right when something needed correction.

Rios always knew the right course, or best decision, after he touched his hairy oracle, as though some divine answer could always be found hidden in the dark folds and strands.

Like Samson, his hair gave him strength and no Delilah would free him of this gift without the loss to her life.

Rios stared straight ahead, focused and determined, yelling forth in his mind to the sea. *'My Love. Why so angry? What can I do this night for you to give us clear way?'*

All seamen and sailors are a superstitious lot with good reason.

When the sea chose to have a spasm, boats and crews could vanish in seconds, without a trace, forever lost, drawn down into the cruel and cold folds of the water's depths.

So be vigilant, be skilled, but most of all, be wary as the sea cannot be predicted or trusted.

Tonight, if Rios could help it, its hunger for more souls would be sedated.

Rios knew this large sea faring craft better than any, from its one hundred and eighty six foot long body to its wooden beams which rode fifty feet high on the water. She held a depth of twenty one feet and had a displacement of over two thousand burthens when fully stocked.

Any good Captain knew about his ship when placing his trust and faith in her, especially when living in her belly for as long as he had. Such devotion was not given blindly. He could tell the men how many slats made up the deck, how many scratches on the rudder and how many ropes it took to hold her steady. She, the ship, and him, were one and the same and like any woman, needed his constant love and attention to ensure fury was not reined upon them.

Hell hath no fury like a woman scorned.

Rios' ship had three primary masts and a square rig. It had an armament of one hundred guns, always ready and waiting for a possible attack, with a complement of eight hundred with thirty men under his command and space for twenty more.

Her sister ship, the Victory, was laid down in 1759 in the Chatham Dockyard and launched in 1765.

Rios' ship, the Serenade as she was called, was launched in 1772 still riding strong to this day.

With such a ship, usually British Captains took the helm, but Rios' reputation and history in helping the royal family earned him much respect and rewards over the years, which included this berth.

He was awarded this ship by royal declaration, something no seaman would ever argue, especially with their Queen, Victoria.

Rios spun the wheel and used his keen sense of the sea to follow the valley of waves, deftly and smoothly moving between their rises and falls with ease and control, knowing the sea was not after his ship this night as had she wanted it, take it she would.

The night was long and stress filled. Rios and his men repeatedly had the sails pulled and raised, from the head to the foot of the sail, to take benefit of wind gusts, bursts and opportunities, but tenderly to ensure the weight of the water did not tear the tightly woven material into shreds leaving them at God's mercy.

The men dragged hard, keeping ropes pulled taut on the masts, but also tied about their bodies and to posts to ensure they were not brushed overboard in the storm and lost.

As time wore on, like any rage, eventually, it subsided.

The winds dissipated, the clouds in the sky lessened, and the sun seemed to melt the fury of the sea's anger, warming her heart and soul, reminding her of the good times, and inviting her to let sailors pass.

Rios smiled openly, having won yet another battle.

Within minutes of the storm's departure, his first officer joined him on deck, Scott MacTaggart, a fine Scotsman, with a five foot eleven height, thick build and a mane of red hair that seemed his scalp was constantly on fire. Unlike his Captain, his face was free of furry obstructions, as smooth as a baby's bottom as he liked to mention.

And liked Rios like to retort. *'And why would any man want to look like a baby's bottom. It was usually always full of shit.'*

This would always be followed by deep bellied laughs, clanking canteens of lager and joviality. This was how it was when living at sea.

McTaggart knew the seas better than most, and had Rios lost his maps, compass and the stars above, he knew, MacTaggart would still find the way home.

He nodded to his trusted crewman as he departed the deck to clean himself up and dry off.

****

A few hours later, Rios returned.

His clothes were clean, his hair dry and his weapons on his sides, at ready. He wore a heavy wool vest over a thin white smock which kept him cool at the extremities, but his chest warm in the chilly sea winds. He had come forth from his cabin and took a deep cleansing breath, filled with salty air and freshness, which invigorated his lungs, skin and his entire body.

He loved the morning after a storm.

Rios nodded to his first officer who maintained the helm at a steady pace.

The sun was high in the sky, the clouds dissipating as though they never existed, and his crew were working hard and diligently to clean the outer ship, dry the decks, examine the hull for damage, secure the masts and review the sails for any tears or rips caused from the night previous that would slow this massive vehicle in its course.

Rios had a fine crew and ones he would trust his life with.

For the past few months, they had delivered a large selection of supplies to the New World, but on the return home, they chose to sail South for the pleasure of it, running along the coasts, searching for new things, and to sail the waters blue.

Most Captains may have a schedule, and orders from their owners, but sometimes, the sea simply called forth, *'Come play with me for a while.'*

And no Captain ever disappointed his mistress.

Owners and companies were bureaucrats with money. People with rubber stamps and ledgers dictating dates and deliveries to their employees. But they, like true sea legged men, knew the sea was beyond control, sometimes slowed movement, caused delays and prevented expedience, which allowed many Captains the opportunity to enjoy the fruits of the seas.

This little tour South was one such dalliance.

As Rios moved up and down the upper quadrants of his ship, examining the damage, a young lieutenant, Thomas Tatum, no more than twenty three, with blond hair, thin build and green eyes which always seemed filled with awe in Rios' presence, intruded on the Captain's inspection.

"Sir?" He spoke so sheepishly, he seemed like he would lose the oxygen in his lungs if he kept talking. "Captain Rios?"

Rios wanted his men to feel comfortable around him, able to talk to him as both a friend, but also a confidante, but always knowing he was still their commander.

However some, no matter how hard he tried, remained intimidated by his rank and stature, which by nature, was hard to overcome for new sailors.

Rios turned, brushing his beard with his left hand, to indicate to the man he was in a good mood.

The sailor, Thomas to his mates, smiled at the gesture. "Sir. We have a ship on the starboard bow."

Rios seemed undaunted by this. "Not hard to imagine with this storm. We may see a few more." He looked across the seascape. "I'm rather pleased at having more than one vessel make it through last night's exhibition."

Thomas paused, seeming to rethink his statement and what to say, but then, knowing what he had seen, offered the truth anyway.

Rios liked that in a sailor. Stand up for yourself as no one else would offer.

Thomas began. "Yes. But I've been watching her through the telescope for the past hour." He paused. "McTaggart let me use it."

Rios sighed inwardly, sad the seaman thought he had to justify why he used ship's equipment.

Thomas continued. "And there appears to be no one on their deck."

At this Rios seemed amused. "Young man. Be assured, even had God himself come down from the heavens to throw water at that ship, there would be someone on the deck to slosh it back off."

Turning in the direction of port, out in the distance, Thomas stared. He waited a few seconds before offering a reply. Once he felt a long enough time had passed, Thomas offered, "In that, I would agree *Sir*." He stressed 'Sir.'

Another pause.

'Nervousness was a bane this man would have to deal with.' Rios thought.

Thomas completed his report. "But I never let my eyes leave her. For the past hour, no one has moved, wandered or even opened a shutter to look out. That and she is heading South, with the tide, not changing the course. From what I see, the ship appears to be adrift."

At this, Rios was now intrigued. He never suspected a crewman to lie, especially about something so easily disproven, and an abandoned ship at sea was always a welcome prize.

Presuming he could convince the crew to go aboard.

Many of them would see an abandoned ship at sea as a ghost ship, a devil ridden scourge to bait unwary sailors, not unlike the Flying Dutchman, travelling the ocean for all who see her to be doomed to damnation.

Rios was not a man who succumbed to such fairytales, believing such things as sea monsters, sea devils or the like.

But then again, because he never saw one before never meant they did not exist.

Rios followed the young Thomas to the helm where he was handed the telescope by the quartermaster. When fully extended, three shafts, the scope could see almost anywhere.

In the distance, Rios spotted her. All ships were a 'her' in his eyes.

Another ship floating on the water.

He recognized her design.

As a Captain of the British Royal Navy, it was his duty to know such things.

It reminded him of the famous frigate from the War of 1812. A ship which due to the American battle, forced the British to build two comparable ships, the Newcastle and the Leander, each of sixty guns, built from fir wood and double banked with massive gun decks.

Sadly, they were built with a soft wood for short term use, which in the eyes of this Captain, was a travesty.

'If you built her to ride the seas, she should be created to last.' He thought.

Equally as sad, these ships were built to initiate and instill hostilities, not maintain peacetime establishment.

As Rios maintained his offsite inspection, he determined, unlike the Newcastle, this vessel appeared to have a length of one hundred and eighty feet, at least based on his first estimates. He could also see three solid masts and a square rig, not unlike his own, with an armament of sixty guns to her sides as expected.

None were at ready, aimed or set to fire.

And like the Serenade, it too appeared to have been battered by the night's storm, but in a worse way. Her sails seemed torn and misshapen, like they were left aloft to bear the brunt of the storm without adjustments or control. Her deck was a mess of debris, which no good Captain would tolerate.

When Rios yelled, "Swab the Decks" he damn well meant it. It not being done was followed by quick and heavy pulls with his right hand on his beard. This was their home, so clean it they shall.

But also unlike Rios' ship, this one was riding higher on the water, unhampered by weight, dampened at many points as Rios could see the sun reflecting off puddles which had formed in areas. She seemed forlorn and lilting, yet luckily still afloat.

And exactly as Thomas had pointed out. Not a single soul was in sight.

'How very, very strange.' Rios thought. Then projecting the question in his mind to the ship. *'Who are you and why are you here?'*

Rios turned to his first officer. "Steer us a course toward that ship. She seems to be in need of assistance."

McTaggart was wary, as Scotsmen were even more superstitious than the normal sailor, on the waters and beyond. He asked, cautiously. "Is that a good idea Captain?"

Rios replied. "It's the rule of the sea. You always help a ship in need."

McTaggart adjusted his course, deep in his mind, thinking. *'God help us all if she is in need of fresh blood.'*

****

They circled the ship once, which was easy as the silent craft was drifting along under very little momentum.

McTaggart pointed out right away when he spotted it. "The anchor appears to have been cut free."

Rios looked out in the direction McTaggart was staring.

The mooring line was indeed shredded and torn, dangling halfway up the side of the ship, the anchor having fallen free from its weakened leash. As Rios could plainly see, it had not been smoothly cut either. It was not like it was sliced by a broadsword, nor an axe, but it appeared as though it had been hacked off, or even bitten off by a sea creature, which had chewed with such ferocity on the ship's lines, it only escaped with the anchor, leaving the rest of the ship barely scathed.

Rios had them drop anchor on her starboard side.

Rios commanded the crew take station on the rails and rope his ship to the opposing ship's side, positioning planks between the two seagoing vessels for his crew to cross over.

Once side by side, ships parallel to one another, bridges built, made for easy access, Rios stared across, his right hand brushing his beard.

His deck was now overloaded with sailors, crew, mess staff, a few soldiers and many of those who had spent the night in battle with Rios fighting the storm, though thoroughly exhausted, they all wanted to see what had led them to this abandoned vessel.

Rios chose a team of his ten strongest men, hardened sailors with rock solid demeanors, excellent reflexes and good temperaments, which when facing the unknown was an asset some explorers did not have.

The armory master, Lt. Curtis Corn, was an older British soldier with pure white hair, green eyes and a small stature. However, his size was nothing compared to the vast stores of knowledge that filled his mind on weapons of any sort. If it could be used to kill, he understood its design, power and use. Corn had a gift to always know which tool, as they were all tools in his mind, as the user made it the weapon, was best fitted for which man. Arming a man with something he could not wield was paramount to shooting him yourself Corn always commented.

Corn outfitted the ten men with pistols and swords, easy to draw, and quick to parry.

Not Rios as he preferred his own.

Corn provided an equal complement of rifles and muskets to a team of twenty more men who would stay stationed on the Serenade, drawn and aimed at the mysterious ship, ready to fire in case anything occurred for which Rios' team was unprepared.

The ship's doctor, Samuel LaFleur, also asked to come aboard. He was a soft spoken Frenchman with a tight pile of short black hair on his scalp, brushed gently into a neat style. He had a solid swimmer's physique, which was well hidden by his long sleeved shirts, matching pants and high top leather boots. He had a small and feminine face with rounded edges, brown eyes and delicate hands which were perfect when performing surgeries or saving the crew.

Rios and his team crossed over slowly, wobbling over the man-made bridges as the waves still rocked the ships up and down, making the walkways move with them.

Some of his men occasionally looked back at the troops and past them, to the men leaned up against the rails on the other side, trying to put as much distance between them and this ship as they could.

Not only had they refused to go aboard, they remained fearful that this was an omen of sorts. An evil dirge brought forth from Hell's depths, running on a crew of unseen demons, tricking sailors aboard to be taken into slavery for an eternity of damnation on the high seas.

McTaggart disagreed, as he theorized, it could be the lost family of Alexander Sawney Bean, set sail on the dark waters, hunting new prey to this day, seeking supplies in the form of unwary sailors.

Beane was believed to have been the legendary head of a forty eight member clan of incestuous and cannibalistic family members, who over twenty five years, off the Ayrshire and Galloway coast, killed and ate what was rumoured to be thousands of Scotsman.

To that Rios replied, "If I find myself someone's dinner, I hope they choke on my bones and my alcohol laced liver spoils the stew."

McTaggart was not sedated by that.

Rios would never force a man to do something he feared, but he made them all very aware, of those of the crew who refused to join the expedition or help move any of the discovered bounty from the mystery ship, they also forfeited their share of the salvage.

Some men still chose their souls over the riches.

Every time.

Rios turned to the first man behind him, William Kale.

British tried and true, thick body, heavy stocky frame, short brown hair and having a small nervous cheek flutter when concerned. Right now, it was twitching a lot. He was an honest hardworking man, quick to take the lead in battles and charges, but devoted to the safety and protection of his Captain.

Rios nodded to Kale. "No staying hampered at my side. The fun in finding a ship such as this is the search."

Kale gave a skeptical frown. He replied back, knowing he was comfortable with his Captain. And with Rios, a man could speak his mind and not be reprimanded for it, presuming he spoke with respect and civility. "Sir. My primary job is protecting you. And if I have to protect you from yourself, I will."

Rios slapped Kale on the back and guffawed. "Son. I don't envy your job because I know I would hate to be trying to keep the reins on me."

****

Once Rios was on the deck of the ship, his boots sloshed and squished remnants of scattered seaweed that had washed aboard in the night. Chunks of wood floated effortless by his feet, dark coloured and saturated, preventing any means to ascertain the source. Pieces of sail lay draped over a few dead fish whose last breaths of ocean ended with the sudden slap of the deck. Rivulets of rope were snaked around wooden pilasters and pilings, ripped and shorn at edges, not unlike the rope once holding the anchor, chopped and chewed as though eaten, not cut.

Again, Rios thought. *'What the Hell happened on this ship?'*

His men fanned out, each planning to search the ship in teams of two. One team was designated to find the stores, one team to search the hold, one to find the crew quarters, one to check the treasure stations and the last, to search for anything that may explain this mysterious ship.

The Captain and the Doctor stayed as a team as they found their way to the Captain's quarters.

Once found, it seemed to be in perfect order, with the exception of the rough rocking of the seas the night prior.

There was a large wooden desk at the rear, adjacent a huge made bed. On the desk were maps and books, with an equal number scattered on the floor. Clothes were in piles and a dinner tray, laden with half-eaten food, lay in a mess near a tobacco can for late night chewing. The windows were clean, the room was undamaged and everything seemed lonely, waiting for her Captain to return.

Rios picked up the Captain's Log, which lay tightly closed on a dresser, wedged between it and a fallen rack.

From the cover, he could read, 'Ship's Manifest.'

Rios opened its leather bound seal and pulled to the last pages where entries could be found. He could give it a more thorough reading later. He perused many of the paragraphs, his eyes squinting a few times at the previous Captain's poor penmanship.

After several minutes, Rios shouted to the doctor, who stood patiently back and by the door providing the proper respect for this room.

Only a Captain can search another Captain's quarters. It was understood.

LaFleur kept his hands clasped behind his back, staying quiet and reserved.

Rios spoke. "The ship is called the Leviathan."

"American?" the doctor replied.

"So it would seem."

"And it's complement?" A doctor was always concerned with the lives a ship carried, not the beams or floors that housed them.

Rios ran his finger down a long list of names, each individually numbered, likely by the ship owner's accountant. Some were crossed off, likely no shows, drunks who slept in too late on departure day or men for who the sea withdrew her invitation.

Others were likely those who simply did not survive the full trip.

And like any accounting ledger, you don't pay those who don't stay, whatever the reason.

Rios finished his counting. "I would say four hundred. Maybe a few more or less. But it seems pretty much up to date."

"With the exception the ship seems to be missing about four hundred, maybe a few more or a few less." LaFleur casually mentioned, speaking sarcastically. He then asked, "Anything in the log as to what happened?"

Rios continued to read on. "They were on a mission of exploration. Travelling along the Southern coasts. From what I read, they pulled into a jungle cove or bay for respite. Somewhere very south as the Captain refers to finding frost on his outer glass one morning."

"South exploring you say." LaFleur was searching the room with his eyes. "Not an uncommon practice. There are a lot of unknown areas in the South." He paused. "Did they find anything?" LaFleur was leading the questions on, hoping to whittle down for more clues to help solve this riddle.

Rios continued to read. "It appears they found an island of sorts."

LaFleur tilted his head curiously. "Of sorts? So the coast they pulled into was an island?"

Rios shook his head. "No. From what I read here, they were on a large land mass. But what he refers to is an island within an island."

"Like a moat?" LaFleur was thinking of old British castles surrounded by a large man made ditches, dug very deep, armed with spikes and talons, and filled with water to hide the dangers beneath. The monarchy would reside inside, behind its precious stone walls like on its own little island nation.

Rios was not sharing the thought. He replied. "It doesn't say. But the Captain calls it the *'Island of Forever Night.'*"

LaFleur's interests were peaked more. "Forever Night? Like the soil was all black? Or that its days were shorter and its nights longer?

I've heard the more South you go, you will find lands such as this with nights and days that run on for months."

Rios was still reading, not following this flight of fancy. "It still doesn't say. In fact, it's like…."

Rios paused.

LaFleur stood ready. He waited, but finally asked again, his curiosity getting the better of his patience. "And?"

Rios clucked his tongue on the roof of his mouth. "Pages are missing."

"Come again?" LaFleur was surprised. "Someone actually tore pages from the official log?"

Rios bristled. Entry into the Captains quarters alone was a travesty. But removing pages from the private memoirs of her ship's Captain was beyond redemption. Besides being a breach of maritime protocol, the log was the official record of a ship's course, its actions and history, as kept by the vessel's master himself. One never touched its pages.

Rios searched the floor with his eyes, now seeing what he had missed before.

LaFleur could see Rios' impatience as his head went back and forth. "Pray tell. What else are we missing?"

Rios gestured to the floor. "The sea charts, maps and guides of their passage."

"And you can tell this how?" LaFleur was genuinely curious.

Rios knelt done, closing the log and dropping it into a satchel he carried with him from his ship. He planned to read it more thoroughly once he was back in his own quarters. "Because these maps are of the Northern seas. I know them well. But the log specifically refers to the South." Rios pushed them all aside, sorting and piling them, not finding any others. "Whoever stole the last pages of the Captain's log seems to have taken all the maps of their route."

LaFleur shrugged. "I guess wherever this island is, someone never wants it to be found."

****

In the corridors, two teams had checked in thus far with Rios.

The supply stores were nearly fully stocked with food. There were some perishable items that seemed to have spoiled, likely over the past month, but most of the dried goods, salted products and bottled items were still salvageable.

Rios ordered them to be brought to the ship.

The second team brought even stranger news. The treasury was fully loaded. Gold and money for the crew's wages was in lockboxes, untouched and unmoved. Silver bars stamped for bank delivery in London were stored, stacked and ready for shipment. The remaining valuables, small baubles and items of special care were set aside to be taken back to America. Nothing appears to have been stolen or pillaged. Piracy was obviously not the reason for this empty ship.

But the treasury team did report one very specific area of which everything was missing. Besides the entire crew not being on board, the armoury was completely empty. All they found were a few bayonets, a couple of long rifles and a selection of old and dull swords. No muskets, munitions or powder.

Wherever the crew was, they went fully armed and ready for a fight.

Rios and LaFleur continued forward in their inspection.

Rios, unconsciously stroking the thick folds of his beard, up and down, ever so carefully, with his right hand.

****

Back on deck, the third team, two former British soldiers, now privateers and regular citizens, called to the Captain to attend to them. They appeared to be circling something on the deck above and to be genuinely perplexed.

'Join the club.' Rios thought to himself as he approached.

The two men walked straight and ridged, like they were still in the Corps, as any army man will tell you, military stayed in the blood. It never died within you.

Rios and LaFleur climbed the wooden stairs while tightly gripping the handrails. Even though the treads were drier than the lower floors by virtue of the height, the wood was still sweating and had warped unnaturally. Once they reached the upper helm, they moved towards the two officers.

The two men stood to each side and allowed for Rios and LaFleur to look.

And look Rios did. He knelt down, staring in confusion.

The area in front of the ship's wheel, which itself was chipped and hacked in thick chunks, was inundated with dozens, if not hundreds of holes thrust into the deck, dug deep in some areas, shallow in others, as though someone thought gold could be found under the floorboards and a team of miners took to finding it.

LaFleur too was down on his knees, running his fingers over what appeared to be masses of stained wood pieces and ravaged paneling. After his inspection, he had another theory for his Captain. He looked right into Rios' eyes and stated quite confidently. "Something died here Captain."

Rios stared at the damage and tried to understand.

LaFleur had drawn a dagger from his belt, a long slender blade with a pointed end which he saved for incisions and digit amputations. It had a pearl handle and a curved shaft. Within seconds, he was digging into the wood and pulling out chips of sharpened stone and edged rocks.

"What did this?" Rios asked staring curiously at the tiny chips.

LaFleur held it up in the sunlight. "It appears to be pieces of a spear tip. From what I can see, numerous spear tips."

"Savages?" Rios asked, knowing many of the Southern unexplored areas were rumoured to be besieged by men of the wild, whose animalistic rages and lack of civilization left them as nothing more than two legged beasts in need of killing.

"One would have to assume." LaFleur looked around. "But they do not seem to have attacked anywhere else. This is the only point on this ship I see massacred in this way. Unless the men discover more."

Rios reviewed the location of the damage and its proximity to the wheel housing. "Maybe they dragged the Captain out here, to stab him into oblivion, to frighten the crew."

LaFleur looked skeptical. "Savages are not known for using such tactics. They treat all prisoners as equals. Rank means nothing to them. So killing one man, leader or not, to tame the others into submission would be a foolhardy act. Plus, consider this, were savages to kill you in such a way, your men would not be cowed into defeat. In fact, it would be like lighting a powder keg."

Rios had to agree. Hardened sailors were not so easily weakened by sights of blood and gore.

The doctor dug out another spear tip, one wedged deep into the wood. He raised it up, turning it over and stared at it with fascination.

Rios could see his doctor's interest. "What is it that has you so impressed?"

"I'm not impressed per say. I'm more confused." LaFleur held it up for Rios to examine.

Rios could see the underside of the tip was soaked in a small amount of a blue liquid, still moist, lined with slivers of green and clear jelly. None of it having been scrubbed away by the storm as the stone points were well protected by how deeply embedded they were in the ship.

LaFleur was intrigued. "Whatever was killed here, as brutally as it was done, it seems to have bled blue."

One of the British soldiers looked aghast. "Royalty?"

Rios quickly interrupted in a commanding tone, to squash and prevent such a rumour from gallivanting through his ship. The last thing he wanted was tales racing through the ship and later the shipyards back in England of an American ship losing a Royal on board. He snapped with some firmness in his voice. "First, Royalty rarely, if ever, travel on American ships. Second, never on exploration missions. And third, and most importantly, I trained two of the princes in fencing back in England some years ago. Sometimes, they could go at one another quite roughly and be assured, though many think the Royal family has blue blood, I assure you, it's a red as my own."

The solider looked visibly relieved.

The other soldier chimed in, listening in from the left of Rios. "Could it be war paint?" Pointing to the stains. "I saw a tribe in the Southern coast of Africa where they covered themselves with blue paint to scare invaders."

LaFleur looked up to the soldier. "I've heard the same thing. But I also must disagree. Whatever got pummeled here was definitively with spears. And the one thing I know about Americans, very few of them find spears more effective than a good pistol or a broadsword."

Both soldiers had to admit, it was more logical.

Why hack away at your enemy with spears when your guns could kill quicker.

Rios was even more curious.

This mystery was getting stranger and stranger.

As the two soldiers and the doctor continued to maul away at the deck to pull out more evidence, Rios saw something at the corner of his eye.

He casually rose and moved to the stern of the ship, using slow and steady strides, to hide any excitement at a new discovery. He took deep breaths, sucking in with some enthusiasm, as he put both hands on the rear rail. He looked out at the now quiet ocean as he listened to his doctor and the men argue theories and ideas.

Using his body to shield what he had spotted, he quickly gripped a strange black curved object rammed hard into the wood of the rail. He gripped it with his right hand, and twisted with some force.

It held firm.

Rios slipped his right boot between the railings, turning it to lock between the rounded cores, giving himself some leverage. Using his full body weight, he pushed it to the left then drew hard to the right. After several back and forth motions, the object finally pulled free.

Rios never turned to give proof of his discovery. He waited and then looked it over. It fit smoothly into the palm of his hand.

It was a rounded object, four inches in length, curved at the centre, wide at the base and pointed at the tip. It was as black as nightshade from outside to core. It had an arc shape to it, not unlike a lion's nail, but he was sure, no lion left this behind unless it grew to fifty feet long. It had two thin and cylindrical hollow centres that ran from tip to tail. And the wide end looked like it had been ripped off something, like a paw or some large finger. It seemed to be a claw of some sort.

Rios kept it keenly hidden knowing full well if any of his superstitious men saw this, they would assume sea creatures, water dragons or the like had left it behind. And he knew he would have lifeboats over the side and men abandoning both this ship and his own for coming aboard and making contact with it.

Most sailors believed in such things as sea monsters, from Kraken to giant sea snakes, or from gigantic forty foot squids to ship length sharks, all with mighty jaws that would maw down the bows of its prey, dining on the soft meaty men inside.

But as Rios was a more pragmatic man, in his years at sea, he never once found hard proof of such things existing.

But he did think to himself as he looked down at the hole made. *And where are your other four claws my monstrous friend? Why only* one in this here ship? What manner of creature has only one appendage for a hand?

Rios spun the object around and accidently stabbed his index finger with the tip. It cut deep. A thin tear ran down from tip to base of his fingertip.

The object was extremely sharp. That and the cut burned. A remnant of yellow puss on the claw's tip trickled down and moistened his finger. There was a numbing sensation that overtook his entire hand.

'Poison?' Rios thought. 'Had the savages actually found the monster that this nail originated from, took it after a kill, attached it to a handheld weapon, soaked it in poison, and used it on its enemies? It was sharp enough. Damn savages.'

He hoped his life did not end this way.

Blood trickled down his hand in thick rivulets filling his fist. Smooth and warm, yet thin, like it could not solidify or scab.

Rios rubbed his fingers together, wiping the yellow fluid away, pocketing the object into his vest with his other hand. He turned to LaFleur for assistance. "Doctor?"

LaFleur ceased all he was doing to attend to the Captain. He spotted the blood right away and wiped it clean with a cloth he carried at his side in a waterproof container for easy access. He sprayed it with alcohol. As he wiped away the blood, LaFleur turned the hand over and back again.

He did it again.

Rios gave him a quizzical look. "What's wrong?"

LaFleur was examining the Captain's hands as he turned it over and over. "Where is the blood from?"

Rios was a tad annoyed his own ship's doctor, a man who was capable of fixing ripped tendons, sealing bullet wounds and stitching up sword lacerations with ease, could not see a simple prick on a fingertip.

Rios turned his hand up and pointed with the damaged index finger. He froze and stared mystified at his tip. Blood was still there, traces of it, trickling down in smooth crimson smears, but the wound the claw had made, deep and thick, was gone.

Like it had healed instantly. That or it was never there.

But if it was never there, like the doctor asked. '*Where did the blood come from?*'

Rios had no answers. He was stunned. But he tried to contain his shock. His beard did that effortlessly.

But as for the wound, Rios could offer no explanation as to this seemingly unprecedented miracle. But he also knew, in his heart, this was a secret he needed to keep close to the vest. He was unsure why, but he knew he had crossed paths with something great and right now, he was not yet interested in sharing until he was sure, he found it first.

Rios looked up at the befuddled doctor and knew, for the first time in a long time, he had to lie. "I tripped on the boards. When I did so, I bit my inner cheek and spit into my palm when I tasted blood." Rios paused. "Sorry. All I wanted was a cloth to wipe it away."

The doctor stared at his Captain, never knowing him to be clumsy or unsure in his steps. But what else could it be? He released the Captain's palm, handing him a cloth, the entire time giving him an offhanded look. He threw in one more comment. "Luckily only blood came out as I saw no saliva."

The Captain and the doctor exchanged looks.

Rios knew that LaFleur suspected he was holding something back. But he was too good a friend to press.

And LaFleur knew, sometimes, Captains kept secrets. And usually for good reasons. Being master of a sea going vessel, filled with numerous personalities, people from different walks of life, likes and dislikes, happy and unhappy, differing cultures and mannerisms, confidentiality was a commodity that Captains kept in abundance and used with little disregard.

Nothing else was said.

Nothing else would be offered.

Rios and LaFleur left the upper deck in search of the remaining two teams.

****

Rios and LaFleur found team four in the crew quarters.

Two Scotsmen, short and stout, were guarding the portal into the sleeping areas.

The men advised and confirmed, they had searched the room from top to bottom and found nothing outside the norm. They reported there were numerous rooms, lots of shelves, bunks made and unmade, trunks for clothes at the ends, most fully stocked, laundry put aside for cleaning, blankets thrown asunder, but more from lazy crew than buccaneers routing for treasure. But beyond that, what they expected.

A well-used ship, but yet, not a single crew member, nor proof of a crewmember, had lived here recently.

Abandoned, without an explanation.

As Rios purveyed the area, one of the men suggested. "Maybe they left the ship as a result of the Plague?"

LaFleur quickly dismissed that notion. "No plague, no matter how deadly, how fast, could ever kill one hundred percent of the crew."

"I have to agree with the doctor." Rios did not feel better. He was sure LaFleur was placating the men with science, a language few seaman understood well. But no matter how he explained it, things did not add up.

Science aside, Rios knew, over four hundred men were missing. He did not want his men frightened by the prospect of sickness or death.

Rios shrugged and turned to the sailor who suggested '*Plague*'. "That and I can assure you, plague is extremely doubtful. Had the ship been infected, before they abandoned, would they not have put the disease ridden corpses on board first?"

The man agreed. Why put your ship adrift due to disease and keep the plague ridden corpses with you.

Rios knew, if such a dire emergency had befallen them, the Captain would have ordered the ship be set ablaze before setting her adrift. Rios had never heard of any Captain putting a ship to sea, plagued by death, to infect any poor vessel that crossed her path.

Rios considered that plus it still appeared to be a fairly fine ship. Older of course, but steady and true. So it's destruction by fire would seem a grand waste when all that needed be done was toss the bodies over the side.

Not that any sailor would do that to one of their mates, but again, depending on the emergency, any action was possible.

Before any other questions could be asked, a gunshot resonated down the empty halls, echoing long and sharp due to the lack of human bodies within them.

Rios drew his pistol and ran toward the sound.

Within moments, Rios entered the galley, LaFleur to his rear, dagger at ready, but wary, as the doctor repaired enough bullet wounds not to be favoured to inflict one.

They found the last team of two men, lantern on the tabletop, standing at two corners of the galley, a full kitchen with pots, pans, knives and other culinary instruments scattered about. They were standing to both sides preventing access to the corner of the room.

Rios demanded. "Who fired their weapon?"

The first man on the left, a tall and hairy fellow with sad eyes, brown hair and lots of exposed muscles. "I did sir. He came out at me from the cabinet." Gesturing to a naked man on the floor. "I think he was sleeping in there."

Rios looked to the floor.

On it was a naked man, as bare as the day he was born, shivering like he lived in the artic winters of the north where no ships fared to tread. His skin was tanned, but only slightly as it appeared he had been out of the sun for some time. He was definitely a Caucasian man, Spanish from his high cheekbones and dark eyes, which seemed to be laced with dozens of deep red veins of bloodshot. The man looked completely healthy, with the exception of the fact, he seemed to be out of his mind.

As Rios reached toward him, the man screamed in a way that would send souls running. Both men to the side of the Captain had their swords drawn, ready to swing.

Rios held his hand high to prevent the assault. This man was the only witness to what happened here, and he had no desire to see him killed so casually for having done nothing more than defend himself.

The second crewman ripped a portion of his sleeve and shoved it in the naked man's mouth, to quiet the screams.

This neither calmed nor relaxed the man. He curled himself into a fetal position, still shivering, crying uncontrollably. His deep moans now dulled by the impediment in his mouth.

Rios looked inside the cabinet.

There was a pile of soiled blankets, dried food and feces. He definitely seemed to have been living here.

Turning back to his crewman who fired the shot, Rios asked. "You said you fired a shot." He pointed to the man. "Did you miss?" Disturbed one of his men could not hit a target so close.

The crewman appeared perplexed. "I honestly thought I hit him. But when I put the lantern to him, he has not a scratch on him. Some blood on his side, so maybe I nicked him. But the odd thing is..." The crewman pointed to the wall. "If I had missed, why can I not find my bullet-hole?"

Rios looked to his index finger and back at the man. *'Even more curious.'*

LaFleur saw what Rios had done, but again, offered no comment.

The second man, a heavy brute with a flat nose, dark eyes, and speaking with a thick accent, handed the Captain some shreds of heavy bond paper. "He was eating these, Sir."

Rios took it from his man and stared at the moist and ink smeared torn pages.

LaFleur quickly pointed out. "I guess we know what happened to the last few pages of the Captain's Log. And the maps."

Rios looked down at the fear stricken man, thinking to himself, not wanting to speak it aloud, as brave as the men were, such suppositions would still chill these seaman to the core. *"What place good sir was so horrible you had to destroy all means of finding it?'*

Rios turned to his two crewmen. "Take him to the Serenade. But try not to hurt him. If you must, put him in chains, but before that, get the man some clothes."

The crewmen nodded.

The larger of the two asked. "What if he's responsible for what happened here?"

At this, LaFleur interjected. "I highly doubt one man could kill and devour a crew of over four hundred. That and we have not found a single blood stain, bone or body on board." He looked down to the shivering form. "No. This man is not our monster. But he likely saw who or what it was. And as far as I am concerned, any witness to something which has cost the lives of four hundred men and left this ship adrift at sea is someone worth keeping." LaFleur looked downtrodden at the man. "Sadly, it also appears, whatever it was he saw may have destroyed his mind in every way imaginable."

Rios nodded agreement.

LaFleur looked to the man and offered one more thing. "The real question is, will our sole survivor ever be well enough to tell his tale?" The doctor stared down into the man's vacant eyes. Dark pools in which many thoughts and ideas likely were long drowned and lost. "In my estimate, likely never."

Rios had one final thought. *'Let's hope not Doctor... As I think he has a fantastic tale to tell.'*

****

Once Rios had returned to the Serenade, while a team of men were now going back and forth with supplies and inventory from the Leviathan, some men still refusing to venture across, he had made a decision.

Regardless of what happened to its crew, he had discovered a perfectly good ship on the open waters, nearly fully stocked with supplies and treasure.

Since the survivor could nary lay claim to his own mental facilities, let alone the vessel, Rios did so.

This ship, its stores and inventory were now the property of the Serenade, in the name of his Queen.

Rios moved to the helm of his ship and bellowed aloud. "Batten down the hatches and rope her firm. We're taking our bounty back to England."

Some men cheered, some shook their heads.

Rios thought. *'Maybe there, I'll have a long discussion with our sole survivor.'*

Staring down at his finger again, Rios knew he had to. If only to determine and solve the mystery of what happened to the Leviathan and her crew. He felt compelled in the deep recesses of his soul to discover the answer. As he was sure, whatever it was, wherever it led, it was well worth it.

2

London England.
October 25th, 1889

The air was cool and heavy laden with chills. The close proximity of the ocean caused larger frost layered edges of ice to form on cobblestone roadways and stone steps leading into homes, etched by traces of salt.

Horses and their masters moved slower in the cooler air, their hooves leaving sloshy pools of slushy prints in the paths behind them.

The animal's snouts breathed heavily with each step, exhaling white puffs as they walked, as though spewed forth from a burning pipe, yet no scent of tobacco followed with it.

The London Dock Strike that broke out in August, which ended in September, still kept the town in an uproar. Its citizens continued to argue with one another, some over labour's rights, while others, the men paying their wages, disagreed. A battle doomed to eternity.

On the outskirts of London, to the West, far away from the civilized world, off a weather-beaten trail layered by mud, hoof prints and horse excrement, housed the fifty room brick-walled structure known as the Royal London Medical Institute.

Or to those who knew it best, the Royal London Lunatic Asylum.

For its inhabitants, the world around them, its news, its travesties and its concerns, bore little interest, or for that matter, any regard.

The facility had bars for windows, steel plates for doors, and a complement of royal soldiers to ensure its guests never posed a risk to any in England.

It was a beautiful place with lush green pastures surrounding it, high trees with large flourishing leaves, yellows and reds with the season, and stone structures from yesteryear encompassing the property and making those inside feel as though they were privileged residents, not simply prisoners.

In one of the upper rooms, the office of the Medical Superintendent, administrator and overseer of this facility, sat one man, resting comfortably.

Captain Rios was in a high back red leather chair, his boot covered feet, one atop the other, rested on a corner of the large ornate desk before him. He was leafing through a report he had found. He was impressed with the handwriting within, delicate and fine, written with a careful hand, each loop and whorl an artwork in itself. One who took serious pride in his record-keeping.

Rios looked up to the window then resumed his reading while he waited patiently.

He was the same man as he had always been, steadfast and confident. Yet now, as a retired Captain of the British Navy, he had lots of time on his hands. His once dark beard was laced with grey with silvers and browns battling in his mane, white fighting to take dominion.

Age and time were enemies many men feared, always losing the battle to keep them at bay.

Rios sat quietly and reflected on his life.

He had crossed the oceans more times than he could count. His accounts were laden with gold and he had more property than many of his peers. He held many commendations as bestowed upon him by the Royal Court, combined with the respect of all who served under his command. He had no family of note, but never sought one.

His only legacy was his satisfaction in living the life he wanted.

With one exception.

A mystery he had never solved continued to gnaw away at his thoughts.

Rios looked again upon his finger, rubbing the tip and reminisced.

"Good morning." A male voice stated, closing the door behind them.

Rios was pulled from his reverie while the other man crossed the office.

The man was wearing a long white coat and a pencil balanced over his left ear. He was a small man, standing at five eight, with short blond hair, brushed back and deftly behind his head, layered with a hint of oil. His gold rimmed spectacles were round and light, resting atop his sharp nose, and framed by a clean shaven face. He spoke with a German accent, smooth and light, as he moved around to the chair to behind the desk revealing the office was his own. He took his seat and saw Rios had been reading the most recent update.

Doctor Sebastian Gerber placed his two hands together, his one finger sporting a University of Munich ring, as he quietly reflected on Rios and his presence. He began. "Interesting reading I presume." Not surprised or bothered to find his papers being rifled through or examined.

Rios smiled but offered no apology. "Nothing eventful with our guest I presume?"

"Not for some time." Gerber offered. "He's been a model inmate. I suspect, in a few years he may even be able to retire outside these walls."

Rios chuckled, doubtful. "From what I read has occurred in London, this is a far safer place. Have they not caught that monster from White Chapel? The Ripper or something like that?"

"I'm afraid not." Gerber replied. "But from recent news, he seems to have stopped. Some believe he's killed himself."

Again, Rios doubted it. *'Monsters don't die. They simply go into hiding.'*

"I knew the third girl, Elizabeth Stride." Rios offered. "She was a fine lass. Made many of my men fit for the seas. I wonder what possible threat she posed to this madman."

Gerber had no answer. Though he understood with the current state of the economy, the reasons for these women selling themselves to sailors and their ilk, he had never conceived a person who felt justified in tearing woman asunder as this *Ripper* did. "Well if they do catch him, I'd want to speak to him. Even keep him here, under secured restraints of course." He paused. "We might be able to learn what makes him tick. And prevent future monsters."

Rios nodded agreement, but he was not really listening.

Gerber and Rios stared at one another, silence growing between them.

Gerber waited patiently for Rios to ask, knowing his small talk was always the preclude to his real interest. And Gerber could wait a very long time, as it was his profession.

"Has he remembered anything new?" Rios queried. "I've been gone almost three months."

"Then I can assume, you chose not to meet with him today?" Gerber asked, already knowing the answer.

Rios nodded, noting his reluctance to do so. He clearly wanted to talk to Gerber first.

"He's offered nothing more than you already know." Gerber leaned back. "We know his crew pulled into a coastal region south of America and they discovered an island for which the sun does not set. Or so he claims."

Rios thought. *'This I know. But I need more. It's been thirty years.'*

"We know they found something. As to what, he can't remember. And in my estimates, he never will." Gerber took a breath, some resignation in his tone. "And I can assure you, I've asked him over and over. He's not lying."

Rios was a man of the seas, not a man of the mind. He could not understand how a man could drown out things he saw and experienced, and in a manner so deep it could not be salvaged. If it was locked away, they simply needed to find the right key.

Gerber offered his hands up and open. "Anything he offers would be equivalent to a guess."

"I'll take a 'guess' over nothing, any day." Rios responded.

Gerber peered out his window. "From my discussions with him, and there have been many, they delivered their stores to a port North of Texas. Upon completion, not unlike your own ship, its Captain ordered the crew South, in search of adventure with no destination in mind."

Rios sighed. *'The world is a big place and everything is South of North.'*

"It was my good friend and colleague, Doctor LaFleur, who referred you to me..." Gerber casually mentioned. "In 1864, I took it based on pure study and his insistence."

Rios turned to him. "You had no difficulty in taking my money each year quite readily when I paid for this man's care."

Gerber did not refute this, but this was not the debate. "Let me ask you this. How many times will you ask him the same questions? How many times does he have to tell you the same answers before you accept them?"

Captain Rios turned to stare out the window. After a full minute of solemn observation, he explained. "He's the sole survivor and the former first officer of a mysterious ship for which the entire crew has vanished without a trace. And to this day, I've nothing to explain what happened."

Gerber raised both his hands. "We may never know."

"I refuse to believe that." Rios stood, putting both hands behind his back. "He has the answers. He simply doesn't know it."

Gerber was always amazed with the zeal in Rios' convictions. "I read the Captain's Log you provided to me, and to him, to help jog the officer's memory. And be assured, it was equally unsuccessful. He neither remembers what was written nor why for that matter he destroyed the pages."

'Not destroyed my good Doctor...Ate.' Rio thought, but offered. "Still, he saw the pages. Otherwise, why destroy them? So he must have known of their content before ridding the world of them."

"Of this I have no doubt. But I must point out, he *knew*, being the past tense."

Rios was frustrated. He wanted answers now, more than ever. "Regardless, if you read the entire log, before the page's *ingestion*, the last entry noted pulling into a cove that leads to this *Island of Eternal Night*. So unless his Captain was insane, there is such an island."

"Writing something does not make it a reality." Gerber noted.

"Captains don't write fiction." Rios bristled at the suggestion an official logbook could be falsified. "As God is my witness, there's an island, and I believe it to be true."

"Yes, that remains a real possibility, but again, these things cannot be forced. He needs time."

Rios clenched his fists. *'Time is a luxury I don't have.'*

Gerber could see Rios' annoyance and offered. "Over the past three decades, each time you took shore leave and returned here to spend time with him, and he considers you a valued friend by the way, you've asked him dozens of questions, in hundreds of ways, to illicit small segments of information. Now with your skill and experience of the ocean, should not all these pieces assist you to assemble a picture of where he went."

Rios did not offer Gerber an answer, nor revealed what he knew. Over the past thirty years, he had carefully and delicately drawn small pieces of information from his survivor of the seas. However at great cost as each time, the man would be drawn back into his nightmares, screaming and regressing back into his mind, useless for more information, forcing Rios to return at another time.

As Gerber had surmised, in that time, Rios had amassed a great deal of information, unbeknownst to the former first officer, all of which he kept close to his vest. The prize would be his and his alone.

"Regardless of his trip, or his route, it's that which took the lives of over four hundred crewman which is vitally important to me."

Gerber nodded solemnly, sensing Rios already had a route in mind. "In the case you had to face them yourself with a crew of only a hundred?"

After a full minute, Rios grinned understandingly. "Then you know."

Gerber was a very intelligent man and what he could not derive by Rios' words, he could from his contacts in the world. "I've been recently informed you've purchased an ocean going vessel. If I'm not mistaken, it's currently being outfitted in Bristol for a *long* crossing. A complement of one hundred men correct?"

"One twenty." Rios felt no need to lie. Plus he assumed, Gerber would see them as such. "She's a small ship, yet sturdy and true. My crew, equally small, are my finest from years at sea."

"And they're men who like a challenge?"

Rios knew Gerber would end every statement with a question. It was a psychiatrist's game. "They like my money and that I make my own destinations, not that of my employers."

Most self-employed men will tell you, it was a marvelous feeling to choose your own fate.

Gerber added. "And you're preparing a cast off very soon?"

"Of that, it's also true." Rios stood firm. "So I was hoping to glean any remaining information I could before I departed."

The doctor remained seated, hands clasped with his two index fingers pressed together, pointing skyward to form a steeple. "And will you say goodbye?"

"He knows I'm a seafaring man. So long departures do not faze him. Why bore him with a story of another?"

"Because this one involves seeking out the very island he has so desperately tried to forget."

Rios looked to Gerber. "If's there's even a shred of truth to what I suspect, I need to find the island, and the answer."

Gerber paused as looked at the Captain. After a moment, he reflected. "I've lived a long and happy life. I have a wife who adores me, children who love me and a career I'm considered distinguished for."

"And you think you're a better man for it?" Rios asked, not seeking an answer. "But what of your legacy?"

"My children will be my legacy. When I move on, it will be under my own terms." Gerber smiled, proud of the life he has lived. "I've absolutely no interest in seeking out that which can do to a man what was done to our friend."

Rios took it in. "That's where we differ Doctor. This mystery needs a solution and I want what he discovered."

Gerber rose and moved until he stood directly behind the Captain. He placed a gentle hand on Rios' shoulder. "Some things were never meant to be found."

Rios grinned. "Then why put it out there."

Gerber pulled away and stood to Rios side. He took a deep breath and offered a profound nod of his head. "A great being once put an apple in a tree and told his two children not to touch it. But the children asked the question, 'Then why put it there?' So they picked it and took a bite." He let the story sink in. "And look where it got them."

"I'm not after the apple..." Rios smirked, causing the slivers of his beard to curl up the wrinkles of his skin around his mouth, brushing it with his right hand. "I want the tree."

Rios loved these philosophical debates with Gerber. It gave him many intellectual things to consider, not unlike his long nights around the conference table aboard the Serenade with LaFleur over a casket of wine.

Rios turned to Gerber. He paused before asking his next question. "And what of his journal?"

"What of it?" Gerber asked innocently.

"May I have it?."

"Absolutely not!" Gerber appeared astonished at such a request. "For him, it's his anchor to sanity. One I can't let you haphazardly pull from the waters hoping it snagged a treasure chest." Using imagery Rios would understand.

"I can purchase him a new one."

"This has been his only way to make real thoughts he is too frightened to voice into reality." Gerber scoffed. "Unlike a pet, one does not replace one's memories put to paper with a blank pad and hope the writer doesn't notice."

"He's still a madman."

Gerber snarled under his breath at the remark and at the suggested invasion of a patient's privacy. "Regardless, he still writes in it. And he has many pages to go. To take it from him now would be to betray any trust he has in me and this institution. And if he truly holds a secret, it'll be lost forever by this one action."

Rios already suspected the answer before he asked it. "And of what has he written?" Hoping the good Doctor had seen something Rios did not.

Gerber motioned, denoting nothing of importance. "He writes slivers of what he can. He's trying to piece together what happened on that island. I suspect before the end of his life, he will."

In that, Rios agreed, but long after he left.

"I wish I had more time." Captain Rios stood, his sword knocking on the edge of the doctor's desk. "I'll be leaving tonight. I may be gone for some time. But I assure you, our patient's expenses will remain covered. I've spoken to the bank and they'll relay the payments to your institution for as long as necessary."

Gerber would have forgone the payments, as the patient was far too important to release into the world simply due to lack of funding. He knew he would personally pay if Rios had not. As regardless of the island, his story, if ever dug up from his mind, would be worth it.

Rios turned toward the door.

Gerber offered up his only warning. "I've seen many men over the years, battle worn with damaged minds and souls. Some are spending the rest of their lives either jumping at shadows, paranoid of everyone around them, or even refusing to leave the safety of their homes."

"Your point Doctor?"

"My point is... Whatever happened to our first officer frightened him to his very soul. And that is a hard target to reach, by anything known to man."

"And?"

Gerber sighed, knowing he was not Rios' keeper. "If you believe the island exists, which you do, then you must believe in the second part, that this island possesses a *Horror*, and that's what he calls it by the way, a *Horror,* lives upon it. One so terrible, our friend lost almost all threads of his essence facing it."

Rios was confident. "I'm prepared for anything any man can throw at me."

"Presuming it was man..." Gerber replied with solid conviction. He hoped he was getting through to Rios, but doubted it. "Combined with the guilt for the loss of his crew, he may suffer for a very long time."

"Time heals all wounds."

"So does dying." Gerber casually inserted

Rios ignored the last statement. "I've shown you my finger correct?"

"Many times."

"Do you know how many times I've cut it?"

"Many." Gerber leaned forward, speaking in a grandfatherly voice, offering a soft and gentle assurance. "I don't deny the miracle. I deny the price."

Rios looked to the window. "I'm prepared to pay it."

"Are you?" Gerber knew this was his final chance. "Whatever happened to that ship, which resulted in the loss of hundreds of crew and drove our mutual friend to the point of absolute madness, in my estimates, is a price not worth the cost."

Rios was confident. "I can afford it."

'God I hope so.' Gerber thought. He gestured to Rios' belt, changing the subject. "I see you still carry that old Flintlock."

Rios massaged the grip. "It's a dependable weapon."

Gerber knew little of weapons, but he did know, each minute he delayed Rios was a minute of reconsideration. "Even at sea? With the salt air? Doesn't it dampen the gun powder?"

Rios placed his hand on the hilt of his weapon, staring into the setting sun on the horizon.. "Paraffin."

"Paraffin?" Gerber started at him quizzically. "You mean wax?"

"Yes." Rios took solace in his ideas. "I put a single drop at the pin and one on the end of the barrel?"

"And what does that do?"

"It keeps air, moisture and salt away from the gun powder. Sure it seems strange, but I assure you, nary has a chance existed when I pulled the trigger did it hesitate to fire. No matter how long I wait to pull it."

Both men took solace in one another's words.

Their decisions were made, and the direction of their lives paved before them.

Rios departed the doctor's office, his hand on his belt, dreams of a discovery men would die to have.

No '*Horror*' would keep him from this bounty.

Rios ship pulled out of port at 9:47 p.m. that evening, its moonlit silhouette shrinking on the water with each mile it sailed from England.

The oceans settled as his ship sunk into the horizon.

Captain Rios, his ship, and his crew were never seen or heard from again.

3

Bristol, Yate.
January 29th, 2012

    Melanie Goodrich, proprietor and owner of the Royal Appleby Auction House, out of Bristol Yate, hated working on her birthday.
    But with the recent liquidation of a bankrupt London maritime museum, thanks to the ailing European economy and people choosing between the need to inspect the past, under glass, or having food to eat always made for tough decisions.
    But she had gotten lucky, having been given first dibs on some of the artifacts and show pieces, and today was the shipment date.
    It appeared trustees did not take people's birthdays into account as holidays.
    She was not terribly bothered. She knew there was no one waiting at home, a large loft in the central core in Bristol. Plus, being alone on this day tended to remind her of the years passing on. She had two children, who she adored and had done fabulously for themselves. She had been married twice, both times ending in divorce.

The first was as a young woman, having met an aspiring Canadian writer on a cruise ship which turned into a five year relationship in Canada and ended equally as quickly when they both sought the address of their own resident countries and thus, parted ways in friendship.

Occasionally, not often, she found herself guiltily hovering in the bookstore, searching the shelves for his most recent published work. He had made quite a name for himself since their parting. He now had a new beautiful wife and two attractive kids. That and two large Labradors for pets, one a burly chocolate and the other a regal charcoal grey. She sometimes looked back with a pang of regret.

The second husband was a matter of the passion fizzling out, nothing more, transforming her work into her one faithful companion.

Her phone chirped.

She quickly looked at her display and waived her fingers over the touchscreen. Two messages, the kids wishing her a happy fortieth.

'*Was she really that old?*'

She turned back to her laptop, scrolling her fingers over the toggle, and reviewed the catalogue of items emailed to her.

'*Doesn't anyone use faxes anymore?*' She thought, not a fan of technology.

As she reviewed the inventory, she found a few choice pieces she knew would fetch an excellent price.

She took a quick break, stood up and checked herself in the mirror. She loved parading before it. Not unlike her first husband who could never get away from it.

She stood at five foot five, long auburn hair which fell into a natural curl. She had deep brown eyes which fit perfectly into her small and demure face. She was lightly tanned by her many months spent in Spain on the beaches of Madrid. She was a sharply dressed woman, with refined tastes and a need to look good in any and all situations, sporting a grey cashmere wool suit, high top boots with a hint of a heel. Around her neck she wore a diamond pendant from a sunken ship in Greece she had acquired in one of her auctions.

She returned to her desk and resumed reading the delivery manifest when she heard a small knock at her door.

Melanie looked up as a door opened and a man peered into her office. He smiled as he entered.

He was five nine, with short brown hair slivered by white. He had sparkling blue eyes, as she noticed such things. His skin was moderately tanned and he was dressed in a black double-breasted blazer, grey turtleneck and matching slacks. What she noticed most of all was he seemed very well built, with his suit accentuating a more than likely chiseled chest beneath.

He stepped forward, extending his hand. "Good day Ms. Goodrich. My name is Anthony Darby."

She took his hand with grace and gestured for him to take a seat.

With the handshake he handed her a business card.

She turned it over and it read, 'Attorney at Law.'

"You're an attorney?"

"You sound surprised?" As he took his seat.

"You don't look like a lawyer."

"What pray tell do I look like?"

She smiled. "A banker."

At that he grinned. "Were my friends here, they'd probably agree with you. However a mere lawyer is all I am."

She doubted by his confidence, '*mere*' was an adjective ever used to describe him. "How can help you Mr. Anthony Darby?"

"First, you can call me Darby. All my friends do."

She repeated herself. "How can help you Mr. Darby?"

He smiled again. "Please, just Darby."

"I'm sorry."

"No need to be. Mister is what I call my father. You can call me Darby."

She found this somewhat charming, especially in the casualness he presented it. "Okay, Darby… What can I do you for?"

Darby reached into his jacket and pulled out a folded piece of paper. As he opened it, he placed a pair of rounded reading glasses over his eyes which he smoothly pulled from the inside pocket.

Melanie watched as he gracefully opened the sheet, holding it before his eyes to carefully read.

She would swear, by the manner and care he took in his motions, he was a surgeon. "My employer has informed me that you have come into possession of some interesting artifacts from a recent museum bankruptcy."

Melanie peered at her computer with some confusion. "Your employer is remarkably well informed. I only just acquired the collection this morning."

"My employer is a thorough. Being informed is one of their greatest assets. And if I'm correct, the collection has already been delivered." Said as a statement, not a question.

She was not sure if she should be impressed or frightened. She herself had not known of the pending delivery until this morning when the courier service called ahead to confirm someone would available to sign the receipt. "Your employer is more than well informed, they're psychic."

Darby offered a smirk. "My employer would like to think so."

'Most lawyers consider the people they represent as clients, not employers.' But she ignored her thoughts for the time being. She could sense with such interest in the acquisition, equal compensation would follow. "I assume if they know I've procured the collection already, they seek something specific from it." Unsure if the employer was a man or a woman.

"You are an astute woman." Darby was direct and to the point. Most lawyers billed by the hour, so time was very valuable. "Specifically, an old journal from a patient from 1906, around the time the Royal London Medical Institute was closed down. Some sort of scandal about a fire and an inmate having perished." Darby looked up, staring over the frames of his glasses. "Stories have it the staff considered him a demon and murdered him."

Melanie shrugged nonchalantly "I've only recently gotten the catalogue over the weekend. I've yet to study all their histories." She kept her cards close to her vest. "But from what I've read so far, there was indeed a fire. Around the time Doctor Gerber resigned his post." She paused for effect. "The new administration was not quite as *caring* with patients as the previous caretakers and somewhat more... religious. The fire that swept through the place was believed to have started when they set a patient on fire. Likely the one you speak of."

Darby winced. *'A nasty way to die.'* But he also grinned inwardly, suspecting Ms. Goodrich was far more knowledgeable than he was originally led to believe. "But the journal survived?"

Melanie rose from her desk, left her office into the back chamber where she had been opening and emptying boxes. After a minute or two, she returned with Darby waiting patiently. She presented the old journal to him, its brown edges charred with soot. Corners of pages were lightly scorched, bent in from the heat with its leather bindings holding tight, seemingly to have protected the pages within. It was tied closed with a piece of matching leather string.

Darby took the book as one would hold a baby, caressing its sides with loving care. He inspected the tome, pulled loose the rope and opened the pages. For about a minute, he was perfectly still. He finally spoke. "How much?"

Melanie suspected this was coming. "I've yet to assess its exact worth. But the auction isn't for a week."

Darby kept his eyes on the book. "My employer finds public auctions like that of farms. Cattle grouped together, baying and grunting on who can get the best corn first." He looked up. "He feels you and he are above such things."

'His employer was a man.' She suspected as much. But for a second, she was both complimented by the elevation of her stature,

but equally insulted in the depiction of her career. She chose to ignore it. Money makes a remarkable agent to heal ailing egos. "What is he offering?"

Darby was equally worldly. "Well, it is damaged."

Melanie interrupted. "I'm sure your employer can procure a new one at a local stationary shop for under ten pounds if he prefers. I mean, if he's concerned with such matters."

The negotiations had begun.

Darby knew full well it was the contents of the journal, not the esthetics that was sought. "I'm sure five thousand would be in order. Including a tidy two more for your indulgence in letting us avoid next week's festivities."

'Yes. *The salve was already soothing her wounds.*' She tried to contain her excitement at the offer, but her cheeks reddened beneath her light selection of freckles. But she knew, rarely do buyers present the best offer first. "I would think ten would be more in order, PLUS the two."

Darby carefully flipped through the pages. "I'm prepared to meet you at eight, including the two to make it ten."

Melanie was not a greedy woman. "American Dollars?"

"I'm actually Canadian." Darby placed the book in his lap, suspecting a deal has been made. "But let it be known, when I make an offer here, I make it in pounds sterling."

Melanie used every ounce of her strength to keep her eyes from widening. She had seen the item on the catalogue the day before and presumed it would have to be placed inside of something from the museum so she could rid herself of it. She never expected it to be an item so ardently wanted. "I accept." She reached under her desk to the drawer to pull out a receipt book.

Darby, in those seconds she turned her eyes, had almost magically placed two stacks of twenty pound notes on her desk, their purplish colour standing out as it etched out the lovely profile of Queen

Elizabeth's face on the top. Each stack was bound with a band which read, '*£5000'*

Melanie had to do a double take trying to figure out where he kept them being his clothes were well fitted and he carried no briefcase.

Darby slid them forward across the blotter. "My employer is not big on record keeping." Clearly implying a receipt was not necessary, nor wanted.

Melanie was still a businesswoman. She understood sometimes, collectors preferred the only ones who need to know they had something of value were themselves. She slipped the stacks into her top drawer and closed it, preventing buyer's remorse, of which she doubted there would be any. She paused. "I'm curious of one thing?"

"I'm single if you're asking?"

Melanie was taken aback, blushing like a school girl, both at the boldness of the response and with the charm it was played, done smoothly as to avoid insinuation. She took a moment to regain her composure. "No. But thank you for your candor." She smiled, seriously considering his suggestion. But she had a lot of work to do. "I'm curious as to how your employer became aware of the journal at all? It was only a casual footnote written in after the liquidation of the museum."

Darby did not feel he was betraying any confidence by answering. "My employer is a man who believes the key to the future is buried in the past."

"A bit cryptic?"

"In that I agree. But to be honest, he spends a great deal of resources seeking out lost things which he thinks tell stories, tales which may lead him to grander prizes."

She wanted to laugh. "You think this journal is a treasure map?"

"Hardly." Darby crossed his one leg over his knee. "One of his recent projects involves the exploits of a ship known as Leviathan."

Melanie was a well-schooled woman, and being one of the few auction houses who remarketed Maritime historical artifacts, she knew the story well. "Yes. The American ship discovered in the South Atlantic in the late 1800's. Its whole crew was lost."

"That's the one. But it was not the whole crew. One survived."

She heard rumours of such things, but with very little substantiation.

Darby continued. "My employer was unable to procure the original Serenade Logbook from the curator of the British Historical Society, but he did purchase a souvenir one online, perfectly duplicated in every way."

Why pay for the real one when the fake looks just like it?' Melanie shrugged with annoyance, knowing such replications only detracted from her authentic products. "She was the ship who discovered the Leviathan. She was under the command of a Captain Rios. This was long before he and his crew were lost at sea three decades later on a private mission of their own."

"You're equally well informed."

"I try to be."

"Well in his investigations, my employer discovered our very own Captain Rios paid for the personal care and maintenance of the sole survivor for many years. In the very same institution that burned down in 1906." Darby paused. "Your historians are fabulous by the way."

Melanie nodded at the compliment.

"Well, my employer assumed all was lost, as there was no mention of anything surviving. But he has many museums under watch, searching for specific code words, especially with sales and receiverships. So when the name Gerber and journal flashed on a web posting, he had me on the first plane out to find what had been saved."

Melanie smiled. "Before I ask you to dinner, I have to be honest with you. I would have accepted your first offer of seven."

Darby winked. "I was prepared to offer fifty."

Melanie felt warm inside, not anger, but amusement. She did not feel cheated, as she was going to dispose of the journal anyway.

Darby offered a casual nod as he stood. "I would love to go to dinner with you, but I have another flight in an hour for Scotland. My employer believes there is a rock with engravings that lead to the Holy Grail."

Oddly enough, she believed him.

"And because I was only asked to procure that which survived the fire, the journal, my job is done."

Melanie held up her hand, gesturing for Darby to wait. She rose and departed for her storeroom.

She returned with a large file folder. "That was not all that survived. The journal was placed with a single medical file from Doctor Gerber. Many of the others were lost or destroyed, but this was the only one he had sealed in a metal box to protect it from destruction."

Darby leaned in with fascination. "This is most unexpected. My employer will be most pleased. He had been unaware of this item."

She handed it to him. "I feel I'm cheating you on the price of the journal, please take this as I cannot imagine it fetching any high price."

Darby looked up to her, genuinely impressed with her honesty. "Do you have a box I can take, to carry this with me?"

"Of course." She returned to her storeroom, talking to him through the empty door while she searched.

Once she found a box of sufficient size, she returned to her office. She froze, as she found Darby gone.

She peered around puzzled.

On her desk were eight more piles of twenty pound notes, bundled the same.

Darby had not lied. *'He did say he was prepared to pay fifty.'*

Far more than she expected to receive.

She felt a pang of guilt though, as she slid the remaining eight piles to join the other two in her desk.

'I'm sure he noticed it.' She thought. *'He didn't strike her as a man who missed such things.'*

As she never had a chance to mention, when she got the journal delivered that morning, according to the description, the last eight pages had been torn out.

4

March, 2012

The morning was cold, yet humid, and invigoratingly fresh. The dewy sweet taste of the moisture on the air filled his mouth with each deep breath he took, like drinking down syrup at a maple sap festival in Canada after it was boiled and poured onto newly fallen snow for succulent ingesting.

He stepped forward, the gentle squish of mud blossomed up and around his hiking boot treads. He didn't even notice.

'God, he loved the South American jungle.'

Miles of trees, vines and plants in every direction, blocking the sun in some areas, shrouding it in twilight, yet bright and open in others, feeding the ground life with rich energy and sustenance.

If he paused to listen, which he had long gotten used to it, he could hear the forest sounds speaking to him, constant squeals, loud chirps and the occasional growl.

'Mother Nature in all her glory.'

He stood in the midst of a ten metre square patch of grass, mostly battened down by his foot treads, which he had carefully mapped out on the ground with over a hundred individual wooden stakes tied together by white weatherproof string to form a gigantic checker board, ten by ten grid, specifically for digging, searching and excavation.

Over the grid was a large green tarp with a white covered layer for sun reflection, suspended by four poles at each of the four corners of the site, pulled taut, but angled high from the centre to allow rain torrents to spill down and away from the dig as opposed to pooling and crashing down on the occupant beneath.

He had examined five blocks so far, having found two arrowheads, a piece of broken pottery and some bone fragments.

The bones appeared to be a Capuchin monkey, based on its large shape and round skull.

Nothing anyone was looking for. Least of all him. But he kept them anyway.

He was Doctor Hayden Lattimer, archeologist and purveyor of the past. He stood at six one, with short blonde hair, slightly askew from his many weeks spent in the jungle. He had bright blue eyes, which could melt a woman's heart, and had done many times, even if inadvertently, framed by a chiseled jaw and perfect teeth. Combined with smooth tanned skin, tinted with a touch of red when the sun was at its strongest, and a well formed physique, he considered himself quite the hunk, trying not to be arrogant about it.

It was simply nature's selection.

He looked well kept, as no matter how many days he spent in the wild, his appearance was something he took pride in.

'Not all animals in the jungle had to look uncivilized.' He theorized.

Today he sported a blue short sleeved collared shirt, a light brown vest and matching khakis, and a pair of well-worn high top hiking boots, crusted by mud.

Around his neck draped a compass on a chain, given to him by his father, with the instructions, with it, he would always find his way home. The only unique feature, his father had it custom made, with North removed and the text "Beer" put in its place.

His father was funny that way.

His current sabbatical from the University of Toronto included his search for ancient tribal life in the Americas as it was considered his archeological expertise, and the only reason the board approved it.

Hayden was not flamboyant like his American whip wielding and fedora wearing cousin to the South, nor his gun toting British baby sister in tight shorts and big breasts to the East. However, if he was correct, they only had one PhD each, whereas he had two. He might be your average run of the mill archeologist out of Toronto Canada, but he was a damn smart one. The mainstay of his studies was ancient societies and his second doctorate was ancient languages and the secrets they contained.

Secrets he always sought to find.

Hayden took a break from his digging. He pulled out his smartphone and smiled. "Awesome. I got a signal today." He liked to talk to himself. When you did lonely jungle excavations in the middle of nowhere, you had to have someone intelligent to listen to.

Hayden turned into the webpage for GTNN news. Global Television News Network out of Toronto, his home town. He was hoping his favourite reporter might be on, Annabelle Veracity. Blonde, beautiful and brilliant. Dumb women did nothing for him. He would rather talk to a post.

He tuned in a lot more to GTNN after they had that huge debacle a few years back. Something to do with a huge meltdown at the station, a police crackdown and the capture of some guy who tried to frame a cop for a crime he didn't commit. Actually dressed up like the cop to do it. Mr. X or something like that.

Whatever it was, Hayden was now a fan.

Once online, he watched for a few minutes. Nothing of any interest and his anticipated reporter was on vacation.

'Maybe in South America?' He thought. *'Yeah, right.'*

He quickly checked the weather prediction webpages.

A storm was coming his way this afternoon.

Hayden rose and moved out from under the cover of the tarp, letting the warm and welcoming air envelope his face and exposed arms. Even in the morning, it felt hot and toasty.

Suddenly, he felt a pang of pain in his lower region.

"Maybe I shouldn't have drunk all that coffee this morning." Hayden muttered. "But then again, Waste not, want not."

Hayden turned and put his one hand on his hip.

The camp was almost a mile away in heavy brush. He had a machete which he used to clear a path over recent weeks, but a mile was still a mile.

He never liked to camp too close to his excavation site. The reason was, in the night, with the pulled up Earth, it tended to attract night crawlers and their like from around the forest, to explore and search for newly dug food and snacks in the soft and freshly turned soil. And imaging a bunch of creepy crawlers prancing all over him while he slept gave him the '*Heebee Jeebees*.'

Archeologist or not, he did not like such things. '*His archeologist cousin hated snakes didn't he?*'

He looked at his watch and considered the time it would take to trek back to the camp, followed by his return for more digging before the predicted storm forced him to quit.

Regardless of all the artificial lighting in the world, sunlight was the safest for digging up ancient artifacts as it did only natural damage to discoveries, unlike the bright halogen radiation of modern luminesce which could scorch delicate and unprotected finds in minutes.

'*Finds*' he desperately sought.

And in South America, a great deal remained unexplored and a mystery to the modern world.

He didn't mind the walk back, as he did it daily, but he only had to piss.

'*What could it hurt? Who would know?*'

Moving away from his excavation, he carefully stepped into the heavier woods, over two well planted logs, under a large moss covered branch and past a pile of boulders. He moved several metres through the trees looking for a private and barren location.

He didn't want to soil his site.

Beneath a heavily tree covered area, he finally reached a private spot and about time as he was ready to explode.

He unzipped his fly and suddenly paused. Right before him was a small metal spike rammed into the Earth with a tiny triangular red flag on it, no taller than a foot in height, etched with the letter "M" on the material.

'What's this doing out here?' He thought.

Turning left and then right, he saw no one in any direction.

He mused. *'I'm in South America after all, who'd know?'*

He took aim and fired forth. He felt relief taking over as he started to empty his full bladder.

At least until he suddenly heard a furious feminine yell. "What the Hell are you doing?!"

Problem was with thick forests, a quick inspection did not mean no one was there.

'All those damn trees'

Hayden stopped urinating mid-completion. He took a breath as stage fright set in. His body started to feel the burn. He figured he might as well be honest. "Trying to take a piss, if you don't mind?"

"I do mind!" The woman's voice snapped. "That little flag you've chosen to mark your territory with by your excrements is my marker for a possible unknown flora."

Hayden wanted to finish, but his intruder was making that impossible. He couldn't turn in another direction based on her position without giving a show. Choking down the pain, knowing he would pay for it later, he zipped up and spun to face her, ready to defend what he did. Before he could fire back, his breath caught in his chest.

The woman before him was stunning, even by model standards. Her long auburn hair, layered by thin streaks of blonde, was pulled straight and tied behind her head in a ponytail, draping down to the middle of her back. She had soft tanned skin, with an almost perfectly shaped face, a short pert little nose, small mouth and a dimple on her left cheek. Her eyes were a deep hazel brown, with flecks of yellow, like pure amber.

Hayden found himself thinking he was lucky he wasn't an insect or he would be spending an eternity trapped in those golden pools.

She wore a long sleeve white cotton dress shirt, brown khakis and hiking boots, obviously for the area they were in. She had a pair of gold wire-rimmed glasses, which appeared more for reading and examining things than visual impairment, resting at the top of her hairline, deeply wedged between her strands. Over her shoulder, a large carry pack with numerous items, a small shovel and a stainless steel coring unit for digging around plants and protecting their roots. Finally, a stack of petri-dishes, pressed one inside the other for easy retrieval and capping, hanging over her belt. Some were filled with dirt and plant life.

Hayden was at a loss for words.

The woman on the other hand felt no such inhibition. "I ask again, what the Hell do you think you're doing?"

"Isn't it obvious?" He stood firm. "I was taking a well-deserved piss. We're in a jungle after all."

She glared at him. "Yes. Miles and miles of jungle in fact. Yet in of all this space, you choose to soil a one inch flag in the middle of this area because it helps you focus your aim?" She took a breath. "What's wrong with you? Bladder issues? Ever hear of adult diapers?"

"No. I..." Hayden stopped. He felt no explanation would justify what he was doing, so why bother. "My name's Hayden by the way. Doctor Hayden Lattimer."

"Did I ask for your name? I asked why you chose to urinate on my scientific marker?"

Hayden figured he might as well be himself. His dad always taught him, always be yourself as it can go one of two ways, they love you or hate you.

"Look. I'm sorry. We can go have a beer back at my camp to make up. And if it was the piss you're worried about, I'll have plenty more pretty soon. In fact, tomorrow morning, I'll have lots."

The woman's eyes clenched. "Did you just proposition me?"

"That depends..." Hayden shrugged. "Are you accepting?"

"I'm afraid I would get pissed on." She snidely offered. "That and I find the inhabitants around us more enticing. At least, they're more evolved."

'Thanks Dad. This time, the latter.' But Hayden had to admit. *'It wasn't a no either.'*

The woman brushed him aside and stared down in the now steaming area. She quickly dawned a pair of surgical gloves, the latex snapped as she thrust them on. "Should I keep my gloves on for when I check the remainder of my markers?"

"No need." Hayden shrugged. "I only found the one."

She shook her head. "So you know, you pissed on a possible undiscovered plant?"

Hayden looked down with a shrug. "It's obviously not undiscovered if you found it."

The woman looked at him with true vehemence. "You said you were a doctor?" She seemed to scoff. "You can't be a micro-biologist too?"

Hayden was never a fan of that area of science, but obviously she was.

"No. I'm an archeologist." Hayden said it proudly.

"Oh" She paused, looking down at her plant carefully cutting around it with a stainless steel blade. "I thought you were a *real Doctor.*" She emphasized the sarcasm in *real*.

He ignored her, knowing many in his doctoral community received such criticism, but they knew and always understood, archeology was the foundation of many discoveries. Those who did not understand the past were doomed to repeat it. He decided to go with the flow. "I never got your name by the way."

"That's because I didn't offer it."

Hayden realized she was not going to offer this readily. "Then why are you being so obviously intrusive?"

"Me being intrusive?" She sneered, standing up and placing the flower into one of her petri holders with a touch of plant food. "My question is more along the lines of, 'Why are *you* being intrusive?' Besides the opportunity to soil one of my scientific research markers?" She looked at him.

"I'm doing an excavation." He pointed back to the tarp and set up.

She let her eyes slide in that direction and back. "So don't you have a camp? A latrine you can use?"

Hayden leaned up against a tree and grinned. "I like to *rough it.*"

"*Rough it?*" She really seemed to take great annoyance in that answer. She drew a circle in the air around them. "Regardless, I have a permit to be doing a scientific investigation in this very area. What about you?"

"So do I." Hayden responded with confidence. "I have a permit to do an archeological investigation." He drew an equally big circle in the air. Then he paused, repeated the gesture, this time making it a bit bigger. "In this very area."

"Impossible." She paused, more in disbelief. "Let me see it."

Hayden grinned. "I'll show you mine if you show me yours."

She bristled, both at his immaturity and his not listening to her order. She turned to rummage through her packsack.

In seconds, she pulled out a yellow piece of paper, with the Government of South America logo watermarked in the corner, typewritten with specific GPS co-ordinates, Global Positioning System, for this very area. "Here is MY permit. From this point and a two mile radius in every direction. All to do my research on behalf of my company, without being urinated on."

Hayden at this point felt obligated. From his back pocket, he withdrew an equally designed permit, stamped in the same way with all the matching signatures.

Both held up their permits in front of the other.

The woman's mouth fell open as she stared at his, appearing shocked. "This can't be right. It's for the exact same area, overlapping one another." She rechecked hers and returned to his. "This is absolute crap. I'm going back to the government offices in town about this." She packed the remaining things in her backpack. "And you're coming with me. If for no other reason than to prevent you from vacating your bowels on my remaining flags."

Hayden happily accepted to join her. He wasn't concerned with the crossover in the designated areas. Personally, he could care less. In fact, when she held up the permit, he hadn't even bothered with reading the parameters of it at all.

He convinced her to show it to him for the one thing he was looking for.

He smiled.

His mystery woman's name was Doctor Danica Swift.

5

During the first decade of the 21st century, South American governments have drifted to the political left, with socialist leaders being elected in Chile, Uruguay, Brazil, Argentina, Ecuador, Bolivia, Paraguay, Peru and Venezuela. Despite this, South America, for the most part, still embraces free market policies like that of the United States. They are also taking a more active role towards greater continental integration as a whole.

Recently, an intergovernmental entity had formed, attempting to merge the two existing unions: Mercosur and the Andean Community, thus forming the third-largest trade bloc. This new political organization was known as Union of South American Nations. Their sole purpose was to establish free movement of its people, improve economic development and build a common defense policy for the country.

But like any government, from sophisticated to third world, there are and always will remain the bureaucracies.

Danica stormed into the office of SAHASE, South American Historical And Scientific Expedition permit preparation and approval division. She let the door drop back on its overly tightened spring, slamming into the frame.

Someone obviously liked having the door kept firmly closed.

Hayden sauntered in behind, dodging the door deftly, hands in his pockets looking exasperated. Having shared Danica's jeep back into town to save on gas, something he was now deeply regretting, he sighed openly. He had never driven for three hours in a vehicle with someone who couldn't stop talking.

Mostly to tell him why *he* was wrong.

'Next time I see one of your flags, I hope I have to take a shit.' But he chose to keep that little thought to himself.

It was a small barren office which consisted of two desks, one phone, a fax machine and a computer that made most typewriters look modern. On the dirt soiled walls, or it might have been its paint colour, were numerous tourist posters defining the wonders of South America, from the world's highest waterfall: Angel Falls in Venezuela to the world's largest river: the Amazon, from the world's longest mountain range: the Andes to the world's largest rainforest: the Amazon Rainforest.

Hayden wanted to point out. *'But we're already here.'* But felt it would fall upon deaf ears.

Behind the desk, boots up on the blotter, hands behind his head, napping comfortably, sat the administrator. A small man, five six, with short black hair, curled and pressed around his sides, with dark tanned skin and brown hair on every exposed area except his face. He wore a light yellow short sleeved dress shirt and matching pants, both sweat stained, and a name tag pinned to his pocket which read, "Diego Mantoya - Customer Service Is Our Mandate."

To the side of the desk, a five foot circulating fan, blowing hard across his face, to which he seemed totally unaware.

Danica slammed both her hands onto the desk, her permit crumpled under her fingers with authority, shaking the four legged furniture until a stapler fell off the side into a tin garbage can beside it. It clanged as it fell.

The man's eyes opened lazily, feet unmoved, not startled in the least. He seemed to get woken up like this a lot. He muttered without looking up. "Welcome to the South American Historical And Scientific Expedition permit office. How may I be of service of to you today?"

Hayden was impressed. No sarcasm at all.

Danica got down right to the point. "You can be of service to me by explaining how I and him..." She gestured with her thumb to Hayden without turning. "Both got permits for the same segment of jungle for the same time frame for two different scientific explorations."

The man already had the answer prepared. "It's a big jungle."

Danica appeared to have been visibly slapped. "You mean it was intentional?"

Diego let his feet drop to the floor. He reached over and opened the first drawer to his right. He pulled out two trays, one with unapproved blank permits and one with stamped and approved ones. He explained with as much patience as he could. "Basically, you come in and you ask for a segment to work. From there, we ask you to show us your credentials and we validate your survey plans. Once confirmed, I check to ensure no one is living on the area you seek or owns it. Once validated it is a public domain, I give you a permit." He held up a recently approved copy. "Viola. And you're good to go."

Danica was flabbergasted. "That's it. All I have to do is point at your map and say I would like to search there and all you do is make sure there are no huts on it and I get a permit?"

"That and no villages." Diego smiled, speaking without inflection. "But essentially, you got it."

Even Hayden found it a bit amusing. This office was more interested in the administration fees than the overlap of scientific teams.

But admittedly, each permit provided for a two mile radius from the point of selection, so too many overlaps was entirely difficult. Plus, how many people really needed to block two miles from being encroached upon by other researchers?

Hayden then turned to glance in Danica's direction. *'Well, maybe one.'*

Danica slammed her hands on the desk again. "Do you know how much money my company has invested in this little project of mine?"

Diego smiled. "In regards to your permit, seventy-five dollars."

Danica seemed insulted. "Maximum Pharmaceuticals invests a Hell of a lot more than that."

Diego pointed to the crumpled paper in her hand. "Not for that permit. It was only seventy five dollars."

Hayden interjected with some annoyance. "I paid eighty."

Diego smiled. "Yours was Canadian. We charge more for the conversion."

Hayden was about to point out if Diego bothered to check a newspaper, he would discover, the Canadian dollar was higher right now. But then again, he felt it was not worth the debate.

Danica on the other hand was not ready to give in. "My company is headquartered out of Toronto Canada."

"Really?" Diego looked visibly surprised at that. "Then I must terribly apologize."

Danica turned to give Hayden an *'I told you so look."*

Which was quickly wiped away when Diego interrupted her with. "Then you still owe us five dollars."

Hayden had to turn away to control the burst of laughter that shot out from his chest.

Danica snapped back to see if he was kidding.

Diego wasn't. His hand was open for the additional five dollars.

Before Danica could make matters worse, Hayden handed Diego a five dollar Canadian bill.

Danica sneered in Hayden's direction. "I could have paid the five dollars so you know."

"I don't doubt it." Hayden slipping his wallet back into the side pocket of his pants. "You look like a woman with money."

Danica was unsure if Hayden was being humorous or sarcastic. "I've written three books."

Hayden shrugged. "I've never read them."

"I'm not surprised. I use very few monosyllables." Danica turned back to Diego, but still speaking to Hayden. "That and I can't picture you getting past page eight without muttering the word 'Duh' at least three times."

Diego snickered loudly. "That was a good one senor." He officially recorded the five dollar bill in his logbook. "Your wife is very funny."

Hayden and Danica both turned in his direction and spoke in unison. "We're not married."

Diego grinned at that. "Could have fooled me."

Hayden leaned against the rear wall and asked Diego pointe blank. "What are our options here?"

Diego looked as his manual, which appeared untouched as it had a deep coffee ring on top from where his drink always sat. "Well, you both can do one of three things." He stared at Danica and Hayden. "One: you both work on the same plot of land, of *two miles*...." He let the word two miles stretch out defining how big an area it was and the two of them fighting over it like bickering children was foolish. "And do your work without bothering the other."

Danica and Hayden said nothing. Both had their arms crossed and providing equally icy stares.

Diego continued. "Two: One of you returns your permit, no refunds of course, and leaves the other to do their work. When theirs expires, you may return and I will provide you a new permit." He looked at his stamps. "At half the price."

Hayden and Danica turned to one another and their facial expressions said it all, neither would be returning their permit.

Diego offered his final suggestion. "Or three, I revoke both your permits and alert my government to have both your passports banned indefinitely, followed by the formal sealing of our borders from both your companies... Corporate and educational." He looked to them both. "Blocked from entrance into South America for the next ten years."

Diego paused to ensure they both understood the magnitude of forcing the administrator to become involved, whose only desire was to stamp forms and nap all day.

Hayden barely waited a second to jump in. "I'm for *fucking* door number one."

Danica stared at Hayden and what she felt was an unnecessary use for swearing. "I'm for number one as well." She glared in Hayden's direction with resignation. "Presuming he can stop pissing on my markers."

At this Diego bristled, turning in Hayden's direction with true annoyance. "Sir. I must point out, urinating on our land is punishable by a very expensive fine."

Danica smiled waiting to see Hayden get himself out of this.

Hayden asked. "How much for a permit?"

Diego looked at Hayden with seriousness in his eyes, then smiled. "Eighty more dollars."

With Danica's mouth wide open in shock, Hayden reached for his wallet.

6

For the next couple of weeks, Danica and Hayden worked in virtual silence, only occasionally crossing paths with one another in the jungle while completing their assignments.

Each time with Danica donning a pair of surgical gloves to check her flags when she spotted him in her proximity and Hayden holding his *special* permit aloft when standing near the flags.

She rolled her eyes every time.

After a while, she did find it a bit funny. Not many men would pay good money to purchase and memorialize on a government document his bad first impression.

She forgave him after week three. She would never tell him though, knowing the smug little grin that would follow it.

Danica did pass by Hayden's camp one afternoon as she was doing some sample cuttings and saw for the first time his work space. It was an aluminum shack situated to the side of a large well cared for denim tent. The work structure was eight feet cubed with an angled roof for water run-off. He was at the side door, seated on a tripod stool with a wooden sand sifter for manually breaking up chunks of piled soil he scooped in, shaking it gently, allowing the finer bits to drop through the wire mesh and letting the larger pieces remain for examination.

Hayden looked up, spotted her and waved her over, offering a tour.

She politely declined with a smooth tilt of her hand.

He winked and resumed his work.

Later in the day, on her second pass, with her return to her camp, this time passing closer, she asked him why no locks on the shack door.

He casually replied. "Most thieves have little interest in old pottery shards, animal bones and dried shit." Before she could question his professionalism in his remark, he added. "Feces being organic make for a better carbon dating of the soil. You'd be surprised how much one manure patty can tell you."

She didn't argue as she knew he was right.

It was the magic of nature.

And Danica, being a field research micro-biologist, was dispatched into the world to seek out such magic. To investigate and find undiscovered animals and flora, at the bequest of her employer, the Canadian conglomerate known as Maximum Pharmaceuticals, as like her, they believed in Gaia, Goddess of Earth, scientifically speaking. They knew full well the power of the planet and the secrets she coveted.

Her executive owners personally funded such expeditions into the wild as they believed all answers could be, and would be found if only someone was looking.

And they wanted their employees to be the first eyes to set upon these very mysteries.

In university, she learned from her favourite professor, Doctor Deryl Ward, who liked to spend his free time bartending at a pub he owned, that secrets could be found anywhere, from deep inside the belly of a shark to the microscopic flecks of moss that grew under rocks beneath a tree, from the hottest steam filled caverns of an active volcano to the icy depths of the ocean where no man had ever tread.

'*It's not much of a secret if you can find it easily.*' was Doctor Ward's motto. That and, "*Don't pour the beer straight up or it'll be full of head.*'

She'd swear he had some Irish blood in him.

And because her PhD was in microbial enzymology and proteins analysis in jungle habitats with specifics to animals and plants, she kept her investigations to the jungles of the world. She had found the claustrophobic environment of underwater terrains to be less than inviting. Also as she only held two Master degrees in underwater aquatic microorganisms, she felt it wiser to keep her focus on where she liked her feet planted, terra firma, as it was her specialty.

****

As the days passed on, Hayden finally took some time to wander over to Danica's camp. He found himself slightly in awe at her set up. Unlike his metal storage structure, all university funded, she had a large ten foot long, eight foot high glass enclosed greenhouse, outfitted with a titanium frame and inch thick glass windows. He tapped it. He would not be surprised to discover it was bulletproof. To the side, a HEPA filter was running constantly on a hybrid solar generator. And finally, at the door, a palm scanning bio reader to confirm identity before opening.

He actually whistled aloud.

And even her tent wasn't standard. It was a modern geodesic dome made from equivalent materials, with exception to the glass, and a high powered air conditioner continually running with an almost silent purr.

He spotted Danica right away in front of a stationary desktop computer, under a white tarp suspended above an umbrella-like cover to protect the precious equipment beneath, with a satellite receiver outfitted to the top of the antenna tip. Like the greenhouse, the equipment was connected to a solar generator.

Unlike Hayden, Danica waved, but offered no invitation to view her greenhouse.

He never expected one. Like her, he understood, in the world of pharmacology and biological research, secrets were hard to keep and expensive to lose.

He returned to his work, once or twice kicking at the ground.

For a few brief seconds, Hayden found himself doubting his career path.

****

A week later, in the midst of their work activities, the sun was burning down hot and heavy. The air was dry and acrid, causing both Danica and Hayden to continually drink from bottles of water, Hayden's water purchased and shipped in on a supply truck and Danica's distilled by an onsite water recycling unit and refilled.

But regardless, the heat was making both their work difficult and uncomfortable.

Danica decided to turn her investigation into the deeper and darker areas of the heavier jungle. And because she was not designated to one spot, one of the advantages of searching for the unknown, she donned a pair of heavier pants and a long sleeve coat for her trip. Regardless of heat, the plants could be harsh, as even in this heat, some discomfort was far superior to deep gouges or cuts from sharp leaves or edged branches. Plus once under the canopy of the high top trees, the shade made it remarkably cooler.

She carried with her a soil sampler and a custom designed handheld bio-screener. It was a comparison analyzer which took a three dimensional scan of any plant she found and uploaded it into the camp server. From there, the scan would be digitized and sent to the company library back in Toronto, where it would be verified as having been discovered or not. This was quickly followed by a text message on her satellite smartphone with the results. Each scan took no more than three minutes as her home database was very comprehensive and easily accessible via her Wi-Fi network at the camp.

A network which her records showed Doctor Lattimer several times using to download movies for his personal entertainment. Out of amusement, she clicked disconnect when he was ten minutes from the end, but she later reactivated it. She really didn't care, but he did piss on one of her flags.

But then again, had it been porn, she would have blocked him permanently.

In the course of the three weeks she had been there, nine remaining, she had discovered six new plant genera. Her company was very pleased. None showed any potential yet, but finding them was the first step. She took samples of each, had them transplanted to the greenhouse for reintegration into her hydroponic bay and prepared for transport back to the main research facility in Ontario for future analysis.

She wandered in the thick underbrush, carefully moving plants out of her way with her gloved hands. Unlike some researchers who used a machete to chop and hack away at the path in front of them, clearing the route like a raccoon searching garbage bags for food, she was more careful. She refuses to rip and tear away with total disregard for her environment. Others, not aware of the irony, sought Mother Nature for help, but shredding her apart as they did.

'Barbarians.' Is how Danica viewed them.

As she got deeper in, the heavy trees above, some centuries old by her cursory view of their bark, shrouded the area in shadows. She held her flashlight at ready as a few times, she was hard-pressed to see the ground.

She came upon a large dirt mound, completely covered in vines, foliage and teeming with plant life. She quickly checked her denim gloves for rips or tears. She had a new pair with her if needed.

Mostly to ensure no skin was exposed when she carefully pulled back at plants. Avoiding thorns or barb as unlike poison ivy, in South America, a newly undiscovered plant could kill if one was not extremely careful.

She always was.

She tugged back on some of the heavier vines, turning them over, reviewing their bellies, truly impressed with their growth rate, especially by their lack of sunlight, when she suddenly froze.

She tilted her head and looked at the hard mound underneath.

It was far more solid than one would expect for a pile of mud and dirt.

She rubbed her hand over some of the wet soil, brushing away rocks and found herself staring at an engraved tablet of stone. Before she could be amazed, she groaned, knowing damn well who she needed to call.

****

Hayden actually thanked her.

And when he arrived at the stone tablet, his mouth dropped in awe.

He turned to her in total shock.

She casually mentioned. "You kiss me, you die."

Hayden ignored her remark as he was on cloud nine. He had no expectation to find anything on this trip, least of all a tablet with ancient writings on it buried in the jungle.

Danica stood behind him while he knelt on the mound. Hayden was now sporting a pair of gold rimmed reading glasses with numerous magnifying lenses on pivoting pins, not unlike a multifaceted screwdriver, each outfitted to twist in front of his eyes to change magnification.

Old school, but to some, very effective.

Behind him were two illuminated tripods he brought back with him from his camp that used low level UV lighting, very bright yet safer on artifacts.

He wiped away a lot of the dirt with a small soft bristle brush, and was about to cut away the vine with his knife when he heard a severe clearing of Danica's throat.

He turned and saw her glaring at him at the prospect of cutting away any form of plant life to get to dead stone.

As she had not needed to show him this, he acquiesced. He carefully and delicately moved the vine to the side, not causing them any harm and examined the tablet with a cleaner view. While he looked, he had put on a pair of white cotton gloves.

Danica stared at him quizzically.

While reading, he sensed her reaction. "Human sweat is far more caustic than any element in my estimate for archeology. Even worse than years of rain and weather." Hayden explained. "Cotton is far superior for absorbing our salt excrements and body acids so I can protect the discovery."

In this, he handed her a pair in case she wanted to touch anything.

For a few minutes, Hayden was staring intently at the stone block while Danica waited.

"And?"

Hayden held up his hand. Not to silence her, but to signal her to wait. He was trying to translate it. Even if it was his skillset, he needed time as he did not recognize some of the symbols.

'A new tribe?' was the first excited thought that came to him.

Danica stood back patiently. As a scientist, she was well aware you could not rush discoveries.

Hayden paused, seemingly confused by what he is reading. "From what I see, this is a story tablet of a travelling tribe."

"Travelling?"

"Yes. They're an offshoot of a more stationary tribe. One that never leaves its home."

Danica was perplexed. "Then why did this one leave?"

Hayden paused in his reading. "Think of it like a teenager. They always want to go out into the world and learn things on their own, even though the parents are happy to live their lives at home." He held his hands up and open. "Ancient tribes are pretty much the same. Their parents want to remain in one area, whatever the reason is, food, weather or even need, while the children have no interest in taking up the family business, so they move on."

"Then why the story?" Danica asked, always happy to learn, but feeling comforted by the ease in which Hayden talked, explaining it in a way both educationally, but not in a manner as to seem he was talking down to the listener.

'He'd make a good teacher.' She thought.

"Well, the younger members eventually grow into adults as well. And as far as they travel from home, they still remember their roots. But like all humanity, they know their time is limited, so to protect their legacy, they document it for future generations, to let their children know where they came from." Hayden paused. "Not unlike we do with history books, but tribes use what's available."

Danica understood.

Hayden seemed to suddenly fill with energy. He started to push away at the remaining foliage, long vines having grown over the rocks, some ingrained into the artwork. He made sure to push them outward, some high and some low, but away from the tablet, all under the confused eyes of Danica.

He finally turned to her. "I'm so sorry. But I need to cut the ones at the left side." He said it with genuine deep remorse, but worse, with sad puppy dog eyes, which Danica hated, mostly because it was working.

But because she had already confirmed the plants were common and well known, she answered he could do so.

Like a surgeon, Hayden carefully and delicately cut away stalks, drawing them away and placing them onto the earth to re-root. He ran his fingers around the edges of the tablet.

Once all the plant life was pulled away, he could see it was three feet tall and two feet wide. Completely covered in individual carvings and patterns.

Danica spotted a vine at the upper edge he missed. She reached forward and pulled gently on it, not noticing it had grown down into one of the pictorials.

Hayden lunged to stop her, but not before she drew it out.

There was a cracking sound. A chip of rock pulled free taking with it a small chunk of the message. Not a lot, but one symbol was now laced with thin filaments of cracks.

Danica froze in shock unaware the edges were that brittle.

"So my pissing on your flag a few weeks back..." Hayden turned to Danica. "I assume this is your revenge?"

"I was only trying to help." She glared at him. "That and I understand plants far better than you do. I was moving it away."

Hayden sighed. He was still extremely thankful for her showing him this at all, so he was not going to get too annoyed. "Fine. But don't pull anything else. At least not yet. I'm afraid of destroying what's underneath."

At this Danica, for the first time in a very long time, felt a wiggle of excitement. In her world, you found unknown plants, undiscovered species and even modern cures. But ancient items were rare and when found, something you passed on to others who were more studied the field, like Doctor Lattimer. So being invited to help on such matters was quite interesting. "What do you mean by underneath?"

At this Hayden smiled. "This is not a tablet." He pointed to two long tracks of stone along the top and bottom. "It's a door. And a sliding one at that." He pointed to the corners of the stone. "Pretty sophisticated too, but not entirely difficult for most cultures."

Danica leaned forward and looked at the divots running along the grooves, filled by dirt and years of moss. She understood growth patterns, but this door design was outside her expertise.

Luckily, not outside Doctor Lattimer's.

He pointed to the plant filled grooves. "I'll need to go back to camp to get some sterile water to pour in, or maybe some natural lubricant. I'll have to get a wood chisel as metal will be too damaging. But if we're lucky, we may even be able to slide it open."

Danica was actually thrilled. "Like a treasure box?"

"I doubt it." Hayden shrugged. "Most tribes found little value in such things as treasure." He grinned with the excitement of a school boy. "But I can assure you of this, it's bigger than a box. In fact, based on the size of the portal, I would say it hides a full chamber."

Danica was hovering around with uncontrolled excitement. "A chamber to what?"

"Based on the tablet, a story chamber."

Danica paused, genuinely perplexed. "What's a story chamber?"

"Like I mentioned, travelling tribes liked to document their past. And the best way to do that was on stone. Most often in deep caves. Because there's certainly no point in going to all the trouble of creating a lifelong history for future generations and then having the weather wash it away in one downpour."

Hayden considered an example. "Imagine if Eskimos carved the stories of their past onto the top of frozen ponds. Absolutely pointless as it would vanish with the rising of the summer sun." He leaned forward and pointed around the dirt mound. "So if a cave wasn't available, the tribe would have to build one. Most often, they dug deep pits and used large flat rocks on the inside to maintain the structure. Once placed, they would compact mud and clay all around it for safety, and to hide its true purpose." He ran his fingers along carvings in the tablet. "But most of all, once dried, they would have lots of interior flat surfaces on the inside to scribe their history, safe from the scorching outside world. Topping it off with a door, not unlike this one to protect it."

Danica, remembering old adventure movies she watched as a child, asked. "Do you think it could be booby-trapped?"

Hayden shook his head. "Very unlikely. If the tribe wanted their youth to know their story, and wanted them to read it, setting off an array of sharp weapons to greet them would really dampen the desire to re-visit their history." He shrugged. "But I'll check. Err on the side of caution if you will."

"So what does the story say?"

"That is what you and I will be the first to find out. The story is inside."

Danica paused. "Then what is written on the outside?"

Hayden turned. "It's reads like an epitaph. It tells us the name of this tribe which seems to mean *Sun Seekers*." Hayden pointed to the symbol which looked like a group of human beings with a sun symbol in front of the figures, but out of reach. "That and mostly simple directions on how to access the chamber beneath. This is how I ascertained right away it was a door, not a grave marker."

"Sure looks like a lot of symbols for directions."

"Well there is a warning."

Danica felt a chill run up her spine. "A warning of what?"

Hayden seemed nonchalant. "That's just it. From what I read, and guess, it says. '*Beware, the knowledge you seek of our ancestors...*' Which by that, they seem to be referring to the parent tribe I suspect, '*bears great peril*.'"

"That's cryptic?" She stated matter-of-factly. "So the chamber beneath isn't dangerous?"

"From this doorway, no. It's the knowledge the chamber contains within that warrants the warning." Hayden smiled sheepishly, excitement in his eyes. "But we'll find out more when we open it."

Danica looked guilty for a second. "Don't we need a permit to do this?"

At this Hayden paused. "Technically, no. First, we discovered it, so we get a lot of leeway there. But once we alert the South American government, we'll have a shit more red tape to deal with. And unlike our visitor and examination permits, the license for excavating an actual find is far more than eighty dollars. We're talking hundreds of thousands."

Danica considered calling back home, but decided to wait, at least until she saw inside. She knew her company would foot the bill if century old plant life lived within.

Hayden continued. "That and we'll have the universities down here marking off places for study. And worse, the government officials watching our every move. And with them weighing and cataloging everything we find, it will be impossible to do what we are best at, explore."

Danica hesitated.

Hayden threw in his ace. "Trust me in this, Maximum Pharmaceuticals will have no claim whatsoever to what's in there once the government takes dominion."

Danica had no love lost for government takeovers of things, but still. "Is this illegal?"

"Definitely not. I'm an archeologist with a permit to excavate here and this is within my zone. Second, you're a board certified microbiologist with equal qualifications, so both of us can be entrusted to inspect a new site." He took a breath. "But if we do discover anything of monetary value, we have to report it right away." He paused. "Then again. If we find something of an educational value solely, we can probably get away with a week before alerting the government."

"So I guess that means we're going to open it?"

Hayden grinned. "Fuck yeah!"

Ignoring his vernacular, she had a quick daydream, imagining herself opening an ancient buried chamber and finding a hidden secret beneath from the past so valuable, those in the scientific world would forever remember her name.

For a few brief seconds, Danica doubted her career path.

****

Hayden returned from his camp with a special tool to chip away all the dirt, mud and natural building up of earth, all which prevented them from simply sliding the door open. That and a compressed air jet sprayer to blow loose particles when he felt his hands were too firm for the delicate work.

He used a natural oil to pour into the grooves, the gentlest organic one the university offered, to lubricate the edges. He had not originally planned to bring any, but, *'Chance favours the prepared mind.'* He was always told.

Finally, once complete, he leaned back with Danica at his side, but not opening the door.

She waited a full minute and finally asked. "Are you going to open it or what?"

Hayden replied. "I think tomorrow would be better. With the night coming, the cold night air and potential rain may make our inspection less than optimal. From my inspections of the designs, it's been here for over four hundred years, so I'm pretty sure one more day won't hurt it."

Danica for the first time since the door's discovery looked perplexed. She mentioned aloud. "That's curious?"

Hayden froze. When an educated person, one as intelligent as Doctor Swift made the statement, *'That's curious?'* you listened.

He asked. "What do you mean by that?"

"How old did you say this door was, based on your initial examination?"

Hayden gestured to several pictorials and drawings etched into the stone. "Until we do some quantitative testing, based on the use of certain symbols, I would say by language and dialect, it would be approximately four hundred years old. Maybe older."

"That is very strange." Danica maintained.

"Why's that?" Hayden paused, genuinely interested.

Danica pointed to the plant life, branches and roots that grew to cover the tablet. "These plants, the base ones, and the roots, even the deeper entrenched ones are only about one hundred to hundred and twenty years old at best. Give or take a decade."

Hayden too found this intriguing, leaning in to look at the plants, but not seeing what Danica saw. "So what are you saying?"

Danica replied. "I'm saying over a hundred years ago, someone else discovered this chamber, removed the plants, opened your door, entered, got what they wanted, closed the door and then chose to un-discover it."

At this piece of information, Hayden and Danica were totally mystified.

But worse, completely hooked.

7

Hayden arrived the next morning to the chamber portal, green duffel bag over his shoulder and found Danica seated before it on what appeared to be a portable ultra-suede lounge chair, inflated for comfort, and drinking a frothy Cappuccino. She was reading a textbook underneath his portable lighting units. He looked down at this cup of instant coffee-like beverage and sneered, trying to suppress his jealousy. "Doesn't your company do anything shitty?"

Danica turned, swallowing her mouthful of steaming beverage and glared at him. "You know you swear a lot."

Hayden shrugged. "My father says swearing is a form of expression." He dumped out his drink no longer able to stomach it.

Danica still in her seat turned a page. "So is farting."

"Sorry about that. I thought I was downwind."

Danica rolled her eyes, closing her book and getting up. "My father told me, people swear when they can't think of something more intelligent to say."

"Really? In my world, swearing is simply words we as a society put taboos upon." Hayden dropped his bag in front of the chamber door. "It's how you use them that define their impression." He looked for the zipper. "Plus, if it wasn't meant to be said, it wouldn't be a part of our vocabulary."

"Having something and flouting it are two different things." Danica continued to drink from her cup. "We have guns, but we don't shoot everything we see simply because we can put holes in it."

Hayden sighed. "Do you know how many cultures over the years communicate with slang and swearing?"

"I would say for certain one. And that I think is still one too many."

Hayden unzipped his bag from top to bottom exposing an array of archeological tools within. "I suppose you never swear?"

Danica knelt down to join him. "Oh I swear. But trust me, when I do, there'll be a very good reason for doing it."

Hayden drew from his bag several shiny spikes attached to a long rope ladder. He reached inside again and handed to Danica a pair of safety glasses with two bright lights affixed to each side. "These are preferential to flashlights. They are brighter, but use softer light bulbs, which will be less harsh on the interior." He pointed to a switch on each side. "That and it keeps your hands free, letting you see in the direction you're looking. This way, we're not jamming or hooking things into the chamber structure more than necessary. At least, until we can better see its construction." He pulled a pair of soft bottomed slipcovers over his hiking boots to cover the treads. He handed a pair to Danica. "Our feet will do enough damage as it is, so let's try to be gentle by wearing these."

Danica nodded her understanding and put them on.

Hayden was the professional here.

Hayden and Danica focused on the door.

Over the evening, Hayden had squeezed the lubricant into all the creases and holes around the door, letting it settle into the edges naturally by gravity. Hoping by morning it would have oozed where they could not have pressed by hand.

But regardless of the oils used, the chamber door was several square feet of solid stone and three inches thick, so it was still pretty heavy.

Danica took the side and Hayden grabbed the top. Using their combined weight, Hayden using his knees in the dirt mound for leverage to push, Danica pulling with her back and shoulders, the two of them applied all their strength on the door. Twice Hayden let out a breath, but resumed his pushing, dirt piles forming behind his feet.

After several minutes, with the rock chipping a bit, small particles of soil rolling down to the base of the mound, Hayden wincing the entire time, the tablet started to move. After a half hour of careful pushing and sliding, the portal opened into a dark expanse.

Hayden wiped sweat from his brow. He reached into his pocket and pulled out a white rubber ball. He squeezed it for several seconds until it started to glow. Inside was a pressure sensitive light emitting diode, switching from red to blue to green every few seconds.

Danica gave him a quizzical look.

Hayden smiled. "My ex-girlfriend had a chocolate Labrador named Zack. I used to come home late from the university, but I still had to give the poor guy a run, so I bought him a set of three to take him to the park for night ball chases. This way, when I threw it, I could still see him. Well, maybe only a bobbing glow sphere in the darkness, but it was always racing back towards me. Zack loved it. So I kept one for luck."

Danica smiled thinking it was amusing to imagine.

Hayden dropped it down the portal. Seconds later, it bounced and rolled to a halt in the corner, lighting a small corner of the room with a dim multi-coloured glow. He peered inside activating the two flashlights on his glasses. After about a minute, he stated, "It's a single chamber. Smells a bit like mildew, but if that's the extent of the damage, then we can consider ourselves damn lucky." He poked his head further and went silent.

Danica waited a minute and then another. She was getting antsy, scientist or not. *Curiosity killed the cat.* "And?"

Hayden pulled his head out. "It's an almost perfect cube. Ten feet by ten feet. The floor has nothing written on it, so we should be safe to walk on it." He winked. "And no traps." He wiped some grime from his gloves. "And before you ask, there are no more doors. It's a single tribal story chamber of a travelling tribe as the door tablet described."

Danica pushed past Hayden to look inside. After a few seconds, she scrunched up her eyes. "What's that in the centre on the floor? Some sort of alter?"

"I've no idea." Hayden switching his work gloves to cotton ones. "But I can't see them erecting a story chamber and then using it to sacrifice things for their Gods. It would detract from its purpose." Hayden offered a tilt of his head. "Whatever it is, it's a part of their story."

Danica reached behind her and slammed the first ladder spike into the Earth. "Then what are we waiting for?"

****

Once inside, Danica and Hayden had carefully placed two low level lanterns in opposite corners, suspended from the door above to prevent damaging the interior and to illuminate the entire chamber. They still wore their flashlight glasses for more focused work, but the background light was helpful.

To Hayden, he was in heaven. Most archeologists do their work from schools, occasionally going into the field, but in today's modern times, rarely finding anything unexpected. So finding this was a dream come true.

He wanted to thank Danica profusely, but she made quite clear, any gesture would be quickly followed by a punch to the abdomen. And as a doctor, she would know where to hit to make it count.

Danica on the other hand was on her knees, examining mosses, small filaments of plant life and molds.

'To each their own.' Hayden thought.

Danica stopped and turned to him. "So where do we begin?"

Hayden pivoted his eye line from left to right, examining the walls. "We need to establish a timeline first. Pick the wrong spot and it's like reading a book by starting in the middle. But be assured, the creators would not want to make it difficult either. They created it with the purpose to be read; and because making a place like this defined a proud race, they would avoid confusing future generations by not making the starting point clear." He turned in the direction of the centrepiece in the middle of the room which first caught their eyes when they opened the door above. "Might as well start here."

It was a stone frame base, surrounded by vines and small foliage as the darkness prevented any major growth from invading. It was composed of the same rock as the walls, three feet tall, wider at the bottom than at the top, but not evenly formed on the sides. Inset into the top, dead centre, was a giant circular disc carved with hundreds of individual jagged lines, connected with one another, created by hand, not accidental, engraved like a giant maze of erratic cracks.

Hayden was perplexed as he walked around the tableau. "There's no writing on it at all."

"And what does that mean?"

"Of that, I'm unsure." He pointed to the blank walls of the base holding the tabletop. "I've never seen a component in a story chamber not used to record information. Tribes prided themselves on using everything, especially when they went to this much trouble to erect the chamber in the first place." He waved around to the walls. "Everything else is completely covered with sketches, etchings and drawings, no space left unfilled, yet this centrepiece is completely devoid of anything at all." He refocused on the centre. "With exception to the strange pattern of cracks and openings on the top disc-like thing."

Danica leaned over. "Maybe they used this as a desk to prepare the work?"

Hayden pointed to the circular inset. "Tribes rarely did rough sketches. Plus this is more a design than a writing surface." He put his finger into one of the cracks and pushed. It slid, but not by much. "What have we here?"

Danica leaned forward. "What is it?"

Hayden was looking down through the cracks. "There is another disc underneath." He tried to move it, but it did not spin further. "It's too heavy to turn." He pushed down the side and it sunk a touch. He put more strength into it, pushing down with his full body weight. It sunk a bit more, but rose again. He did it at several points along the circumference, each time it sinking in the same manner until the rim met the wall. He shook his head.

Danica asked. "Is there a problem?"

"No. I thought it might be a lid for a container, but they're too heavy to turn and too well balanced for hiding something inside." Hayden gestured. "That and based on the edges moving down and back up, there is some sort of central point or pin which the discs are balanced upon at the bottom. Taking into consideration of how tight fitting it is, I can't push it very far. It's designed to prevent all the discs from falling free."

"All the discs?"

Hayden pushed his finger deeper into one of the cracks. "From what I can feel, three minimum, possibly more?"

Danica was intrigued. She suggested. "Maybe it's a work of art or a mosaic."

Hayden shook his head. "Tribes made things with intent. Esthetics was never a factor. They didn't decorate for decorum's sake. So this little table had a purpose. I simply have no idea as to what."

"Maybe it was once filled with water." She pointed to the spacing around the sides. "Over the years, it probably evaporated or leaked out. I mean, if it were filled, would it not turn easier?"

"Not likely." Hayden offered. "Three reasons why not. One, the discs weigh about twenty pounds each by their shape and weight. And as a man who has dug up a lot of rocks, I can be pretty sure of my assessment. So even with salt water from the ocean to increase buoyancy, it still wouldn't allow it to turn by a single hand." He walked around the centre. "Two, we're too far from the ocean to keep this thing full as needed to use it. Tribes rarely wasted water on art forms, so keeping it filled would be a large waste of resources." Hayden ticked them off using the fingers on this left hand. "Third, there are no divots or pointed tips on either side of the discs to allow resting one atop the other to allow for turning using a water based medium. It's designed to be removed and stacked only. As to the how or whatever it's meant to reveal, someone didn't want this easily deciphered."

"So there goes your theory they wanted to make it easy."

"That or some parts of their story they didn't want to tell, but felt obliged to." Hayden grimaced. "But to inspect it, we'll have to pull all the discs out."

Danica grinned. "In for a penny, in for a pound."

****

Over the course of the next hour, they carefully lifted each disc out of the foundation frame, making sure to note the order they were removed, until there were a total of seven, lined up and around the centerpiece.

Each one was carved differently, but completely filled from side to side with a new series of cracks and engravings.

Danica used her portable 3-D scanner to photograph and create images of the discs which she communicated back to her laptop at camp. For good measure, she repeated the action using her Smartphone with imaging software.

'No harm in having a back-up' she thought.

Danica pointed to the discs after photographing them. "What kind of rock is it? It doesn't match the one in which it was housed."

Hayden shrugged. "I've no idea. I'm not a geologist." He leaned over the centerpiece and examined the interior. "Even the bottom is different. It's painted."

Danica peered inside the opening.

At the bottom of the now empty cylinder, a foot deep, in the centre, was a pointed triangular like stone, painted black, much wider than expected as it filled one third of the hole, also shaped oddly and uneven like some type of mountain, and not unlike the base itself in which it was housed. It was surrounded by a giant yellow painted circle with weird engravings in the red paint. The yellow paint did not reach all the way to the outer edges, as it left a good few inches of unpainted stone around the entire circumference of the yellow circle which did lead to the edges and some carved divots.

As Hayden suggested, the mountain pin appeared to be the pivoting point for the bottom disc which confirmed its sole job was balancing the others above. The rims kept them from tipping regardless of the weight on any one side.

Hayden continued to examine the centre.

Danica ran her fingers over each of the differently carved discs. "It almost looks like a human brain and the circulatory system within it."

Hayden whistled. "If it is, then this tribe had an insight into medical science far beyond their years. Presuming that's what we're looking at. But I doubt it. I'll have to bring a team down here to study it."

Danica paused, but Hayden already suspecting her reaction spoke first.

"But not before you can send the details to Maximum Pharmaceuticals. I'm just an interpreter." He turned to her. "You found this place, so I will delegate all decisions to you. I'm simply very happy you allowed me to share in this."

Danica blushed as he spoke with such genuineness, she was almost at a loss for words.

Until he ruined it. "Plus, I'll let you sleep with me and we'll be square for the translations."

Danica knew he could not help himself. She responded with. "Unless you can find me the secret of the universe on these walls, you can keep dreaming."

Hayden smiled thinking inwardly. *'So, it's not a definitive 'no'. And as long as I know there's a goal line, I have something to strive for.'*

Men are like that.

****

"Absolutely nothing?" Hayden said in frustration. He stopped after another half hour of his examination of the centerpiece. "This is so very strange. Not on the base, not on the discs and nothing inside the cylinder."

Danica made no comment, leaving him to his work. She could tell he was more talking to himself than her.

Hayden had each of his fists on the sides of his waist, almost posing. He turned around to the walls of the chamber. "Since the centrepiece is blank, there's no point in wasting any more time on it. There might be more information on the walls that explains the reason for the stack of discs and mountain tableau."

For the next hour, Hayden moved back and forth around the room until he found what he believed to be the beginning.

Over the next few hours, as Danica worked to remove plant life and catalogue possible new fungi, she occasionally peered up to watch as he worked.

Hayden was talking quietly to himself, carefully moving his hands over the chiseled and painted designs, but never touching them. A few times he would raise his left eyebrow, pause, shake his head and move on.

Finally, as evening was setting in, Hayden spoke up. "I think I have the gist of what the core language is."

Danica asked. "Can you read it?"

Hayden continued to look over the designs and colourful engravings in the wall for several seconds. "Yes and no. It's old, but definitely a form of the Maya writing system."

"Looks like hieroglyphs?"

Hayden responded with amusement. "Egyptians used hieroglyphs. Mayans and most of the ancient South American tribes used a logographic writing system. It's basically a combination of phonetic symbols and logograms to form a *logosyllabic* language."

Danica remained silent.

Hayden added. "Are you about to say '*Duh*?'"

Danica took that on the chin. She had it coming from what she said back at the government office.

Hayden did not press the issue. "It's not completely identical. But so you know, the known scripts have more than a thousand different glyphs, which vary from tribe to tribe, and some are confined to particular localities. It is not unlike Canadian French and Parisian French, the same language but yet very different." Hayden took position at one of the corners. "Whoever, and I mean the tribe as a whole, wrote this was pretty segregated from the other more popularly known bands, as some symbols I've never seen before."

"So what are we looking at then?"

"We're looking at their story for sure. From the design, a true story, but told in the form of folklore. Very strange."

"How so?"

"Tribes normally write an account of events chronologically, like history. This one does the same, but only more as a tale. This aims to tell readers to consider it with care. Meaning, read it only, but do not get involved."

"That is strange. What's the story telling?"

"The story of their tribe, at least the one they broke off from, their original mission, life and death, and from what I can discern, long life and the prevention of death."

Danica was extremely interested with that last part. "How is that possible? Preventing death?"

"It's not." He smiled. "But some tribes had belief systems beyond our cultural knowledge. Some believe in life after death, or some, even immortality."

"Which is it?"

"I can't say. It does not offer specifics. Only that life can be sustained by some means, but not explaining the how. And I've read all four walls, it very carefully avoids the how, only offering the what. And funny enough, it definitely avoids telling us the where."

Danica turned to look at Hayden.

He had to turn his head as her lights went right into his eyes. "Hey."

Danica turned away. "Sorry."

Hayden rubbed his sore eyes and gestured to the right wall, behind their rope ladder. He walked towards it and took a confident stance which told Danica he was quite impressed with this part of the story structure.

Hayden pointed. "This wall seems to be the most important. The others talk of how the tribe was formed, how they lived and their religion. They believed in one benign God and one evil one. I'm sure Catholics would love them."

Danica looked at the wall and all she saw was gibberish. "And this helps us how?"

"Well. This wall expands on the core of their story. It details more of the tribe's mission, which by the thick paints and vibrant colours, it was designed to last for years, to ensure it was never forgotten. And most of all, what was important to them."

"And what was that?"

"Well, get this. The most important thing was also their greatest fear."

She paused, wanting to let Hayden explain it; he was telling the story as he read it, but she could tell he was also stringing it out for dramatic effect. "You still haven't answered the question."

Hayden turned to her and smiled. "From everything I read, it always leads back to one place."

Danica glared. "What place?"

"An island."

"What island?"

At this Hayden shrugged. "That's just it. It offers a lot about an island as a whole, but it is almost intentional not to explain where it can be found."

"So does it exist?"

"The tribe believes it does."

Danica looked to the picture Hayden was examining and pointed to the engraving of a mountain under a dark circle, surrounded by water symbols. *'Island.'* She at least understood that much. "What does this mean?" Pointing to the dark circle.

"Normally, a circle in the sky means the sun, but as it is black, it seems to denote an island without sunlight, or since it is depicted in the sky, an island of constant night."

"How is that possible?"

"I did mention I was an archeologist, not an astrologist right?"

Danica shook her head. "It's cosmologists that handle the skies. Astrologists handle your horoscope." She glared at him in annoyance. "And you're right, I've noticed, you're not a lot of things."

Hayden grumbled quietly under his breath. "For example, infinitely patient for certain."

Danica leaned in. "What was that?"

He smiled. *"Interesting paintings for certain."*

She was sure that was not what he said, but as she didn't hear him, so she couldn't refute him either.

She turned back to the centerpiece. "Maybe the discs depict lightening?" Danica waved her hand over the crackling patterns. "Maybe this island is so inundated by electrical storms, it feels like an unending night?"

Hayden had to agree, as it had some logic to it.

Tribes did not have hundreds of thousands of symbols to depict their tale, so sometimes, they had to paraphrase and group things into one, which could summarize a long event as seeming to be longer than it actually is.

Hayden clucked his tongue. "Either way, based on this, the island is both their greatest discovery and their most terrible fear. And the original tribe was tasked to the monumental responsibility of protecting this island from the world..." He waited a good second before finishing his train of thought. "Or vice versa."

"What do you mean vice versa?"

Hayden stared quizzically. "There are several dichotomies in the symbols."

"Dichotomies?"

"I mean lots of the symbols about the island seem to conflict." Hayden pointed to several pictures. "These ones describe protecting the island from the world, yet this symbol..." A picture of several stick men with shields facing the island spears held high. "The tribe here is looking *at* the island in an aggressive capacity as though what is on it must be fought."

Danica looked at it and did agree, it seemed to imply the tribe in the design actually considered the island their opponent. "So the island was the enemy?"

"That or whatever was on it was."

"How come there are no pictures of anything on the island then?"

Hayden rubbed his chin. "A lot of cultures believed drawing or recreating an evil on paper, stone or in any form, gave it strength, and by not noting it, they are actually weakening it."

"Sounds like a lot of crap."

"I never said it would all be logical." Hayden took a step back. "And there's more."

Danica moved in behind him.

"Some symbols, though I have to give weight I could be reading it wrong, seem to directly conflict with one another." He gestured to two patterns of circles and a person within them. "These two are side by side. One means 'gives life' while the other notes 'takes life'. Or 'at the cost of life.' And in direct relation to this symbol." He pointed. "The island."

Danica stared at it. "So the island takes life."

"Yet gives it."

"That is odd."

"That and some portions appear to be reversed?"

"How so?"

"Some languages are read right to left. Rare, but it exists. Most of the designs appear to read left to right, but then there are instances where things seem written in the wrong order."

Danica was trying to figure out which ones.

Hayden gestured to some. "This one describes a broken bone in two halves, and the second one, a complete bone. The next series is an open palmed hand with a long black line in it, with red fluid painted around it, obviously an injury, but the following icon was the same hand, no line."

"It appears to imply the reverse order to harm. Break an arm, it repairs, harm yourself, it heals."

"That's basic biology One-Oh-One." Danica pointed out.

Hayden remained puzzled. "That's just it. It's not something worth noting on a story wall unless this healing had some significance." He gestured. "But again, every picture leads directly back to the island as the central part of the story."

Danica turned to look at the centrepiece. "Could that mountain thing in the lake of yellow be the island?"

Hayden leaned in. "It could. But the water is yellow." He pointed to the walls. "The pictures on the wall define water was blue, so they knew the colour of water. So I have no idea why this water is yellow."

Danica aimed her index finger at the red marks in the yellow. "That's fire right?"

"You would be correct. But water does not catch fire."

"Maybe it was blue at one time." She pointed to the door above. "It's not exactly waterproof. What if rain over the centuries pooled in here and wrecked the colours."

Hayden looked skeptical. "But only this one item and one surface being wrecked? Leaving all the others safe?"

Danica held out her hands. "This is like a cup shape. It could have held the water."

Hayden pointed to the corners and tiny divots in the rock at the base of the cylinder. "See those small holes. They lead to the soil below, like an ancient irrigation system for leeching off the rainwater away from the centrepiece. And if you look around the full floor, it's the same thing, but from the chamber." He continued to look at it for a few seconds. "It is designed to draw all water away, from the centre and the story chamber." He nodded. "Pretty ingenuous if you ask me."

Danica had no answers having seen this herself.

Hayden seemed to have one more thing to offer. Pointing back to the main story wall, he described. "And this is the weirdest symbol of all."

Danica looked at it.

It was a cloud-like drawing inside the core of the island. In the centre, one stick man surrounded in a white trim that almost seemed to encompass him. It seemed liked he glowed.

"What does it mean?" Danica asked.

"I think it refers to the light of eternal life."

"How is this strangest of all? We saw pictures describing immortality did we not?"

"We did." Hayden pointed to the dark cloud above the glowing man in white. Dark black with dark rain drops pouring down. "Because above the immortal man is an evil so pure, it will live for all eternity."

Hayden ran his fingers along to the next picture.

The stick man now in a cloud of grey, him still glowing white, but his belly is expanded and filled with black paint.

Hayden explained. "It reads. 'The island will infuse you with its evil.' One so strong, it forever becomes a part of you. Yet it says it feeds on you in return." He stared. "Very weird."

Danica took a moment to think about it. "Maybe like possession?"

Hayden seemed to think it was as good an explanation as any. "A good possibility. A lot of cultures believe in such things. Including modern day Catholics."

Danica stood straight. "So we discovered a tale of an island of no sun or constant night. And with it, prospects for immortality and something to do with healing properties being the central core?"

"That's what I read." Hayden stood up beside her. "I've a lot more reading to do, but that's the basics." He waited a second. "But you can't forget the most important part."

"I'm not."

"Then when you report back to your bosses, you have to include everything on the walls. Including the fact the tribe who wrote this thinks the island is pure evil."

"There's more about the good. Maybe the evil is exaggerated."

"If you believe in one part of the story, you have to consider the other. Why would the tribe write all the truth about the miracles and make up all the evils. Doesn't make any sense."

"To scare people away from their treasured island?" Danica chuffed. "Maybe their miracle was so good, they feared if they told everyone about it, it would be used up."

"Then why write about it all?"

"You can't scare people away then. I mean, it's not a good story if you don't have monsters." Danica grinned. "Plus, I'm a scientist. I don't believe in such things."

Hayden started to climb the rope ladder and offered with some sarcasm. "For your information, scientists taste just as good as us archeologists and forgotten tribe members." He turned back and smirked at her. "The question is, will the scientist in you know when to run when a monster is coming your way."

She followed up the ladder in pursuit. "Trust me. I'll know."

****

After two hours, Danica completed her report on the chamber and its discoveries, including a summary. She attached all the pictures she took to the email.

She sighed as she included the 'evil' parts.

She entered the subject line. "Island of Constant Night."

She clicked send on her laptop, forwarding it to her research team back in Ontario.

She closed the lid and got into bed, her muscles sore, but her body still slightly energized by the day's events, excited about tomorrow.

Sleep took her quickly.

****

At one of a hundred South American network ISP protocol networks, run through several proxy servers and maintenance sites, ones not as well protected as some of the US and Canadian Government traffic hubs and central processing stations throughout their land masses, Danica's email travelled.

What she was unaware of, at one such site, a copy of her email, her report and all her photos were duplicated on a secondary network point, and a second email was sent.

Not to Maximum Pharmaceuticals who still got the original.

But to someone who spent a great deal of money monitoring the electronic communication world within the internet highways and data streams, specifically searching for such keywords as: *Island, Constant* and *Night*.

Plus many others found in her detailed report and synonyms defining the same thing.

But this second email would not wait until morning to be read.

As the new recipient kept his computer operating twenty four hours a day with a loud alarm mechanism to alert him, awaken him or page him, no matter where he was, what he was doing and when, with the specific instructions to inform him such information had been found and on its way into the world.

Tonight, Danica's email arrived.

All his bells went off.

8

The satellite phone rang on her night table.

Danica groaned.

It rang again.

She turned to look at her digital clock.

It read 5:22 a.m.

'*Are you serious*?' Is all she could imagine. She was usually an early riser, but she also normally did not spend her days climbing in and out of ancient stone chambers in the middle of the South American jungle with an eccentric archeologist learning the stories of long lost tribes and mysterious islands.

Today, she had planned to sleep in.

It rang for a third time.

She presumed those plans were lost, not unlike the tribe and the island.

Danica reached over from her bed, back still flat on the mattress, her one hand holding the covers while the other crept along the tabletop and pressed the speaker button on the base. Once activated, she curled back under the covers.

"Good Morning Doctor Van Altena." She answered.

She was addressing the director of medical operations in Toronto and her superior. His friends called him '*Mom*' because he always took care of those under his watchful care, regardless of their activities.

"A little early for a wakeup call isn't it?" Sarcasm lacing her tone.

"I prefer to get up at five a.m. myself." It was a deep resonate voice, but not that of her director. "But we all have our vices."

She sat right up, muscles rigid, pulling her covers over her like she was worried she could be seen in the confines of her cabin sporting only her underwear and bra. She responded with a bit of annoyance. "This is a private line specifically outfitted for Maximum Pharmaceuticals."

The man laughed, deep and heavy. "I would certainly hope so, considering how much I pay for it."

Danica was silenced. She suddenly flashbacked to all the town halls, the big television interviews and online video conferences with him as the main speaker. His voice was like a storm, able to encompass everyone in earshot and saturate their minds with his energy. It was so distinguishable, it was impossible to believe she did not immediately recognize it.

"Doctor T-Thorne?" She stuttered, sleep weighing down her tongue.

"The one and the same." Doctor Maximus Thorne replied, CEO and president of Maximum Pharmaceuticals.

She was at a loss for words. She offered the first thing that came to mind. "I'm so sorry… I thought…"

Maximus cut her off. "You've nothing to be sorry for. I called *you* and unexpectedly I might add. Not all of us find the early morning hours as refreshing as I do." He paused and spoke with more authority. "That and the fact I find apologizing is an act for the weak. Personally, I never apologize. I do what I want because I can and let the rest of the world learn to work around my actions."

Danica held quiet, unsure how to respond, knowing after that, another apology would be unwelcome. She didn't have to wait long.

"Might as well get right to the point." Maximus stated. "I hate wasting time with idle chit-chat or impersonal platitudes when we both know damn well you could care less how my day will go or what I plan to have for breakfast."

Danica was about to ask him just that, so luckily, she had not spoken.

Maximus explained. "Last evening, you submitted a very strange report to Maximum Pharmaceuticals."

Danica was suddenly wondering if the last few days she spent in the chamber and on its excavation detracted from her real assignment and now she was about to get reprimanded for it.

'But by the CEO himself. She barely wasted two days. She would gladly allot them to vacation time if that was the issue. She was owed much more than that. Was this not overkill?'

"The report and pictures you returned to us last night..." Maximus declared. "And your discoveries are absolutely amazing."

Danica smiled, her fears quickly subsiding. "Thank you sir."

"Call me Maximus."

Danica froze. She was too overwhelmed to cross that line yet. "Can I call you Doctor Thorne for now and maybe later, change to Maximus?"

Maximus laughed, friendly and open. "Whatever makes you comfortable."

Danica quickly asked. "I thought Doctor Van..."

Maximus cut her off. "Is no longer the one you're reporting to. From now on, you report directly to me."

"Is he okay?" Danica felt some concern.

Maximus gently confirmed. "He's fine. I felt this project was better handled by me."

"And me." A second voice joined the conversation, deep and heavy, but decidedly female. It was obviously the company's Chief

Financial Officer and ironically, wife to Maximus, Doctor Maxima Thorne.

Danica could offer nothing but nervousness. She balled both her hands into fists and thanked the stars she had grabbed her sheets before answering or her nails would be digging holes into her palms instead of tearing the material. "Of course."

Maximus spoke with enthusiasm. "I see a bright position in your future young lady."

Maxima added. "Very bright."

Danica beamed. She had never spoken to her executive team before. Not even an email for questions to the anonymous Human Resources box for companywide staff meetings in the form of webinars for those questions to be presented and answered by the CEO. She considered herself a confident woman, but these two people who ran a multibillion dollar medical organization totally intimidated her.

Danica shyly inserted. "Thank you."

"Thank you again?" Maximus sounded surprised. "It should be us thanking you."

Danica never imagined having the two highest executive officers of her company call her and being so… *thankful.*

"It was dumb luck. Nothing more." Was all Danica could add.

"Chance favours the prepared." Maximus explained. "And let me tell you, that little site you found is something vitally important to both myself and Maxima."

'Really?' popped into Danica's head, but she kept it to herself.

"I want every drop of information you can derive from it. Bleed it dry. Some say there's no blood in a stone. But I think if anyone can find it, it'll be you."

Danica never heard such passion from her CEO, not even in his public forums. "Absolutely."

Maxima spoke again. "Some of the files you sent were corrupted, so I will need you to send it again."

"I'll do it the moment I terminate this call."

"Excellent." Maxima replied.

Danica asked with some reservation. "But technically, we only have a permit to search for biological and scientific evidence. Not a historic landsite. Should we…"

Maximus cut her off again, a bit of a habit, and applauded her quick thinking. "Have no concern. We've already dispatched our senior legal counsel to the South American consulate in Brazil. I have been assured by Mr. Darby that by the end of the week, that site will be the exclusive property of Maximum Pharmaceuticals." He chuckled "At least for the time being."

Danica was shocked.

Mr. Anthony Darby was the Chief Operating Officer as well as Senior Legal Counsel to the company, so his being sent personally meant this was very important to the Thornes'.

"Pardon my asking." Maxima spoke. "But in your report, you've translated a good deal of the symbols." She waited a second to pose the next query. "I've seen your resume and consider you a talented bio-specialist, but it does not note your skillset of interpreting South American ancient dialects?" She sounded puzzled.

"Hay…." Danica froze. "Doctor Lattimer has been able to translate…"

Maximus interjected. "Doctor Lattimer?"

"He's an archeologist who was working another site near to my own for South American artifacts. Upon my discovery, I took advantage of his knowledge."

Maxima jumped in. "You procured an archeologist who can read the text?"

Danica replied, voice soft, filled with deep concern. "Yes?" Hoping she had not overstepped her authority.

Maxima sounded proud when she replied. "Dear God woman, you're amazing. I assume you can get him to sign a non-disclosure agreement. I will email one immediately. Standard incentives apply."

Which was usually money, products or favours in the future.

Danica understood. *'Protect the site, protect the discovery, and most importantly, protect the secret.'*

Danica was about to ask a question before Maximus cut her off.

Aggressive personalities tend to interrupt others without thinking.

Maximus asked. "But what about a location? Your report makes no mention of it. Does the chamber tell us where we can find this *Island of Eternal Night*?"

'Island of Eternal Night?' Danica paused. She never called it that in her report. *'Guess he feels he can name the discovery since it is his company and all.'*

"No." At this Danica sighed. "Doctor Lattimer said it is one of the most detailed tableaus of a tribe and their history he has ever found. He explained that the walls talk much about the island itself and its people, but with all the details, he claims the storytellers seemed to go out of their way *not* to reveal where it can be found."

Maximus could be beard talking to Maxima in the background.

Quiet, not for Danica's ears, but he seemed unaware how sensitive his speaker unit was.

Maximus whispered. *"Not unexpected. But combined with the other pieces we have, this chamber is a Godsend."*

Maxima whispered next. *"Finally another piece."*

"We'll see." Were Maximus' last words to Maxima.

Maximus returned to speaking to Danica. "Good work. Doctor Swift."

"Thank you."

"You can now consider yourself the Director of this operation." Maximus declared. "Whatever you need, you shall have it. I've had a same day courier dispatch to you a corporate credit card with no limit. Whatever equipment is needed, sought or wanted, do not hesitate, have it brought to you."

Maxima paused and quickly suggested. "In fact, I want you to hire your archaeologist friend as a consultant for this project. If he can read what he found now, we'll need him."

Danica was about to add. *'We're not friends, but she held it back.'*

Maxima made very clear. "Whatever he asks, you're approved to pay it."

Danica chuckled, knowing Hayden. She jokingly replied. "What if he asks for half a million dollars or something?"

Maxima replied. "Then ask him what currency?"

Danica was silenced by the seriousness of that last response.

This was obviously far more important to the Thornes than Danica realized.

9

"I'm not calling you Director." Hayden stated matter-of-factly, standing with his back to her. He was focused on a selection of symbols he had difficulty reading in the chamber the morning before. He was carefully chiseling around one with a small wooden pick and a rubber mallet.

"I'm not asking you to." Danica replied, rolling her eyes as she was closely examining the mountain island centerpiece surrounded by the circle of yellow. "I simply told you. Maybe so you could, I don't know, congratulate me?"

Hayden waited a few seconds. "Congratulations."

Silence grew between them.

Hayden removed a chunk of dirt. "'You're welcome' by the way."

Danica turned. "For what?"

"I said congrats. Aren't you supposed to say 'Thank you?'"

Danica shook her head. "Not when I have to tell you to do it." She continued in her examination, her teeth grinding.

Hayden could feel the room cooling and it was not the temperature.

He finally threw in when the silence was getting to him. "I'm just saying I'm still not calling you Director."

Danica sighed.

After a few minutes, Hayden brushing and wiping mold remnants away, queried aloud. "You know, you did accept my offer of twenty-five thousand to work for your company pretty quickly? Should I have asked for more?"

She laughed quietly to herself. "You'll never know."

Hayden could be heard grumbling, regretting he had not thrown up something ridiculous like one hundred grand or something to test the waters.

After a few minutes of working in relative peace, Hayden spoke up again. He couldn't help himself. Why be silent when you had company. "You know, Director is a pretty big promotion in a day. Are you sleeping with him or something?"

Danica scowled without looking in his direction. "Is everything sex and swearing to you?"

Hayden shrugged. "I also drink."

Danica bobbed her head in annoyance. *'It's like working with a child.'*

"Oh. By the way. I would avoid the corner over there." Hayden gestured with his head to the section by the third disc they removed.

Danica raised an eyebrow and looked. "Why, did you find a trap?"

"Nope." He smirked guilty. "I *expressed* myself over there. Give it a few minutes."

"Charming." Danica commented with heavy sarcasm. She changed her original assessment. *'It's like working with a child... and a pig.'*

For the rest of the day they worked diligently, Hayden twice asking Danica to examine a design, if only to try and make peace between them.

It wasn't working too well.

He admitted to himself, *'He could sometimes be a bit of an ass.'*

Over the final hours, Danica was now working with a selection of individually sized paint brushes and a bottle of desalinated water with misting sprayer which she had been using to carefully wipe away years of grime and dirt to reveal the vibrant coloured pictorials beneath.

She had finished six so far.

It was far harder than she thought and equally rewarding.

At the end of the evening, they packed up their work tools, turned off the lights and climbed up the ladder and out of the chamber.

****

By nightfall, the two of them were back in Hayden's camp over a roaring fire after finishing a selection of fire-roasted chicken and potatoes.

Hayden had two cold bottles of local beer beside him and Danica was drinking casually from a bottled cooler she had delivered that afternoon.

Seated around the fire, snaps and pops crackling within, Hayden rubbed his hands together and held them over the flickering flames. "You should cheer up. We found an ancient burial chamber in the vast jungle of South America, which helps my university immensely and you found at least a dozen plants within the structure you haven't yet identified which may be to the benefit of your company who sent you down here."

Danica finished a mouthful of her drink.

"That and I'm getting paid twenty-five thousand to be *your* consultant." He chuffed and stressed '*your*'. "This is a win-win-win here."

Danica glared at him. "What makes you think I'm down?"

"You've paused to relax, unwind and have a drink." He winked. "And you haven't insulted me once since we finished dinner. So something must be off."

Danica adjusted her camp stool, a three legged collapsible seat with polyester fabric. "They're going to send down another team of recovery specialists to retrieve the plant specimens. That means once we're done with the chamber, they're going to move me somewhere else."

Hayden held out his hand. "You worried you'll miss me?"

Danica looked at him with annoyance. "That's the silver lining."

Hayden withdrew his hand with a shake of his head.

Danica continued. "I happen to like it here."

Hayden took a chug of his beer. "Then tell them to go fuck themselves and stay."

Danica gave him a withering look for the swearing. "They're my bosses. I go where I'm told."

"Quit."

"It's not that simple." She looked to the sky. "I have bills to pay. A home to take care of."

"You have kids?"

"No."

""Husband?"

"Nope."

"Boyfriend?"

"No."

Hayden smiled. "Girlfriend?"

Danica scowled. "No. I'm happily unattached."

Hayden finished his first beer and was on his second. "Then what the Hell is holding you back? My God woman, you're a brilliant research scientist and I bet, you can get a job anywhere in the world."

Danica went completely silent at Hayden's question.

The only thing she could hear now was the fire sizzling due to the dry twigs Hayden had tossed in.

She honestly didn't know why she hesitated with such decisions. She liked the security steady employment provided, but she could easily handle change. It was one of her father's greatest gifts handed down to her. That and his creativity. He taught her that no matter what the world throws at you, it can be caught and thrown back. *'You control the game, nobody else.'*

She missed his voice. She might even call him tomorrow morning, if he wasn't down in his office writing his next best seller. But then again, Mom always had a knack for dragging him out of there to take the phone. She missed her too. That and her banana bread. She had to be careful with Mom though. Mom could keep her on the phone for hours. Not that it mattered about the bill. Dad's last book raked in over four million. And they still lived in Waterdown. God, she loved them dearly.

She knew if she wanted to quit everything and travel as a hobo she could. Her father long ago told her that his money was hers. He even gave her a bank card to his accounts, but she wanted to make her own way in the world and turned it down.

But she couldn't stop her mother paying all her bills when she wasn't monitoring her accounts. Her parents were annoying that way, but loveable nonetheless.

Hayden could tell Danica was tuned out. She was not enjoying this tour down *'personal reflection road.'* So he decided to change the subject or he knew his campmate would be leaving sooner as opposed to later. "Remember that series of symbols on the lower quadrant of the chamber, near the North West edge?"

Danica came out of her reverie. "The ones about the water surrounding the lake?"

"Yes." Hayden replied.

Danica looked at Hayden with her interest now refocused. "Did you figure them out?"

Hayden shook his shoulders. "I think so. From what I was able to derive from the other symbols, it describes their far ancient past. From a time before the island. And from the story, it explains why the tribe painted the inset yellow with red marks."

"Why then?"

"Well, the symbols seemed to note their evil God, of no name, put the darkness on the island, whatever the Hell that is, but their benign God discovered what the evil one had done and in return, did something to the water to forever trap the darkness there for all eternity."

Danica felt like a fan of her father's books, sitting on Hayden's every word waiting for the next part to reveal itself. "Like what?"

Hayden shrugged. "I've no idea."

The winds escaped from her sails leaving her feeling deflated. At least her father did not do that in his books. "Then why did you mention it? I thought you knew what their benign God did?"

"I wasn't actually there you know?" Hayden stated with annoyance at her expectations. "He probably did whatever benign Gods do to lakes around evil islands. Maybe he pissed in it."

"Why? Did the evil God accidently put a flag in the water to be aimed at?"

Hayden rolled his eyes skyward. *'I'm never going to live that down.'*

Danica stood and brushed wood chunks from the back of her shorts. "On that lovely note, I think it's time I settled in."

Danica turned in the direction of her camp. "Goodnight Doctor Lattimer."

"Good night Doctor Swift." Hayden paused and quickly threw out before she was too far. "Going alone?"

"Of course not."

Hayden's eyes perked up.

"I have my gun with me."

Hayden let out a defeated breath.

Danica added. "Just in case anything creepy tries to get into my cabin, and more importantly, in case it's drunk."

"I highly doubt two beers count as drunk." Hayden retorted. "Plus you had two of your fruity cooler drinks as well. And yours have a higher concentration of alcohol than mine."

Danica smiled. "The difference being is I had mine one at a time. You opened them both and drank from them at the same time."

"Ever hear of two fisted?"

Danica looked down in the direction of Hayden's groin area. "Well tonight, I'm decidedly sure you can make do with one."

Hayden frowned as she vanished into the darkness.

He shouted. "I'm still not calling you Director."

He snapped open two more beers, swearing under his breath.

'You'd be surprised. I might need two fists.'

Then suddenly thinking to himself. *'Not helping.'*

****

4:00 a.m.

Early the next morning.

Hayden was awoken when he felt a giant *'whump'* under his cot.

Several items on his side table fell off and clattered to the wood flooring with a bang and a rattle.

Hayden sat up. He pinched his nose and took a quick breath.

"Goddamn local beer." He swore loudly. His head was ringing. He rubbed his temples for a few seconds to get the blood flowing.

He hated hangovers, especially cheap ones.

He listened again.

Nothing.

He was exhausted; having spent the last two days down in the chamber doing carbon sketches of the unrecognized symbols to send back to his department in Toronto and then drinking six beers before bed.

He thought to himself. *'Six qualify as drunk. Not two.'* He pinched his nose again. *'Dumbass.'*

He paused, shaking the cobwebs out of his brain.

A second *'whump'*, even louder this time.

His lantern shook on the nail that held it. It dropped to the floor and extinguished.

All Hayden could think was, *'Explosion? This isn't a war ravaged area?'*

He exited his tent and stared across the night sky.

The South American morning was not fully night covered. The sky was a light blue, shaded with deep greys and filaments of purple blurs. The orange glow of the rising sun could be seen in the distance over the trees, as well as a black billowing smoke cloud funneling skyward from the jungle.

Hayden started to run. *'The chamber!'*

****

Danica was reading in her bed, an article on 'Dominant DNA re-sequencing within a zero-gravity environment.' On her night stand was scientific journal with the headline, 'Plant hybridization and recombinant RNA cross breeding with radiation infused fungi.' Both had bookmarks in them as well as yellow sticky tabs to mark sections for rereading later.

She had the covers pulled up and over her knees, her one pillow resting behind her back and the second under her feet. She was clicking a pencil between her upper and lower teeth as she read.

She was unable to sleep, still thinking about the call from her company's CEO and CFO the morning before. Even now, a day later, she was feeling nervous.

Being promoted to Director of this operation was so unexpected, she kept thinking she was dreaming.

At least she had Doctor Lattimer to keep her grounded. Well more than that, he dug her a deep hole and covered her with a few shovels of dirt to keep her humble. *'He could be an ass sometimes.'*

She reached for her glass of warm milk, situated on a coaster on her bedside table.

Whump!

She immediately stood up. She had been in the jungles of Africa and Northern China and she knew an explosion when she heard one.

And it came from the direction of the chamber.

In seconds, she was out of her bed, flashlight in hand and out the front door of her cabin.

Once there, she froze.

Directly in front of her greenhouse was a large male figure, clearly identified by his shape and stature, six two in height, but his boots seemed to have deep treads by the deep impressions he left in the mud behind him. His back was to her, dressed from head to toe in black fatigues, his face covered with a ski mask and wearing night vision goggles, at least from what she could see in the moonlit reflection on the greenhouse glass.

He pressed a button on a handheld device he was holding before he pocketed it.

A second *Whump!*

Danica turned in the direction of the chamber as the ground shook. This was followed by a geyser of dirt and smoke shooting skyward.

'*The chamber!*' She knew right away based on the smoke's origin. '*Please don't be working overtime Doctor Lattimer.*'

She turned back to the more immediate threat. The man was now trying to break into her greenhouse.

She watched as he tried to use a screwdriver to disengage the front touchscreen reader plate keeping the security lock engaged and the door shut.

She waited a few seconds and spoke. "Even if you get it off, the bolts are titanium, all fourteen of them, so unless you brought an arc welder in your fanny pack, you might as well leave my property alone."

The man went rigid. He turned slowly and stared in Danica's direction, the single mounted eyepiece of the goggles aimed right at her, both hands glove covered, but empty. The man replied with a low heavy voice, muffled by the mask. "I do not seek to do you harm, but I need everything you've found."

Danica started raising her hands up in surrender letting her body shiver with fear. "Of course." As her hands came up, she flicked her wrist and pivoted the flashlight in her hand in an upward arc from the ground directly into the eyepiece of the assailant's night vision goggles.

Night vision goggles are basically high tech glasses with a large diameter objective. They have lenses designed to gather and concentrate ambient light, intensifying it by optical means, enabling the user to see in the dark with the naked eye using as little light as possible. Problem was, they were designed to be used in a midnight environment with little to no light at all. So any sudden burst of luminesce, especially into the light intensifying eyepiece, directly into the pupils of the wearer, with a minimum of thousand times of amplification, would be like staring into a solar flare without protection.

The man let out a scream as he fell forward.

Danica, in the span of a second, spun around on her right heel, pivoting and using her left as a catapult, spinning it back and around behind her body, to the side and using her momentum to bring her heel across the shrouded man's face and jaw with a perfectly placed roundhouse kick.

She sent him face first into the titanium frame of the door which he bounced off with a bone crunching thud.

He dropped and tumbled into the dirt.

In those same few seconds, she drew her weapon, a high capacity .45 pistol with a double column magazine and supported chamber barrel. She removed the safety and targeted the black clad man reeling on the ground.

His night-vision goggles dangling broken around his neck.

She quietly stated. "Don't move. "I do not seek to do you harm." She mocked. "But you move and I will."

He was rubbing his ski mask covered jaw, his eyes still shadowed by the evening light. He got up from his fallen position.

Danica grinned. "Seriously. I'm a third degree black belt. What I can't do to you with this gun, I will with my fists."

He seemed to be shaking off the blow, trying to reorient himself.

Danica watched him as she could see he was tensing up for a pounce.

In self-defense training, you were taught to recognize when a body shifts, how it changes for motion and when someone was about to make a move so you could defend against it.

She warned him. '"Don't be stupid."

He was.

He lunged.

Danica fired, one shot, perfectly aimed, directly into the man's lower right leg, the one he used to shift his weight, obviously the strongest one.

He dropped like a lead ball with a heavy groan.

She sighed with annoyance.

"I did warn you." Danica held the gun steady. "And consider yourself lucky. I chose only to graze your tibia." She looked around. "Now when my friend gets here, we'll be calling the authorities. They'll help you get some medical attention and they will hopefully teach you some proper manners about touching other people's stuff."

The man rose, his body straining under the pain of the shot.

Danica kept her weapon trained right on him, prepared to shoot him again, impressed with his fortitude.

"The next shot goes into your forehead." She raised and took aim. "I don't want to have to deal with all the paperwork of killing someone outside of Canada, but be assured, I will if you move on me again."

The man heard someone running through the brush towards them. He spoke, his voice still muffled, but wanting her to understand. "You're making a grave mistake. Some things were never meant to be found."

Danica was shocked by his words. *'How the Hell do you know what we found?'*

But before she could ask, the man turned and ran in the opposite direction, disappearing into the heavy plants and trees, limping heavily the entire time and vanishing into the jungle brush.

Danica was impressed. His not wanting to be caught by the South American authorities was incentive enough. But she stayed where she was. She had no intention of chasing anyone dressed from head to toe in black through thick dark underbrush for which she had not memorized the terrain.

Hayden came running in from the darkness, wearing only a pair of boxers and a T-shirt, his bare feet bleeding from the rocks he ran through. He was wielding a long shovel before him. "I heard gunshots?"

"You heard *a* gunshot." Danica corrected. "I only fired once." She holstered her weapon back into the rear waistband of her pajama shorts.

Hayden looked at her. "What did you shoot?"

"Some guy dressed in black. He was trying to break into my greenhouse."

Hayden looked at it and then her in amazement. "What's in there?"

Danica shrugged. "Nothing you can't find on the ground or around here if you looked long enough."

"Son of a bitch." Hayden leaned forward and took a deep refreshing breath, his body exhausted.

Danica deduced he had obviously run all the way to the chamber before he heard the gunshot and ran to her aid. *'My hero.'*

Hayden stood and leaned on her greenhouse wall.

"And I should point out, from I saw, he had a remote detonator with him. He depressed it seconds before the second explosion."

Hayden's face seemed to fill with sadness as he turned to look to her.

Danica felt her shoulders sag. "Don't tell me."

"Well whatever he was after in your greenhouse, he felt destroying the chamber took precedence."

Danica looked at the sealed door of her greenhouse. In the dark, it looked more like a house than a gardening unit. "I think he was after all the data we had procured on the chamber. When he arrived, he had two choices, my geodesic cabin or the greenhouse." She paused. "He probably presumed it was in the greenhouse based on the security. I guess I can thank the stars he didn't choose my place first."

"You should." Hayden nodded.

Danica took a breath and then explained to Hayden the mysterious attacker's final words before departing.

"You're making a grave mistake. Some things were never meant to be found."

Both Hayden and Danica stiffened.

'How had their discovery gotten into the world so fast?'

'And worse, who did not want it discovered?'

Both of them started to relax after the assault, but deeply wondering, *'What the Hell had they gotten themselves into?'*

10

Danica had her hands clasped in her lap, her face in the direction of her cabin ceiling, eyes closed tightly. She was silently hoping for a dimensional vortex to open above her and pull her from the room and into the multiverse, forever taking her away from this world, but more importantly, from this exact moment.

As she had no desire whatsoever to be here in it.

But sadly, the laws of physics stayed intact and remain she did.

She looked down and lowered the volume on the phone base. Hoping the weaker decibel level during the conference call would subdue any potential yelling through the speaker after she relayed her report.

Over the next few minutes, she walked the Thornes through everything that had happened. When she was done, she took a deep breath and waited.

Maximus spoke first, his tone tempered by disappointment. "So the chamber is completely destroyed?"

Danica felt chastened in having to tell him this. "I'm so terribly sorry." She was in total disbelief at being both made director of this operation and in less than twenty four hours, calling to brief her superiors on her failure.

"Why are you apologizing?" Maximus asked. "Did you blow it up?"

"Of course not." She was shocked at the implication.

"Then it's we who should be apologizing to you." He paused. "And trust me, I don't apologize."

Danica waited a few seconds.

He still didn't. But Maximus then declared. "This is our fault."

Danica was dumbfounded by the statement. She was about to ask, 'How could this be YOUR fault?'

But Maximus resumed his tirade. "Knowing the value of the discovery, we should've dispatched a security team immediately." He spoke quietly away from his speaker for a minute and returned. "Whoever this assailant is, he moved far faster than we anticipated."

Maxima joined the conversation. "Be assured, there will be no opportunity for a next time."

Danica was unsure how to read that, nor offer a reply, so she chose silence.

After a few seconds of scribbling sounds, Maximus asked. "Tell me. Is anything salvageable?"

Danica did not relish this part, but she had to explain it eventually. "The attacker used a very corrosive acid on the paintings inside the chamber. He obviously climbed down the ladder, sprayed the place with it and then placed his explosives."

"Explosives?" Maxima stressed the fact it was plural.

"Yes." Danica continued. "He set two individual bombs, activated by remote. At least I assume both were by remote as I only observed him detonate the second one."

Maxima interjected. "You're certain it was a he?"

"Of that I'm sure." Danica added. *'Only a man could get up after the hit I gave him.'*

Combined with that, as a doctor, some things were unmistakable.

Maximus could be heard whispering aside again.

Danica waited for him to finish, but Maximus spoke up. "Please continue Doctor Swift."

Danica almost stuttered, unaware Maximus was listening at the same time. "The first bomb exploded inside the interior of the chamber. It was likely designated to destroy the centerpiece and the surrounding carvings the acid could not eat off." She took a quick breath. "The second detonation was designed to collapse the structure in on itself from the outside." She sadly sighed. "Doctor Lattimer said it will be months before they could dig it out. And worst of all, the acid will be in there burning away the entire time, disintegrating whatever survived the shockwaves of the explosion until searchers reached it."

"How does he know about the acid?" Maximus asked with interest.

"Doctor Lattimer found several empty bottles of it, one of which was outfitted with a handheld spreaying tool." Danica replied. "He saw no other purpose for it outside an ancient chamber, even if baffling."

Maxima could be heard fuming. "The bastard was really thorough."

"He obviously did not want anything else to be found." Danica replied, deciding quickly not to offer up the specifics of what the man said to her. It was as if the assailant was implying something far different should not be found than the chamber itself.

For the moment, she kept this one card back.

'You control the game, nobody else. So don't play all your cards in your initial hand. You may need some for later….'

'Thanks Dad.'

"I wish I could've seen that centerpiece." Maximus offered up.

Danica queried in confusion. "But I included pictures of it with my report?"

Maxima replied. "Those were the corrupted files we spoke of the other day."

Danica had not realized. But she had resent them. Maybe her Smartphone did not save them properly for transfer to her laptop. She would have to check into that.

"We also had our own problems last night in regards to the chamber." Maximus stated rather dramatically, but not as loud as before, obviously not comforted by sharing their failure.

Danica leaned closer to the speaker. "What problem was that?"

"We were hacked." Maximus sneered venomously. "Rather sophisticatedly, at least according to our I.T. department. It appears all your data and the report you emailed to us has been systematically traced, stolen and all remnants of it have been erased." He took a hard fought breath. "Including the corrupted ones for good measure."

Danica was shocked. She assumed their firewalls were impenetrable. "All of it?"

"All of it." Maxima replied. "It seems they tracked it from your original IP address and then used it to infiltrate ours."

Danica felt even guiltier. "Was it something I did?"

Maximus consoled her. "Absolutely not. Whoever did this had access to both our servers and seemingly all servers your email travelled. They inserted themselves somewhere along the line and wormed their way into our network. And in their electronic travels, wiped everything from source to finish."

Danica was shocked with the speed, as well as the technical knowledge required to pull off this expansive form of data theft. "This can't be coincidence.'

Maxima replied. "We're sure it isn't. We assume the attacker got your laptop?"

Danica was proud to offer her response. "Of course not."

Maxima let out a gasp, sounding elated. "What?"

"The attacker tried to take it last night..." Danica noted.

Maxima cut her off. "And you still safeguarded it?"

"I'm a third degree black belt." Danica answered matter-of-factly, no arrogance in her tone. "And trust me, he'll regret that decision to seek the laptop for some time."

Maximus laughed loudly. It sounded like a boom through her speaker. After a few seconds, he proclaimed. "You my dear have earned your bonus. In fact, I'll personally see to it that it is deposited by tomorrow."

Maxima could be heard in the background. "In fact, I'm keying it as we speak. Don't ask how much, as tomorrow, you'll be floored."

Danica was smiling broadly from ear to ear. "Thank you." She was glad there was no camera in her cabin as she was blushing.

Maximus could be heard on his cell phone in the background dialing someone. In seconds, he quickly interrupted. "I have I.T. on the line. They told me to have you get the laptop right now. Seconds are vital."

Danica grabbed it instantly. "I have it."

"Excellent. Now underneath it, near the battery pack, disengage the Wi-Fi network connectivity capabilities."

Danica pressed the switch. "Done."

"Now under no circumstance should you either reactivate the device's roaming or connect it to the internet in any way. We're not sure if the hacker is still in our system. We have I.T. working overtime to purge any and all traces of their presence, but until such time, your laptop must stay offline."

"Will do." Danica felt confident now her executive team had taken charge and things were back under control. "What should we do for now?"

"For one thing, under no circumstance are you to have that laptop out of your sight. Not even for a second." Maxima stated. "We've no desire to lose our last vestiges of that chamber."

"Understood." Danica felt like the guardian of a great treasure.

Maximus declared. "We need you and Doctor Lattimer back in Toronto on the first flight out. Use your procurement card to get the two quickest flights back."

Danica was shocked at the request. "But what about all my research here?"

Maximus replied with authority. "My private plane has been boarded with a clean-up and moving crew to take care of everything. Both your camps will be cleared, packed and ready for re-opening anytime in the future for your return. Mr. Darby will oversee everything."

Danica smiled. She knew her COO was nothing if not meticulous.

Maxima pointed out. "All your plant experimentation and discoveries will be catalogued and prepared for transport by Doctor Feller."

Danica knew him. He was a good research officer from development. She knew he could be trusted immensely to care for her acquisitions.

"So there is no other reason for the two of you to stay is there?" Maximus pointed out.

Danica admitted, she had none. Then one question came to her. "What about the chamber?"

Maximus answered. "Well it seems, as Mr. Darby has informed me, having a historical discovery destroyed *before* reporting the find and getting a permit to investigate it has caused a few issues for Maximum Pharmaceuticals."

Danica felt terrible all over again. "I should have…"

"Done exactly what you did." Maximus cut her off. "Had you reported it, we'd never have gotten all the details as quickly and as accurately as you were able to procure them." He paused and added with some rigidity in his tone. "And trust me, had we been forced to deal with the government from the onset when you had the unique opportunity to search the site beforehand and chose etiquette over curiosity, then I can assure you, we'd have been disappointed."

Danica felt better in her decision.

Maximus finished his thought. "So your hard work and getting all the information you did for us without all the red tape is exemplary. And don't you forget it."

Danica felt recharged again.

The dips and troughs of an emotional corporate roller-coaster.

"Plus, let Mr. Darby worry about the ramifications. It's what I pay him for." Maximus declared with confidence. "As for you and Doctor Lattimer, my *directors* of this operation, see you in Toronto."

With that, he terminated the call.

Danica rolled her eyes, happy Maximus could not see her right now.

Her only thought being, *'I'm can't tell Doctor Lattimer he's now a director too. He'll be unbearable to fly back with. She could see him now, in all his glory, demanding I call him Director Lattimer.'*

Danica grinned inwardly. *'I'll never call him Director.'*

She pulled out her cellphone to book the flights.

All she could think was. *'What possible discovery from a hundred years ago warranted all this trouble? None she could imagine.'*

She dialed the airline customer service and let her mind drift as she prepared for a long hold time.

'Maybe I simply need more imagination.'

11

Danica turned to the empty seat beside her.

The laptop was safe and sound, resting upon an airline pillow and leaned back against the blue leather backrest.

She turned and peered out the window of the aircraft, raised the power footrest on her lounger with the remote and took a sip of her espresso from a china cup as she watched the carpet of white fluffy clouds flow beneath them. The entire time, her hand was laid gently on the computer, not letting her fingers leave it.

She knew they were making good time.

They would be in Toronto in under a few hours.

She felt a sudden shift of her seat and felt the laptop being lifted. She turned with a snap, almost spilling her drink into her chest and onto the white wool blanket she had wrapped around her bare legs.

She let out an annoyed sigh when she found Hayden seated beside her, laptop in his hands and giving her a nasty glare.

"Nice work by the way." Hayden sneered. "Booking my ticket in coach and yours in first class." He turned to her. "I assume the guy beside me smelling like cheese was an unplanned perk."

"I asked specifically he smell like ham." She retorted. "Guess I'll be calling customer service upon my return for a refund."

He ignored her response as he looked around at the several empty seats. "You told me they didn't have any first class seats left."

Danica smiled demurely. "I told you the truth. There are no more first class seats. These are business class." She shrugged. "Plus I thought you said you liked to *rough* it?"

Hayden offered her an annoyed shake of his head at her using his own words against him. He dropped the laptop into the leather fold of the seat in front of theirs with the emergency procedures and Duty-Free catalogue.

Danica chided him. "Careful with that."

"Relax. It's a laptop, not a dozen eggs." He gave it a quick kick for good measure to Danica's dismay. "See. Durable if you ask me?"

Hayden gestured to the stewardess, a pretty little thing with light brown hair, a short cut skirt, tight vest and bright red lips, to look his way.

She did.

With his hands, he provided the universal signal for '*beer.*'

At least in Hayden's dictionary of hand motions anyway.

The stewardess smiled, her name tag reading Sabine Biagoni, seeming to understand. She nodded, indicating she would bring it right away.

Danica watched the exchange in annoyance. "While we're on the subject, how did you get up here anyway?"

It was Hayden's turn to smile. "I told them I was your doctor." He held up his archeological identification. "They never did ask what kind of doctor. One of the perks of having the letters D.R. on my passport."

Danica stared at him in disbelief.

Hayden continued. "I told them you were my patient and I needed to keep you under observation. Just in case you had one of your…" He made quotation marks with his fingers. "*Episodes*."

Danica looked horrified. "You told them WHAT?!"

"That and there was an obvious seat mix up as they certainly didn't want a schizophrenic patient up here in business class without her doctor." He winked. "You know, if something were to happen."

Danica was sure one of those episodes would include her choking him to death.

Hayden continued. "So of course, they upgraded me right away."

Danica refused to believe him.

She could not conceive he would do something so infantile over being booked in economy. *'Would he?'*

The stewardess brought his beer.

Hayden took it with a smile.

Danica knew these next few hours would be long now. She motioned to the stewardess. "Can you bring me a white wine?"

The stewardess turned to Hayden. "There won't be any conflicts with her medication will there doctor?"

If looks could kill, Hayden would have dropped to the floor of the aisle in a pool of cold imported beer clutching his heart and gasping for oxygen as Danica locked her pupils on him.

He winked to the stewardess. "No conflicts. She can have wine." Hayden then leaned in, whispering to the stewardess conspiratorially, but loud enough for Danica to hear. "But let me know if she swears loudly or jumps up and yells she's a chicken again. That means she thinks the demons have taken her."

The stewardess gave Danica a frightened look and rushed to go get her the wine.

Hayden turned to Danica with a confident grin. "You were saying?"

Hayden would have thanked Danica for cooling his beer at that moment as the cabin temperature felt like it dropped thirty degrees, at least in his mind.

For the next hour, they flew in silence, Danica choosing to stare out her side window, fearing if she yelled at him, she would be subdued by air marshals.

Finally after twenty minutes, Hayden spoke first. "Just to be fair, you took the low route first by putting me back with the cheap section. So what other option do you think I had?"

Danica turned to him, still annoyed, but she knew what she did was pretty lowball. "You could have paid for the upgrade, like I did."

"On your boss's money..." He remarked. "So don't give me that."

Danica had no response.

Hayden challenged. "And plus, admit it, this was more amusing."

He locked eyes on her and she did the same.

They stared one another down, but after a minute, the anger waned.

She finally let an edge of a grin wiggle out.

She had to give him his due, he got a business class seat free of charge, and on the back of the one who had put him in coach.

For now, the score was tied.

"But that does not mean a tiebreaker is not in the works.'

Once Hayden realized she was getting more amicable, he asked. "What's with the laptop anyway?"

Danica took a drink of her second glass of wine, happy a new stewardess was attending to them and not the original one, knowing what Hayden had done. She explained to him everything she was told by Maximus during their conference call after she relayed her report.

Hayden whistled, finding himself genuinely perplexed. "Seriously? Breaking into the international servers of numerous transfer points between South America and Canada? Do you know how many there are?"

"A lot."

"A lot? We're talking thousands." Hayden leaned back. "Not to mention breaking into the Maximum Pharmaceuticals mainframe database to boot. If only to get a single email and its attachment. It's totally unbelievable."

"Believe it."

Hayden took a moment to theorize. "Obviously, someone really wants to stop us in our tracks."

"Someone almost did."

Hayden rubbed his chin with his fingers. "Could it be that hacker group called Anonymous? Maybe they have a thing for your company?"

Danica defended them, *Anonymous*, only because it was not logical. "No. This is not their style."

'*Anonymous*' was a name originated in 2003 which represent an amalgamated force of electronic users who used their combined technical intelligence and the electronic medium of the internet to disable websites, hack databases with the intent to post controversial political imagery and statements to broaden the minds of the world. To basically create discord for institutions which the group felt were not playing by the rules of society or fairly for that matter.

Most corporations and government entities found them annoying, but for the most part, they were activists using the strengths they had.

And they used it well.

Danica added. "Maximum Pharmaceuticals is a research company. Nothing more. We have no political capital whatsoever. We have shareholders, but the Thorne's hold the majority. That and *Anonymous* protest using the World Wide Web to give publicity to their causes. They have an agenda, and from what I've read, they don't sneak around and destroy information. Far from it. They copy it and post it. This is not the case." She then pointed out. "Plus *Anonymous* does not send thugs to do their dirty work physically."

Hayden agreed. It did not fit the mold.

This was a theft plain and simple.

Well, not so simple.

Hayden asked. "What did your bosses say when you told them what the attacker said to you?"

At this, she blushed with embarrassment.

Hayden grinned from ear to ear. "You didn't tell them did you?"

"I didn't think it was pertinent. It was the ramblings of a terrorist."

Hayden shook his head. "A terrorist without a weapon, besides the explosives, who specifically targeted the site, not us, and when put in a position of attacking or running, he chose running."

Danica snapped. "He tried to attack me."

"Right before he told you he meant you no harm."

She admitted to that.

"So I suspect his intention was to subdue you to get the laptop. Not hurt you."

"Well he failed."

"Yes he did." At that Hayden nodded, but not before stating. "The real question is. Is he one of those, 'If at first you don't succeed, try, try again kind of guys.'?"

Danica felt a cold chill.

In her mind, remembering the conviction of the assailant's words.

'You're making a grave mistake. Some things were never meant to be found.'

She had no doubt in her mind he was one of those.

12

Clearing Canadian customs, the two doctors retrieved what little luggage they had from the spinning turnstiles, the female never once letting the laptop out of her grip, the male not offering to carry it.

He followed them closely, but staying out of sight.

Twice he blended into groups, the first being the third wheel on an eclectic couple of Spanish tourists waving washcloth sized Maple Leaf flags on paper sticks as they pranced forward to immigration. The second by pretending to be escorting his elderly grandmother from behind down the escalators.

What the two doctors did not see was him, when he reached the bottom, pushing the old broad aside because he couldn't squeeze past her huge bottom while they were going down without turning the moving stairs into a comical game of human dominoes.

Thus attracting attention he did not want.

At least until he had the laptop.

His employer tried to access it remotely the night previous, but it appears the female doctor was one of those people who thought turning it off at night saved battery life and of course, cut off internet accessibility because it was not simply in '*sleep mode.*'

He kept pace, quietly and confidently, knowing all he had to do was bide his time until they were alone.

He had almost lost them on board.

He was watching for a couple, never having seen the male in his assault and only having seen the woman through the green haze of his night vision goggles. That was only seconds before she almost fried his retinas with her flashlight which she aimed directly into the amplification lens and then leveling him with a kick that could have taken down an oak tree.

Luckily his employer had a doctor in South America to handle such things, like a cracked nose, bruised face and bullet torn ligaments, all quickly and more importantly, discretely.

He would be riding the codeine high for a bit, but not by much as it tended to cloud his focus. The pain allowed him a reminder of how dangerous she was.

How could he have known a bio-research specialist was also a highly trained martial arts master?

He would not underestimate her again.

As for the male, who would have the thought he would put himself in economy.

'Cheap prick.'

At first he assumed it was a tactic they employed to lose potential pursuits by splitting up and making themselves into single travelers thus to the trained eye, giving them a more dangerous edge, showing intimate covert knowledge of deception and thus, making them deadlier opponents.

He changed that assumption on board when the male, obviously regretting his cost cutting decision, got up, approached the stewardess and within minutes, charmed his way forward. By the big deal he made to get upgraded, clearly standing out in every way, he was either an amateur at being followed or he really had no idea.

He went with the latter.

But he had to admit, sitting downwind of the guy beside him at the time, smelling of old gym socks or someone who ate shit for a living, it would have had him quickly paying for First Class too.

Regrettably, he couldn't follow them forward and be upgraded as well.

It was again, attention he did not want.

He had to remain in coach, inhaling each rotten stench filled breath.

He seriously considered after they landed, putting a bullet in the brain of the sweat smelling man, if for no other reason to save future travelers from him, including himself.

But this was not allowed within the mandate.

But then again, this rush job laughed in the face of professionalism.

Normal protocols of such an assignment included photos, a dossier and information on his targets.

But due to the urgency, all he got was a set of coordinates and a window of time. With the specific instructions to destroy the Indian art cave they discovered and steal any and all the technology on site belonging to Maximum Pharmaceuticals, specifically a laptop which his employer claimed was the only item he could not patch into to get the last of the data he sought.

And all with one serious handicap.

'No bloodshed.'

He was told, if one drop of blood was spilt by his actions, he would neither be paid and the next blood lost would be his own.

Some people couldn't take the wet work required.

Considering all the money the old guy had spent, he could have easily had the two doctors killed, dropped inside their precious cave, dousing them with all the excess sulfuric acid he used to destroy the artwork, and finally burying them with the explosive debris for the next archeologist to find.

But no, instead he was down one laptop and up one broken nose, one chipped tooth and one hole in his calf.

His job was only fifty percent finished. He still needed to get the laptop or he was not getting paid.

He followed them past arrivals, through a crowd of wide-eyed onlookers at the gate, all waiting for missed friends and associates to give them a ride, and into the main hall.

They wandered along the brightly lit corridor of the airport, seeming to be arguing about something.

He couldn't hear.

They finally reached the pre-arranged pickup area by the lower first floor front entrance. They had a limo waiting for them.

He was amused for a second when the male doctor seemed to wait for her to open the door for him.

She actually slammed it behind her, forcing him to enter from the other side as she locked it behind her.

'Lover's spat?'

They pulled away.

But his car was waiting for him as well, a black import, rented and brought up by a valet service to ensure no delays.

His employer was anything if not thorough.

He followed them out of the airport, along the Highway 401 until they exited onto Yonge Street, turning south, heading towards the city core.

After fifteen minutes, they reached a pretty posh hotel.

The name of the place meant nothing to him as he wasn't planning to stay.

'Just get in, get the laptop and get out'

He parked the car in a green labeled parking lot, prepaid with a disposable credit card provided by this employer and moved along the sidewalk until he was standing outside the property.

He pulled out his handheld tablet PC with encryption software. In seconds, he accessed the hotel's mainframe. After a few minutes of sorting, he had their room numbers, adjacent to one another.

'*Obviously not a couple.*' He thought.

Penthouse suites, with two tier access, one for the guests and one for visiting staff.

He would use the staff entrance.

He donned a new pair of night vision goggles, this time it had flat lens and automatic shut off function when exposed to high energy light.

'*Once, shame on you. Twice, shame on me.*'

He moved toward the rear alley.

Upon his arrival, after having parked, he carefully changed until he was again dressed in complete black. Sweater, gloves, pants and boots. As he skulked, he drew a black ski mask over his face and he pulled from his matching satchel a handheld stun gun.

This time, he would ensure the woman did not get the drop on him.

He slipped along the fence, running his fingers over the ringlets of wire until he was almost at the back employee entrance of the hotel. He waited until a casual smoker dressed in a tuxedo extinguished his cigarette and went back inside.

He moved forward, completely hidden by shadows, ready and able, until he felt a huge pair of arms reach around his neck and pull him back into the darkness of the alley wall.

Had there not been flesh on those forearms, he would have assumed they were tree trunks by how thick they were.

The man slammed the stun gun in the gigantic forearm of the attacker and pulled the trigger.

His attacker tensed up and released.

The man's turtleneck had a rubber polymer inside the material, more to prevent rain or moisture, but it did well to prevent the stun gun's effects from penetrating him.

The man spun around and found himself face to face with a muscle bound thug dressed in a black tracksuit, grey muscle shirt and runners.

The attacker was six foot one, at least two hundred and fifty pounds and all muscle. His hair was sparse, if any and his face was pock-marked by long scarred acne.

The huge attacker shook off the stun effects and smiled. "That tickles."

The man was about to lunge again with a second blast when an equally large set of forearms grabbed him again from behind, this time squeezing so tight and so fast, the air burst from his lungs.

The stun gun dropped to the ground with a clatter as he held onto to what little oxygen he could, preventing himself from passing out.

He felt like he was inside a garbage compacter, pressing bags and recycling into smaller and easier to transport cubes. Blackness started filling his vision.

Then out of the blue, the second assailant released his firm grip and let him breathe.

The man turned his head and saw an exact duplicate for the first attacker he hit with his stun gun.

'Twins?'

The one in front of him chuckled. "We were told to watch this hotel for any uninvited guests."

The one behind laughed. "Guess we found one."

The man, still gasping for air, replied. "I'm…"

The first attacker cut him off. "Dressed completely from head to toe in black with a ski mask because you were cold and looking for a good place to ski?"

The second assailant laughed so hard, the man's whole body shook in his grip.

The first attacker reached forward and pulled the ski-mask off the man and chucked it to the ground. He tilted his head to check out his face. "You look like someone kicked the shit out of you." He smiled. "Just as the boss described."

The second assailant mocked. "We could be wrong. Maybe we should check his leg?"

The first attacker swung his massive leg back and snapped it forward, thundering into the man's lower appendage.

The man nearly crumpled over due to the pain, but the huge arms held him up. No codeine in the world would hide the level of hurt that fired up and down his spine. Had his leg been a football, it would have been a field goal.

The second assailant nodded. "It's our guy all right."

The first one brought his face in close. "You destroyed something very valuable to our bosses. And you tried to steal from our two docs who found it."

The second assailant tightened his grip. "We were told to ensure the message was made very clear, you would get no such opportunity to do it again."

The man would have nodded, but his head was held tight.

The first attacker pondered for a minute and asked. "My first question is, who do you work for?"

The man was considering lying when the second one tightened his grip.

The second attacker snarled. "You can lie if you want, but then I'm gonna squeeze until you go unconscious. And then maybe, just maybe, you might wake up with something long and hard up your ass."

The first attacker picked up a beer bottle off the ground and held it up to assailant number two, who nodded his agreement, as they both tried to imagine how to best force it somewhere.

The man could sense by the look in their twisted eyes, they would very much follow through on their threat.

"I've no idea who he is. Some old guy. All he gave me was an email address to confirm when the job was done and the money would be wired to my account in the Caymans."

Both men seemed to accept that as truth.

Standard rules in operations such as this.

'Don't keep the help in the loop.'

"What's the email?" The first attacker asked.

The man knowing there was no point in lying, provided it.

The second assailant asked. "Have you given him your account number yet?"

The man froze suspecting why he was asking. "I did. Standard protocol. You will not be able to give him yours."

The second assailant shrugged, shaking the man with each amused convulsion. "Oh well."

The first attacker was clenching and opening his fists. "So basically, you came up here to steal the laptop and kill our docs."

"No." He resigned himself with the truth. "I was paid specifically not to harm them. Simply get the laptop and destroy it."

The first attacker grinned as he turned to the one holding the man. "That's too bad."

The man replied, suddenly fearful. "Why is that?"

The second assailant from behind replied. "We were not given such *specific* directives." Then the second assailant wrapped both his giant forearms around the man's neck and with one violent twist, followed by a crack not unlike ice breaking on a lake on a warming winter day, and with such force, had he been a beer bottle, the cap would have been wrenched right off.

The man, his mission, and his plans to steal the laptop ended instantly.

For a moment, there was complete silence.

Then the first attacker growled. "What the Hell did you do that for?" He offered a look of total incredulity. "It was my turn."

The second assailant argued back. "You let him go."

The first attacker retorted. "He hit me with that little electric pop stick of his."

"And then what happened?"

The first attacker glared, his shoulders sagging as he sighed. "And I let him go."

"That's the rules; whoever holds him can kill him." The second assailant offered a peace offering. "But I promise, you can have the next one."

"That's what you told me the last time." The first attacker took a deep exasperated breath. Then he suddenly lunged forward and yanked the draping corpse off his brother and threw it over his left shoulder with a solid thump. "Then I get to feed him to *my* dogs."

The second assailant chuffed. "Hey. It's Fluffy's turn."

The first attacker mocked. "What just happened?"

The second assailant gave a dirty scowl. "I let him go."

They both faced one another down for a good minute, eyes squinting and most of all, not relenting. It was then followed by a burst of double belly laughs.

"How about we each take half? We can use the band saw back at the farm." The first attacker offered.

The second one shrugged non-committing. "Fine. Just don't bruise the body too much. My dogs hate it when we soften up the meat."

Both men laughed again, happier now.

The first attacker tossed the body into the back of his truck and covered it with a blue tarp. "Want to wait and see if anyone else shows up?"

"Sure. My dogs can get pretty hungry up in Milton." The second assailant grinned. "But I pretty much think he'll be the only one. The docs report was pretty specific."

The first attacker offered a smile. "What's the worst that can happen? We might *accidently* kill one wrong person or two?"

The second assailant shrugged. "I guess so. But then again, innocent and guilty people taste the same to my Fluffy."

Both men laughed heartily as they slipped back into the shadows to wait until morning.

13

The next morning, the limousine picked up Danica and Hayden at the front entrance to the hotel.

The concierge assured them both their luggage would be well cared for and waiting for them at the airport.

'*Airport?*' Hayden questioned internally. '*Are we leaving so soon?*'

Driving up Yonge Street, past Bloor, over the 401 and into the northern region of Toronto, the industrial district, past several manufacturing plants and one newspaper distribution centre, they continued to coast at a steady pace.

Hayden resumed his dispute from the evening before while walking through the airport. "All I'm saying is we could've stopped for a sandwich."

Danica was reviewing a government report. '*National mortality rates and statistics within the pharmaceutical industry in relation to interventions and prevention protocols.*' She raised her one eyebrow.

"As I mentioned last night, all you wanted was to stop for a beer. And like I said, you could do that at the hotel."

"At hotel prices?"

"It sure didn't stop you."

Hayden snidely replied. "I was still thirsty."

She resumed her reading without saying anything else.

The limo turned right onto a long stretch of road. To both sides were thick green lawns. Directly before them were large healthy maple trees, planted perfectly along the road's edge with uniform grace, their foliage so thick, their leaves seemed to nearly encompass and block out the sun above them as they drove. Directly behind the trees ran a seven foot high chain link fence with barbed wire coils at the top.

'Worried about entry...' Hayden mused. *'Or escape?'* He got bored of it pretty quickly as it ran on for almost a mile. He chose to open up his journal on the ancient symbols from the chamber at this point. He withdrew a pencil from his satchel, placing it upon his right ear for easy retrieval, and started attempting to decipher some of the unrecognized text. He looked like a commuter on his way to work doing a crossword, with the exception, he could not flip to the back of the book for the answers.

Danica took a bottle of water from the fridge in the armrest and nursed it slowly.

After ten more minutes, Hayden looked up from his journal in frustration and found himself distracted by a huge enterprise in the distance. He commented almost immediately. "They sure chose to build this place far from the city."

"And prying eyes." Danica interjected, folding her booklet closed. "There's temporary lodging on site in the southern quadrant for delicate experiments that require constant observation, but other than that, it's really not that far. Plus I think our limo driver has been riding under the speed limit since we left."

Hayden proudly stated. "Your employers obviously don't want to risk us getting injured."

Danica laughed. "More likely the laptop."

They passed a giant grey and white marble monument, ten feet tall, with the deep set engraved text of 'Maximum Pharmaceuticals'. Several spotlights were placed strategically in front of the sign, but not illuminated at this time as the sun was shining bright.

To the rest of the world, Maximum Pharmaceuticals was the third largest medical conglomerate in Canada, housed over ten acres of land with the main complex consisting of laboratories, research and development labs, animal housing shelters and business offices.

A few smaller units responsible for more confidential research resulted in more difficult access routes and thus, not attached to the main structure, but again, also not easily seen from the road.

The limo only stopped once at the main gate to provide the security clearance, and once shown, they were back in transit to the primary facility.

Arriving at the front of the building, obviously the Head Office, a ten floor azure blue glass encased structure with solar paneling interspersed between windows, to maximize solar absorption on all sides, the limo came to a stop.

Both Danica and Hayden exited.

Surrounding the office was a five foot wide reflecting pool which traced around the entire building with a single black stone bridge leading across to the main entrance only meant for foot traffic.

Danica and Hayden found their way inside, past three security checkpoints, six guards and into the private lift leading to the penthouse offices.

Hayden even found the elevator to be elegant with its solid walnut paneling, brass fixtures and beveled mirrors on the ceiling. The only thing he found out of place was the small tinted sphere in the corner with a security camera hidden inside and locked on the two occupants.

Danica had resumed reading her report, trying to appear nonchalant, but her stomach was dancing like butterflies over a field of posies.

They reached the tenth floor and the doors opened. They were greeted right away by a pretty young executive assistant, Amy, with long blonde hair, a slight British accent and well-shaped physique. She asked them to follow her to the conference room, gently noting the president would be with them shortly.

Hayden chuffed. *'President is how you address the U.S. leader, not business CEO's.'* But he kept his thoughts to himself.

They entered a large meeting chamber, at least the size of a 747's interior cabin, with lush tan carpet and a huge mahogany table that ran from one end of the room to the other, framed by twenty five comfortable red leather executive styled chairs pushed in for easy retrieval.

The walls were adorned with numerous sketches placed in thick brown marble frames. They appeared to be all of Leonardo Da Vinci's inventions, recreated masterfully on crisp vellum paper and inked with black India ink, all hand drawn, from the Ornithopter Flying Machine to the Armoured Car, from the Eight Barreled Machine Gun to the Artillery Park, giving precedence to the achievements of the imagination, but more importantly, a telltale sign this company believed the past held many things of importance to the future.

Both Danica and Hayden were asked to take a seat neat the rear of the room and directly before a sixty inch flat screen plasma television inset into the wall for conference meetings online.

At the end of the table sat a sterling silver tea set, positioned on an ornately designed tray, with coffee percolating inside a single decanter and matching cups for drinking. The scent of freshly ground beans permeated the room.

The executive assistant poured them each a cup, prepared it to their liking, without having asked, and placed it before their chairs as they took their seats.

Hayden took a sip of his drink and was thoroughly impressed. The only thing he could offer was, "Nice spread."

Danica was a little awestruck, speaking directly to Hayden. "I've never been up here myself. Most of my work is in the field. I mean, I've been to the fifth and the seventh floors, the seventh being where my lab is, but other than that, I've never been invited to the penthouse offices."

"And that is something we shall very much see rectified." Bellowed the deep voice of Maximus as he entered the room from the side double doors leading from his private office.

Hayden turned and for one brief second, his mouth dropped. He quickly snapped it back up.

Doctor Maximus Thorne, Chief Executive Officer of Maximum Pharmaceuticals was a massive human being, standing at six foot three, with sharp and intelligent brown eyes, thin blonde hair and three hundred pounds of solid muscle. His black suit, custom-made, stretched around his limbs like a parachute, revealing a man, if he so chose, able to crush boulders with a simple squeeze.

All Hayden thought was, *'Is Mr. Universe in need of a champion?'*

Following in his wake, the company's Chief Financial Officer, his longtime bride, Maxima, also equally formidable. Only one inch shorter at six foot two, deep brown eyes with a hint of blue, vibrant red hair with dark tanned skin. In all appearances, she was a walking tank.

In deference to Maximus, Maxima wore a low cut velvet red dress which barely passed her thighs, but only as a result of huge quadriceps which pulsed and flexed with each step she took. She dressed classy, yet provocatively, but clearly to show off her form where any skin was revealed.

They were obviously a couple who spent all their free time in the gym, pumping weights, exercising constantly and maintaining their near invincible physiques.

Maxima nodded to them. She smiled with eloquence and refined sophistication, stating firmly. "Good morning to you both Doctors Swift and Lattimer."

Hayden and Danica returned the greeting.

Hayden stood to offer his hand, but Maximus waved it off. "Friends don't need to shake hands. But since we're not yet close enough to offer a hug, let's be civil."

That and Hayden imagined he would be crushed like a bug in this behemoth's grip.

They all took their seats.

Maximus had his assistant bring him a protein beverage, as did Maxima.

Hayden suddenly felt awkward drinking coffee.

Maximus seemed to sense his discomfort. "Doctor Lattimer. I've already had three cups of coffee this morning at four a.m. before my workout. I find too many more this early and I would be less a hospitable host as I would be a twitching lunatic."

Hayden relaxed and took another drink.

Maxima turned to Danica, getting serious and down to business. "Doctor Swift. I assume you safeguarded the laptop?"

Danica smiled and placed it before her on the table. "As promised."

"Excellent." Maximus declared. His eyes glowed with genuine pleasure. He motioned to his executive assistant. "Please have it brought down to Mr. Grover." He turned to Hayden. "He's our I.T. director. He'll have it downloaded to a server, one not on the network I assure you, copied a dozen times onto numerous backs-ups so we can review the data later, now forever safe from…" Maximus grinned. "Future annoyances."

Maxima gave him a wink.

Hayden provided a quick '*thumbs up*', not sure what else he could offer.

Danica smiled at Hayden's discomfort.

The room was silent for only a few seconds as the assistant disappeared with the computer.

Maximus cut through it all. "Time is valuable, and I admit, not to be arrogant, mine is the most. So there's no point wasting it on idle bullshit or asking about flights when let's be honest, none of us give a shit." He clasped his large hands together. "So let's get down to brass tacks shall we?"

Hayden was actually warming up to Maximus.

Maximus looked out his window at the expanse of Toronto. In the far distance, the CN Tower needle poked up through the horizon. He asked loudly across the room, but directed to Hayden. "Do you believe God created the Earth, Doctor Lattimer?"

Hayden felt that warmth start to ebb away at the sudden shift in the conversation...

'A Bible thumper! Just what I fucking needed.'

Hayden knew he had to tread on eggshells, especially because he was still being paid very well by this *thumper*'s company and more importantly, the deposit had not yet arrived. He replied carefully. "I believe in a lot of things."

For a few seconds, everyone waited on bated breath for Maximus to either agree or disagree.

"Good answer." Maximus replied. "Personally, I do."

A genuine exhale oozed quietly from Danica in relief.

Maximus continued. "While I don't expect everyone to share my faith or agree with my ideals, I do expect compromise. That and I believe the ends justify the means, so I will work with believers and non-believers alike to achieve my goals." He looked to both Danica and Hayden. "But I also expect, if you're paid by me, you'll follow orders when given."

Hayden offered a positive shrug of compliance, but in his mind, he held no doubts he would dispense with his employment in seconds the moment those orders did not agree with his personal morals.

Maximus was not finished. "Many of my scientists disagree with my belief, but then again, they're not the CEO." Spoken matter-of-factly, not with arrogance. "But if we can work together to make a better world, who cares really. I'll let God do the judging when we all reach the pearly gates."

Hayden felt far more comfortable. A man of belief who also shared a desire for science was usually a better man for it.

Maximus got down to his main point. "So in that assumption, I refuse to believe God would create a world as unique as this, populate it with man, such perfect beings, and then saturate it with incurable diseases like Cancer, Lupus, Multiple Sclerosis and so many more, and with a single salute, wish us well and watch us fall."

Hayden agreed the theory had some merit. It did not sound like the plan of an all loving God. But as he was unsure where this was leading, he turned to Danica for help.

Danica had heard rumours of the Thorne's religious ideologues, but they never let it intrude on their work or into the media for that matter. She returned Hayden's look for help with a look of. *'I'm sorry?'*

Maximus continued without having noticed. "To me, it's like imagining Michelangelo painting his Mona Lisa on a sidewalk with chalk or carving his Statue of David on the beach out of butter..."

"Da Vinci." Hayden cut Maximus off.

"Pardon?" Maximus paused, not accustomed to such interruptions.

"Mona Lisa was painted by Da Vinci, not Michelangelo." Hayden corrected, thinking to himself. *'Spoke a lot to who had any influence in decorating this board room.'*

"Thank you." Was all Maximus could offer, his voice lowered slightly. He took a breath, glaring at Hayden and resumed where he left off. "For me, I refuse to think God has us so easily washed away by disease without providing us a means to protect ourselves."

Hayden admitted, based on that presumption, it was not entirely illogical. But he did not understand its relevance or its relation to their discovery. "And this has to do with the chamber how?" Hayden asked with a small amount of trepidation.

"That's the question we brought you up here to answer." Maxima threw in.

Danica intruded on the conversation. "And me?"

Maximus offered. "You both found it. I'm not a man who breaks up a good couple when he sees one."

Maximus and Maxima leaned forward and shared a deep solid kiss between them, their opposing hands holding tight over the tabletop.

Danica knew of the stories of their refusal to deny their love for one another, regardless of being on a television interview or at a business conference, as they wanted the world to know it.

Hayden found himself feeling slightly uncomfortable.

As did Danica.

When they parted, Maximus looked at the awkward expressions of Danica and Hayden. "A good team demands energy, direction, passion and expression. It's a part of who we are as humans."

Hayden again, gave a quick thumbs up and thinking. *'I need a beer.'*

Maximus smiled. "Me and Maxima...." He trailed off for a few seconds. "Let's simply say, we were born to be together."

The two of them shared a look, smiling at one another in a way to confirm they shared a private joke.

Hayden mused. *'I guess when I meet a girl with the same name, I should marry her too?'* But again, he kept such thoughts to himself.

Danica shyly pointed out. "We're not a couple."

Maximus stated. "In this endeavor, you are." He spoke with such finality, Danica had no rebuttal. "The two of you have discovered in ten days what my company has been unable to do for ten years, if not more. And I will not make the mistake to mess with that... Shall we call it...Karma."

Danica sighed, realizing the implication.

Where Hayden went, she would be forced to follow.

Maxima pulled out from under the table two small stacks of bills, tightly bound, listed with '$100' on the top one in yellow text, wrapped to depict five thousand on the band. She slid one of each of the piles to both Hayden and Danica like she was shooting a puck over ice into their goals.

They both caught it deftly.

Maximus took on a very serious look. "I have a proposal for you two. All you have to do is listen. If you still think it's crazy, you can walk out of here with your five grand and resume your work." Maximus turned to Danica. "And it will not affect your future in this company in any way. I assure you."

Danica found the words empty.

Maximus ended his statement with. "But ask yourselves this question before you answer. Do you want to walk away now and never know? Of a secret which hundreds of men have died for over centuries and continue to do so to this very day?"

Hayden and Danica exchanged looks.

To them, all they had found was an ancient story chamber speaking of a lost tribe and their unknown island of no sun. And small referrals to miracles balanced by equal evil.

Yet since that discovery, they had been attacked, threatened, their discovery blown to smithereens, but not before it was soaked with acid and all accessible data stolen by sophisticated hackers.

And now, they were being offered a huge chunk of money to simply hear a man out, a powerful business leader, if only before ending their quest.

Both Hayden and Danica slipped the money off the table into their respective laps.

'In for a penny, in for a pound.'

Maximus slapped the tabletop with authority and excitement. "Excellent. I knew you were my kind of people." He turned to Maxima and back to them all. "Now that I have your attention, I have a story to tell. And unlike most campfire tales, mine is *real*."

14

"Before I begin..." Maximus turned to Hayden and asked. "Do you believe in destiny Doctor Lattimer?"

Hayden paused, unsure how to answer. Then he offered. "Do you mean were we put on this planet with a higher purpose?"

"Exactly." Maximus responded with some enthusiasm.

After a moment of serious thought, Hayden replied. "I do and I don't. In my studies of history, I've read numerous accounts of cultures and their beliefs, mostly in their striving for destiny, some even having achieved their lofty goals. But by that same token, I've seen those same predictions in others, yet their civilizations fall." He leaned back. "Rome for instance is one such happenstance."

"But Rome was great for a very long time." Maximus retorted. He was enjoying this educational tit-for-tat with someone would could speak to it.

Hayden shrugged. "If destiny was meant to have an expiry date, then I would agree with you, Rome did a great job."

Danica turned and looked around the room to see what happened to Hayden as the man speaking now is not the same piss shooting, beer swilling, trash talker she met in her camp.

"My sentiments exactly." Maximus replied with energy.

Hayden gave Maximus a quizzical look, not having thought he had provided any form of mutual agreement.

Maximus resumed. "Destiny can be temporary and easily lost if not properly sought out, pursued and most importantly seized."

Danica joined the conversation. "What exactly are we expected to seize by the way?"

Maxima entered the discussion. "Something of the utmost importance, which we feel…" Maxima and Maximus shared a look. "…has been around since the dawn of time. And I must clarify, not since the dawn of man, we mean of time."

Hayden was a specialist in this area, yet he was hesitant to agree. "Treasure hunters have been around for centuries. What makes you so sure *your* treasure is any more real than another?"

"Destiny." Maximus replied with such finality, he seemed to feel no other explanation was necessary. But he did offer more. "We're not looking for gold, sapphires or piles of diamonds. We seek miracles. The kind that can change the world as we see it."

Hayden chose to add some reality to the conversation. "You're not the first people to think you can change the world."

Maximus relaxed, changing the subject. "Did you know most of the staff here fears me Doctor Lattimer?"

Hayden had no idea. He had only just met him.

Danica said nothing. She admitted to herself, she was one of them.

Hayden replied. "Well I don't. You asked me here as a consultant. You can't have a frank discussion being scared of the answers."

Maxima leaned forward and spoke to Maximus, loud enough to be heard. "I like him."

"I absolutely agree." Maximus never let his eyes waiver from Hayden. "We're regular people like everyone else. We're simply better at seizing opportunities and willing to take bigger risks."

Danica re-asked the question, getting more confident with Hayden at her side. "What risks are we talking about?" Sensing the mentioning of the word *'risk'* had importance since from the start, Maximus had stated, he was not willing to waste time.

Maxima drew a small cart from under the table, one Hayden and Danica had not seen upon entry. From it, she withdrew two books, both old in appearance, wrapped in cellophane and a third, newer, obviously a photocopy. Maxima introduced them. "The two on the left are the originals. We will keep those. The copy here, we will also keep." She gestured to Amy as she returned to the conference room with three large pre-printed binders filled with papers and files. "Amy here will provide you a copy of all three of these sources."

Amy handed all three manuscripts, bound in heavy stock paper, two distributed to Hayden and one to Danica.

Maxima continued. "Your three copies are for you to read. You should have plenty of time on the plane."

Hayden found his thoughts from the morning resurface. *'This is why our luggage was returned to the airport I suspect.'*

Maxima threw in a small warning. "But do it quickly as all three are copied in 'Phantom' ink, a trademark product of Maximum Pharmaceuticals, one which cannot be photocopied in any way and after seventy two hours will evaporate in its entirety, taking all the text with it." She smiled proudly. "Unrecoverable by any means of scientific reparation. We have a contract with the CIA in the US Department of Defense to provide them an unlimited supply."

Hayden was surprised at the efforts taken to secure this information. "What are they?"

Maximus turned very serious. "The first is the original logbook of the ship known as Leviathan. Discovered in 1863 adrift in the Southern oceans." He flipped to the rear of his copy. "As you will see in yours, it is missing several pages, all having been ripped out and destroyed by a former crew member before the ship was salvaged."

Hayden and Danica moved closer together to review and share the first tome.

Maximus pointed to the second one, the copy and quickly proceeded. "The second is a digital copy of the ship's log of the Serenade, written by the one who discovered the Leviathan at that time. One Captain Rios. The original logbook is in Belfast, with a museum that refuses to part with it." He provided that last statement with a snarl under his breath. "Irish Idiots." He clenched his fists and released. "There was really no need to copy it in 'Phantom Ink' since you can still order a copy online for less than ten dollars, but for continuity's sake, we did."

Hayden looked at the cover and slid it to the side for Danica to examine.

Maximus ended with. "The third and final one is the partial journal of a madman from the end of the century who is rumoured to have been the Leviathan's sole survivor and the destroyer of the Leviathan's logbook pages."

Hayden drew the three books together, stacking them one atop the other. He carefully asked. "Not to repeat myself, but what does this have to do with the chamber?"

Maximus replied. "The same reason I asked my first question. I believe for every cause, there is a cure. And God has tasked mankind to find it. I believe your chamber and these books will lead me to one of them."

Danica sat idly by, watching their exchange, unsure what she could offer at this point. They were debating history, for which she was not as well armed as Hayden.

Maximus continued. "Did you know Maximum Pharmaceuticals funds over three million dollars annually into the expeditions around the world, from oceans to jungles, from mountains to ravines, all searching for such secrets?" He spoke with proud satisfaction. "If there is something to be found, I want Maximum Pharmaceuticals to be the one to find it."

Hayden and Danica shared a quick look.

Danica motioned for Hayden to hold the lead.

"I'm not saying I believe or not, but how can you be so sure it even exists?" Hayden asked kindly, turning to face Maximus, not knowing what *'it'* is.

Maximus took a deep cleansing breath. "God helps those who help themselves."

Hayden interjected with. "Hezekiah 6.1"

For a long moment, Maximus was very quiet. Finally he spoke. "I underestimated your knowledge of the Bible Doctor Lattimer."

Hayden brushed it off.

If you asked, most archeologists knew the Bible. It was considered standard reading for anyone who researched the past as no other book has lasted the test of time as well.

With the exception to the Quran, but Maximus had not referred to it.

At least as of yet anyway.

Hayden knew the Quran as well. It spoke to equally great stories, with just a different view of the world in its interpretation.

Good archeologists read them both.

Great ones supported them.

In fact, during his studies, his professor demanded, out of respect for those who worshiped the Quran, it only be read wearing cotton gloves. The reason was clerics and worshippers alike in the Middle East felt it was disrespectful to read it with your bare hands. Hayden may not share their faith, but he understood their desire for respect and honoured it.

Hayden added. "My mother was a Catholic, as were my grandparents. They taught me that one cannot choose to disagree with something unless they understand it first. While I don't agree with all its views, I also don't disagree either."

Maxima looked impressed. "They sound like smart people."

Hayden replied proudly. "I think so."

Even Danica found herself looking at Hayden in a different way.

Maximus took a breath and resumed. "So I need the two of you to help me find one of God's secrets."

Hayden turned to Danica and back to both Maximus and Maxima. "Sounds like a daunting task?" He offered. "What makes you think we can really help?"

Maxima took over at this point. "Your discovery of the Tribal chamber for one. It describes an island we believe has been discovered before, but for some reason, is now lost."

Danica, knowing she was a part of this team, asked again. "Okay? But why us?"

Maximus stated. "Destiny."

As a scientist, Danica had no response to that statement.

Hayden did. "Destiny notwithstanding, how?"

"We have a specific mission in mind." Maximus offered carefully. "But before we get to the specifics, have either of you ever heard of the ship called Leviathan?"

Both Danica and Hayden exchanged looks of confusion.

Neither had a clue.

Hayden did not keep himself apprised of European history, least of all, Maritime history. It rarely conflicted with his work in tribal South America.

Danica on the other hand, avoided history altogether. Not because of the subject matter, but because, if it was not under a microscope or analyzed by dissection, she never needed to look.

Maxima explained. "It was an American ship found adrift in the late 1800's, 1863 as my husband said to be exact, with all crew lost with the exception of one."

Hayden and Danica sipped at their coffees, cooling with each minute they listened.

"To this day, no one knows what happened to that ship, its crew or why?" Maxima pointed out.

Hayden threw in. "The Bermuda Triangle had many such stories. Why is this one so special?"

Maximus leaned forward, his weight pressing on the table until it actually groaned. "The Leviathan's Logbook of course. From what we've been able to procure, it appears the survivor went to great lengths to destroy the path they took *before* their crew was lost, by eating the last eight pages. So unlike the missing ships from the Triangle, this one did not want to be remembered."

'*Eaten the pages?*' Hayden was getting intrigued. "But this helps us how?"

"Well, before the pages vanished, the previous ones referred to an Island of Eternal Night."

Danica now knew why her boss called it as he did.

Hayden took a sip of his coffee. "But we don't know where it is?"

"Yet..." Maxima let that word trail off. "But we now have a starting point. Admittedly, without the location from the logbook's missing pages, we chose the next obvious route. The survivor." She pointed to the journal. "From our research, he was placed in a mental institution upon Rios' return to England. From there the reports are sketchy, mostly due to records being lost in the fire."

Danica was deeply entrenched now in the story. "What fire?"

Maximus found himself feeling elated as he could relate to others what he had learned over the years, like a story teller around a campfire telling the scouts about the world they live in, and of course, eventually, the man with the hook. "At the turn of the century, when the facility closed due to a suspicious fire that broke out, it was rumoured the patient had written and kept a *complete* journal of his survival, including more on this Island of Eternal Night."

Maxima continued where Maximus left off. "As stories would have it, before the fire, his original doctor finally convinced the patient to provide the location he remembered into his journal. Making real what he feared most."

Hayden gestured to the journal on the table. "If you have the journal, what do you need us for?"

Maxima smiled demurely. "The patient tore out the last eight pages before he was killed and of course, with it, the location of the lost island."

Everyone was quiet for a good solid minute.

Hayden looked around the room "And how do you expect us to find an island neither of you can find, with two books missing the directions?" He opened his hands in mock surrender. "Unlike the movies, us archeologists are actually quite tame."

Maximus laughed. "Yes, but your knowledge is invaluable."

Hayden leaned on the table. "But these books are written in English right? What do you need *me* for specifically as it's obviously not to translate?"

Maximus pointed to the items. "With the journal, we have learned a great deal. Hopefully when you read it, you will also. But with a new set of eyes, you may see something we missed. And with your direct insight into the chamber, maybe even make connections no one else could."

"Is eight of any significance?" Danica threw in, to be part of the discussion, referring to the pages.

Maxima shrugged. "Likely not. The nut probably got full. Good quality paper at that time was pretty thick."

Hayden asked the question both Danica and he were thinking. "Where are we flying? Back to South America?"

Maximus smiled. "England."

Hayden was surprised at that. "What's in England?"

Maximus looked like the Cheshire cat with his wide smile. "It seems, as of yesterday, in London, there is an auction taking place. A collector has found and offered what is believed to be the remaining eight pages of this very madman's journal."

Even Danica was confused. "And you want to send us?"

Maximus' mood darkened momentarily. "It appears the owner, an eccentric pest, will only sell the pages to a reputable institution of learning."

Hayden understood now. "And because I'm an archeologist..." He turned to Danica. "A real *doctor*..."

Danica rolled her eyes.

"And part of a revered institution of learning for Canada." Hayden continued. "You want me to get it."

"Exactly." Maximus interjected. "We will provide you everything you need, including a blank cheque to pay the collector whatever he wants for these pages."

"What's on them?"

"If I knew that, you wouldn't be going." Maximus smiled. "But if it adds more yellow bricks to the road, I want it."

Hayden was amused for the first time since they started talking. Maximus said 'I' not 'we.'

Danica listened intently and she too heard the very same thing, but she was not as amused.

"So all you need to do is fly to London, get us the pages and then when you return, either join us..." Maxima posed the offer. "Or leave and return to your lives."

Hayden found this too sparse an explanation, flying him and Danica across the world to purchase from a nutcase eight pages written in a century old mental institution, followed by asking them to join their crusade when they did not know what they were after. "You have to at least tell us what these pages lead to."

Maximus leaned back in his chair and took a few long moments to consider. "Okay I'm a fair man. That and I need you. Something most people will never hear from me." He gulped down his protein drink in one pull. "So let's get down to it. Quid Pro Quo Doctor. I tell you something, you get me something."

Hayden smiled. "Done."

Maximus asked. "As a scholar and specifically an archeologist of South American lore, have you ever heard of the Fountain of Youth?"

Hayden wanted to make a joke, but once he saw the look in Maximus' face, he knew he was dead serious. He held his control to mock Maximus and answered. "Like as in Ponce de Leon?"

"Yes. But our former Puerto Rican governor never found it." Maximus retorted.

Hayden waited a few seconds. "But most stories refer to the Fountain being in Florida, or at best, in Bimini in the Caribbean."

"Yes. But all have proven to be dead ends." Maximus smiled, obviously having paid a great deal to search out these very avenues. But he was very impressed with Hayden's intelligence. "But if I had to look to all leads, Hereodotus of Ancient Greece referred to it being in Europe. But we can't chase all the stories out there can we?"

Hayden could not help himself. "I've also heard lots of stories about the Easter Bunny, but I don't sit up on Sunday with a net in my hand hoping to catch him."

Danica's neck snapped sharply in Hayden's direction, shocked at his remark.

Maximus stared at Hayden and let out a large heartfelt laugh. "Doctor Swift mentioned your sarcastic side. I actually find it refreshing. I truly appreciate when I can speak to someone who sees me as a person, not a CEO."

Hayden grinned. "I still respect you, don't get me wrong, but you have to understand, I try to work within the parameter of my studies."

Maximus asked the question. "But what if?"

"What if what?" Hayden replied.

"What if the Fountain of Youth exists?" Maxima interjected. "Would it not qualify as a part of your studies?"

Hayden was struck silent. He thought about the question and answered. "Technically yes. But these are stories told by soothsayers and dreamers. People's word passed down through the generations.

There has never been any tangible proof of such a thing as the Fountain of Youth. At best, only rumours."

"Is not all archaeologies the study of the past's stories as they are passed down, verbal, written or otherwise? As well as its rumours?" Maximus gently prodded.

"And not only that, because none of us were really there at the time, isn't all history simply the word of another?" Maxima added.

Hayden could offer no argument as both were essentially right. But he did point out. "You refer to this as one of God's miracles. But I've studied the Bible and know it well. And I've never once seen reference to the Fountain of Youth."

Maxima smiled. "Do you know how many chapters were considered for the Bible before it was constructed, edited out for the simple fact the creators knew full well no one would carry around and worship from a fifty thousand page book?" Maxima stated matter-of-factly. "The Catholic community had to choose the best and the brightest stories. The ones to garner the greatest following. While I'm not saying the Fountain of Youth was in those ones either, I'm also not saying it was not. So not having it in the Bible does not speak to its significance."

Hayden found himself stuck for an answer.

"But let's look beyond the miracle of youth." Maximus gestured to move the conversation forward. "What if it also heals all wounds as believed? And I mean ALL? Can you imagine the medical potential?"

'And the profit margins.' Danica mused.

Hayden offered up. "The Holy Grail is known to do the same thing."

Maximus shrugged it off. "Yes, but the Holy Grail is lost somewhere in Europe. I already have a team in Scotland in Kilwinning on that and they have reached a dead end for the time being."

Hayden would have joked again, but he could tell, Maximus was serious.

All four of them sat and took a drink from their respective beverages, Amy having replaced Maximus's quickly and quietly.

Maximus took control again. "Do you know how much money Adolf Hitler spent searching out legends and mystical artifacts?" He paused for a few seconds to let that sink in. "Millions."

"And yet he still lost the war." Hayden sanswered. "Plus we're not comparing ourselves to him are we?"

Maximus dismissed the comment with his hand, but still answered the question. "Of course not. All I'm saying is leaders throughout history have also believed in such tales, and on less evidence than we have. So, can all these people be wrong?"

"Doesn't mean they're right either." Hayden shot back.

Maximus nodded. "I'll give you that. But what can it hurt to look?"

Danica and Hayden shared a quick glance and shared the same thought. *'It really can't hurt to look.'*

Danica took a quick drink of coffee for a burst of energy. "But in the chamber, it refers to an evil that inhabits the island."

Maximus took another deep chug from his glass. "Yes. I've heard this tale before. I've also heard the island is haunted, or cursed or stained by sin. My personal favourite is the devil himself created that which lives on the island and God had to come down from the heavens to make the island its prison."

Hayden was amused as that was almost exactly how the travelling tribe had put it.

Hayden finally knew Maximus's mind was set. Hayden threw out the gauntlet. "So what do we have to do?"

Maximus proudly clenched both fists knowing Hayden was hooked.

Maxima pulled from her interior jacket two envelopes. "You're going to fly to London tomorrow. Inside each envelope is an invitation to the auction, a new corporate credit card without the Maximum Pharmaceuticals logo, in case the collector has any issues with you being with a corporation, a reservation card for the hotel and finally, a one way First Class airline ticket each."

"One way First Class?" Danica chipped in.

Hayden sarcastically threw in. "You'd be surprised how few people book economy if given a choice."

Danica shook her head with a glare. "I meant the one way part?"

Maximus smiled. "Your return ticket will be electronic, waiting at the airport for when you leave. Just in case anything happens and you need more time. So we left it open."

Hayden could not imagine what would delay them, but then again, he was being asked to find the Fountain of Youth too.

Maxima slid the individual envelopes to both of them. "I want you both to procure for us the last eight pages from the madman's journal and bring it back here immediately. Price is no object and as you can understand, failure is not anticipated."

Danica grinned with tightly held teeth, not yet understanding her role in this. She finally offered her opinion. "I was planning to return to South America."

Maxima shook her head. "To a destroyed burial chamber in the midst of a South American mess with lawmakers seeking blame. No Doctor Swift, your skills are best teamed up with Doctor Lattimer. Considering what the two you have accomplished thus far in such a short amount of time, separating you now would be paramount to bad luck."

Danica crossed her arms and leaned back in her chair. *'Great. I'm a walking rabbit's foot.'*

Hayden turned to Maximus. "I'll go. But do you honestly think a few missing pages from a century old journal written by nut-job will point you in the right direction?"

Maximus stood up motioning for them the meeting was coming to a close. "I find a quote befitting this situation: 'In every madman is a misunderstood genius whose idea, shining in his head, frightened people, and for who delirium was the only solution to the strangulation that life had prepared for him"

Hayden retorted. "Tell that to his psychiatrist.'

Maximus smiled. "I don't need to. I have the files from the institution when it closed down. It included not only his doctor's assessments over the thirty years the patient remained with him, but his personal theories as well. It included an unexpected diagnosis of one Captain Rios, who though not a patient, visited enough times to be considered as such. According to the good doctor, Rios' obsession with the dark island and what he believed was a mystical place that healed all wounds was evidently clear. It's real."

Danica could understand Maximus' need to seek out the island, especially if it truly existed.

As a pharmaceutical giant in Canada, a mystical healing source would be worth millions, if not billions, especially if they found it first.

Hayden casually mentioned. "Before we leave, you should know, nowhere in the chamber did I see reference to the phrase the Fountain of Youth."

Maxima also rose. "But you did see the phrase *Eternal Life*?"

Hayden shrugged. "*Eternal Life* to indigenous people means lots of things. The world's ability to restore itself, the afterlife, and many more."

"She did not ask for your opinion of it." Maximus for the first time was hard in his response. "She asked if you saw the phrase *Eternal Life*."

Hayden nodded, slightly chastened. "Yes I did."

Maximus seemed to relax again. "Let's be honest, I'm willing to fund this little expedition to London, pay you an exorbitant consulting fee, and make a substantial donation to your University towards whatever you deem is needed. What really have you got to lose except a few more days, presuming you don't join us after?"

Hayden stood and took Maximus' open hand. His palm almost seemed to vanish in it. "You sir are a salesman. I accept."

Danica knew in his acceptance, she would be forced to do so. She got up with a small touch of defeat. "I guess you can count me in too."

15

"You know this is insane right?" Hayden mocked, twisting the cap off his beer and pressing himself into the headboard of his king sized bed.

Danica was sitting in a high back lounge chair in Hayden's hotel room, facing him, legs crossed, nursing her cooler.

It was the early evening hours and they were both waiting for the ride to their flight, long after departing Maximum Pharmaceuticals.

Her room was adjacent to his with connecting doors. She could have gone home for the night, but elected instead to be closer to the airport rather than drive all the way in from Burlington for the morning flight to Heathrow.

"I admit, from what I've heard, the Thorne's can be a bit… unique." She defended.

"Unique? They're flying us to London to buy a century old diary, scratch that, a few pages from a century old diary, written by a guy they *think* was the survivor of a ship tragedy in hopes it leads them to a mystical island which no one can find and hides the Fountain of Youth."

The way Hayden put it, she had to admit, it did sound insane. She took a quick sip. "They're paying you aren't they?"

"That's not the point."

"Then why did you accept?"

"I never said I wasn't greedy."

Danica rolled her eyes again. She figured if she spent too much more time with him, her eyeballs would be able to press weights. "So you're doing it for the mission, not the money?"

Hayden paused and then smirked. "All right fine. It's the money. But you're more of a scientist than I am. You can't tell me this is how you planned to spend your career. I might study legends and folklore as it relates to the past, but I certainly don't take it as gospel."

Danica did agree as her world took a rather odd twist recently. Last week she was hunting for plants and tree sprigs in the middle of nowhere. This week she was looking for a legend no one really believed existed.

Danica reconsidered that last thought. Two people did and both were her very wealthy employers. "I figure the sooner we get them what they want, the sooner we can return to our lives and do what we did before."

"Before we were almost blown up in the middle of rural South America?"

Danica glared in his direction. "I highly doubt a chamber being destroyed half a kilometer away from your camp qualifies as '*almost blown up!*'"

Hayden crossed his arms. "It still shook my tent. Woke me up with a headache."

"I think the beer did that." Danica got up and opened Hayden's fridge for another drink.

She froze. "Did you empty the entire mini-bar?" She asked incredulously.

"It's in my carry on." Hayden replied. "What's the issue? It's comp."

"Comp?" Danica turned to face him, her eyes wide with shock. "My company is not a casino. You can't just empty the mini-bar?"

Hayden looked at her with a guilty grin. "Then I guess you'll want me to put back the towels and the bathrobes huh?"

She slammed the fridge shut. "You're incorrigible." She left the room and returned with a cooler from her own fridge a minute later.

Hayden waited a few minutes for her to cool off. Once she looked more relaxed, and after a few pulls on her drink, he resumed. "It's not how I pictured I would be consulting? That's all."

"What did you think they were going to have you do?"

"Translating maybe. Help recreate the chamber in a 3-D virtual environment for examination?" He chugged half his beer in one gulp. "Not flying to London England to trick some old antique collector out of eight pages torn from a book a hundred years ago written by some insane guy." He pursed his lips. "I don't know. I assumed it would be more… archeology stuff."

"We're not exactly being asked to trick him. We're paying him what he wants." Danica still felt empty in saying it.

"On the presumption it is being taken to an institution of post-secondary learning." Hayden challenged. "And using *my* credentials I might add."

Both of them stopped for a few seconds to take a drink of their respective beverages.

Danica was curious, as he had brought up the subject, and they had several hours to kill before their flight, so she asked. "Why archeology?"

Hayden replied. "Why not?"

"That's not an answer."

Hayden took a second to consider telling her. "My father."

"Your father?"

"He taught me history was the key to everything. It was his major in university. He went on to be an executive at a bank, but if you ever sat with him around a campfire with a beer, he never once talked about interest rates, mortgage holdings or foreclosures. He talked about history."

Danica listened with rapt interest.

"As a kid, he would sit me in bed and tell me the stories of all the legends of old, from Hercules to Thor or Zeus to Poseidon." Hayden grinned. "He loved Greek mythology most of all. And oddly enough, American Civil war. History was his passion and his love for it was so all encompassing, it also became mine."

Danica smiled. She liked that. It made Hayden seem more human. "But you went with South American tribal history?"

"I had to set myself apart from my father in some ways. He was great and all, but I wanted to be my own man. Plus I found South American culture to be very addictive. That and the way all these different tribes lived their lives, independent of one another, teaching many things and yet were still able to communicate with other tribes with ease and in such unique and wonderful ways. I had to follow where their steps took them as I fell in love with it."

Danica smiled. After a few seconds, she asked the question. "What if, in fact, their steps lead to the Fountain of Youth?"

Hayden finished his beer. "I'll believe that when I see it."

Danica stood indicating her intention to return to her room. "We're getting up pretty early tomorrow."

Hayden grabbed his pillow and shoved it under his back. "You can go to sleep. I'm still wired. I might watch some television." With a smooth gesture, he had the remote in hand and the plasma screen flickered to life.

Danica turned to leave. As she walked, she shouted over her shoulder. "Don't order any '*comp*' movies that I have to explain to management upon our return." She grabbed her door handle. "And you know which ones I'm talking about."

Two seconds later, Hayden turned off the television. "I guess there's nothing on then."

'A child and a pig.' Danica was closing the door behind her.

Hayden shouted as he shoved his face into his pillows. "If they tell me my next mission is looking for the Ark of the Covenant, then I'm really going to gripe." He paused. "And ask for another twenty five grand."

Danica thought to herself sealing the door. *'Don't suggest it. Chances are, if they thought you could find it, they'd be asking.'*

16

London, England.
Twenty seven hours later.

Standing in the lobby of the hotel, surrounded by walls adorned with beautifully aged English art, framed in antique wood frames, emblazed with colours most eyes could not help but be drawn towards. The floors were layered with smooth black and white Italian marble running from front to end and smelling of Parisian perfumes, roses and sugars, elegant and fine, like an aroma-laced velvet cloth had been lightly graced under ones nose.

Even with all this beauty, the hostess frowned in annoyance. All the while, she gently tapped harder on the keyboard in front of her computer hoping for a different message. She sighed.

Danica on the other hand was glaring, both elbows up on the counter, trying to see the screen, even though it was facing away from her. "You have got to be kidding me?" She almost snarled, jet leg and exhaustion weighing down her limbs.

The hostess, a pretty little brunette with hazel eyes, skin as white as alabaster and a soft voice hinting of a slight Portuguese accent, her name tag reading '*Donna Lopes*' smiled very sweetly, customer service seemingly born in her bloodstream. "You have to understand, the auction is very popular. It runs for three days. You coming here unexpectedly after the end of day one cannot always guarantee a reservation."

Danica lightly smacked her passport on the desk, imagining all the things she would do to Amy when she returned home. "I was told we would have two rooms. Adjoining rooms, but very specifically, two!"

Danica turned and looked at the politely waiting Hayden, hands at his sides and sporting a goofy grin, having slept comfortably on the flight the entire way, unaware his snoring kept most of the first class cabin up and the front seven rows of economy, not to mention, herself.

He shrugged and mouthed the words. '*Shit happens.*'

Danica ignored him and turned back to the hostess. "What about a broom closet or a trunk?" Gesturing to Hayden behind her. "He likes to *rough* it."

The hostess smiled, looking up and winking innocently at Hayden, as though considering putting him up for the night at her place. She returned to Danica with a downtrodden look. "I'm truly very sorry. There's only the one room. But it's still a suite." The hostess keyed a few buttons. "But as compensation, I will have a generous gift basket brought up for the inconvenience."

Danica sighed with defeat. "Is there at least a sofa?"

The hostess frowned again. "I'm afraid not. But there is a dining table?"

Danica turned to glare in Hayden's direction.

Hayden tilted his head at her like you would a child who needed to be told something important. "You don't even have to ask. Of course you can have the table." He looked past Danica to the hostess. "I presume it comes with a blanket and pillow?"

The hostess blushed, not having offered it for that purpose.

Danica spun back to the hostess without a word, knowing who was getting the table. "Can you also please have the '*paid*' movie channel deactivated for the term of our stay?"

The hostess acknowledged the request and returned to her keyboard to add the instructions while encoding their keycards.

Hayden looked insulted. "Hey. Did I not pay you for the movie at the hotel before we left?"

Danica gave him a dirty look. "Yet, I still had to check out. You sticking a ten dollar bill in my pocket *after* the concierge asked me if we enjoyed our stay and him seeing your *selection...*" She emphasized 'selection' with distaste. "Does not qualify as having paid enough. I paid with my pride."

"I told you in the elevator down I owed you ten dollars." He answered defensively.

"I thought it was for room service."

Hayden grinned with amusement. "Technically it was."

Danica's eyes widened for a second and squinted tight. She offered him no answer, as her father once told her, '*If you don't have something nice to say, don't say anything at all.*' She instead returned to watching as the hostess prepared the keycards.

Hayden remained equally as quiet.

After a minute, Danica casually mentioned. "Plus it was fourteen dollars, not ten."

"Would it make any difference if I said I didn't watch the whole thing?" Hayden asked.

Danica turned back around very slowly.

Hayden's smile froze on his face at Danica's look, the corners of his lips being drawn downward by the gravimetric forces of a woman's fury. It was like invisible death rays seemed to shoot from her eyes and melt his precious grin into a puddle of sloppy frowns.

When Danica felt she had wasted enough time on him, her eyelids loosened and she rerturned her icy gaze to the front desk.

After a full minute, realizing Danica was no longer glowering as she was, Hayden spoke up. "You know I'm kidding right?" He offered apologetically.

She ignored him.

Hayden waited a second. When he got no response, he stated, speaking louder. "I did watch it all."

Danica wanted to turn and slug him, but in doing so, she knew she would still have to touch him. Ignoring him seemed to bother him the most, so she kept it up.

After another minute, Hayden offered. "I'll give you $ 4.00 when we get to the room if you want."

"Keep it." Danica replied curtly, not wanting to touch anything his hands held.

The hostess reached forward and held up the two keycards to be taken, held apart as she suspected they wanted to grab their own.

Danica grabbed hers, followed by her luggage.

Hayden picked up his bag, grabbing the second key from the hostess and passed Danica. As he did so, he said aloud for the hostess to hear. "I hope you don't snore because I'm a light sleeper."

Danica stormed in behind him with her cardkey in hand, remembering the sound of Hayden on the plane like a chainsaw in the forest bringing down a barrage of redwood trees without the courteous *'TIMBER!'*

They reached the elevator in relative quiet.

"You're still not getting the bed." Danica declared.

Hayden chuckled to himself. *'Hopefully not to myself anyway.'*

Danica scowled suspecting what he was thinking.

'Not a hope in Hell.'

17

The next morning, Hayden exited the bathroom, showered and smelling of something sweet, a combination of cinnamon laced with lilacs. A selection from the gift basket Ms. Lopes had sent up, which included a generous quantity of sample colognes from all over Europe, Swiss dark chocolates and more importantly, imported beer.

Technically, not imported from here anyway.

Hayden chugged half of one down quickly after brushing his teeth.

'Breakfast of champions' as his Dad always said.

He cracked his neck and stretched his shoulder muscles, having slept on the couch all night, which in his estimate was not all that bad.

Though not a sofa bed, which normally had a pull out mattress hidden within, the three coushioned couch of the hotel was remarkably large and comfortable.

He adjusted his grey turtleneck and pulled on his black double breasted blazer, the kind he loved to wear.

Some said it was out of style, but he always replied. *'Archeologists bring the past back to life.'*

After a few more tugs and twists, he felt he looked perfect.

Hayden shouted to Danica who was in the bedroom chamber getting dressed for the auction. "Are you not ready yet?"

"Unlike men, women pride themselves on their appearance." She replied through the walls. "So give me a minute."

He ran his leather belt around his waist. Once snapped into place, he asked aloud. "I assume you were trying to be funny by placing one of your scientific flags in the middle of the toilet?"

She laughed. "I used to live with a guy. He could never get it all in the bowl. He always missed and hit the floor." She went silent for a second. "Plus I figured you were used to the target."

Hayden chuckled as well as he brushed his hair back with a touch of mousse. "It's called marking our territory. Dogs do it all the time."

"Dogs only do it once." She retorted. "Men do it all the time."

Hayden finished his beer. "We like to remind those around us of what's ours."

Danica offered no rebuttal, obviously not dignifying that with an answer.

Hayden moved into the front foyer, having called down minutes before to the concierge desk to have a cab waiting.

Danica came around the corner.

Hayden turned to say something, but quietly gasped, his breath catching in his throat.

Danica looked absolutely stunning. Her hair was untied, loosely drifting past her shoulders, flowing like feathers in the wind. She wore a white cashmere long sleeved sweater, V-neck, which accentuated her lightly tanned skin from the South American sun. With that, a pair of almost skintight grey wool slacks that ran to her ankles, creased sharply with military precision. On her feet were a pair of grey leather high heeled shoes, open toed, that went perfectly with her outfit.

For accessories, Danica sported a pair of small green emeralds framed in gold on each ear. The emerald was both her mother's and her birthstones, as she had relayed to Hayden on the plane, *May babies*. Around her neck she wore a gold heart pendant which her grandmother had given her mother before she passed away, one which Danica held very dear, refusing to wear anything else with it.

Finally, a perfume so succulent, had Danica been a mermaid, Hayden would have found himself diving headfirst into the sea, swimming downward to drown in the icy depths and not caring in the least.

For several seconds, there was only silence and quiet breathing. Finally…

"You look…" Hayden stuttered. "… Nice."

Danica smiled, sensing his true thoughts. "Thank you." She grabbed her purse and gave him a quick look over. "You look very handsome yourself."

Hayden grinned and grabbed his wallet, cardkey and the invitations, all the while thinking, *'You actually look awesome.'* But he felt what he had said was enough.

Danica stepped forward and past him, opening the door for him to go. "Now let's go buy a madman's missing diary pages and go home."

18

The London Constabulary Auction House, North of Trafalgar Square, off Charing Cross Road, was a hundred year old former police station now turned business. It was also considered a secret storage haven for collectors, enthusiasts and truly unique hunters of treasures from around the world who would gather annually and acquire things of note, rarity and of course, without the publicity.

During this season, numerous boot sales, inventory clearances and auctions took place all over London, but the LCAH, as it was called, prided itself on only offering one of a kind items. Truly rare acquisitions passed onto them through either greedy family members selling prized heirlooms for cash, collectors in need of rarer items for which capital was sought, through the sale of their less favoured items in exchange, or like tonight, when collectors wanted to see institutions of higher learning get their chance to have that which they had found, acquired or collected over the years so others could benefit. The latter usually only a result of the owner either having no family members or none worthy of the prize. Thus the collector, for whatever reason now felt, and believed, their wares were meant for the world.

For a price of course.

The LCAH was a beautifully decorated British building with lots of art defining the monarchy in all its history and glory, combined with its current and modern day presentation in the form of painted plates, rare photos and differing stamps and coins.

Each room, and there were many of them, was immaculately cleaned, with small tables, some with snacks, drinks and British treats, delicacies only a true '*mum*' could make, the LCAH's '*mum*' being a master chef hired out of Bristol.

The auction had yet to begin, so most of the visitors were still milling about the bidding halls, examining items up for grabs and looking over displays. Some were guesstimating as to the remaining artifact's highest bid potential while others simply seeing things they either wanted or needed to have.

Hayden and Danica had walked around the room three times, twice passing the journal pages on display.

When Danica tried to examine more closely, Hayden carefully, but forcefully dragged her around to other items so they did not seem overly interested.

Hayden whispered to her. "We're under the watch of trained psychiatrists as we speak." He took a breath, pointing with his eyes as not to reveal what he knew, noting the globe shaped camera units hidden in the corners. "They're trying to ascertain levels of interest. In doing so, they will determine values and even provide fake bidders in the audience to drive the price up."

Danica found herself genuinely surprised, unaware of the secret workings of a private auction and its nefarious affairs. However when she put more thought to it, she had to admit, it was a brilliant idea.

Hayden found himself pausing before several items of note. Though not South American in origin, he was still an aficionado of history. Though, he found seeing such items up for bid so easily and haphazardly surprising. Some treasures would give any archeologist pause.

Danica looked offhandedly at most of the items, as to her, it was all old junk old people wanted to buy and let it get older.

Hayden silently hoped they read Danica as the buyer as her lack of interest would help keep the bidding war to a minimum.

Danica gestured to an old comic book for Hayden.

Hayden's eyes widened when he looked, but only for a second until he saw the price. "Maybe another day." He whispered, downtrodden he did not have a hundred thousand pounds on him.

Danica resumed her tour of the remaining items.

Twice Hayden had seriously considered if his twenty-five grand paycheck could buy him anything. So far, he was sure, from what he saw, if he was lucky, he could buy the velvet blanket which lay under the precious items up for grabs. And maybe the label.

Danica finally gave in and returned to the pages.

Hayden followed reluctantly.

The pages were housed in a red walnut case with brass fittings bolted tightly. Inset was a sealed glass cover, ten by eleven inches, composed of a polycarbonate shield to prevent penetration and coated with an elastomeric carbon-based polymer to avoid scratches. The item beneath being only the top page of the missing eight pages from the journal, the same single page as shown in the auction catalog, with the remaining seven pages stacked beneath, hidden from view.

Danica carefully, and discretely, snapped a shot with her Smartphone. When she looked at the photo, she noticed it was a glittery haze.

Hayden looked at the screen with some confusion as well.

"Besides being bulletproof, it's carefully designed by the manufacturer to include a prismatic element to prevent photography." Resonated a voice from behind them.

Hayden and Danica turned in the direction of the voice.

The voice continued. "I figured the first page would entice the appetites. But showing the remaining seven pages in an easy to copy format would devalue the prize."

Danica smiled warmly.

Standing before her was a handsome older man, about sixty in her estimate. He was six foot one with short black hair slivered by grey and executively styled. His skin was a reddish brown, recently tanned or having spent some time in the sun, with Mediterranean features, either Spanish or Greek. His most pointed feature, his hazel eyes, flecked by blue and some yellow, giving it a most unique and distinguished quality.

The man gently took Danica's hand into his own. "You normally should not be taking pictures at all, but for one as beautiful as yourself, I will keep my lips sealed."

Danica blushed.

The man introduced himself. "My name is Carlos. Carlos Santiago." He then kissed Danica on the back side of her hand softly, caressing her skin, gentleman-like.

Hayden looked at the act and tried to hide his displeasure.

Carlos didn't notice with his eyes locked on Danica.

Hayden reached forward, gently disconnecting Carlos' grip to give him a firm handshake. "Good afternoon Mr. Santiago. I'm Doctor Hayden Lattimer." Making sure '*Doctor*' was emphasized.

Carlos shifted smoothly into a military stance and returned the firm handshake. "Good afternoon Doctor Lattimer."

Hayden gestured to Danica. "And this is my assistant..." He turned to her with a confused look. "What was your name again? Michee? Erin or something?"

Danica glared at Hayden.

Hayden added as he spoke to her, but looking at Carlos. "And while you're here. Would you mind getting us something to drink? Maybe a beer? Or Mr. Santiago may like a coffee?" He nodded to Carlos. "What do you take in yours?"

Danica never moved, her eyes filling with ice.

Carlos on the other hand returned to grip Danica's hand with a huge smile. "Be assured." Holding her palm firmly. "With a woman as enchanting as yourself, your name would not be one I'd have easily forgotten. In fact, I would have it etched into my skin with a burning ember if for no other reason than to say it again long after you were gone." He smiled and kissed her hand again. "And if you wish, I'd be pleased to get *you* a beverage of your choice."

Danica smiled in Hayden's direction.

Hayden scowled.

Danica took Carlos' hand with her free one. "It's my pleasure. I'm Doctor Danica Swift by the way. Excuse Hayden." She made special note to not use the word '*Doctor*.' "The university is doing an exchange program with the mentally handicapped autistic archeological society. As you can see, we got the raw end of the deal."

Carlos had to put his fist to his mouth to maintain decorum and not burst out in laughter.

Hayden on the other hand pursed his lips and mouthed the words. *"Hayden... Four, Danica...Two."*

Danica smiled in a way that clearly communicated. '*The game is still far from over.*'

Once their little unseen battle was complete, Danica and Hayden resumed their positions before Carlos.

No drinks would be retrieved by anyone at this point.

After a moment of awkward silence, Carlos looked at them and elected to break the ice. "And what brings you both here?" He asked with genuine interest.

Hayden as the specialist in this area spoke first. "We're here seeking treasure."

Carlos grinned and replied quite quickly. "Then you've come to the wrong place."

Both Danica and Hayden shared a quick quizzical look without turning in one another's direction.

Carlos offered to explain himself. "We sell unique items, even rare items; collector pieces some despise and want to get rid of, yet others want so desperately, they'll stop at nothing to acquire them." He motioned to the room. "But as for treasures, they're few and far between. Most things here are academic in nature and if sold on the open market, you would get money more for its rarity than its value."

Hayden responded, deciding to go for honesty. "We've come for those eight pages." He pointed to the locked case. "My employer is a nutcase who thinks something written by a madman a hundred years ago will lead him to something insane."

Danica was a bit shocked at Hayden's bold declaration, but she trusted him, so she decided to let Hayden direct the game.

Carlos turned to examine them with a genuine look of surprise. "I admire honesty in people." He waited for several seconds. "But I thought you were here with the University of Toronto?"

"I am." Hayden replied, a bit suspicious that Carlos had this information without having asked. "I was sent here as a consultant. With one job. To get those specific eight pages." Hayden pointed "My employer is under the assumption the original writer knew secrets known by no other."

Carlos paused to consider this. "Treasures in one's eyes could be fairytales to others." He mused, remaining stoic. "But I believe your intents are pure."

Hayden smiled at the confidence.

Carlos asked though. "But what possible treasure would an old diary such as this lead you to?"

Hayden wanted to explain, but he knew the rules of the game. *'Don't show all your cards on the flop.'*

In Texas Hold'em, short of folding, you bluff.

Hayden asked with a statement of his own. "I wouldn't refer to eight pages as a diary, unless the author only lived nine days."

"Fair enough." Carlos smiled at having his argument snuffed out. "How did you even learn of these pages?"

"My employer."

"And that would be?"

Hayden smiled. "The one who hired me."

Carlos grinned realizing this information was not forthcoming. "At least, tell me where you're from?"

Danica chimed in. "Canada." Happy to be a part of the discussion finally.

Carlos looked to the pages. "And you both flew here all the way from Canada to buy some old pages from a half complete diary?"

Hayden offered, "I was told what might be written could prove important."

Carlos finally admitted. "I've had these pages for some time and the only thing I have derived from it is that I should get newer reading material."

Hayden suddenly realized, he was talking to the eccentric collector Maximus referred to. The one who would not sell to anyone but academics.

'Did I just screw our chances for the bid?' Hayden asked himself.

Danica thought the same thing.

Hayden decided to go *Full Monty* for honesty sake. *'What possible harm could it do?'* "I guess you have me on that. My employer thinks it leads to the Fountain of Youth?"

Carlos stared at both of them, twice looking back and forth, hoping for a hidden camera to be revealed and a pretty young hostess to jump out and yell, "You're on 'Got-You' Camera." He finally burst into laughter, slapping his knees as he doubled over.

Danica turned to Hayden and offered a confused look.

Once Carlos regained control, he resumed his military stance. "Please accept my apologies. I've never heard such nonsense. But to be honest in return, you're not the first to think such things. Back in the late 1800's, a sea Captain thought the same about this diary. One

Captain Estefan Rios. He purchased a boat, I believe it was called the Watercress, to cross the ocean and seek out this very same legend."

"And what became of him?" Danica asked with interest

Carlos responded sadly. "Captain Rios and his entire crew vanished in 1889. Never to be seen again."

Hayden took a moment. "Do you think they ever found this Island of Eternal Night?"

Carlos smile froze on his face. He frowned for a second and then smiled again. "Who can say? The sea has taken many a man long before they found their destination. Rios and his ship could have sunk shortly after leaving England for all we know."

"You sound like a man who worked on the waters." Danica noted.

Carlos mused. "I dreamed of being Captain once. Worked my way up the ranks. Never made it. Some things were never meant to be." He stared outward, silent for a second. "I have no regrets. I returned to land and became an investor. It has served me well."

"So how did you come to possess these pages?" Hayden asked, genuinely interested.

Carlos smiled. "I acquired the estate of Captain Rios, long after he vanished."

Hayden appeared confused. "Based on what I read, the Captain disappeared before the institute fire. How did the estate come into possession of the journal *after* Rios vanished?"

Carlos shrugged, dismissing the question. "How am I to know? From what I read about the good Captain, he had a long standing relationship with the administrator. It is very possible it was sent to him by the doctor without knowing Rios had not returned."

Danica reviewed the top page again and turned back to Hayden and Carlos' discussion.

"As I recall, you would only offer the eight pages to accredited academics and their institutions." Hayden turned to Carlos. "I'm a man who respects such things. Do you want us to leave?"

Danica found her jaw nearly dropping, but she held it firm.

For a long minute, Carlos stared into Hayden's and then Danica's eyes. He answered with genuine pride. "No. I stated only those I trust in academia should have acquisition of this purchase. And something about you two…" He smiled. "I trust."

Danica beamed with pleasure at having given him that vibe. This was followed by a friendly nod to Hayden.

"But you still have to win." Carlos added. "My liking you won't help you at the auction. Here, money talks and bullshit walks."

Hayden grinned. "Bullshit doesn't have a credit card."

Carlos offered a genuine laugh. He looked to them both. "Don't thank me yet." He smiled. "There are a lot of nutcases out there that think the Leviathan found an ancient and mystical treasure which this patient described as invaluable."

Danica asked. "What do you think?"

Carlos was silent for several seconds. "Whatever they found, it must have been terrible, as no one who has ever sought it since has returned."

All three looked at one another in quiet contemplation of the steps to be taken.

A bell rang in the hallway, indicating the auction was about to begin.

Carlos excused himself with a small bow and vanished behind a thick black velvet curtain.

Hayden threw in as he departed. "May the best man win."

Danica corrected. "Or woman."

Hayden rolled his eyes. "Fine. Person."

Danica grinned, thinking to herself. *'No. I meant woman.'*

19

The LCAH bidding room 'C' was a smaller room on the Southwest corner of the facility, down two small flights of stairs and behind an Egyptian sarcophagus with a single mummified hand extended out and directing people to the left.

Rooms "A" and "B" which were located in the North part of the property, in the upper echelons, were much larger in size, capable of housing up to three hundred patrons, whereas the "C" only accommodated seventy-five to a maximum of a hundred.

Along both sides of room "C" were long wooden bookshelves, from floor to ceiling, constructed from a deep dark walnut. They ran from back to front and were filled to capacity with first editions from Charles Dickens to Edgar Allan Poe, from Lewis Carroll to Jean Austin, all shielded by airtight and tinted UV resistant glass doors protecting the books inside.

The room had eight red velvet chairs lined up side by side, with a total of ten rows of them, starting from the rear door and extending forward, each row separated by three feet of room with a bidding paddle placed upon each seat and a small writing table attached to the armrest, one which flipped up, for placing drinks, stationery and wallets.

At the front of the room was a podium with a small reading light and platform for the auctioneer. To the left of this were four large black leather high back chairs, for sellers to observe the proceedings and validate the actions taken to sell their wares.

Above them were two massive big screen plasma televisions suspended on bars, one to each side to provide for larger views of smaller items and to prevent bidders from having to come up and personally inspect the items, though some still did.

To the right of the podium was a small oak table with a pivoting video camera, fastened to a radial arm which could be adjusted or moved to any position, hardwired and linked to the televisions to display anything before it.

It was professional auctioneering at its best.

Hayden and Danica took their seats in the middle of the room.

As Hayden put it, *"We don't want to look too anxious, but we certainly don't want to appear too lax either."*

Danica shook her head at the elaborate measures Hayden was taking to dupe the '*shrinks.*' She had brought with her the auction catalogue which listed the order of items to be sold, the pages of the journal being fourteen on the schedule.

Hayden grabbed his paddle and placed it against his knee, holding it tight, his hand lightly twitching in preparation to hold it aloft and bid like a quick draw at sundown outside a western saloon.

Danica on the other hand casually slid hers to the seat beside her, giving that patron two to use as she could care less.

The room started filling in.

There were a few men in three piece suits, some in casual attire, one sporting a Christmas sweater to Hayden's amusement, one woman in a nicely wrapped wool shawl seeming hand spun and another with a pink jogging outfit, yet carrying a briefcase.

An eclectic band of shoppers in my instances, but not in this world of treasure hunters.

Everyone took their seats, some opening books, reviewing catalogues, pulling out pens and pencils, donning eyewear, while others simply sat back and waited patiently.

Danica looked up at Carlos as he entered from the back area, taking a seat on the upraised stage in one of the spectator chairs.

Carlos winked in Danica's direction once again causing her to blush.

Hayden blushed as well, but not with embarrassment, but annoyance. *'Did he not see she was with me?'*

Hayden turned to Danica as she was reading the program. "Anything you like? Your company is footing the bill."

"No thank you." Danica's eyes squinted tightly when she looked in Hayden's direction, trying to avoid responding to his cavalier attitude in spending her employer's money. Not to mention forgoing their trust. "Just the pages. It's not comp."

Hayden chuckled at that. "I'm just saying. We could get a couple of things and charge it all as one. Maximus never said he needed a receipt."

Danica knew he was kidding, but she decided not to give him the satisfaction of an answer. She took a breath and changed the subject by pointing to the booklet and querying. "There sure are alot of artifacts from sea disasters?"

Hayden nodded nonchalantly. "This is Europe. If it didn't sink after leaving dock, no one cared. You'd be surprised how few of the successful voyages got any press." He turned to her. 'Not unlike today's news. Unless it bleeds, it never leads."

In that, Danica agreed, today's news was most often a bloodletting in written form.

The auctioneer came in last, a thin reed like man with long bony fingers and pale skin, almost like the Grim Reaper chose to retire and sell antiques. He had short spiked red hair and thick circular eyeglasses with deep black frames, ones which made his eyes seem to expand outward under its magnifying effect, making him look like an owl perched on his podium in search of prey. He placed a clipboard down, adjusted a small microphone on his jacket lapel and tapped it lightly.

The speakers around the room popped.

Looking satisfied with himself, the auctioneer softly reminded the room to take their seats as the bidding was about to begin.

Hayden pivoted around. He could see at least two other professors he knew, by reputation only, one from Bern in Germany whose field was ship faring routes and aquatic salvage and the second from Israel, a specialist in ancient biblical texts. Neither individual would be here for the eight pages.

Based on the catalogue, there were numerous other treasures they were here for.

Danica elbowed Hayden gently. "Look over there."

Hayden turned as two very large men entered the room.

The men were both six feet tall, short brown hair on one, the other balding, with long term acne scarring their faces. They had solid muscled physiques, looking a lot like spinning tops as their upper bodies were disproportionate to their waist and legs beneath. The appeared to focus too much on the chest and shoulders areas when they pumped iron. They were dressed in weightlifting T-Shirts, blue jeans and combat boots, looking like two body builders in need of a bench press, but none were on the schedule to be sold today.

Danica could tell right away, they were identical twins, as they looked like mirrors of one another, and equally ugly. She asked Hayden. "Are they professors too?"

Hayden scowled. "Not to judge a book by its cover, but the only school I can see them representing is Fuck 'U'."

Danica turned sharply. "Seriously. Can we not go just one day? One single day without you swearing?"

Hayden smirked. "Come on. It was funny."

Even though Danica did agree, she felt the timing was rude. "Funny yes." She replied. "But not necessary."

Hayden acquiesced. "Fine Princess. What would you have preferred I said?"

She glowered at him and waited a solid thirty seconds without speaking. "Screw *U*." She turned and faced forward again.

Hayden sat there quietly with his mouth firmly closed, having felt he was silenced for some reason.

'Did she just give me a suggestion… or make one?' When he thought about it harder. *'Likely the latter.'*

After several minutes of quiet and everyone had taken their seats, Hayden gave Danica a quick gentle elbow to her side.

She looked up, no longer annoyed with him, as his childish antics were somewhat entertaining, though she would never tell him, and noticed what Hayden was pointing at.

The two thugs had taken different seats, one near the group at the front and the second, nearer to the back, but closest to the largest group of people there.

Individual buyers remained seated, alone, but within the sightlines of the podium.

"Remind you of anyone?" Hayden asked softly under his breath.

Danica looked at them again and imagined Maximus and Maxima. She shook her head. "Why would they send another team of bidders to bid against us?"

Hayden shrugged. "Maybe it was destiny." He mimicked Maximus' voice perfectly, down to the same arrogant tone and heavy self-righteousness.

Danica smiled. She saw the way the twins stalked around the room before taking their seats, like lumbering gorillas in a pen trying to find a place to dominate. "I'm not sure. But they don't look like antique collectors in my mind."

Hayden added. "Unless we missed something on the list and they're auctioning off bananas."

Danica suppressed a giggle that time as the bidding began.

Over the next hour, numerous items came and went, some with long bidding battles, while others sat untouched and uncalled upon for several minutes, at least until someone finally bid simply so they could move on to the next item.

Nearing the bottom of the second hour, the eight pages were placed upon the pedestal and before the cameras.

Hayden had his paddle at ready, the number '0509' etched into the middle of it in bright red letters, face down on his lap and ready to be snapped up like a Jack-In-The-Box.

Danica looked at Hayden in amusement, seeing his excitement to begin.

The auctioneer took a drink from a bottle of water he had hidden beneath his podium shelf. Once refreshed, he activated the big screens to reveal the pages to everyone.

Hayden was ready.

The auctioneer quickly described the item, mostly a quick medical history and a short story on the night of the great fire. Finally, he spoke to the meat of the tale. "We have eight pages torn from a century old diary of an inmate from an institution long destroyed." He paused for dramatic effect. "Nothing else survived. And some rumours have it, the madman went insane because he found something of immense value." He smiled viciously like a gargoyle on a church edifice leering down at his audience. "It was either that or he was simply as nutty as a German fruitcake." He took a breath. "Let your bidding decide."

The auctioneer barely noticed the lack of response to his joke, giggling to himself. He paused and declared loudly for the room to hear. "We start the bidding at ten thousand pound sterling."

Hayden was ready.

But before he could lift his paddle, a voice from the background, a young woman, brown hair, jogging suit and briefcase, sitting near the last row, lifted her paddle and offered thirteen thousand.

Hayden countered with fifteen thousand. He turned to the woman and smiled.

She winked in return and offered eighteen.

Hayden responded with twenty.

Danica elbowed him in the ribs. "Can you not bid in increments of one, not two."

Hayden gave her a sad nod, not sympathetically. "Winners don't pace. They thrust."

"Thrust in ONES!" Danica snapped. "Ever read the Tortoise and the Hare?"

The woman bid twenty two thousand.

Hayden raised his paddle, offering twenty four. "The Tortoise never had a credit line."

Danica bristled. Before the next bid could be offered, she turned and saw one of the two thugs, the one near the rear, facing in the direction of the female bidder.

He seemed to whisper something Danica could not hear.

The woman on the other hand paled. She put her paddle down on her lap, letting it go and appearing not likely to bid again.

A man in the front row raised his paddle, suspecting the sudden flurry of bids meant something was worth acquiring. He shouted. "Thirty."

The auctioneer gave the man a quick nod.

As the auctioneer turned away and called for another bid, the second thug had changed seats, moving in behind the last bidder.

The second thug whispered something into the bidder's ear and sat back.

The bidder froze, his face ashen. He looked about the room hoping for a higher bid.

Hayden was focused on the auction, thus he offered thirty two.

Danica kicked him in the lower shin, whispering. "I said one."

Hayden scowled as he rubbed his lower leg. "Baby steps are for infants. I'm a man."

Danica sighed. *'Not in her books.'*

A third man twitched near the front and seemed he was about to bid when the second thug had moved again and whispered something aloud behind the seat, but not close to his ear to allow all of those around him to hear.

Danica still was out of earshot.

The man dropped his paddle and remained quiet.

Hayden at this point was seeing what Danica saw. "Did you see that?" He directed to Danica.

"I certainly did." Danica pulled back and jerked her head to the one at the back. "They've been doing it since we began."

Hayden got a horrible feeling. ""I don't think they're here to bid against us. I think they're here to limit the bidding entirely."

"I know." Danica was shocked, but she was pointing to the stage. "But this has not gone unnoticed."

Hayden looked up to see the anger filled eyes of Carlos.

****

Carlos was staring from the sidelines, stunned at what he observed.

Worse, he was disgusted beyond measure.

'Who brings thugs to an educational artifact auction to intimidate bidders'

Carlos suspected something like this would happen by offering the pages, but it was still surprising to see.

And based on the targets of intimidation, they were supporting Doctors Lattimer and Swift.

Carlos found this surprising as they did not strike him as the kind of people who would employ such tactics.

Then again, the purported Fountain of Youth legend could draw all comers from around the world and not all of them were what they claimed to be.

Carlos rose from his seat, adjusting his jacket and walked up to the auctioneer, who had slowed the auction, as he too suspected something odd was happening in the audience by the sudden slowing of interested buyers and bids.

Rarely do bidders start a bidding war for an item and stop when the momentum gets good.

Carlos whispered something to the auctioneer.

The auctioneer appeared out of sorts, turning to glare in Carlos' direction, stating loudly. "This is highly irregular sir." He paused to listen to Carlos whispering. "Yes I'm well aware of the special circumstances you employed before the auction." He paused again. "Of course. But don't expect a lot of bidders next time if you put the item up for grabs again."

Carlos nodded his acceptance at that.

The auctioneer threw in. "That and be aware, you'll be paying the fee for our services regardless." He motioned to the display with the eight pages. "You might as well remove them now."

The auctioneer drew a key from around his neck to unlock the housing unit that kept the pages from being stolen and handed it to Carlos.

Under the watchful eyes of the bidders, Carlos unlocked the case, slipped the rectangular block containing the eight pages out of the inset and into his briefcase, custom designed to hold them.

In seconds, both he and the pages disappeared through the dark velvet flaps of the rear curtains.

****

The auctioneer took several seconds to consider how to explain what happened and then turned to the audience. He offered a sheepish grin. "The seller has chosen to withdraw his collectible from the auction. And as per his contract, it's his legal right to do."

The room groaned.

To some, it sounded like gratitude.

The two large twins stood, anger evident in their eyes, fists clenched and glaring at all of the patrons around them.

Many seemed to shift away, while others ignored their gaze.

Hayden and Danica stared at both of them with steely eyes, not intimidated in the least.

The thugs departed quickly through a side entrance.

Hayden and Danica rose from their chairs as the auction resumed on item number fifteen.

Hayden turned to her and casually asked. "Does this mean we have to give back the five thousand?"

Danica forced a smile. She wanted to have here spirits lifted, but simply could not.

In the span of a few weeks and being entrusted to help her company in unique and prolific ways, she had failed.

Twice.

20

Back at the hotel room.
Later that evening.

Hayden jumped up and into the bed, slapping his back to the headboard, banging it against the rear wall with a solid crack, ruffling pillows and wrinkling blankets in the process. The shaking sent a towel tied swan decoration, folded by the maid, at the base of the bed, flying to the floor. He crossed his legs before him with his feet on the quilt, still wearing his shoes and chuffed in annoyance.

He turned in Danica's direction. "Well that was a total bust."

Danica was leaning against the marble column in the corner of the room, staring at the ceiling in quiet contemplation, not moving.

"And who the Hell were *Tweedle* Dee and *Tweedle* Dum?" He continued, referring to the two thugs intimidating the other bidders, which ended the auction for the pages with the owner taking them back and leaving.

More silence.

Hayden looked in Danica's direction when she did not answer and realized she was still ignoring him. "Come on. You can't still be mad?"

Danica glared in his direction. "Do you know how lucky you are that guy outbid you on that comic book?"

"I knew he would."

"You were aware we used the corporate credit card to secure our credit line to do the bidding right?"

"I was well aware of that." Hayden replied casually. "Why do you think they accepted my bid in the first place?"

Danica stared at him with awe. "And yet you still bid on it?"

"The guy looked at me funny. It was like he was daring me to do it."

"And you thought that *look* was worth eighty thousand pounds?" She asked with incredulity, imagining the horror of having to explain to her bosses after losing the eight pages, they thought buying an old comic book about a caped crusader for under a hundred thousand pounds might be a nice compromise.

"The guy still bid eighty two." Hayden replied with satisfaction.

'Thank God.' Danica shook her head and stormed away. She moved into the kitchenette to grab herself a cooler. Once she found it, she twisted off the lid and gulped down a sweet mouthful of a raspberry vodka mix.

Hayden waited patiently in the bedroom.

After serious consideration, she returned to answer his earlier question. "As to Thing One and Two, I've no idea as to who they were. But I sure bet they didn't imagine Mr. Santiago would, or could, pull the pages from the auction after he saw what they were doing."

She laughed a bit at that. "Did you see the look on their faces?"

Hayden had and was equally amused. "They were pissed."

Danica took some solace in knowing at least the twin gorillas had also not won.

"Makes you wonder if they failed, who they'd have to report that to."

She had asked that of herself already. *'Who sent them? They sure as Hell weren't there to bid.'*

Hayden then pointed out. "And being how bullish they were today, you'd also have to wonder, how far would they go to get what they wanted?"

Danica had not considered this. *'Were they dangerous? Or just bullies?'*

Most bullies were like a balloon, a lot of hot air until you poke them where it hurts.

Dangerous ones were stupid.

They kept attacking until they could strike no more.

Danica took another chug of her drink, her nerves and disappointment starting to wane away under the warming effects of the alcohol.

After a good minute, Hayden voiced it, knowing Danica was thinking it. "They did look a lot like our benefactor's people."

Though Danica agreed, it did not make sense. They had the credit line, unlimited they were told, and Hayden being very aggressive in his bidding, would have won. What possible motivation would they have to sour everything with intimidation? She refused to believe Maximus and Maxima would taint the bidding process so boldly. Unless, they felt, no matter the cost, they had to have those eight pages.

Bringing her back Hayden's original point. *'So with the pages slipping from their fingers, how far would they go to regain them?'*

Hayden had left the bed, tapped the mini-bar and opened himself a beer. Once he finished it, he produced a second one and retook his place on the pillows. *'Two-fisted.'*

Danica ignored it and changed the subject. "Do you actually believe?"

"Actually believe what?" Hayden took a deep swallow of second beer.

"That there is a Fountain of Youth? And we're chasing it."

Hayden paused, leaning back with a casual smile. "Who's to know? But who's to care really? I plan to live my life to its fullest, enjoying every minute of it. It's the price of mortality. We die eventually. So no, I won't waste too much time looking for a way to extend my life when each day I use looking brings me that much closer to the end." He shrugged. "Throwing away your time dreaming for more time is worse than wasting it on nothing at all."

Danica sighed. It was true.

"But if they want to pay me crazy amounts of money to travel the world with a beautiful chick, trying to find pieces to a century old puzzle, I'd be an idiot to turn it down."

All Danica heard was, *'beautiful chick.'* She smiled inwardly at that remark.

Upon her return to the room, Danica had rechecked their copies of the manuscripts given to them by the Thornes to look for more clues. But as Maximus had warned them, *'The Phantom Ink'* had a short lifespan. Once she opened the pages, she discovered, everything inside had evaporated and with it, all the text.

Now they truly had nothing.

They both drank their beverages in peaceful reservation.

Hayden finally offered up a suggestion. "You know. Carlos knew we were serious bidders about those pages right?"

Danica turned to him. "So?"

"So... He must have seen the look on our faces at the *monkey boy's* tactics."

Danica admitted, Carlos had looked at them both from his seat in surprise, watching their dumbfounded gazes as the events unfolded.

Hayden added. "And since we came all the way to Europe anyway, why don't we call the auction house tomorrow, get his address and number. With that, we can drop by and make a bid for the pages personally if you will."

Danica stared out the window in the direction of Buckingham Palace, her spirits perking up. "Why not go tonight? It's better than sitting here all evening and doing nothing."

Hayden winked, rubbing his hand on the sheets. "I can offer up some suggestions… instead of nothing." He said it seductively.

Danica rolled her eyes. "Even if I was so inclined, what would we do after the two minutes?"

Hayden leapt off the bed in mock annoyance. "One of these times, I'm going to take the offer off the table."

"Make this one of those times." She replied.

Hayden froze mid-stride, his eyes tightening with a widening grin. "Wait a good Goddarn minute." Trying to control his swearing for Danica, but sounding more sarcastic in its presentation. "What do you mean *tonight?* We've no idea where he lives?" He smirked like the cat that ate the canary, asking with sexual innuendo. "Unless… Do we know where he lives Doctor Swift?"

Danica smiled and held up a small rectangular piece of paper. "Carlos slipped me his home address on his business card before he departed our meeting in the lobby area."

Hayden laughed. "You little minx you."

"Shut up." Danica replied, grinning to herself. "He wanted to take me on a tour of London."

"Starting at his flat?"

She squinted now. "Shut up."

Hayden held his hands up in surrender. "Hey, I'm not saying anything. I paid for a tour like that once, but mine *ended* at my apartment. His must be much better."

Danica turned away, pleased that Hayden was a little jealous. She had no idea why.

Hayden grabbed his wallet and keys.

Danica reached for the cellphone and dialed. After a minute, she hung up. "It's his office number. I guess we have to do a pop by."

Hayden grabbed his coat. "I'm for one of those."

Danica pulled on a warm sweater and a pair of hiking boots, happy to have her uncomfortable high heels off. "Maybe if we explain to him what we found in South America, he might let us see the remaining seven pages."

"What can it hurt?" Hayden interjected. "We came all the way to London and I've yet to ride the subway. Now's my chance"

Danica corrected him. "It's called the Tube."

"I thought that was the TV"

"No. That's a *Tell-Aye*."

Hayden rolled his eyes. "Fine. Let's stay with pub, lager and lass. That's all the words I need to visit England."

Danica laughed aloud and thinking, for Hayden, that really was all he needed.

They locked the door to the suite and took the elevator directly to the London Underground connected to their hotel.

For them, the auction was far from over.

21

Carlos found himself feeling deeply annoyed, seated in his London flat, his grey wool sock covered feet laid to rest on a black leather footstool, in his hand a single malt scotch on the rocks, his wrist gently swirling it around in a crystal glass, the ice jingling against the sides, yet not once taking a drink.

Having exited the Stockwell Tube Station to the south of the city core, he had stormed towards his home, feet shuffling one in front of the other, counting his treads like an anger management student counting to ten, yet his seven hundred and sixty-two step jaunt from the subway to his apartment had done very little to cool his demeanor.

He had picked up the bottle of Scotch from a local shop in hopes it would calm his frayed nerves. He deducted the forty-seven steps to get in, line up and purchase it from his primary count.

He would have hit his local pub for some bangers and mash, followed by a cool lager, but tonight, he felt his mood was not befitting company.

He chugged the first glass of the sour amber liquid in one mouthful. It burned going down. He wasn't worried about getting drunk. His tolerance was deep and his control was stronger.

His apartment was a small five room property which consisted of a kitchen, bathroom, living room, bedroom and office, more than most single residents in London had. His home was modestly decorated with antiques, books and Victorian furniture from the turn of the century, all immaculately cleaned and polished, thanks to a weekly visit by his maid.

He started to relax as the strong high quality booze settled in his veins. The buzz came and went quickly. He had imagined today going differently. He was both surprised at the interest in the eight pages, but moreover, the arrival of Doctors Lattimer and Swift from South America.

Upon meeting them, he felt guilty at having pulled the pages from the auction. He actually liked them. They seemed so genuine and honest, even if constantly at odds with one another. It had been a very long time since he had met two people that amused him as easily as they did.

He ran his hand over the edges of his briefcase which held the pages at the side of his chair.

'Safe and sound.'

'If Doctor *Swift calls...'* he thought, he may even offer her another chance at the pages. *'Maybe even.'* He sighed.

Doctor Swift was an extremely attractive woman.

That and he was an old man. Whatever interest she would have for him at best would be friendship.

But as he weighed it out, having a friend such as her was well worth it.

And Doctor Lattimer of course, as he seemed to come part and parcel with Doctor Swift.

He did admit to himself, they appeared genuinely shocked at the barbarian's intervention.

He leaned back in his chair, readying himself for a drink, when a cool draft blew across the back of his neck, his hairs rising, like he left a window open.

'*What the...?*'

Before he could turn to look, he felt a wooden object, flat and solid, barrel into the back of his scalp and lower neck, like a baseball bat going for a homerun, his brain feeling like it was lit on fire, sending Carlos flying from his chair, his half-filled Scotch glass skittering into the hallway of his apartment, and him, face first into his wall. He saw stars for several seconds, but quickly regaining his equilibrium, he turned around.

This was followed by a second blow across his forehead.

They hit so hard, the room seemed to spin around him.

Carlos got up into a crawling position before he heard the first intruder speaking.

"He's still awake. Tough old bugger."

Carlos looked up from the floor; his one hand behind his head, holding it like he feared it would fall off and observed two intruders having entered via his patio door.

There were two men, both dressed from head to toe in black matching pants, shirt and leather gloves. Both sported ski masks with only their beady eyes and mouth being exposed. They could be twins as they were of equal size, that being gigantic.

They were six foot tall with heavy triangular upper torsos, short arms which hung off the shoulders, unable to fall straight down due to extreme nature of their wide shoulders and what seemed like tree stumps for legs.

Carlos counted himself lucky his head hadn't come off.

The first intruder leaned forward, asking directly. "Where are the journal pages old man?!"

Carlos should have known. *'The thugs from the auction.'*

Carlos replied. "I stopped for some fish and chips on the way home. They ran out of paper to put the fries in. Luckily I had the eight pages." He grinned. "Once I was full, I tossed them in the trash. Just a few blocks back. You can probably still find them, assuming you don't mind the mushy peas."

The first intruder kicked Carlos hard across the jaw.

Had his head been a football, Carlos thought, *'Field goal.'*

Carlos felt his whole body pivot as he was launched from the floor into the wall of his home for a second time. Books tumbled off shelves and a small glass model ship shattered on his hardwood floor. He held his head and neck with fiery burning shooting through his back and spine. He was in pain, but he had had enough.

Carlos jumped up and catapulted his body forward into the first intruder, sending both him and his attacker over the dining room table, through a clay handcrafted centerpiece and busting two chairs behind it.

The second intruder was dumbfounded, standing at ready. "Wow. A lot of juice for an old guy."

Shocked or not, the second intruder took action. In seconds, he was around the table, grabbing Carlos from behind and pinning his arms behind his back, leaving Carlos' chest and stomach exposed.

The first intruder rose, fury in his eyes and cracking the knuckles in his fist. He pulled back and sent a gut wrenching fist into Carlos' abdomen.

Carlos let out a gasp of air, thinking this is what a building must feel like when hit by a wrecking ball.

For what felt like an eternity, likely no more than ten seconds, the first intruder punched away furiously into Carlos' chest, switching hands, him feeling like a leather boxing bag for match preparation before the big challenge, until they let him go and he sagged to the floor in a heap, instinctively curling into a fetal position.

The second intruder laughed. "Maybe he is one of those SAS guys. You know the British version of the Navy Seals. They can always take a good beating."

"Seems that way." The first intruder leveled another hard punch into Carlos from a standing position. This was followed by a second right swing across Carlos jaw.

Carlos swallowed hard with the impact, nearly choking on his own blood.

The second intruder snapped. "Careful. We need him alive. Father will be pissed if he dies before we found the pages."

Carlos tried to ignore the pain flooding through his body.

The first intruder bent down and lifted Carlos from the floor with the ease of a ragdoll.

Before Carlos could be asked any more questions, the second intruder pointed to the end of the couch to the sealed briefcase and shouted. "That's what he stuffed them in at the auction house." He moved over to it and picked it up. He tore open the flap and declared. "Bingo."

Carlos moaned.

The second intruder pulled out the plastic case and the eight pages inside. "We got'em."

The first intruder with a double handed throw tossed Carlos, across the foyer and back first into his apartment front door. It broke from the frame, splitting the door in half and sending him into the hallway with a body crushing slam.

Carlos lay on his side, face bleeding and trying to catch his breath.

The first intruder moved forward to finish what he started, yelling to the second. "You promised. It's my turn now."

The second intruder acquiesced. "I did. Kill him and let's be on our way."

The first intruder flexed his muscles and started toward Carlos.

Carlos had rolled up and into a seated position in the hall, his chest was heaving deeply at the exertion. His eyes were hazed by blood and he was trying to regain his breath. He knew he was unable to put up much of a defense. His eyes lowered. *'I guess this is it.'*

As the first intruder bent forward, hands in front of him, a big malicious smile on his face to level the killing blow, he found himself shocked to get a front Tae Kwon Do kick, directly under his chin and into his nose, sending him flying back into the apartment.

Carlos heard the crack of foot to face connection and looked up from his position, refocusing his blurry eyes to see Doctor Swift retracting her leg.

He then saw Doctor Lattimer coming in and around her.

"Remind me not to piss you off." Hayden stated as he stepped into the apartment first. He turned to Carlos. "Top of the morning to you. Hope you don't mind if we crash your party."

Danica followed suit with a smile and a wave. "Morning Carlos. Don't mind us. Appears something ugly followed you home. But I'm sure we can rid you of it."

Carlos found himself speechless at their unexpected and welcome arrival. He simply nodded his acceptance at their offer as they both entered his flat.

'Glad I paid my property insurance.' Carlos thought, as it appeared his apartment was about to become a battle zone.

22

Hayden came forward, moving to the left of Carlos' couch, snapping his head back and forth like a boxer readying himself for the title match. He turned to Danica as she took the right side. "You know, since I met you, I've had things blown up around me, been flown around the world in search of pages from a crazy man from a hundred years ago, and now I'm being dragged into a house brawl." He pursed his lips. "I'm trying to figure out, is it me or are you the common denominator to disaster?"

Danica opened and closed her fists. "Before I met you, I didn't have to have a stewardess ask if I was hearing voices before serving me a second beverage. I could walk out of a hotel with dignity and without having to explain my movie selections, and best of all, I didn't have to wash my hands every time I retrieved one of my scientific markers." Danica retorted. "So there's no question to where the link is."

The fallen intruder Danica had struck on their way in had gotten himself up, shaking his head to clear the stars, all the while, snarling with moist sounds as he held his open palm to his face. He rubbed his lower jaw through the mask and within seconds, saw his own blood trickling between his fingers. His nose appeared to be broken.

His consort in behind him looked equally furious through the open slits of his face covering.

Hayden turned towards the two figures, but speaking to Danica. "It appears we've been rather negligent with Carlos' guests." He gestured to them both. "Us having a private conversation in front of them and all. It must seem rather rude."

Danica took a *ready stance* to station herself for the incoming attack. "Let's rectify that shall we?"

Hayden quickly asked aloud to the masked men. "Are those getups for you or for us? I mean, if you're the ugly mugs we saw at the auction this afternoon, I'm thinking for us, so before we begin, let me say thank you for sparing us another appearance."

Danica chuckled inwardly, amazed at Hayden's bravado.

The two intruders on the other hand seemed to shake violently, losing any sense of control.

The first intruder pulled his hand away from his mask and seeing the blood for the first time. He stared at it, wide eyed and filled with rage. His eyes locked on Danica. "You whore!" He hissed.

"That wasn't very nice." Hayden responded. Then he paused, casually turning to her and back to the bleeding first intruder. He spoke to her again. "Unless..." Hayden smiled. "When we first met in the jungle and you turned me down... was it simply a matter of money? I mean, it would have been a long drive in all, but I could have found an ATM?"

"Hayden..." Danica said through clenched teeth. She waited a few seconds. "Remember on the way in when you told me to remind you when you were *really* pissing me off?"

Hayden envisioned how easily she delivered that front kick and replied. "Point taken." He winked at her. "But I do have twenty five thousand dollars now."

Danica responded with. ""For you, it would have to be a Hell of a lot more than twenty five thousand."

Both intruders annoyed with Danica's and Hayden's comical discussion in front of them motioned to attack.

Hayden lowered his body frame for a fight. "So it's only a matter of price. I can work with that."

Danica grinned at his persistence, grateful he was at her side. He was the kind of man she would want with her in a fight.

The first intruder charged, head down, body compressed, directly at Danica.

Hayden dived downward at the first intruder's legs, as his former rugby coach Robert Radway taught him. *'No matter how big a tree is, it can always be brought down if you chop the base.'*

The first intruder not expecting such a low aimed assault found himself falling forward, directly into Danica's knee, which she delivered upward into his turning cheek, followed by a *palgup chigi* elbow strike to the back of his head sending him face first into the coffee table, crushing it beneath him.

The second intruder was already in motion, running forward, launching up and off Hayden's crouched form into the air at Danica, perceiving based on her martial arts training, she was the more imminent threat.

Hayden let out a grunt at the weight of the attacker as he shoved off him. "Come on now. What am I? A stepping stone?"

Danica saw the second intruder catapult towards her. She pivoted off her right side, shifting all her weight low to deliver a *too sul* maneuver, which diverts the attacker's force against him, driving him downward. She spun around with him sailing past, face first into the library shelves, sending books everywhere. "And me without my Matador's cape." She challenged. This was followed quickly by, "El Toro!"

Hayden was up and back at Danica's side. He yelled out. "Carlos, we may be doing some damage in here."

Carlos fired back from the hall. "It's all replaceable. I have insurance."

Hayden grinned.

The first intruder was back on his feet and swinging hard at Danica.

Danica dodged under his fist, it still grazing her shoulder, which based on his sheer size, sent sharp pulsations down her arm. She did an uppercut motion with a four knuckle strike directly into his chin, causing him to twist back and slam into the wall.

Two plaques dropped to the floor with a crash, sending broken glass everywhere.

The second intruder was acting on instinct, dazed from heavy books slamming into his head. He moved toward Hayden, both hands before him. He swung haphazardly, only to miss, his momentum carrying him past and into a second shelf unit, this one filled with booze; fine wines, expensive Cognacs and some very old scotch.

Hayden sighed at the loss.

The second intruder was already in motion again, pure reflex. He pulled himself out of the liquor cabinet, wiping chips of splintered wood and chipped glass caught in his sweater out of the way. His clothes were soaked with booze. He fired back at Hayden, furious as his having missed twice, murder in his eyes.

Hayden spun left, shifting back and shoving his body forward, as he leveled a right handed haymaker punch directly into the attacking behemoth's lower chin.

The second intruder staggered back, rubbing his face for a good ten seconds, holding himself up. He shook his head and muttered almost amused, "Is that the best you…"

His sentence was cut off when he was hit across the chest and chin with an oak dining room chair Hayden had grabbed in those seconds, breaking it across the second intruder's unprepared body, sending him up and into the apartment hallway.

"That's nowhere near the best." Hayden chanted dropping the broken pieces to the floor, finishing his sentence for him.

The first intruder was standing, holding his busted nose, blood filling his mouth. He took a football stance and charged at Danica again.

Danica pivoted on her rear ankle, parrying aside and around, leveling her elbow into the closest shoulder blade of the intruder as he shot past and under her arm. Using his momentum, due to his immense size, unable to stop the kinetic force, she sent him into the television.

The unit cracked beneath the attack. The fifty two inch LCD television flipped down off the brackets, falling forward, and cracked across the intruder's back which was followed by a heavy grunt.

Hayden saw it and yelled. "I really hope good insurance Carlos."

Danica casually swung around, stared at the splinters of wood, broken glass and pools of expensive booze she missed before. She yelled. "Sorry Carlos."

Carlos was on his feet, amused they were more worried with his property than themselves.

The second intruder rushed towards Danica, but this time, Carlos was in motion, using both fists like a battering ram, he cracked them across the chest of the second attacker, sending him up and over the couch, tipping the frame of it with him.

Hayden brushed himself off. "I'm feeling a little neglected here guys. Always going for the girl?"

Danica hopped up and delivered a bone crunching roundhouse kick, striking the second intruder mid-chest and sending him back through the open patio door. He caught the railings before going over. "Guess they find me more attractive." She declared.

Hayden dropped an elbow across the back of the first intruder trying to get back up. "I find that extremely sexist. I should file a complaint."

The second intruder furiously reentered the apartment. "Don't you two ever shut up?!"

Police sirens wailed in the distance through the open patio doors.

Hayden piped up. "The local constabulary."

The two intruders slowly came together in front of the doors, the eight pages held tight in the second man's hands. "We got what we came for! They can go... For now..." He exited quickly over the side.

The first intruder limped to the patio door as the police sirens increased in volume, glaring at both Danica and Hayden. "This isn't over."

Hayden offhandedly shrugged. "Of course it is. You're scurrying away like the cowards you are."

The first intruder's eyes went tight, his fists clenching and opening, preparing to race back in when he felt the hand of the second intruder on his foot through the bars. "Father would be most displeased if we were caught and lost the pages."

The first intruder obviously fearing that more than seeking revenge disappeared over the railing and into the night.

Hayden and Danica came together and relaxed.

"So." Hayden said, turning to Carlos. "Is this what you Brits do for fun? If so, would you perchance have cold beer?"

Danica rolled her eyes. "If you don't give him one, I'll hear about all the way back to the hotel."

Carlos smiled in total disbelief. "You both intrude here uninvited, fight off two men trying to kill me and when they run off, the only thing you ask for is a lager?" He slapped them both on the backs and let out a huge laugh. "Canadians. Who can't love them? Follow me to the kitchen. I have a keg."

Hayden was overjoyed. "Am I glad I suggested we drop by."

Danica was thinking to herself. *'The only thing is...Our assailants took the pages. Like the auction, too little, too late.'*

Failure number three.

23

4:00 a.m.

Carlos reentered the apartment, jovially thanking the police for their diligence and timely arrival, having filed a witness account of the evening festivities and sending them on their way. As they departed, he had informed them he trusted them to find the men responsible, but knowing in his mind, they were likely already on the first flight out of England with their treasured prize.

The landlord had come up shortly before, interrupting the officers, to assure Carlos he would have a new door and any damage repaired by noon of the following day.

No expense would be spared.

Carlos knew why, it was his expense.

As Carlos returned to his flat, he found the two doctors sitting on the floor, since they had busted up most of the furniture and now had nowhere to sit, drinks in hand and seemingly overly depressed for this early in the morning.

Hayden was rubbing his sore fists and Danica was massaging her shoulder where the first intruder connected.

Carlos was standing before them a bit confused. "Why the long faces? You both won. I even got in a few punches myself, but you pretty much sent them scampering." He did a few stretches, pumping his arms and legs, breathing in with heavy cleansing breaths, grimacing slightly.

Hayden looked up at him in amusement. "Guess the guys who attacked spent most of their efforts pounding on us? I mean who would attack an old guy right?"

Danica interjected. "They seemed to focus a lot on me if you didn't notice."

Hayden turned to her with no sarcasm in his voice this time. "I saw it. Even when they had a shot at me, they went for you."

Danica leaned back and let her sore muscles relax. "They had to know who we were and of my training as they kept their attacks directed to disable me first."

"Hey..." Hayden looked insulted. "I'm a pretty big threat."

"And I'm sure they're regretting having underestimated you." Danica consoled.

Carlos chuffed. "I took as many punches as you did, if not more. I simply find exercise and motion helps get me back on my feet quickly. It's an adrenaline thing."

Hayden smiled at his exuberance and then frowned. "Even so, you can pump and twist all you want, they still got the pages."

Danica lowered her chin at that. "Too little, too late."

Carlos stared at the both. "They were simply forgotten pages from an old diary."

"That may be so, but our job was to get them. And we failed." Danica stood up, feeling her body twitch a little. "Who'd have thought they'd hit a lady."

Hayden smiled to her, rising at the same time. "With the way you hit, they probably thought you were a machine."

Danica smiled, then quickly winced thinking she would need to chew down some acetaminophen soon.

Carlos retrieved from his fridge a fresh glass of juice and chugged it down. He choked for a second, leaning forward, holding the centre of his chest to clear it.

Hayden spoke. "Me thinks our host is hiding the severity of his injuries in a show of bravado for you my dear." Gesturing to Danica.

Danica stepped forward, motioning for Carlos to take a seat to examine him. "Come on. Let me see that upper torso of yours. They threw you pretty hard through that door." She moved in. "I'm a Doctor so you know."

Hayden offered. "So am I."

Danica winked to Hayden. "Yes, but he needs a *real* doctor."

Hayden glared, but offered no insult as she was focusing on Carlos.

Carlos politely declined, gently removing her hands. "I'm fine. Honestly. More my pride hurt than anything else."

Danica remained where she was, ignoring her patient's manly show of strength.

Carlos moved away from Danica's probing hands of concern, holding his back and groaning. "Trust me. I'll be fine. Just give me a few minutes."

Once Danica and Hayden realized Carlos was holding firm on his privacy, they reached for their own drinks and quietly savoured them, thinking of how to move forward.

Hayden finally asked, turning to Carlos, hope in his eyes. "Please tell me you brought a fake set of pages with you to the auction and the real ones are in a safe hidden under your bedroom pillow."

Carlos replied with resignation in his voice. "I'm truly sorry. They got the real ones."

Both Danica and Hayden's demeanor softened again by the disappointment.

Carlos coughed into his hands, a speckle of blood appearing on his lips.

Danica moved forward, trying to forget being bothered by the loss of the pages, again putting her hands on Carlos' chest.

Carlos winced, his eyes moistening.

Danica shook her head back and forth, stating matter-of-factly. "I think you may have broken a rib."

"Honestly. I'll be fine." Carlos backed up and motioned kindly for her not to be bothered.

The trio stood in the kitchenette, staring at one another, no one moving.

Hayden spoke first. "I guess this ends it."

Danica sighed with resignation. "We've got nothing else. The chamber is destroyed. We lost the pages. The logbooks are all erased and all my reports are on my laptop in Toronto in the possession of the Thornes. We might as well return home and resume our lives as Maximus and Maxima will not allow us to continue with three failures on our record. I'm surprised they let us continue beyond two."

Hayden responded, trying to be supportive. "Danica. You're one of the best scientists I have met in years and be assured, the only failure today is the lack of information. I still feel this was a set up."

Danica smiled warmly, happy at his confidence in her.

Carlos took a deep breath and walked to his patio door. He stared out for a good solid minute, both hands clasped behind his back. He finally turned with a serious look on his face, tempered by confidence. "How far are you both willing to go for this mission of yours?"

Hayden and Danica both shared a look and turned back to Carlos, speaking in unison. "To the very end."

Carlos grinned. "You both saved me tonight. I suspect they would have tried to kill me without your timely arrival. So I owe you. And I'm a man who repays my debts. And ironically, in balancing my books with you, you'll be in turn, helping me yet again."

Danica and Hayden stared at Carlos, unsure how to decipher his cryptic answer.

Hayden asked Carlos the first thought that came to him. "Is there more than the eight pages?"

Carlos nodded. "Yes and no. Technically, though they have the eight *original* pages, I have something better."

Danica looked up at Carlos with sudden energy filling her veins. "You photocopied the pages?"

Carlos shook his head. "Absolutely not. I would never allow them to be copied. It would bring down their value."

Hayden raised his eyebrow. "You can't be serious. You memorized all that stuff?"

"Not exactly." was Carlos' mysterious reply.

Danica had leaned forward, hands out, palms up. "Then what exactly?"

Carlos paused to trade looks with Danica and Hayden, his mind seeming to wrestle with an internal conflict. "What indeed."

Carlos looked one last time out the window, across the English countryside, down grassy meadows, old structures and the world beyond, seeming to give himself the strength to speak. He remained poised, considering his next words and move carefully.

"The reason I never photocopied them and the reason I had no need to memorize them was…" Carlos paused and started to unbutton his shirt. "I think seeing is believing."

Hayden was first to respond, his face taking on a somewhat annoyed look of displeasure. "Can we get the version where you keep your clothes on?"

Danica smirked. "I'm okay with this explanation."

Hayden gave her a glare. "If it's like the prison escape television series and he tattooed everything on his body, I'm not translating it."

Carlos chuckled. After a few seconds, he opened his shirt to reveal his chest and abdomen beneath. His stomach and body were covered almost completely in thick purple bruises, some almost black at the centre, but yellowed at the edges.

Danica was appalled, her mouth opening wide. "My God Carlos. Look what they did to you." She moved in, examining the outer edges in disbelief Carlos could even walk around with damage such as this. "This looks like you have been attacked before?" She looked harder at him. "A few days ago from the level of healing. And you took a second beating tonight? Did you know they were coming?"

Carlos responded. "No. And these injuries are from tonight."

Danica was about to argue when the words froze on her lips, her eyes opening wide in total astonishment, staring at his upper body.

Even Hayden, with no medical training whatsoever, stared dumbstruck with shock.

While Carlos held his shirt open, showing all the damage, Danica and Hayden observed the skin at the edges were turning yellow and tightening before their very eyes. The redness of his skin was coming back, filling in with pink, overpowering the yellow and purples as they started to dissipate.

Danica, as a medical doctor could offer nothing more to say than, "That's impossible."

Carlos smiled. "There's more."

"If it includes your pants coming off, I'm out of here." Hayden peered up and into Carlos' eyes.

Carlos almost laughed. "My pants will stay on, I assure you."

Hayden looked relieved, but still in wonder.

Carlos started buttoning up his shirt. "Now yes, the information the thieves stole is accurate. But like I said, I have something better."

"What?" Danica asked with some trepidation.

"Because though they have the eight pages..." Carlos spoke with quiet conviction. "I wrote them. That and the rest of the journal when I was an inmate in the asylum."

Hayden's face started going slack, uncomprehending. "But that was over one hundred and ten years ago."

"I'm aware of that." Carlos said matter-of-factly.

Danica was doing the math. "But that would mean…."

Carlos cut her off. "My name is not Carlos Santiago. My real name is Carlos Diaz Montenegro, the former First Officer of the Leviathan, the ship found off the coast of South America in 1863." He took a breath. "And before you ask, I'm one hundred and eighty six years old."

Hayden and Danica stared at Carlos, mouths open, trying to think of something to say. Nothing came to them.

Carlos spoke instead. "And as I said, they may have my partial memories and thoughts to find the island on paper, but I myself know exactly where the island is located, as I've been there before."

Hayden asked the question that had been on his mind since he first found the chamber. "Then tell me this. How the Hell can there be an Island of Eternal Night?"

Carlos shrugged. "Because there is no sun."

Danica was even more confused. She followed that question with. "But how is that possible?"

Carlos nodded to them both. "Because it's subterranean. The Island of Eternal Night sits on a lake two miles beneath the Earth's surface. No sun, no daylight, thus eternal night."

Danica and Hayden shared a look, never having considered that possibility.

Hayden finally asked Danica. "Come on. Surely I should be allowed to swear now."

At this Danica acquiesced. "I submit to you on this."

Hayden looked Carlos in the face and declared. "Holy Fucking Shit!"

24

For a good several minutes, no one spoke.

For Danica and Hayden, their world had turned upside down in a matter of seconds. They were still thunderstruck by the revelation Carlos entrusted to them, as it not only gave weight to their recent adventure, but also explained the forces that had been brought to bear against them resulting in their recent failures.

Their lack of belief had put them at a serious disadvantage, whereas they assumed they were acting as two people playing a game. One with money behind them, provided by an eccentric couple, only to discover, they were in pursuit of something for which mankind would devote their lives to find and sacrifice others to get.

Now having seen the hyper healing on Carlos' body for themselves, Danica and Hayden knew their mission was more than they had originally estimated.

Far more.

Carlos, understanding the two doctors were still stunned by this change in their course, if not their reality, knew he needed to keep them on track. "First. I never lied to you. I simply omitted the truth."

Danica and Hayden were not angry. Far from it.

Hayden asked him. "How have you been able to hide your past for so long?"

"It was easier than you think." Carlos looked offhandedly at them. "In fact, I've changed my name several times. The last being in 1946 to Santiago. It seems, when your birth certificate reads 1825, you get a lot of questions. And I didn't need the scrutiny. And unlike today, reinventing yourself in Europe, especially at the end of World War II, was remarkably easy with all the chaos. But with modern technology today, I may not be so lucky the next time."

'Next time?' Danica thought. She asked him with some awe in her voice. "How long do you expect to live?"

"I honestly have no idea." Carlos replied. "But I suspect I'm not immortal. In fact, since 1899, I have aged significantly, if not somewhat slower. I used to look thirty around the turn of the century. Today, I pass for a good and healthy sixty-five." He flexed his left and then right muscles. "That and the speed of my healing you see today was remarkably faster then too. It's slowed more since the early fifties. I once could heal a broken bone in minutes and wounds in seconds."

"Amazing." Danica moved around him, running her fingers over his bare skin, searching his upper body where he had left his shirt open at the top, Hayden looking on with annoyance.

All the bruises, scratches and exterior damage on Carlos were gone.

Carlos pointed to his chest. "I suspect my ribs may still be fractured, but by tomorrow, they should be reforming the calcium layers."

Hayden took a seat across from him on the counter, sipping his beer, grimacing at its warmth. "You have a fresh one?" He held up the bottle.

Danica turned to glare at Hayden. "At least some things are still normal."

Carlos grinned and gestured Hayden to the fridge.

Once Hayden had a new one, he returned to his seat and asked the next biggest question on his mind. "So, there really is a Fountain of Youth?"

Carlos paused, looking skeptical, regardless of his advanced years. "I have no idea what's on that island, but it's obviously something remarkable." He turned to both Danica and Hayden. "But I can assure it's not the Fountain of Youth in the sense that you think."

Hayden took a gulp of his beer. "Excuse my French, but you being here is already beyond my sense."

Danica leaned against the counter next to Hayden. "What is it then?"

Carlos shrugged his shoulders. "I haven't the foggiest idea."

Danica and Hayden exchanged another look of confusion. "How can you not know?"

Carlos offered them a resigned look, seemingly more annoyed with himself at his answer. "All I can tell you is whatever happened; I wasn't regressed to a younger age, waking up a teenager aboard the Leviathan. Mind you, I have no recollection of having been found on board either, but this is what I was told on how they found me." He took a breath, thinking back. "I remember our voyage. It was remarkably uneventful at the time. We had pulled into a cove in the lower quadrant of South America. We went ashore and made camp. Our plan was to explore for a few weeks. It turned into three months. We stocked supplies, hunted, fished and much more. It was truly a good crew." Carlos eyes drooped a little imagining all his lost friends. "I remember us coming into contact with the island tribe that guards the island."

Danica gave Hayden a quick look.

Hayden shook his head as he spoke. "This would more likely be the *original* tribe. Not the offshoot that built the chamber."

Carlos could offer no confirmation. "They welcomed us into their camp. And of course, we later betrayed them by seeking out the island." He rose at this point and retrieved a bottle from his kitchen cupboard. He poured himself an amber coloured liquor from an unmarked bottle. It appeared he needed something stronger to speak of this part of his past.

The drink's stench was powerful, nearly burning the kitchen air with alcohol fumes.

Danica put her hand to her nose. "What the Hell is that?"

Carlos held it up. "Dark rum. One hundred and fifty proof. The only thing that can help me relax. My body metabolizes normal booze so fast; it might as well be drinking water. This holds firm for a good hour. Presuming I drink the whole thing."

"And you don't get drunk?" Hayden was baffled. "You poor bastard."

Danica did not think that deserved sympathy. She knew the liver considered alcohol a poison in the body, so any accelerated healing would remove toxins quickly.

Carlos took a drink and sat back down. "From there, I remember our search of the caves. It took weeks until we found the bottom. The tribe offered no assistance. I remember sailing across the underground lake to the island itself and….." He paused, his body involuntarily shivering.

Danica stepped forward and put her hand on Carlos' shoulder.

Carlos placed his hand on hers and held it there for a good minute. "And the next thing I know, it was 1887 and I was a guest of the Royal London Medical Institute in London."

Hayden gave a low end wolf whistle. "Seriously?"

"Seriously." Carlos replied. "I was later told my ship was found at sea, the entire crew was lost. I was never blamed of course officially, but it was noted my destruction of the Leviathan's log and charts was deemed suspicious. But I was also diagnosed as mad, so any criminal proceedings faded away over time. It was all simply attributed to another tragedy at sea."

Danica was saddened by Carlos' plight. The thought of waking up, two decades later, all your friends gone, institutionalized and being suspected of having some small part of it had to be horrifying. "You were found alone at sea aboard the Leviathan?"

"Based on the logbook..." Carlos remembered. "Ship damage and the dates *before* the missing pages, combined with the date of discovery, it was assumed I was at sea for a good two months before I was found. Not including the three months on shore. I was told I was living in squalor in a kitchen cupboard, living off of dried meats and food stuffs which had not spoiled."

"Terrible, but still pretty amazing." Hayden noted.

"And the very reason Maxima and Maximus want it as bad as they do." Danica added. "Longevity, miraculous healing and who knows what else. It really doesn't matter. I can guarantee you, a millionaire would pay thousands, if not millions of dollars for even one extra year of life. Some would sell their souls for it."

"Some did." Carlos threw in, sounding very grave.

Neither Hayden nor Danica chose to speak to that last remark.

Danica took a moment to broach the next difficult subject. "When we were researching the journal, it referred to a fire and you having been killed?"

"They tried. Believe me." Carlos eyes darkened. "When the good Doctor Gerber, the original administrator retired, his replacement was, shall we say, a bit more of the archaic religious kind. When he discovered my very slow aging and healing factor, he presumed I made a deal with the devil himself." His muscles tightened. "And he very badly wanted my journal. He felt it was the origin of my deal and he needed to destroy it to break the contract. But I kept it hidden from this point. And did this infuriate him. He finally chose to return me to my deal maker in the clutches of fire."

Danica's face was aghast. "That's horrible."

"I would never want to do it again. They roused me from my cell, and trust me, in those days, as comfortable as they make it, anything with a lock on the door and window is a cell. I got wind of the new doctor's plans from inmates as the guards found it sort of exciting. They were like housewives on a lonely street, they talked. Before they took me, I ripped out the last of the pages with the directions to the island and buried them in a stone in the wall. The rest of the journal was placed under the floor. I figured he would find one, likely not the other."

"So that's how they survived the fire?" Hayden looked at him. "But what about you?"

"That evening, they dragged me outside and I was tied to some trees. I had no idea what they had planned exactly, but I assumed it was another one of his failed exorcisms with more enthusiasm."

"Barbarians." Was all Danica could muster.

"But oddly enough, though the fire was painful, they had tied me with rope instead of chains. And the ropes were less resilient to flames than I was. I broke free and in my hysteria of the burning, I was grabbing at walls, furniture and anything not lit. Their actions ended up costing them the institution as I tore through the halls. The guards were in a panic to get away from what they perceived was a fiery devil that could not die."

Danica and Hayden exchanged looks of astonishment.

Carlos seemed to shiver at the memories of that terrible night. "I escaped in the chaos and the collapse of the building. As the flames took to the walls, I finally was able to extinguish myself at a horse trough. I raced back inside to get the pages before they were lost. I have no idea why, but I felt they should be retained."

"What did you do after that?" Danica asked with deep curiosity.

"I hid in the city for a good month, living off scraps and doing menial labour. No one was looking for me. After the heat involved, they assumed I was ash." Carlos found himself drinking another glass of his powerful brew. "Later, I sought out the good Doctor Gerber. In fact, he told me he was expecting me. He was not surprised at my survival. In fact, at that time, he used his vast network to change my name for the first time to Carlos Castillo."

Hayden gestured around the room. "And with a new name, you acquired all this over the years?"

Carlos shook his head. "No. Before I changed my name, Gerber informed me Captain Rios bequeathed his entire estate to me in his absence... or his death. It seems Rios felt I was as close to a son as he would ever have."

Both Hayden and Danica were poised on the edge of the counter, hanging on Carlos' every word.

"He included a letter." Carlos said. "In short, he felt if he found what he was seeking, he would be indebted to me more than he had given. If he didn't, he would die trying. Either way, he felt he owed me and would not accept not paying for it. And based on his vast holdings, it was quite handsomely."

After a few seconds, Danica queried. "Do you know what happened to Rios?"

Carlos shoulders sagged. "In that, I have no idea. He vanished in his pursuit of the island. I fear if the sea did not take him, which though dark, I hoped it did. I do dread he found what he was looking for."

"I think Rios may have found the chamber and resealed it before ultimately seeking out the island." Danica mentioned, pointing to Hayden. "From what we discovered."

Hayden nodded his agreement.

Carlos pursed his lips. "Rios was a dedicated man. I have no doubt he could have. Though I have no recollection of our crew ever finding the chamber, my journal specifically noted a tribe in the area and their appearance. Had he found the travelling one matching my description, I could see him stalking them until he found their precious chamber or their living ancestors to find the cave entrance down."

Hayden asked. "So when you said by helping us, we are helping you, how is that?"

Carlos pondered for a second. "I've not been back to that island in over a hundred years. My irrational fear has kept me from doing so." He sighed. "And I certainly couldn't proactively bring others with me unprepared for what they may face because I couldn't remember. That and being the length of time it took me to get over it, it was far too dangerous to bring along unwitting parties. Yet I couldn't return alone. It was a Catch-22." He raised his head and looked to Danica and Hayden. "But since you already want to go and I owe you, I feel it's time I return to the Island of Eternal Night and face my fear, but with you both at my side."

Hayden smiled. "Sounds like we have ourselves another expedition."

Danica felt a glimmer of hope. "I have to inform Maximus and Maxima."

Hayden rolled his eyes. "Must we?"

Danica turned to Hayden. "They're the ones bankrolling this operation. And paying us quite handsomely I might add."

Carlos seemed to hesitate. "I was always aware of who employed you both, but I've had my reservations about Maximum Pharmaceuticals and its two principles, the Thornes." He said no more.

Danica looked to them both in surprise. "I'm honour bound to my word. They did hire me after all." She sneered in Hayden's direction. "And you!"

Hayden returned the look. "I have my suspicions our employers may be more involved in this than you think. Combined with the *Tweedles* who were here not more than a few hours ago, and may I state again, who remind me a lot of our employers."

Danica shook her head, refusing to believe they had been duped. "Well what can one email or one call hurt?"

Hayden surrendered his position. "I leave it up to you. But be wary. If there is another secret group after this island at exactly the same time, using the very method we are, then I will eat my words."

"I will hold you to it." Danica replied.

Carlos placed his hand gently on Danica's, staring into her eyes. "I'll not ask you to lie, but I will ask you to omit any reference to me. Until I can feel more comfortable with whom they are."

Danica agreed as the Thornes had not paid her for that information.

Danica logged into Carlos' laptop and tried to remotely access her account at Maximum Pharmaceuticals. After several minutes of keying several things, she found herself confused. "We must have been hacked again?"

Hayden came over. "Why do you say that?"

"All my data on the chamber and the island is gone. Unless they moved it off the network." She checked again. "But why keep me from accessing information I've already seen?"

Carlos leaned in. "It was not hacked a second time. I initiated the first one and I promise, I made no second effort."

Both Danica and Hayden turned to him with a look of shock.

Carlos waved the issue away. "I will explain my reasoning later. Let's finish what we started so we can move this forward."

Danica gave Carlos one lasting look and resumed her work. In seconds, she tried logging in through her employee ID. "My access is also gone?"

Hayden took the laptop and asked her for her password.

Danica reluctantly provided it.

"Seriously. It's Babygirl?" Hayden smirked.

"It's Babygirl101. Other than that, shut up and type it." Danica shot back, slightly embarrassed.

'USER UNKNOWN' Appeared on the screen in bold text.

Danica suddenly had an unsettling feeling.

Hayden held the words, '*I told you so.*' in check.

Danica called the hotel and then the airport.

After twenty minutes of arguing, Danica hung up and turned to Hayden and Carlos. "Our airline tickets, the return tickets were never purchased. My corporate credit card, the one they gave us, is no longer valid. We're being checked out as we speak."

"I knew I should have taken those bath robes." Hayden sneered, followed by his shoulders sagging. "Great. So I guess I'm not going to get paid am I?"

Danica offered Hayden an annoyed scowl. "It's amazing how you can turn this whole situation to be about you."

"It's a gift." Hayden remarked.

Danica rolled her eyes. "Anyway, I called back to the office. Thank God Amy with reception still knows who we are. I informed her what has happened and she is trying her best. But she claims she can't do much because both the Thorne's have taken an impromptu vacation in the corporate jet."

Hayden's eyes widened. "What? To where?"

"They never registered a flight plan. Mr. Darby is having a conniption fit about it." Danica took a breath. "And they have no idea why our access is offline or why the credit cards have been closed. Amy is saying it has to be an administrative error, but without Maxima, they don't have the authority to approve another one."

Hayden's eyes tightened. "They paid us ten thousand dollars to fly out here, buy eight pages they have been pining for years to get and then on the cusp of us losing them, they decide it's high time to take that vacation they're owed?"

Danica's shoulders slackened, trying to see excuses for her employer's actions, but finding none. "Maybe they…" The words died in her throat.

Hayden looked to Danica, amused at her innocence. "As a man who understands immaturity, this is intentional. They're trying to shut us down. At least, slow us up. Each hour they delay us, allows them to bank up the only commodity they need in this little race for the island. Time. Every hour they have on us, they can use to find the island before anyone else and steal its secret."

Danica felt her life spinning. "But…"

Hayden waited several seconds before asking. "But what?"

Danica looked to both men forgetting the '*but*.' "Well, wherever they're going, they're meeting their children there and expect to be out of communication for several weeks."

Hayden looked furious. "Children? Let me guess."

"Don't bother saying it." Danica cut Hayden off. "Amy confirmed they have two sons. Both twins and fully grown adults. The secretary calls them the ape brothers, but she asked me to keep that on the down low."

Carlos asked, already knowing the answer. "Where are they coming from?"

Danica knew it as she said it, the pieces now falling into place. "They're flying in from England on the second corporate jet. And like Mom and Dad, they have no flight plan with a destination."

"Son of a...." Hayden hissed.

Carlos asked. "What about GPS?"

Danica rocked her head. "Maximus has sole authority over security. Not even Mr. Darby can override that to track the planes as the Thornes own them personally."

"Come on..." Hayden turned to Danica. "You must want to swear now?"

Danica shot back. "As I said, when I swear, there will be a good reason for it."

Hayden chuckled.

Danica on the other hand did not. She was angry. No. She was more than that. She was furious. Most of all, she felt betrayed.

Danica remembered the first intruder's final words as he disappeared over the railing. 'This isn't over.'

In that Danica agreed.

'*Not by a longshot.*'

25

As Danica came to grips with her employer's deceptions and game playing, Hayden had shifted gears, turning his focus to Carlos.

Hayden leaned back, accusation in his eyes. "Back to the item you so quickly glossed over..." His eyes drilling into Carlos. "You said it was in fact *you* who hacked Maximum Pharmaceuticals?"

"Yes." Carlos replied, simple and direct. "Not me per say, but someone I trust, paid very handsomely to recover any information I deemed should not be in the hands of anyone."

Hayden waited in silence. When he realized he was not getting anything more out of Carlos, he challenged him. "Why is that?"

Carlos held his hands open. "Besides the fact I felt no one should have to suffer as I did, I never trusted the executives at Maximum Pharmaceuticals with the information."

Hayden seemed to share the sentiment, as did Danica now, yet this was still new information to them, so he had to ask the question. "Why not?"

Carlos stood and moved about the kitchen. "Originally, I only had possession of my eight pages, which I kept safely here for decades. I had assumed my diary was long destroyed in the fire. Ironic now that I think about it." He was pacing. "When I discovered my diary had survived, I was stunned. I later discovered a smaller museum had found the original journal a few years back, how I will never know, but I tried my best to get it back." He paused with resignation. "But to no avail."

Danica had now turned into the conversation and was listening intently. "So what happened?"

Carlos smiled that Danica had proven interested. "Well from my investigations, I determined the journal was not considered all that important, thus the museum had it stored. It seemed they'd rather keep it in a box out of the way than to display it or sadly, sell it to an interested collector."

"You being the collector?" Hayden remarked.

"Yes." Carlos replied emphatically. "But to my good fortune, not theirs, the museum later failed in its operations, forcing them to put its acquisitions up for sale, including my memoirs. I knew I had my chance to get it back."

"But you didn't get it?" Danica asked, already knowing the answer.

"At the time, I played fair." Carlos sounded regretful he had done so. "I attended the Bristol auction as scheduled to purchase it, if for no other reason than it was rightfully mine. And I felt my declaration of it having been mine one hundred years after my reported death might have proven an uphill battle."

Hayden found some amusement in that. "You were outbid I assume?"

"You can say that." Carlos seemed to get angry as he said it. "The item was sold *before* the auction, a week prior."

Hayden looked confused. "How is that possible? I thought once sale items are put to auction, or placed in an auction catalogue, it's sold at the show without deviation. From what I know, missing items from a potential sale could damage an auction house's reputation."

"Normally yes, but money talks." Carlos showed his annoyance at the act by clenching his fists and holding them. "It's uncommon, but possible. That and though my journal was a part of the inventory, it was considered shelf filler, not a true prize, so it never made it into the auction listing. It was to be included with one of the actual items according to the young lady running the show. So by the time I arrived, my journal was long gone."

"How did you find it again?" Danica queried.

"It took a small fortune and a lucky break after a few weeks of private eye work to later discover, Anthony Darby, Maximum Pharmaceuticals current COO had purchased it and to my dismay, my original medical records." Carlos stated.

Considering their own observations of Carlos healing, the notes by the medical doctor who had cared for Carlos over the years had to be a phenomenal acquisition, Danica surmised. If for no other reason, it supported the treasure at the end of the quest by an unbiased source through documentation of an unexpected origin.

For the Thornes, it had to be an addictive morsel to continue their mission for the prize, and as proven, at any cost.

Carlos then declared out of the blue. "Some things were never meant to be found."

Danica's blood ran cold. *'That's what exactly the attacker in South America said in front of her greenhouse on the night of the chamber's destruction.'* She rose from her seat, staring icily at Carlos, backing away from him.

Hayden seeing his partner's reaction also rose to side with her.

Before they could continue, Carlos raised his hands in surrender. "Please. Don't be alarmed. I'm well aware of what I just said."

Hayden was not, as he had not been present with Danica at the attack in her camp. Though she had told him prior, he had focused on the act itself, not the conversation.

Carlos turned to Hayden. "I should begin by apologizing to you Doctor Lattimer."

"Me?" Hayden looked confused. "Why me?"

"As Doctor Swift has deduced, I was the one who had the chamber destroyed." Carlos said it with such calm and reserve, it was like he had archeological treasures destroyed every day. "I paid a mercenary to find its location and destroy any and all existence of it, including any possibility of it being rediscovered."

Hayden now understood the reasoning for the acid wash used on the chamber walls. But still, he was not impressed. "You sent a man to attack us and destroy the chamber on a whim?" Hayden stated in dismay. "Do you know how old that chamber was?" More concerned with history than his well-being.

"It was not a whim. And yes, I did and I would do it again without a moment's hesitation." Carlos felt no remorse in his declaration.

Hayden was open mouthed. "Your man nearly blew us up."

Danica turned in Hayden's direction. "I told you before, we were half a kilometer away."

Ignoring Danica's last statement, Hayden challenged. "But he did attack Danica."

Carlos shook his head. "He was given very specific instructions not to harm you." He turned to Danica. "But as I was informed, it was to *you* I should have given those instructions."

Danica grinned remembering her satisfying kick and gunshot having sent the man running.

"Plus I had no idea who you were at the time." Carlos defended. "I was trying to destroy any path to the island. The longer the chamber remained open, the better the chance someone could have found the route. I had no idea what was written in there and I couldn't take the chance."

"How did you find out about it so quickly?" Danica asked. "We barely only discovered it before it was assaulted upon."

"Your report." Carlos answered matter-of-factly. "It was remarkably detailed. The internet is nothing if not a perfect pool in which to fish. With the right filters for certain words, text or lines, at strategically placed servers around the globe, no matter how encrypted, information can be netted, redirected and reviewed."

Hayden was impressed with Carlos' network. "What happened to your guy?"

Carlos gave them both a puzzled look. "I've no idea. I lost track of him in Toronto. He was supposed to intercede at the hotel and get the laptop. He never checked in. Chances are, the worst."

"Just so you know we didn't get rid of him or anything." Hayden added.

Carlos smiled warmly. "I didn't suspect that in the least. Once he failed to check in, I put the pages up for grabs as fast as possible, making special care to email details to your company." Looking to Danica. "Baiting the snare."

"Why them?" Danica asked. "Just because they bought your journal?"

"I have been investigating many avenues for years in regards to paths leading to the island." Carlos took a breath. "And using Rios' vast fortune made it easy." He looked up to Danica. "And at almost every turn, I found Maximum Pharmaceuticals right ahead of me. Buying books, acquiring maps and absconding with any evidence of the island they could. That and of my original trip in the 1800's. Amazingly, once in their possession, the information vanished. So I suspected they were after the island. I had no desire to share in their hunt until now." He turned to both Danica and Hayden. "But I believe the only reason for your involvement is your discovery of the story chamber. A rather lucky find for them. And of what I know of them, they are ruthless in their endeavors, so you should count yourselves very lucky they chose not to rid the world of you both already with what you know." He leaned back. "Presuming they have not already planned it."

Hayden and Danica found that entirely discomforting.

Hayden was suddenly more interested in the dirt on his now former employers than the loss of the chamber. "What did your private investigators discover?"

Carlos gritted his teeth, almost like he was disgusted at what he found. "You're aware Maximus and Maxima are twins right?"

"You mean there is another set of them out there?" Hayden chuckled. "Great more two bible thumping muscle bound punks to contend with."

Carlos shook his head, cutting Hayden off. "No. I mean, they're fraternal twins. Brother and sister."

Hayden's joke died on his tongue. His felt his facial muscles scrunching up. "What? But they said they've been married for over twenty years."

Carlos shrugged. "I never said they weren't also married."

Hayden grimaced even more. "But that would mean their boys are incestuous children?" He said it with such disgust, he looked like he was going to lose his own lunch. "Though that would explain their looks."

Danica burst with a sudden laugh, amazed at Hayden's ability to see the funny side of the situation.

"What about their parents?" Hayden queried. "They had to see what was happening."

"I'm afraid not." Carlos replied. "Both their parents died when they were very young. They assumed control of the company when they turned eighteen. They spent a great deal of money covering up their past, but I've been around for a very long time and have connections far beyond theirs."

Hayden got a chill thinking back to that conversation in the corporate head office. *'We were born to be a couple.'* He shivered inwardly. He quickly looked in Danica's direction. "Don't you research your employers before you apply?"

Danica was offended. "First, they head-hunted me ,not the other way around. And second, you'd be surprised how few times the question doesn't come up in the job interview. 'Oh by the way, love your wedding bands. Are you two also brother and sister?'"

Carlos laughed, continually amused at Danica and Hayden's intelligent, yet comical arguments, even if somewhat childish. "Look. We still have an advantage. The island is two miles down from the surface, preceded by a maze of caves far longer. Even if they beat us to the cave, they still have to find their way down and let me assure you, it is not a simple feat."

"Do you remember the way?" Danica asked with hope in her eyes.

"Honestly no." Carlos replied, watching as Danica's eyes dropped a touch. "The cave system is too massive. When we first explored it, it took us weeks to find our way down. And we had a team of fifty men working in shifts of six hours, twenty four hours a day, dropping coloured rocks to mark dead ends to prevent doubling back. I have no doubt the guardian tribe has long since removed them."

Hayden grimaced. "Even if we get there, the chances of us not crossing paths with them in such a system is remote. And considering what they were willing to do to get the eight pages, imagine what they would do to us when they're within spitting distance of the prize."

The trio remained silent, suspecting the dire consequences of being caught in an underground cave system with the Thornes who already proven their willingness to lie, cheat, steal and very likely kill to get what was on that island."

Danica sighed. "This does not bode well for a starting point."

Carlos tried to cheer them up. "Well, I can tell you this, if we find the natural stairways down, it means we're going in the right direction. There are only seven to find."

Hayden's ears perked up. "How many sets of stairs?"

"Seven." Carlos responded. "The caverns and corridors do drop significantly over distances, but I do remember seven specific descending natural stairways, if you could call them that, dropping us a good amount at each point."

Danica could see Hayden's excitement and asked right away. "What is it?"

"The seven discs we hadn't deciphered." Hayden replied. "The ones layered one atop the other which we thought looked like a lightning storm or you thought could be art?"

Danica envisioned them. "Of course."

Hayden pumped his fists. "What if it was a map? A map of the cave system as it leads down to a small mountain in a lake beneath it. Remember, the discs were suspended on a mountain like tip at the base."

"I read about them in your report, but they weren't attached to it." Carlos piped in, the excitement becoming infectious. "I searched the Maximum Pharmaceutical database and it wasn't there."

Danica had a smile that went from ear to ear. She held up her Smartphone. "That's because I could never get it to attach to the message. In fact…." She keyed her photo library in the memory. With a few swipes of her finger, she held up a selection of fourteen photos, from different angles, depicting the seven discs. "I still have the only copies."

Carlos held out his hand. "May I see your phone?"

Danica handed it off with ease.

Carlos took it gingerly and asked them to follow him to his office where he kept his computer.

It was a vast room of certificates, photos and maritime art. Carlos was not a minimalist decorator. If there was a space, it was filled. He took a seat in his large leather chair and with a tap of his fingers on the screen, the thirty inch monitor blazed to life. He attached a USB wire to the phone and in seconds, downloaded all the photos.

Carlos explained as it uploaded. "We will use my 3-D imaging program to scan them. And based on my quick look at them, reposition and stack them in order."

"How will we know the order?" Danica asked.

As they scanned, Hayden gestured to a small symbol on each disc, rear side, near the edge, which was the only odd point. "Line those symbols up."

Carlos did, layering the seven stone discs from the stone temple at the bottom upwards, in the order Hayden had carefully remarked at the time, using the ancient symbols to centre them, one atop the other, spinning them until they lined up with the upper spaces to reveal a clear route down.

The trio was filled with positive energy.

"The Thornes will take weeks to find the bottom based on this system." Hayden pointed to the map with a huge grin. "And only we have the key."

Danica smiled too. "Now, we can beat them to the island."

Carlos hesitated and then smiled. 'Yes. With this, we will get there first."

Carlos quickly uploaded the completed map back to Danica's Smartphone, and again to his and Hayden's. "I will keep a copy here as well, safe and sound."

Danica turned to both Carlos and Hayden. "We've been lied to, attacked, flown across the world and abandoned and all disguised with the purpose for us to deliberately fail." She scowled. "I for one am pissed and in need of some payback."

Hayden grinned. "Need to kick someone?" He turned to Carlos. "You'll heal faster. Want to take one for the team?"

Carlos smiled back. "I appreciate your volunteering me, but I think our Doctor Swift has something else in mind."

"Do you Doctor Swift?" Hayden said with some sarcasm in his tone.

"I think we should not only beat our former employers to their treasure, but I think we should take it from them and give it to the world for free."

Carlos, now part of the team, raised his fist in support. "It's been a long time since I went on an adventure and returning the favour of the Thorne's disreputable actions only sweetens deal."

Danica warned, speaking directly to Carlos. "Are you prepared to return to an island that took you thirty years to remember?"

Carlos paused. "It was inevitable. I have long felt I lost more than I gained on that island and my return was something I would eventually have to do." He turned to them both. "And bringing allies such as you with me only secures my feeling I will succeed this time where I originally failed."

Hayden shrugged. "I like all your devotion to the past for justice and all, but I'm for simply sticking it to Maximus and Maxima, so inevitable or not, I'm coming." Hayden pumped his fist too. "Plus as *Tweedle* Dee and *Tweedle* Dum said, 'This isn't over."

Danica and Carlos exchanged a look of satisfaction.

Danica announced. "Carlos. You call your contacts and I'll call mine. Let's get this little adventure on the road."

Carlos nodded. "Agreed."

Hayden stood there with his hands in his pockets. "While you do that, I'll get myself another beer."

Danica scowled and walked away, taking her cell phone to the patio to make some calls.

Carlos returned to his bedroom.

Over the next hour, after numerous calls, bookings and more, all the arrangements were made and the trio returned to the kitchen.

Danica smiled. "A car is on the way. We have an hour. We'll be driven to the airportand be on our way back to South America by sun up."

"Fountain of Youth." Hayden announced. "Here we come."

Danica interrupted. "Carlos told you it was not the Fountain of Youth."

"What should we call it then?" Hayden asked with innocence. It was a logical question.

Danica turned to Carlos, unsure how to respond.

Carlos looked slightly uncomfortable. After a few seconds of consideration, he responded. "I have memories, but mostly from my dreams." He shivered involuntarily. "I'm sure they're of the island, but I don't remember many specifics. And what I do recall is deeply disturbing."

Danica placed her hand on Carlos' shoulder. "Anything you can remember will only benefit us."

Carlos relaxed at Danica's touch. "In my dreams, when I get close, real close, I wake up in a cold sweat, pushing the visions back down again." He took a deep breath. "I remember it being hot. Very hot. So much so, it felt like it was almost hard to breathe." More deep breaths. "And it smelled. Like death. Not recent death, but death nonetheless."

Hayden and Danica tried to imagine, but the images did not blossom in their minds without any reference of comparison to something this dark and foreboding.

Carlos continued. "But one thing always comes back to me. The most horrible thing of all. I remember hearing whispers in my head and all around me. Everywhere and yet, nowhere. No words I can discern. It was unintelligible, but it was always very loud."

Hayden stared at Carlos. "That's sounds almost contradictory. Loud whispers?"

Carlos shrugged. "I can only tell you what I remember, not the why or the how. And to this day, when I hear people whisper, my blood runs cold."

Danica asked. "Were you alone?"

Carlos tried to remember back to his nightmares, as that was what they were to him. "I don't think so. I remember eyes peering at me from the darkness. Empty and devoid of life, yet not dead. Lost souls left to suffer and live on."

The air seemed to chill around Danica and Hayden.

"And of courses the screams." Carlos added. "Loud and constant screaming when the whispers were at their loudest. But when I think hard about that, I'm pretty sure some of it was my own."

Hayden and Danica had nothing to offer as it sounded terrible.

Carlos ended with one more thing. "If I had to give it a name, absolutely must, I would say I was in *Hell*."

26

Maximus liked to stand. It made him feel powerful. He stood before the full length mirror in the *Caxias do Sul* central hotel, his arms crossed above his chest, his forearms resting on his large pectorals like they were shelves, admiring himself for a good solid minute.

At one point, he winked. Maximus absolutely loved his body. His God-given massiveness which he used endlessly to intimidate others in his presence.

In board meetings, Maximus would hover over competitors, standing before them like a golem waiting for them to capitulate or simply rising to walk around, showing off his monumental mass, reminding them, they were in the presence of greatness.

Most acquiesced.

'With the exception of Doctor *Lattimer.'* Maximus thought, thinking back to his first meeting with him in his boardroom, his home turf as it were.

Doctor Lattimer's natural inclination to challenge authority was starting to give Maximus serious cause to very much dislike him, regardless of his intelligence.

But then again, his plans for Doctor Lattimer in the near future included making him something a future archeologist would have to dig up.

Maximus smiled at that, the muscles in his face tightening with the grin.

But like Doctor Lattimer, Maximus' size also gave little pause to his wife Maxima as she was equally as imposing.

Maxima was lying on a couch with blue and black leather stitching for cushions, swallowing strawberries dipped in chocolate, whole. She rose, creeping over to Maximus, taking his mouth into hers. For several long moments, they held one another in a deep embrace.

Maximus loving the sweet taste of his sister's lips.

"Mother would be so proud." Maxima smiled as she pulled back, her hands moving up and down Maximus' hardened biceps.

"As would Father." Maximus responded, his arms coming around her torso with a lasso like hold. "They both would have been, presuming they lived to see us."

Maxima smiled. "Of course, assuming they would have been comfortable with our being together."

Maximus kissed her hard. "We were born to be together. Blood is thicker than water and our bond goes beyond being brother and sister."

Maxima smiled. "Which is why our parents couldn't be allowed to live."

They laughed ruthlessly and resumed their tongue wrestling.

After several minutes, they pulled back their upper torsos, keeping their lower bodies intertwined in a standing position looking like a giant letter "Y."

Maximus took a breath. "After years of searching, investigating and numerous expeditions, we're finally within grasp of the Island of Eternal Night."

"And it's precious secret." Maxima smiled. The corners of her lips dropped slightly as she considered their recent team alignment. "I've no idea why you bothered with Swift and Lattimer in the first place."

Maximus chided her with a look. "Because fate had them find the chamber. I couldn't risk interfering with such happenstance and Karma. If their luck held true, I estimated they would also help us to acquire the final eight pages of the journal." He provided Maxima an *'I told you so look.'* "And now we have them."

Maxima could not argue the point as the two doctors did lead them to the pages. "Yes. But our boys are a tad worse for wear."

Maximus shook his head in annoyance. "Damn fools they were. We told them not to engage the good Doctor Swift. Power may be their strong point, but intellect is not. You're far better suited to deal with Doctor Swift."

"My meager hand-to-hand training is nowhere near as high as Swifts'." Maxima was still complimented at the remark, yet argued. "But from the call, Doctor Lattimer did some damage as well."

Maximus frowned. "Well, I could almost applaud the fact they attended Mr. Santiago's flat, sharing our idea of retrieving the pages. I almost wonder if they had the same plan as us to dispose of him and take the pages."

"Doubtful." Maxima grinned. "They probably thought they could buy them. Innocent fools."

Maximus and Maxima kissed again, shorter this time.

"We still have yet to find out who sent that attacker to destroy the chamber and after the doctor's back in Canada." Maximus noted.

Maxima shook her head. "Who cares. We have the books and the pages. There's nothing left. Even if someone else was in pursuit of the island, they'll never beat us to it now."

Maximus agreed with that assessment. All the aces were in their deck. He pulled apart from Maxima and took to the bar at the corner of the room. He poured himself a generous serving of vodka on ice. He chugged it down in one pull, swallowing the ice cube with a single gulp, chilling his larynx as it clattered down his esophagus. He poured himself a second. "Once we find the island and take its secret for our own, we can make the world ours."

Maxima started to undress. "With our boys at our side."

Maximus muttered. "Presuming they are not stupid enough to get lost on the way."

Maxima slugged Maximus hard in the bicep, slightly under the *Coracobracialis* muscle beneath the shoulder on the exposed inner arm, sending him back with a wince. "Those are your children you're talking about." She defended.

After several seconds, Maximus lowered his gaze. "I apologize."

Maxima pulled him in and kissed the point she struck. "Plus, they have us to direct them. No matter how stupid they are."

They both laughed again and engaged in another passionate play of facial fluids.

After several moments, Maxima breathily spoke. "The boys are on the second jet into Brazil. From there, they will meet us at Point One."

The first point they had derived from the Leviathan Log.

Maximus removed his pants. "From there, we'll move in the direction of Point Two."

Point Two having been determined by the theories of Captain Rios after his many years with the young first officer from the Leviathan. Information gleaned by Doctor Gerber and recorded in the medical files. The documents had revealed numerous conversations between Rios and the survivor. It appeared Gerber's ability to eavesdrop and his meticulous note taking over the years were far more comprehensive than was ever known.

Maxima reached her hand down into Maximus' boxers and grabbed his large and throbbing member.

Maximus let out a soft gasp. "And with the pages, we'll move in the direction of Point Three. Based on what the boys read to us over the phone, this is where they all intersect, thus triangulating on the cave leading down to the island."

Maxima was pulling Maximus' boxers downward, anticipating taking him into her. "Who would have ever thought, the island was beneath the earth itself."

Maximus grinned as he put his hand down Maxima's pants and grasped her frontal area with his meaty fingers.

Maxima moaned deeply, bucking back and shivering uncontrollably.

Both of them lunged forth and embraced, sharing a deep and lust filled kiss.

After a good minute, Maximus leaned back. "You looked angry at the airport today my dear."

Maxima clenched her teeth. "Did you not hear that little baby crying in his car seat? For God's sake, he cried for almost ten full minutes. I so wanted to walk over there and smash my foot into that basket and grind him into paste while telling his mother for the next child, buy a gag."

Maximus pulled away, his face stricken in shock. "What is wrong with you?" For a good minute, he glared at her. "I paid three hundred dollars for those shoes."

They both stared at one another and burst into laughter, passionately grasping at one another again, imagining the carnage.

Maxima pulled back and started to chuckle.

"What now?" Maximus asked, truly interested.

"It reminds me of that clinical trial we ran last year."

Maximus laughed viciously. "Of course. What was it? We paid two hundred young mothers in Toronto one hundred dollars each to let us do a free amniocentesis test to determine chromosomal abnormalities in their fetuses."

They shared an amused look.

"They had no idea we were syphoning off stem cells to help improve our wrinkle creams for our age research division." Maximus remarked.

"And with those ironclad releases they signed, despite those sudden miscarriages they sadly suffered, ensured they had no legal recourse."

Maxima's eyes perked up. "One of them survived though. Even if endowed with permanent mental retardation."

"There should have been a test for that."

They both laughed in unison, holding onto one another for support.

Maximus threw out. "But don't forget, they still got a hundred dollars."

"That and we sent them all a wonderful Maximum Pharmaceuticals basket a year later. If I'm right, you even included a sample of the cream they helped create."

Maximus smiled. "Giving them back a piece of those children they lost."

They both burst into hysterics at their own evil humour, nearly tumbling over.

Maxima pulled free and sauntered toward the bed, her naked body and its taunt form rippling with each step from the mass of muscles under her skin, motioning for her husband to follow.

Maximus strode toward her and in seconds, relieved himself of any remaining clothes. He took Maxima into his arms and lifted her from the floor with ease.

Maxima quickly asked. "What about this *"Evil'* we've heard so much about on the island?"

"Nonsense." Maximus threw Maxima down and in seconds was on top of her, penetrating her body perfectly, causing Maxima to gasp. "Stories to keep true believers away. I'll not allow a superstitious fairytale to keep me from immortality."

Maxima choked and thrust with Maximus. "Still, we can't allow what we think we've found to be seen by too many others. Until we make it our property."

Maximus was moving in tandem with his wife and sister. "Anyone who gets in our way will be removed from the equation."

Maxima grinned as her orgasm was building. "What about Doctor Swift and the archeologist?"

Maxima smiled viciously as he too felt the fire of his body building up for release. "They're smart. I'm sure by now they figured out it was us who had the pages stolen. But what does it matter. They have nothing but three blank books and no one to chase. We've won."

Maxima let the rivers of energy flow through her ecstasy filled body. "But what about the collector who had the pages?"

Maximus was holding back, waiting for Maxima to burst with him. "An old man with nothing to show for the auction but a beating and knowing he was defeated. What can they get from him?"

Maxima was getting hot, her body and skin filling with pins and needles as she was reaching the finish line. "But like you said, what IF, our good doctors have fate on their side?"

Maximus was about to explode. "Sounds like the *Evil* may have itself two more victims coming their way."

Both exploded into one another, power, energy and sexual passion as they laughed at their planning.

Once they were done, they continued violently over the next two hours, twice with knocks on their hotel room to lower the volume.

They did not.

Hours later, as they were passing out from exhaustion in the wee hours of the morning, Maximus sighed. "Maybe we'll be together for all eternity."

"I do hope so." Maxima smiled blissfully. "Fuck the rest of the world."

27

"It's not really *Hell*." Danica sighed, shaking her head. "Carlos was describing the island using a commonly known term from historical and biblical reference for comparison, not naming it specifically."

Hayden leaned back in his leather seat on the private jet and let his muscles relax, letting his mind remain in action. "Hot, dark and foreboding. That and constant screaming combined with lost soul's voices calling out." Hayden chuffed as he crossed his arms over his chest in defiance. "Sure sounds like *Hell* to me."

Carlos continued to read his book, casually ignoring them, amused at their debate from his rendition of events. He drank from a cool juice glass in his armrest.

Danica held her hands up in exasperation. "Carlos said *whispers,* not voices, Doctor Lattimer."

Hayden grinned and he sat forward. "Ever notice when you agree with me, I'm Hayden. But when you don't, I'm Doctor Lattimer."

"I figured Doctor Idiot would be rude." Danica retorted.

Carlos had to muffle his laugh into his the crux of his arm at that.

Danica turned in her seat and stared at Hayden. "I highly doubt the almighty God when he was making Heaven and Earth chose to make *Hell* a single subterranean island miles beneath the jungles of South America."

Hayden signaled to the personal stewardess to get him a beer. "I guess I studied a different bible than you did. Mine must have been the abridged version, the one that didn't include the maps."

Danica let out a breath and counted to five. Ten would be needed if he kept this up. "*Hell* is supposed to the vast expanse filled with evil souls having passed on for millennia. This island according to Carlos, and on the chamber wall I might add, only describes a place as about a mile and half wide and likely as deep. If God was to banish his fallen angels somewhere and populate the place with demons, I'm sure he had found a better spot."

Carlos chuckled as he listened. Two intellectuals fighting like children, but with the combined knowledge between them of Einstein. He was sure they liked one another.

Hayden curtailed that argument. "But what if it was simply one demon. *Legion* for instance. He would fit the bill of Carlos' description."

"Seriously?" Danica argued, her two palms squeezing the armrests, trying to envision how her life's recent choices had led to this moment. "You want to insinuate its *Legion*?"

Legion was a group of evil spirits referred to in the Bible having originally possessed a man from Gadarenes. The demons begged to be spared from being sent back to Hell. Jesus cast the demons out of the man, granting their request and allowed them to dwell in a herd of pigs. The pigs later drowned themselves in the Sea of Galilee.

"Since we don't know what it is, we can't rule it out." Hayden disputed. "I'm not saying it is *Legion*, I'm simply saying, it could be anything."

Carlos lifted his head and nodded to Danica. "I would have to agree with Doctor Lattimer on that point. Without knowing what we're up against, with the exception to the Thorne's, nothing is beyond the realm of possibility."

Danica turned to Carlos. "Don't help him."

Carlos smiled and raised his hands in surrender. He returned to his reading.

Hayden pushed left on his armrest, pivoting his entire seat around on the spinning axis of his chair to face Carlos behind him. As he looked around at the single cabin cruiser jet, Hayden counted sixteen seats, all executive, two tables, both capable of seating eight, a plasma television inset into the wall and ten windows of a larger than average size on each side.

In the back, behind a swinging wooden half door stood a pretty red-headed stewardess wearing a crisp brown uniform matching the colour scheme of the aircraft. She was adorned with small tanned freckles and a pert nose under a gentle smile which seemed to warm the cabin. She had a bounce to her step that made you want to get up and dance with her.

"So..." Hayden queried. "You just happened to have a private jet lying around?"

Carlos lifted his head from his book again. "You would be surprised at the price of gold nowadays. That and do you how much compound interest your bank account can accrue over a hundred and fifty years?"

Danica grinned. She asked the stewardess for a soda water. She turned to Carlos. "Back in London, you said you've been aging since the fifties. At what rate?" Asking as a scientist.

Carlos gave her a perplexed look. "To be honest, I can't really gauge it. For a while, it seemed to be at a standstill at the turn of the century." He looked to Hayden. "The first one."

Hayden bowed his head in amusement at that.

Carlos continued. "But definitely more so in the past decade. I was holding my thirtyish appearance until the end of the forties and then it seemed to increase. Not by a lot, but I would say I currently age one year in appearance for every seven."

"Like a dog?" Hayden threw in, instantly regretting the analogy.

"It's only in how I personally perceive it." Carlos did not notice Hayden's remark. "And like I mentioned, my rapid healing is much slower. But in the scheme of things, it's still very fast."

Danica found herself genuinely intrigued. "It makes the unique connection between aging and healing, as though the very act of aging is in fact a form of injury. And with the island healing wounds miraculously, it implies by its retarding aging, it is in fact preventing the harmful effects of growing old. Thus our old age is a result of our inability to heal."

"You're far smarter than I, Doctor Swift." Carlos smiled at her. "As all I presumed it meant was more birthday presents."

Hayden raised his beer to that.

Danica had been watching Carlos a lot since they left London, impressed with his resolve and healing of course, but noticing some odd quirks as well. "You don't sleep much do you?"

Carlos peered in her direction, impressed she had noticed that.

Danica remained locked on Carlos. "Since we left, I and Hayden slept a good hour or two in power naps, yet you've remained awake the entire time."

Carlos took a slow drink of his juice. "Besides helping me to catch up on my reading, whatever happened on the island, has infused me with energy which sometimes, prevents sleep from taking hold. I do sleep, I assure you, but less often than I used to."

Danica could not imagine such a monumental change in a human's physiology to induce all these changes, yet here Carlos was, proving nothing was impossible.

Hayden turned to Danica, changing the subject. "And how did you get us back into South America by the way? I figured we were still banned after not reporting the chamber, followed by its destruction."

Danica paused and replied. "When I called the office this morning, it seems Maximus and Maxima were not entirely honest with us."

"No shit." Hayden retorted.

Carlos raised his left eyebrow. "You're right my dear. He does use a lot of colourful expletives."

Hayden tilted his head. "Et Tu Brutus?"

Carlos smiled.

Danica continued. "It seems Mr. Darby had not been flown down to South America to secure our permits. In fact, when I spoke to him, he had been unaware of the chamber entirely. He was indeed asked by Maximus to fly to South America, but he was told it was to handle all the paperwork to secure and privatize our camp area for a ten mile radius. As far as the South American government is concerned, the chamber never existed."

Carlos looked up. "As I said, some things were never meant to be found."

"Wonder what they had planned to do to keep us from telling?" Hayden stated quietly.

No one spoke, suspecting the dark prospects of the Thorne's original plan.

After a long moment, Hayden tried to lighten the mood. "Regardless of Daddy Warbucks here." Hayden gestured to Carlos. "What are we going to do for equipment?"

"I already called my Dad." Danica replied with conviction, as though this was the ultimate answer and the only one needed. "He said when we land we'll have everything we need for cave exploration, supplies and camping gear. Including an all-terrain vehicle to take as far as possible before going the rest of the way on foot. It is being same-day couriered from Vancouver to the airport where Carlos said we're landing."

"And your Dad paid for all this?" Hayden asked incredulously.

Danica smiled. "I told you he writes novels right? He said if he can spend a thousand dollars on a comic book, he can pay for his daughter to go hunting ancient monsters on lost islands."

"And he believes you?" Hayden asked innocently.

"Without question." Danica replied shocked at the accusation anyone would conceivably lie to their parents. "This is why he warned us to be careful." She turned to him. "And for you to stop trying to get me into the sack."

Hayden looked chastened. "You told him that?" He was suddenly embarrassed.

"I tell my parents everything." Danica nodded with self-satisfaction. After letting Hayden stew in it for a minute, she added. "Plus he wired an additional fifty thousand USD in case we need to… shall I say… smooth the trail."

Knowing sometimes what you could not accomplish with paperwork, you could with bribes.

"I should have asked for more for my consulting fee?" Hayden offered under his breath, referring to Maximum Pharmaceuticals.

"What would that have mattered? Whatever you asked for, they were still planning to stiff you?" She grinned. "You should have asked for half a million."

"Yeah. Like they would have paid me that?" Hayden mocked.

Danica remained silent.

"What did dear old dad think about your employers doing all this stuff?" Hayden asked.

"He wasn't impressed. But then again, he told me to quit a long time ago." Danica replied. "I told him once I beat them to their prize, I'll be giving it to the world." She shook her shoulders. "Plus he said when he writes his next book, he'll make them the villains."

Hayden smirked. "Yeah right. Like people are going believe a couple of bad guys named Maximus and Maxima. A bit crazy to me."

Carlos turned to stare out the window as they closed in on their destination.

Only a few more hours and they would be back in South America.

And from there, several days of driving and a good two days trekking into the barely explored depths of the Amazon jungle.

Thinking back to over a hundred and fifty years ago, Carlos' blood still ran cold, not knowing what he was returning to, but fearing it with every fibre of his being.

'There is nothing to fear, but fear itself.' Carlos thought.

Then added. *'Oh yeah, and the island.'*

28

Carlos terminated the call on his satellite phone as the plane came about. He let out small sigh. "It appears our competitors have already arrived. They landed approximately two hundred miles south of here." He dropped the phone into his jacket pocket. "My contact with airport security confirms four walking gorilla's without hair passed by earlier this morning with enough equipment to start a new civilization."

Hayden paused to consider that. "But if they're working alone, just the four of them, how do they plan to carry everything?"

"Do you not remember what Maximus looks like?" Danica gave Hayden a mocking look. "I wouldn't be surprised if he slapped whatever they had on a skid, strapped it to his back and dragged it through the jungle behind him like an ox tilling a field."

Hayden admitted, if it came to manpower, they had the advantage.

Carlos on the other hand was more optimistic. "Doctor Swift has already arranged transportation and for our supplies to be ready for us as we land. And from my calls, it's already on site and being loaded."

Danica gave Hayden a self-satisfied smile.

"At most, they have a twelve hour lead." Carlos stated.

"That's a lot of time." Danica noted.

Carlos smiled. "True. But they're using my journal pages to decipher the location. I never wrote an exact path, only what I remembered along the way to find the cave entrance. I on the other hand know exactly where it is, so our search will be more direct. And trust me, it's not simply a mile from civilization, it's very far into the uninhabited areas of the jungle."

"And even if they beat us, without the cave map..." Hayden threw in.

Carlos completed his sentence. "...they'll be scurrying about like rats in a maze and a giant one at that."

Danica acquiesced to their exuberance.

Carlos gave them both a solemn look. "But remember, they can still get lucky." He wanted to prevent them from underestimating their opponents. "Though I find that doubtful, no matter how convoluted the caves are, eventually, they will find their way down to the island. In this, it's inevitable"

Hayden challenged. "Then we'll simply have to ensure we find it first."

Danica zipped up her jacket as the plane banked and started its descent.

"When we land, the vehicle will meet us at security." Carlos paused. "It will be a few days drive before we even get to the part of the jungle we have to traverse on foot."

"How did a ship's crew find it so far in?" Hayden asked curiously.

"Excursions on land were rare." Carlos replied. "So after many months at sea, when we did pull ashore, it was always a drawn out affair. Plus anyplace where supplies are abundant can easily give cause for a month or two of settling." Carlos had a faraway look in his eyes, looking back into the past. "Plus like I said, the tribe made an error. One we capitalized on."

Hayden was about to press the subject when Carlos suddenly padded his pocket, his face revealing he had forgotten something. Something important. He reached in and drew out a red velvet pouch, tied tightly at the top with a lace like ribbon.

Carlos motioned to Danica. "Doctor Swift?"

Danica turned in her chair to face him. "You know you can call me Danica right?"

Carlos offered her a grin. "In my day, one always addressed a doctor with respect by including their title. For all the years of training you worked through to achieve it, one must be rewarded equally, even if only by a simple courtesy."

Danica could not argue that. He was a man of a different time. "Understood."

Carlos then gently handed her the bag.

Danica gave him a quizzical look. "For me?"

Hayden was curious. "I don't propose you have a bag for me?"

Danica rolled her eyes in Hayden's direction.

Carlos had sat back. "When I took Rios' estate, this was left specifically for me to find. In a cherry wood box on his writing desk with a single sentence written on parchment. It read, 'May this mystery be solved by my return.'" He sighed. "As you know, he never did."

Danica found herself wondering what Rios left. She pulled the string upwards and opened the top of the bag. She reached inside and pulled out a red satin handkerchief wrapped around a small hard object. She gingerly laid the satin covered item in her lap with Hayden peering over with baited breath.

Hayden extended his fingers forward to help.

Danica gave him a dirty look, causing him to withdraw his hand. "Patience." She said.

"Not one of my strong points." Hayden replied.

'Don't I know it.' Danica thought, keeping the remark to herself. She pulled back the four corners. For several seconds, both she and Hayden stared at it. She tilted her head to the left, completely unsure of what she was looking at.

"Captain Rios found it embedded into the railing of the Leviathan. Some sort of nail or claw I presume?" Carlos explained. "But be very careful, it's extremely sharp."

Danica turned it over and examined it under the lighting of the plane. She was impressed it maintained its shape over the century Carlos had it, especially for an organic item. She held it up and stared down the two cylindrical hollow tubules that ran from tip to tail.

"What is it?" Hayden asked Danica, deferring to her expertise.

Danica shook her head. "I haven't the foggiest idea. From what I gather, based on its size and shape, it's a nail of some sort. Or like Carlos said, a claw."

"From what?" Hayden asked turning to Carlos.

Carlos offered no expression of having the answer. "What I know you know. Rios claimed in his letter it was stuck in the wood and very deeply. And his most important point, it was dripping a yellow fluid which he claimed instantly healed his finger when the claw cut it."

Danica looked to Hayden. "The lake?"

"What about it?" Hayden not making the connection.

"According to the chamber centerpiece, under the discs, the water at the bottom is yellow." Danica reminder him.

Hayden nodded. "True. But the diagrams specifically noted the *Evil* on the island is the key to life, not the lake that surrounds it."

"Unless you read it too literally." Danica theorized.

Hayden was not offended as translating ancient text did not always mean perfect transitions into everyday language. "Until we find it, we're only guessing."

Danica rewrapped the claw and placed it back in the bag. She reached out to return it to Carlos, but he held his hands back, not taking it.

"You're far more able to discern what that is than I. I prefer you keep it." Carlos declared.

Danica bowed her head with an unspoken '*Thank you*.' She slipped the bag into her jacket pocket.

The intercom hissed to life above them. "Ladies and Gentlemen. Please fasten your seatbelts. We're coming in for our finally landing position. The local time is 2:12 p.m." There was quiet pause filled with white noise. It was followed with, "Welcome to South America."

"More like, welcome back." Hayden declared.

Carlos peered out his window, thinking. *'God protect us.'*

And he was not talking about the plane landing.

29

Upon arrival at the small rural airport in Manacapuru, a somewhat backwater location for an international hub in Danica's estimate, sporting hard packed earth for a landing strip, haphazardly hung backyard lights for illumination and several corrugated aluminum shacks to either side for arrivals and departures.

The only thing missing was customs, which was seemingly replaced by a single military officer with an overly tucked green shirt, an ill-fitting hat and a gun which if drawn would fire more rust than lead.

Carlos' private jet looked completely out of place among the dust flyers, freight delivery craft and planes so obvious they were used for drug running, they were only missing a logo painted along the side advertising, *'Cocaine. Fastest High Anywhere.'*

Once free of the airport, Carlos signaled for the pilot to take it home, and quickly, before he found the hubcaps and the wings for sale in the local airplane chop shops.

The jet was off the ground even before they were outside the property.

The trio were met by a rental car courier at the exit. He adorned in white shorts, a matching collared T-shirt and Sahara hat, having driven one hundred and forty-two miles to bring them the vehicle. He was provided a second bundle of funds to take a bus home with a generous tip for his efforts.

Once inside their four-by-four all-terrain vehicle, designed to carry six people, or three with lots of equipment, the trio felt they were ready to get going. There had been no need to load any gear as Danica's father saw to it that everything was ready and stored upon their claiming it.

Having only lost an hour in their arrival, they spun the tires and raced forward in hot pursuit of the Thornes, eager to close the gap between them.

The next two days were long, spent with them driving deep and hard into the heavier jungle areas of South America. Most of the travelling conversation being more theories, continual conjecture and the occasional request by Hayden whether they would be passing a bar anytime soon.

Hayden was thankful for the air conditioning, as he spent a good deal of his free time draped over the rear seats in snoring bliss.

The trio exchanged turns driving, for maximum distance, over the days and nights they moved.

Numerous times they found themselves stopped by locals crossing with cows and horses. Twice they were forced to get out to move trees and fallen brush. And once even to allow a squad of ducks to pass to safety in front of them.

Carlos felt it was bad karma to kill innocent animals for a few minutes of road time.

On the third morning, Carlos pulled over into a large tree covered area and parked. He had warned them of this in advance, but reminded them the next two days would be on foot as the vehicle could not reach the cave entrance by any artificial means.

Once the vehicle was parked, Danica found her way to the hatchback where she found the long aluminum crate her father had informed her about. Dragging it from the back, she angled it downward at a forty-five degree angle against the rear bumper and opened it. Inside was an array of weaponry for the three of them to distribute amongst themselves.

As her father told her, the permit requirements in this part of the world were somewhat far more lax than Canada.

Danica sorted quickly through the rather comprehensive arsenal. Quickly thinking to herself, she knew she would have to have a long discussion with her father as to how he acquired such arms contacts, regardless of his novel research. She selected a handgun, three clips, and a leather holster. Her weapon was a 9mm Parabellum with 98mm barrel, six rifling grooves and an eight round capacity. She dropped the magazine at the heel of the butt and slammed it back into place, satisfied with its easy to hold weight.

Hayden chose an equivalent sized weapon, three clips and a leather holster which was worn around the waist. His firearm was of a UK design, with a 9mm IMI, 94mm barrel and fifteen round capacity. The magazine catch hung to the left side of the butt behind the trigger.

Danica warned Hayden if he started twirling it on his finger and re-holstering it into his side holder, she would take it from him and he could carry a sock filled with dimes to defend himself.

As Hayden secured his weapon, he double checked the case to ensure there really were no rolled dimes in there. He would not put it past Danica to have asked for it.

Carlos on the other hand hefted a high powered bottom-loading, side-ejecting shotgun with dual action bars, internal hammer and a slide release that could hold eight rounds in the tubular barrel. It sported a leather strap for over his shoulder and a sling to slip it into.

Filling a small satchel of cartridges, thirty in total, he felt prepared for their incursion.

Once the trio was fully loaded up, most of their gear could be carried in packs, they engaged the auto locks on the vehicle and were back on their way.

Over the first day, the terrain was arduous and hard. Even the muddy areas were slick and difficult to traverse. Combined with heavy tree cover, though attractive and shielding them from the hot sun, it was still thick and annoying to pass through. Despite the generous use of a razor sharp machete in Carlos' hands, there were still significant delays.

The trio suspected the Thornes would be equally burdened by such tasking hurdles as they were forced to suffer, or at least they hoped.

The constant jungle sounds, a blend of insects buzzing, animals growling and birds squawking made for a musical melody of nature which Hayden found to be overrated when tromping through it seeking an unknown destination.

When they did make camp, the rainstorms and high winds made sleep hard to achieve, leaving them deprived of energy for the next daily trek.

With the exception of Carlos of course, who always woke up smiling with bacon and eggs cooking over an open fire.

Hayden did make the generous offer to snuggle each evening, but Danica made clear, she preferred to be cold.

When Carlos held his arms open for Hayden's embrace indicating he was a tad chilly, Hayden found his body quivering, explaining his physique was uniquely calibrated to only provide heat for the opposite sex. So he offered Carlos a sweater.

This was followed by the tent filling with loud laughter by two, and eventually three comrades.

The next morning, three hours in, Hayden finally asked, "Why did we not simply take a helicopter? For my own information really?"

Carlos shook his head. "Though South America is not known for its militant factions, there are sufficient criminal activities to warrant prevention of flight access. That and the local authorities have little belief you're not trafficking when travelling in such a manner."

Hayden recalled news stories of such things. It was understandable.

"Plus," Carlos added. "No matter how far away we would be dropped off, the helicopter pilot would still have to file a flight plan. And however it's explained, three would-be adventurers dropped off in the middle of the Amazon with nothing known in the area would ignite interest pretty fast. People still believe in cities of gold, ancient Mayan chambers of jewels and other more fantastical theories like…"

"Like the Fountain of Youth?" Hayden sarcastically cut in.

"Yes. Equally silly notions." Carlos commented with a grin. "So in no time at all, we'd have a horde of treasure hunters following suit. And in my estimate, in under a few weeks, no matter how hard I tried, the island would be discovered."

Danica walked for several more steps and asked. "Ever think the island was meant to be found?"

Carlos stopped dead in his tracks, bringing their little human train to a stop. He turned, his eyes seeming to chill Danica's bones as they bore into her. "Not for a solitary instant." He offered nothing more, turning back around and moving forward, hacking away with his machete and clearing the path.

Hayden whispered from behind. "You've been told."

Danica swung around and hit Hayden in the arm, causing him to wince. He muttered under this breath.

The trio trudged on.

After a few hours of Hayden's continued and unwelcome, 'Are we there yet?' Danica suggested he be quiet.

Carlos checked his compass and confirmed they were moving in the right direction.

Hayden dodged downward as a leaf stalk narrowly missed his face. "Can I get in front of you?" He asked, speaking to Danica.

"Why's that?" Danica replied.

Hayden used his forearm to knock the next one to his side. "Because I've been slapped at least six times by all the branches you keep pushing my way."

"Slapped?" She let another sail back. "Must feel like you're on a date."

Hayden ducked under the next one with a scowl. "With you anyway."

"Keep dreaming." Danica replied, smiling to herself. She turned and looked at the somewhat stomping Hayden. "For an archeologist, you sure complain a lot about being in the field. I thought you'd be made of sterner stuff."

"Know a lot of archeologists do we?" Hayden shot back. "Plus if you ever watch all the movies with *us* archeologists, when they seek out a destination, they usually drive. Or fly or at least have a horse. Ever see them do a lot of walking in films? No. What makes us archeologists is we live in modern times. We look back at the past and think, '*I bet they wish they had a car.*'"

Carlos laughed quietly to himself as he pushed through the heavier plants and trees moving deeper into the jungle.

Trekking through the underbrush and heavy marsh for another hour, Hayden asked. "How do you remember the way so well?"

Carlos hacked some tall grass away in his path. "My memory is quite good. In fact, back in the day, I could recall the entire crew complement of the Leviathan by name. This was why I found having forgotten what happened on the island so trying and why I was so reluctant to return. At least on my own anyway."

Danica was swiping some insects away from her arms. "Well we thank you for coming with us. After having Maximus and Maxima stab us in the backs like they did, I feel it is only fitting we beat them to their prize."

Carlos smiled. "The question is, is it a prize or a punishment?"

Hayden yelled from the back. "Nice upbeat conversation. Makes me keep wanting to go all the way people."

Danica and Carlos laughed.

After clearing into another small open meadow, Hayden asked. "Would it not have been faster to come in from the cove point where your ship came in?"

Carlos shook his head. "Yes and no. In today's present, the cove is a large shipping port, with less than admirable individuals running it. The last thing we need is to have a group of criminals following us through the jungle with all our gear. We'd be sitting ducks."

Hayden understood the thought pretty well. South America was well known for its brutal criminal element.

Carlos continued. "And as I said, at the time, we were establishing a settlement. We originally came up river for fresh water. But once anchored, we stayed for a while. We took trips to and from the ship, which in some cases, took half a day."

Danica brushed a mosquito off her arm. "But the Thornes are using the cove aren't they?"

"Probably because they're criminals." Hayden remarked. "Would you want to try and overpower that lot alone in the jungle?"

Danica admitted to herself, she did not.

Carlos took a moment to rest. "What no one ever knew was we actually came ashore on the coastal side of Peru." He stated. "These were part of the pages I was informed I had destroyed in the Leviathan Logbook."

"You don't sound too sure?" Danica commented.

"Of our arrival on that side of the Americas I'm certain." Carlos replied. "Of my destruction of the logbook, I have no recollection of doing so. But I knew my Captain. He would have seen it written accurately in the log. So destroying it to prevent its location was the only logical reason I could surmise. Presuming logical was my mindset at the time."

"This was when you went insane?" Hayden asked.

Danica gave Hayden a dirty look, but Hayden held his hands up innocently, mouthing the words, *'What? It's a fact.'*

Carlos replied, having no regrets. "Yes. When I went…." He paused for a better word. "When I found myself outside my mental comfort zone."

Hayden nodded. "No chance of finding yourself relapsing outside your comfort zone anytime soon I hope?"

"You'll be the first to know Doctor Lattimer." Carlos replied. "Presuming I don't eat *you* first."

"Nice Carlos." Hayden shared. "Real nice."

Danica inhaled deeply to swallow hard the laugh that almost followed.

The trio moved deeper into the heavier habitat. The machete now taking several swings to clear an opening where it originally only took one.

"I've imagined my return many times." Carlos began, starting to reminisce as he moved forward. "And this route is the most unimpeded route to our destination."

Hayden and Danica let Carlos talk knowing he was obviously extremely nervous at his return.

"I've used online topographical maps, three dimensional grid schematics and a GPS mapping system to find the most ideal path to the cave island entrance with the least amount of human contact." Carlos commented. "Though mine is not the most direct route, mine is the best way to get there undiscovered." He sighed. "And remember, my journal describes only keys landmarks I observed at the time, which may have been eroded, if not lost, over the past century. It was never meant to be a point A to point B situation, point B being the cave entrance."

Hayden and Danica followed in accepting silence.

Hayden tripped and fell into a large packet of wet marsh, which was followed by a sucking sound as he pulled his leg free. He rose, brushed some wet dirt off his knees and cleared his throat. "I know you hate this, but is it much farther now?" He growled. "We've been walking for almost two days."

Carlos turned. "Not much farther."

"Are you just saying that?" Hayden asked.

Carlos grinned. "Yes."

Hayden groaned.

After two more hours, Carlos finally turned to Hayden. "Now I can honestly say it's not much farther now."

"How did you even find this cave this deep in *Shits-burg*?" Hayden asked.

Danica glared. "This cave does seem to be in the middle of nowhere. How did you ever find it?"

Carlos' shoulders drooped slightly and his eyes sunk into his face. "Purely by accident I assure you. And of course, our deception." Carlos clarified, guilt lacing his voice. "When we pulled into the cove and moved inward, we were simply hunting prey for stores. It was then we came face to face with the tribe that guarded the island."

Hayden threw in. "The original one? Not the one who built the chamber?"

"Correct." Carlos answered. "Surprisingly, they were very welcoming. We ate with them, drank with them and even danced with them over several nights. We enjoyed their company, shared our foods, even if we could not communicate that well."

Danica seemed confused. "If this is the original tribe, why would they tell you about the island? Based on the renditions of the chamber, they guarded its secret quite devotedly."

"They didn't tell us anything." Carlos seemed to lower his gaze with shame. "Like I mentioned, they made an error and we capitalized on it. To this day, I still have not forgiven myself for having betrayed their hospitality."

Danica and Hayden exchanged a quick look.

Danica reached forward and softly placed her hand upon Carlos' shoulder. "What happened?"

Carlos had stopped moving again. He let out a breath, planning to unburden himself upon them. "It was a different time back then. Suspicion of savages was easy, regardless of their kindness." He took a moment. "The first inclination was after one of their ceremonial dinners. Our Captain felt they were hiding something. You see, during one of the meals, they were preparing their warriors for something special, but they wouldn't tell us what. So, after some of us returned to our ship for the night, a few of stayed back in hiding to find out what was going on. And yes, I was among them."

Hayden almost asked a question, but held it in check at Danica's look to let Carlos continue.

Carlos took a sip from his canteen. "After the fire died down, the inhabitants returned to their leaf covered huts. The warriors left the camp, with us in pursuit, unknown to them."

"No one spotted you?" Danica was impressed.

Carlos answered with. "Surprisingly no. But they were very focused on their mission. We followed them for a good hour, until we found ourselves before this small but oddly defined cave entrance."

Hayden ducked under a tree branch as it sailed over his head and smacked the tree behind him. He glared at Danica who had held it for just that purpose.

Carlos was still telling his story. "We waited outside the caves. For hours. We almost left. At least until we heard the screaming."

"Screaming?" Danica asked with curiosity.

Carlos turned to her. "Screaming so terrible, you felt your soul shiver."

Danica gulped, followed by Hayden.

Carlos continued. "It was not until the next morning, but when they finally returned, the youngest warrior came out shaking spasmodically, being carried by the others out of the caves and back to the camp."

"And you felt after seeing that, your team wanted a piece of it?" Hayden asked sarcastically.

Even Danica found imagining that horrible a vision would be more a deterrent than an invite.

Carlos face went taut, thinking back to that day over a century ago, still regretting that night's decision to enter that cave unprepared which resulted in thirty years spent trying to recover. "When the warrior was carried out, he broke free from the others. He was frantic, running around in a frenzied display. The other warriors tried to subdue him, but the escapee's rage was fueled by madness."

Hayden asked again. "And you all felt, 'Wow. That's for me?'"

Carlos finally gave Hayden a cold look. "It's was what happened next that grabbed our attention, not his insanity." He was quick to answer. "After a good solid minute or two, they realized the frightened warrior was beyond negotiation, so one of the warriors used his spear to stab the crazed warrior, right below the lower shoulder, near the armpit, with a vicious thrust."

"My God." Was all Danica could say.

Carlos looked defeated as well, momentarily. "We honestly thought they'd killed him." He paused. "But it did not. Even with the pain, the warrior remained animate, flailing about manically. But eventually, he was brought to rest. The warrior dropped to his knees and the spear user withdrew the tip."

Hayden mentioned. "And...?"

"It was when we all saw it. The warrior's wound healed right before our very eyes." Carlos remembered with amazement.

Danica understood immediately.

Even Hayden could imagine the sailor's astonishment at seeing that happening in the late 1800's, not unlike he and Danica felt in London when Carlos unbuttoned his shirt, like they were witnessing a miracle.

"We had no idea what was down there." Carlo pointed out. "But for us, we envisioned invincibility and even immortality. Maybe in the back of our minds, likely as you originally surmised, something fabled like the Fountain of Youth. But whatever it was, on that night, we knew we had to have it, no matter the cost."

Danica and Hayden moved forward a few more steps, no words offered, waiting for Carlos to conclude.

Carlos ended his explanation with. "And like I told you before, some things were never meant to be found."

Danica noted. "And you were never welcome to return."

Carlos shrugged. "We figured that out the next day. Our intrusion had insulted the tribe. Thus our invitations were quickly rescinded. And from this point forward, we were on our own. Ironically, our hosts became our watchers. For some unknown reason, they chose not to intercede at the time."

"I wonder why?" Danica queried.

"I've no idea." Carlos was genuinely unaware. "And though I recall reaching the bottom, from that point forward, it's a total blank. As I mentioned, I've flickering visions of things, but none with enough clarity to tell you what I saw, what I did or what happened to me."

"You still have your dreams." Danica added.

"More like nightmares." Carlos stated. "Part of me wants to know what happened. Another part of me does not. After having spent three decades of my life in a blur of therapy, drugs and experiments makes me wonder if facing my fears is a wise decision."

All Danica heard was, "Experiments?"

Carlos nodded sadly. "Mostly by the lower staff. Experimenting in the form of beatings to see how fast I healed. Not more than that as the administrator was being paid very well by Captain Rios. So any harm I befell was without his knowledge. And bearing in mind how fast I healed, it was always long gone before he could find out."

Hayden looked annoyed. "That had to be horrible."

"Well, the advantage was, when I got a chance, and I got a little payback, my energy levels were always charged, so I could go for a long time. Most never tried again after one bout with me."

Hayden had to admit, it would be a very one sided fight.

The trio resumed their trudging for another half hour. They reached a very dark part of the forest when Carlos suddenly froze.

Carlos raised his closed fist up to the side of his head and opened it wide into a flat hand, fingers expanded, signaling for Hayden and Danica to come to a stop, which they did instantly.

The trio each turned and looked in every direction.

They were in a particularly dense area of jungle, the sun shrouded from above by high top foliage, with plants, bushes and greenery surrounding them from nearly every angle.

Carlos slowly turned his head around and whispered. "We're not alone."

Hayden and Danica unholstered their weapons, unlocking the safeties.

After several passes of his eyes, Carlos entire body stiffened. He stared into a thick canopy of leaves and tree branches.

Danica sensed it before she saw it, but having Carlos' gaze locked on the spot, she saw the silhouette right away.

Even Hayden had to do a double take.

Standing near the trees was a tribal warrior, clad in a brief amount of animal skins for clothes, but every inch of his skin covered in green and brown body paint, distributed and covered so perfectly, he seemed to be a part of the background itself. The only evidence he was not in fact a picture was the slow and hesitant breathing motions of his chest rising and falling.

Hayden kept his weapon aimed downward, motioning the others to do the same. He whispered. "Do not make a show of aggression. He wanted to be seen as he moved enough to alert us. Also chances are, he's not alone."

Within seconds of the words leaving Hayden's mouth, seven more warriors stepped out of the jungle, one from every side forming a circle around them. They were each adorned in the same war paint and outfits, bare feet and strong hands. All of them were holding long bamboo shafts with a wickedly sharp spear tip fastened to the end. The final piece, a decorative shield at their sides.

Danica kept her weapon down, but spoke to Hayden. "Any ideas what to do now?"

Hayden was examining the symbols etched on their skin, looking for anything identifying. His eyes widened when he spotted a symbol on the tip of the shield, a dark moon over a triangular shaped object beneath. "It seems we're on the right trail."

Carlos casually nodded. "I already told you that."

"True." Hayden responded. "But so did they."

"How's that?" Danica asked.

Hayden used his eyes to direct Danica and Carlos to the icon engraved into their shield. "Based on that symbol, this is the guardian tribe of our lost island."

Danica was speechless. For seconds she held her breath until she asked with some confusion. "How can they still be alive today?"

Hayden smiled. "That's something I'd like to find out."

The warrior group remained stationed around them, spears held at ready.

Hayden threw in. "Presuming of course, they don't eat us first."

"Nice. Doctor Lattimer." Carlos mocked. "Real nice."

30

"I don't recall you mentioning the tribe being cannibals?" Danica whispered with trepidation, speaking to both Hayden and Carlos.

Carlos replied. "I assure you Doctor Swift, from my time spent with them, none of my crew ever found themselves as a part of the menu."

"It's been over a hundred years." Hayden shrugged his shoulders. "Who knows if culinary fads have changed? Maybe eating *people* is the new gluten-free here?"

Danica let her eyes lock in Hayden's direction with a scowl. "Not funny." She said, staring forward at numerous sharp spears aimed in their direction.

Carlos tilted his head back. "Regardless of the tribe's dietary habits, it appears we have ourselves in a Mexican standoff, colloquially speaking, no better than being between a rock and a hard place."

Hayden let out a quick breath. "Presuming they had intended to kill us, they would have done so already. And with the stealth they recently exhibited, they could have done so easily." He acknowledged, then looking at Carlos. "Maybe with the exception of you."

Carlos smirked, but was seemingly unsure if he should share the sentiment.

"They revealed themselves more as intimidation, not assault." Hayden looked to Danica and Carlos. "So I want you to follow my lead. Tribes are extremely territorial. And based on history, each time this tribe comes in contact with modern society, they get the shit end of the stick, so they will be more wary than most."

Carlos felt the hairs on the back of his neck prickle knowing he was one of those Hayden referred to.

"We have to provide them a show of good faith." Hayden continued. "Proving our trust in them that they will not hurt us. In turn, showing our proof we mean them no harm." With that, Hayden carefully allowed his weapon to dangle on his one finger. He slowly and meticulously holstered it.

Danica repeated the gesture, putting her weapon under her arm pocket, yet easy to pull out in a moment's notice. Her hands curled slightly, not forming full fists, but ready to strike if necessary.

Carlos had only his machete in his hands, the shotgun still tightly snug in his back sling. He opened his fingers and let it drop straight down, the blade tip piercing the ground and sinking deep into the moist earth, remaining upended for easy retrieval.

For several long moments, the tribe remained silent, unsure of how to react, expecting a different result. One of them muttered something aloud to the others. After several more seconds, one of the warriors stepped forward, seemingly the leader of the pack. He took a stance and stood before the trio.

The leader was six foot three, dark leathery skin from years under the sun, green eyes flecked by brown and a muscled physique that would put most body builders to shame. He was painted like the others, spear in hand, but with a bone embedded through the lower of his nasal septum.

All Hayden could think was *'Ouch.'*

The warrior leader muttered a loud series of sounds, composed of mostly blurbs, clicks and grunts, followed by an aggressive gesturing with the spear toward them.

"Tell me you understood that?" Danica queried hesitantly.

Hayden looked behind them. "They're asking us to turn around and leave."

"You speak their language?" Carlos was visibly impressed.

"Mostly. It's a blend of the Aztec and Mayan language combined with some things I've never heard. Likely unique to their culture alone." Hayden replied. "The people of this area tend to use gestures and sounds to fill the void of the language barrier." He held steady. "But their movements and the fact the ones behind us have now strayed forward to form a more solid line of bodies in front of us, opening the rear, is designed to clearly communicate to us our only option of egress is back."

Danica and Carlos turned their heads and confirmed the open area they had entered through was now devoid of enemies, fully exposed for a quick departure.

Carlos spoke first. "We've come too far to turn around now."

Hayden smiled. "I've absolutely no intention of turning around. I was just explaining their generous offer. Now it's our turn to reject it."

Danica had her hands and body poised for a quick attack. "What do you want us to do?"

Hayden held his two hands up and open. "I want you to remain firm where you are. Under no circumstance are you to back up, even by one step. We must hold a position of strength. We will get no respect if we do not show our intentions to proceed, unhindered by them."

Danica and Carlos nodded their understanding.

The warrior tribe were getting restless, unable to understand the conversation of the white people before them, but holding strong, protecting their land from the trio's invasion. Their spears were rising and falling in a slow, but threatening manner.

Hayden then declared. "I'm about to provide a show of strength. Nothing physical, just verbal, but it will catch them off guard, especially at having an interloper speak in their tongue, even if not one hundred percent accurate." He turned to his partners again. "Once done, remember, we need to hold our ground, no matter what."

Danica and Carlos calmly motioned for Hayden to do what he did best, piss people off.

Hayden turned to the warrior leader and spoke back to him in his language, slower, but being very careful to enunciate everything he understood. *'We're staying and we're moving forward. Now move out of our way. We seek no trouble from you."* Hayden announced with authority.

The warrior's eyes widened, shocked to have an invader speak in his tongue, but more angered by the trio's defiance at his order to leave. In seconds, a slur of angry sounds and motions spewed forth from the warrior, maintaining his eye lock on Hayden, refusing to turn away as it was considered a show of weakness.

Like the warrior, Hayden locked his gaze on the leader, followed by a quick wink, which only confused the warrior more.

As the tribe argued, Hayden, Danica and Carlos formed a circle, backs to one another, facing out as the tribesman moved again, re-surrounding them all, spears pointed forward and their rock edges held at throat level.

"True to form." Danica sarcastically pointed out as she was now staring at an angry tribe and the business end of three spears targeted on her. "I guess the option to turn and run is off the table."

Carlos retorted. "It was never on there to begin with."

Danica had her body coiled to strike at any moment perchance a sharp edge moved too close.

Hayden could see her charging her body for an all-out black belt assault, but he raised his hands to them to remain relaxed.

The trio did.

The tribal warrior stepped forward, his bare feet crunching on the dried leaves and grass, with his equally armed battalion of spear wielders behind him for support as he moved before Danica.

Hayden stepped forward and with one left step, was standing directly in front of Danica, shielding her.

Carlos moved as well, but to stand in front of both of them.

The warrior was making a snarling sound as he came face to face with Carlos. He let his teeth grind and he sputtered some sounds, obviously their language, to which the other men nodded their acceptance.

Hayden commented. "He said, 'We can kill them now and drown them in the pools.' And if I'm correct, he used the phrase 'As for the woman, we can keep her as a slave.'"

Danica turned to Hayden in shock. "They did not just say that did they?"

Hayden smiled. "No. That's for *'It's not far now'* from yesterday."

Danica was tempted to turn and punch Hayden, but felt it would trigger the wrong response from the tribe. She held it in for later.

The trio originally suspected the Thorne's has been through here first, obviously unimpeded by the native populace, but by the tribe's obliviousness and surprise at their arrival, the Thornes were still long behind them.

While both sides stared one another down, the leading warrior shoved his spear tip forward towards Danica, within inches of her cheeks, revealing what he was capable of and noting to her, he understood who was being protected by the men.

Carlos reached out and grabbed the shaft of the spear, behind the tip, stopping the forward motion toward Danica. He clenched his muscles and held it firm.

The warrior's eyes tightened with anger, surprised by the action, taking it for aggression. He snorted and with one vicious yank, pulled the spear back and free, taking a deep slice out of Carlos' open hand. The warrior let out a mean spirited laugh, followed by the others behind him clapping like an audience enjoying a show. He was about to lunge again when he watched as Carlos rubbed his hand casually, showing no shock or pain, on his side jacket pocket.

Carlos smiled as though it was commonplace.

As Carlos wiped it away, the warrior's eyes expanded wide when he observed Carlos' palm and the gouge he had made within it was smaller than he presumed. And in total disbelief, getting smaller by the second, as the skin started slowly knitting itself back together before their very eyes.

The leader shouted something to the others. They all paused, confused by what they were being told.

Two of the warriors, appearing genuinely spooked turned and disappeared into the trees.

Hayden spoke again. "He said, 'Get the Chief. He is… 'something.'" He shook his head in annoyance. "Sorry, that last bit was word I've never heard before."

Danica piped up from behind. "Up until a short time ago neither had we."

The trio held their position, hands up and exposed, awaiting the return of the two warriors and very likely the Chief.

The rest of the tribe had stepped back, somewhat frightened by Carlos' rapid healing.

'Thank God for small miracles.' Hayden thought.

After a few minutes, Hayden whispered to Danica. "Would it be awkward if I asked the first warrior dude if I could reach into my pack for a beer while we wait?"

Danica slowly turned to Hayden. "If you pull it out, I'll personally take a spear to you myself."

Hayden returned her look and replied back. "So yes…it would be awkward."

Danica rolled her eyes as she let out a breath, counting to seven now. She started to think her eyeballs would freeze in a upward stare if she stayed with Hayden much longer.

Carlos offered a quick chuckle, for which the tribe observed them all in confusion, shocked the trio could find anything funny in their position.

The tribe and the warriors were holding firm for a good hour until out of the woods, two warriors split the grass weeds apart, holding it open for an older man to join and pace toward the trio.

The older man, obvious the Chief by how the warriors acquiesced to him, appeared to be almost eighty, small in stature, slightly bent forward on his spine, likely from time and old age. He had long white hair which ran down past his shoulders and was tightly tied in a simplistic braid filled with small decorative stones and feathers. He had thick sunburned skin, but not painfully so, and deep piercing blue eyes like sapphires. The most amazing thing was he walked like a teenager, energy in every step.

The warrior leader moved aside for the Chief.

The Chief stepped up and before Carlos, his appearance seeming to solidify into a position of strength. He stared deep into Carlos' face, tilting back and forth as he examined the wrinkled features and muscled form. After a few seconds, his eyes went wide with amazement. Without turning to his comrades, he yelled something in a fast and furious series of grumbles and grunts, using words Hayden had never heard.

The entire tribal army locked eyes on Carlos, muted gasps and conversations in the same language spoken a moment before, this time; all aggression in their tone was gone.

Within seconds, every single one of the warriors, including the leader, lowered their weapons, fell to their knees and bowed. One hand forward and the other across their heart, faces and eyes on the Earth, they chanted and moaned.

Danica stared at Carlos, who was looking back at the tribe dumbfounded.

Hayden was the first to speak. "Forget to mention to us when you were here last, you also happened to be their God?"

Carlos mumbled. "If I was, I have absolutely no memory of it."

"Well whoever they are, they've been to our island." Danica stated.

Hayden turned to her. "And how do you know that?"

Danica pointed to one of the tribesman on his knees.

The kneeling figure had cut himself on his spear when he knelt as quickly as he did and like Carlos, the wound was healing right before their very eyes.

Hayden gave a satisfied smile. "Guess that means we're really on the right trail."

Carlos interjected. "I was never in any doubt.'

The Chief smiled, signaling for the others to rise. He spoke to them all with another series of sounds and motions.

Hayden translated. "They're inviting us back to their village to share a meal. They feel this re-union is long overdue" Hayden looked to Carlos.

"I wish I could remember." Carlos stated.

"What about the island? Is not time of the essence?" Danica asked.

Hayden relayed a quick question to the Chief.

The Chief turned to the others, posed a question and once responded to, turned back to Hayden, shaking his head and replying accordingly.

Hayden nodded, turning to Carlos and Danica. "He said the island entrance is currently under watch. No one has entered or even approached." He took a breath. "They would take our decline as very offensive. And personally, having a tribe of fast healing warriors who have been to our mysterious island being on our side would be an asset."

Danica sighed. "Fine. Dinner it is. And us without a bottle of wine."

Hayden offered a grin. "Don't worry. I brought plenty of beer."

At that, Carlos laughed.

Almost immediately, so did the rest of the tribe, unsure what was said, but sharing in the jocularity.

Hayden accepted the invitation to the Chief, followed by declaring in their language. "Lead the way good sir. We're all hungry."

Danica quickly mentioned. "And make sure to note, it won't be us they're eating."

Hayden winked. "If they do, I'm sure I'd be the tastiest."

The trio resumed their laughing, following the tribe into the jungle.

31

Night had fallen. The evening sky was clear of clouds and devoid of any stars. A gentle wind blew softly, swishing through the trees with a graceful dance over leaves as small stages and the moon as its spotlight.

The nocturnal insects were rising from their protective hidey-holes, buzzing melodiously as they sought out the shadowed world of the evening in search of freedom and food.

But this natural wonder was quickly overpowered by the thunderous slams of callused hands slapping the tops of animal skin-covered bamboo drums as they pounded out a raucous beat. This was joined by the whistling wail of tribal pipes, in the hands of skilled fighters, not musicians, tempered with the occasional moan to music from the happy and pleasure filled crowds of the tribe.

The trio of Danica, Hayden and Carlos were positioned around a roaring fire, the largest of ten such flaming set ups, with the Chief holding dominion over theirs.

Before dinner, after a quick walkabout of the camp, Hayden had returned and explained the tribe consisted of two hundred and fifty members approximately. The men did the hunting and gathering and the woman and children cared for the camp. The Chief, or Elder as Hayden determined he preferred to be called, was part of a team of four such Elders, each responsible for a portion of the tribes' political structure. The one who introduced himself to them that afternoon was the oldest and the one having the most authority. When Hayden asked for his age, it was met with amused laughs and heads turning away without answers.

In the centre of their barbeque was a huge spit, suspended over wickedly powerful flames, cooking the council's dinner.

Female tribe members were decked out in soft draped sheets and feathers, attending to the diners.

Hayden asked Danica if she would feel more comfortable serving them. This was followed by a quick punch to his shoulder with such speed and sharpness it had Hayden holding it tightly for a good ten minutes wishing for Carlos' healing ability.

Danica looked up at the scorching beast cooking within the blaze as the dancing flickers of fire reached up and licked the animal with tongues of heat, forcing her to grimace. "Please don't tell me that's a jaguar."

Hayden whispered to her. "They'd be very offended if you turned down their food. Trust me when I say it, this is very precious to them. They don't take a life casually. They either had nothing else to offer or they paid homage to its spirit to thank the animal for its sacrifice."

Danica shivered with revulsion. "Do they have vegan Gods?"

Carlos chuckled when he overheard. He smiled to Danica. "Try to look past the animal and imagine only the food. It tastes no different than beef."

Danica sighed. "It better not be offensive to turn down seconds."

"For a field research biologist, I thought you'd be made of sterner stuff." Hayden commented.

Danica ignored him, reaching for some corn bread, hoping if they saw her eat enough of it, they would understand her being too full for a fresh slice of jungle cat.

Over the course of the next hour, the tribal women would approach the individual fires, each carrying large clay bowls of ground *maize,* an Indian corn used in most of their dishes for dipping with cooked tortilla breads. They also served smaller portions of beans, wild rice, sweet potatoes, avocados and surprising to Danica, chocolate.

Danica ravaged many of the individual dishes, finding herself impressed with their combination of wild spices and cooking blends, some with fire, others boiled or the rest pan-fried in peanut oil, creating unique and wonderfully exquisite dishes. She finally choked down a small piece of the jaguar, very thankful Hayden made a gesture to share his plate with her so he could eat most of it knowing her displeasure of having to ingest it. Though it tasted like beef as Carlos suggested, she could not get past it being a feline.

The meal ran for a full two hours, the fire attended to by young teenage men with happy expressions, pleased to be allowed to partake. They all ate, drank and eventually relaxed. Everyone was feeling full and the camaraderie was beginning to build.

The tribal Elder at their fire rose from his log seat. He gestured to a tree trunk, a stool by its cut and design, placed in the ground at his side. He gracefully moved around to come closer to the trio.

Two warriors rose quickly, lifted the stump from its resting place and carried it to where the trio was seated. They placed it firmly before them, allowing for the Elder to take his chair again, regardless of where he moved.

The trio leaned back on their much larger log, shared by them all. It had been brought forward by a series of men before dinner, anticipating this conversation.

Before anyone could speak, the music started low and began to build. Two of the female tribal dancers approached. In seconds, the music gained a feverish pitch as the dancers moved around the large fire, displaying passion and pride in their actions. They came completely around the hot coal pit and took positions to both the left and right of Danica and Hayden. Their bodies were moving in tandem with one another, almost choreographed, waiving their feathers over their heads, lightly tapping each of Danica and Hayden's shoulders, followed by blowing them both a kiss filled with smoke they had inhaled from handheld pipes passed to them by two other entertainers to the sides. Within seconds, the music ceased and they all vanished into the night from whence they came.

Carlos for the first time since he left London actually felt like a third wheel. "What? No dancing girls for me?"

Hayden turned to him. "Having the whole tribe bow to you was not enough?"

Danica smiled at Hayden's retort.

Carlos withdrew his complaint with a grin.

Danica turned to Hayden with a look of confusion, coughing into her hand to hide the question. "What's the dance supposed to mean?"

"Don't be alarmed." Hayden held up his hands in surrender. "But I think they observed us sharing our plate and so… they may have just married us."

Carlos spat up a mouthful of beans he was trying to swallow in his attempt to suppress his laugh.

Danica turned away with annoyance. "You wish."

"I'm just saying." Hayden replied. "We're guests here and we have to respect their traditions. So if consummating the union is a part of their culture, we may have to...."

Danica cut him off with a look. "Praying mantis's have a tradition too ...Want to see if the tribe likes that tradition more?"

Carlos smiled sheepishly knowing the praying mantis was known for killing its mate.

Hayden grinned. "We can talk about it later.... Mrs. Lattimer."

Danica scowled and then smiled. "Be assured, if I did marry you, it would be you changing *your* name to Mr. Swift."

Hayden remembered their discussion back in Carlos' flat in London during their fight with the Thorne's twin sons. "So it's both price and wearing the pants. I can still work with that."

Carlos laughed aloud, finding himself more entertained than he had been in decades, pleased to have made friends with these two.

The warriors around the fire joined in the hilarity, none having a single idea why they were sounding so joyous.

Danica on the other hand was blushing, moving her face closer to the flames to hide it with the pulsing heat.

The Elder gestured with a slow motion of his right hand. Within seconds the music stopped, as did all the dancing and celebration.

Many of the warriors from the other fire pits had risen and quickly approached, forming a large circle around the sizzling and popping fire pit. All of them stood behind the Elder with them as an audience and him as the circus master.

Hayden raised his hands, gesturing a welcome greeting to them all.

Danica and Carlos followed suit.

The tribe all bowed their heads in acknowledgement, pleased with the respect accorded to them.

The Elder too smiled at the understanding of their ways displayed with such skill, thanks to Hayden.

Danica looked to Hayden before the discussion could begin and whispered. "How can they live like this?" Referring to the tribe and their ancient ways.

Hayden smiled. "Let's say they're a proud people and one not easily swayed by the acumen, '*Since everyone else is doing it...*" He pointed around. "Plus it's a hard life maintaining their traditions in a modern world. Personally, I envy them."

"How so?" Danica asked, genuinely interested, Carlos listening intently.

Hayden was serious for the first time in a while. "They don't compromise for anyone. They're their own society and if the world doesn't like it, they aren't invited."

Carlos found it somewhat inspiring himself.

Hayden waved his hand over the entire camp in a symbolic gesture. "There are lots of ancient cultures throughout the world living as they did hundreds of years ago. This group, though small, is not uncommon."

Danica had traveled the planet, seen many things, but always found the past and its existence in a modern world somewhat perplexing. Interestingly so.

The Elder let them speak amongst themselves, according them equal respect.

Hayden gestured for Carlos and Danica to listen as they were invited guests and their discussions could be had long after the dinner celebration disbanded.

As all activities had ceased, everyone in the tribe was now focused on this fire at this time, wanting to be a part of it.

The Elder rubbed his hands together, crossing his leg over the other. He spoke slowly, knowing Hayden could understand his words, but only if not rushed or in a flurry of their own idioms. He also spoke loudly so all around him could hear.

Hayden looked to the Elder and nodded for him to begin, but explaining he would have to translate his words for his friends who did not share their tongue.

The Elder looked to Danica and Carlos and bowed his head, followed by the words, which Hayden translated. *"Too bad they're so far behind the times."*

Both Danica and Carlos smiled, as did the Elder, both understanding his intro was his idea of a joke.

Everyone around them chuckled lightly, but holding it to a soft minimum with respect for the Elder.

The Elder spoke, slowly at first, but ending quickly.

Hayden turned to Danica and Carlos. "He first wants to thank us for sharing a meal with them. This is a very important tradition to their tribe. I missed a bit, but it's an old language, like I told you. It's very much like Mayan, but I can now hear pieces of Olmec and Mixtec in it. In itself, it's still unique, which I can translate for you, but it may be choppy at points."

Danica put her hand on Hayden's shoulder. "As far as I'm concerned, he ordered a pizza, so anything you offer will be brilliant."

Hayden smiled at Danica, sharing a look. He turned and resumed his conversation with the Elder, returning hand gestures and actions.

The Elder appeared confused at several points, but after a few seconds, he comprehended that Hayden was trying.

Hayden motioned for the Elder to resume.

After the first series, Hayden turned to Carlos. "He wants to welcome you back."

Carlos looked surprised. "Glad I left a good impression."

Hayden relayed the response.

The Elder let out a good laugh. *"You're always welcome here. Though it has been a long time, the last time, you were valiant and trustworthy. We take that very seriously and something we do not easily forget."*

"Obviously I do." Carlos joked. "What happened to me?" It was the only question on his mind.

The Elder frowned. *"I'm not surprised you do not remember. You were in poor shape when we saved you from the island. And the...."*

Hayden listened for a full second. He gestured for the Elder to repeat it. He took on a quizzical look as it was said again. After a second, he explained to Carlos and Danica. "He advises the island is home to something they call.... the *Horror*."

"Great." Danica's shoulders sagged.

Hayden turned to her with some confusion. "What's wrong?"

"I've heard the island is inhabited by evil, by darkness and even by monsters. So to now to hear the tribe who guards it calling them the *Horror*..." Danica sighed. "I don't know. I was hoping someone, would say the island was inhabited by large cuddle fairies for once."

"Sorry to burst your bubble." Hayden responded.

"Hoping and dreaming is still allowed right?" Danica queried nonchalantly.

"Of course." Carlos answered for Hayden.

Hayden motioned for the Elder to continue, not explaining the side conversation, as the Elder simply presumed it was Danica and Carlos trying to understand what was being said.

The Elder looked to Carlos. *"The Horror are many."*

Danica grimaced. "We're not back on *Legion* again are we?" Looking to Hayden.

Hayden shook his head. "I doubt they'd understand the concept, but this is what they're saying."

"Concept or not, let's not forget it's still a single island miles underground in the middle of nowhere." Danica was a scientific woman and willing to concede some things. "I'm not saying I believe it's actually *Legion*, but I will agree what they're describing could be considered *Legion-like*."

Hayden accepted this.

The Elder was still looking at Carlos. *"Have you returned for another infusion of the island's power?"*

Carlos turned to Hayden, unsure how to reply.

Hayden reminded Carlos to relax. "Just be honest."

Carlos nodded. "All I've come here for is answers, to discover what happened to me and nothing more."

The Elder understood. *"Having you return is somewhat unexpected. Even some of our bravest warriors will not risk a return to the island, even after only one visit. And many of them only shared a few hours on the island. You were the only man to have ever escaped the island alive after spending the longest time in the Horror's clutches."*

"The longest time?" Carlos asked with concern. "How long was I... In the *Horror's* clutches?"

"Almost eight days." The Elder stated.

In so much that Carlos was unaware of what the *Horror* was, eight days did not seem like a lot to have cost him thirty years of his life. "How did I escape?"

"You didn't." The Elder replied emphatically. *"I dispatched five of our best warriors to the island to find you and bring you out. And luckily for you, they did."*

Danica looked to Carlos, his expression unreadable, while he tried to remember.

The Elder continued. *"You were extremely fortunate. It was the time of their great sleep, or otherwise, regardless of our indebtedness to you, you would've been lost."*

Carlos took a labored breath. "Indebtedness to me?"

"Yes." The Elder nodded. *"Some of your crew took a fancy to our women, but not a liking to their disinterest. You saved three of our woman by having these men placed in your brig. We do not take such actions lightly. We owed you a great debt for this. And we are a people who repay our debts."*

Carlos was stunned. He was trying to grasp what had happened on the island, but with this, he now understood other memories were lost as well. It was disheartening. "What happened to my crew?"

At this, the Elder's smile faltered. *"Your crew was a remarkable group. Never in our time has anyone been able to capture one of the Horror alive. Your crew did. Even our warriors were shocked."*

"How so?" Carlos asked.

"We presumed none could remove them from the island as the lake is their prison. But your crew not only got it over the lake, but through the caves and as far as your ship." The Elder sat up straight, almost seeming to solidify into rock. *"But our vow is firm. None of the Horror can leave the island, dead or alive. By the time we arrived at your ship, it had already escaped. And as we warned, your ship was totally unprepared for such an enemy. We cornered it on the highest point and dispatched it, taking its remains back to the island."*

"You came aboard and no one interfered?" Carlos seemed baffled.

"Most of your crew was dead at that point." The Elder stated matter-of-factly. *"Any remaining ones were killed shortly thereafter."*

"By the *Horror*?" Carlos asked.

"No." The Elder's face was impassive. *"Your Captain was most obsessed with having the miracle of the island for himself. He and the remaining crew were unwilling to leave without one of the Horror. Especially after having lost a third of the crew to the Horror initially, when you first breached the island's shore."*

Carlos was stunned, as were Hayden and Danica, unprepared for the tribe's rendition of events. "We lost over a third? That's almost one hundred and thirty men."

"Your group was ambitious to steal the prize." The Elder replied. *"And your crew felt no less could secure it. Once they discovered the true danger of the enemy they faced, it was already too late. They were quickly defeated."*

For several long moments, Carlos was taking deep breaths. "But you said most of the crew was dead when you approached the ship. If one third was lost on the island below, what happened to the remaining two hundred and seventy men?"

Silence.

"It was our duty." The Elder replied decisively, remaining stoic.

Carlos feared the answer to his next question. "What was your duty?"

The Elder looked to his audience and back to Carlos. *"As to the fate of your people, we were forced to kill them all."*

At this, Carlos gasped. He turned to Hayden. "I think I need one of your beers now."

Hayden reached for his pack.

Danica added, the shock still evident in her eyes. "No kidding. Grab me one while you're at it."

32

"You killed them all?" Carlos asked with genuine shock in his voice. The beer did little to help strengthen his resolve as his liver absorbed, processed and metabolized the alcohol in the seconds it was ingested.

"We did not go looking for a fight." The Elder paused, looking skyward as though seeking answers from some unseen entity. He seemed to reconsider something and began speaking again. *"I spoke an untruth. We did expect some resistance to dispatching the Horror they had captured, but when we arrived, it was after your Captain received the reports of what happened to the first volley of men to the island."*

Carlos remembered his Captain and got a sick feeling in his gut.

"He was beyond negotiation. He blamed us immediately for having withheld the information and costing him the lives of countless men under his command." The Elder explained. *"We told him he was warned, but he felt it had not been enough. He ordered our tribe be killed. And worse, he declared our women and children were to be taken and used as the vengeance seeking men deemed fit."* The Elder

was sharp with his response, speaking with command, defending the actions of the tribe from over a century ago. *"We had no choice but to protect ourselves. And more importantly, the world from the Horror. Were the circumstances repeated, we would do it again."* The Elder's eyes were locked on Carlos, not deviating. *"Without hesitation."*

The trio found themselves looking back and forth from the Elder to the army of warriors surrounding them, seeing them now in a different light.

The Elder suddenly sensing their rising fear quickly interjected. *"It was a different time and a terrible circumstance. You have my solemn word no harm shall come to you now."*

Hayden turned to Carlos. "To YOU anyway."

"All of you." The Elder added, guessing what Hayden had said.

For several long seconds, which felt like hours, a calm settled back into the fireside pow-wow.

Carlos had long come to grips with the deaths of his friends, but the not knowing had left an empty feeling in his belly over the decades. Now having discovered the truth and his own Captain's involvement in bringing about their end, it did not satisfy nor fill the hole.

"Be assured." The Elder tried to explain. *"We tried to convince your crew to retreat, but they were duty bound to their Captain and the memory of your lost men. Within minutes, your armoury had outfitted the remaining crew and attacked. And because they considered us savages, they expected an easy fight."* The Elder hesitated for a second. *"In that assumption, they were wrong. As protectors of this island for over a thousand years, we have fought before and I suspect will again."*

"But your warriors barely topped a hundred." Carlos stared around at the camp, sporting a look of incredulity. "My crew was at least two hundred and seventy men, fully armed and filled with fury… How could you have…?"

Danica cut him off, as a scientist and a woman of logic. "An army of a hundred warriors, trained in basic hand-to-hand combat and who can heal from almost any wound in seconds, energized as you described by the power of the island…" She softly argued. "Your crew could have been a thousand and they'd still have lost."

Carlos bowed his head. He had to admit, the odds were against the crew. Once they saw the warriors healing from the attacks and still coming, their superstitious natures would have taken hold, causing untold havoc on the assault. Combined with the *Horror* and having already lost a third of the men, they would have been forced to believe they had found the camp of the devil himself.

The Elder remained quiet, allowing for Carlos to take the events in.

Carlos was calming down, his fear subsiding at the tribe's long ago actions. He knew, in equal circumstances, he too would have defended his own people under such an onslaught. "What's done is done. Let us return to my past. How did I get back to the ship? And how was I found in the middle of the ocean?"

The Elder gestured to the air. *"With your crew dead and having saved you from the island, we knew we were poor caretakers for you. Unlike our warriors who intentionally seek out the island for its life giving power by stealing it from the Horror, you were completely unprepared for the danger and the repercussions. Combined with the time they kept you in their lair and fed upon you…"*

Danica interrupted with a disturbed expression. "I'm sorry. Did you say fed upon him?"

"I did." The Elder replied. *"The island is barren of food. Mostly stone and rock. No sunlight means no flora. And of course, the Horror are not plant eaters. What they eat, they must capture. And most importantly, while the Horror feeds upon you, you feed upon it."*

All three of the trio exchanged a look of confusion.

"How is that possible?" Hayden asked.

"Sounds like a parasite." Danica replied. "Likely some form of symbiosis."

"Sybi-what?" Carlos asked. Not being a scientist, the term escaped him.

"Symbiosis." Danica repeated. "It's basically a relationship in nature where one organism lives off another with both partners sharing their endeavors with survival being the ultimate goal. An evolutionary *give and take'* if you will."

Hayden turned to the Elder. "Then why not let those things on the island starve? If they're so evil, letting them die of hunger sounds like a great plan."

The Elder shook his head sadly, like he was lecturing a young child. *"Believe me when I tell you, we have tried. Many things, over many moons, and no matter what is attempted, the Horror survives. Always present, undying, unrelenting and forever breeding more of them."* The Elder for the first time since they started, looked defeated. *"And worse, hunger can breed the instinct they have coveted so well...Survival. We determined a long time ago, as long as we keep them fed, even if only a little, they are kept satisfied, and more importantly, contained. A prisoner will not attempt escape if they have what they need and don't know what awaits them beyond."*

Carlos asked again. "But I've not yet heard how I was found lost at sea?"

"We placed you back on board your ship of course" The Elder answered. *"We presumed your own people would be better suited to care for you. That and as a group, we voted that sending you back in your state would be an added warning to anyone who would attempt a return to seek out the island. It would let it be known for all who might try; the reward for such an incursion would be a repeat of your condition and the fate that befell your crew."*

Hayden gave a soft wolf whistle. "Message delivered."

"As for the ship, some of our finest warriors took your boat back to the ocean, as some of your men had taken a shining to them and

showed them the ease of sailing it. Teaching us savages if you will." The Elder cracked his neck with a quick jerk. "Once free of the shore, we pushed her off and let the winds carry her where they may. She rode steady and we ensured the ship was fully stocked with fresh foods and fluids for you. As for your mind, that was yours to find again." The Elder clapped Carlos' knee. "And by your return today, you did."

Carlos felt he learned all he wanted to know on how he got to the ship, so he posed the next question that had always eluded him. "Can I be killed?"

The Elder laughed. ""Of course you can. Though it is much tougher, death can still take you. A blow to the head or heart will work if strong enough. The importance is stopping the flow of blood. When that river fails to run, your life will come to a certain end."

Danica had never expected to get so much information so easily. She had a question of her own. "When you speak of the Great Sleep, do you mean the *Horror* hibernates?"

"I know not of this word." The Elder replied. "Call it what you will. The Horror goes into a deep sleep, not unlike death, unable to awaken for many, many moons. Two full seasons."

Hayden nodded to Carlos and Danica. "I would conclude that to be about six months."

Danica pursed her lips. "With the lack of food, it is logical. Eat for short periods and sleep for more, slowing down the metabolism in hibernation to savour the little they have."

"In fact, you're very fortunate..." The Elder interrupted, looking to the trio and back to Carlos. "Fortune follows you a lot."

"Tell that to my psychiatrist." Carlos smarmily shot back.

The Elder stared in some confusion. "Your who?"

Carlos waved his hand. "Never mind, it was a joke."

The Elder rubbed his hands to the fire for warmth. "Well this time you have chosen to visit is only a few moons into their Great Sleep. They will remain this way for many more moons."

"Thank God for small favours." Danica commented. "Can any of the tribe help us, maybe even lead the way?"

"*No.*" The Elder replied instantly. "*We must always pay great homage to our God before making such an incursion into the Horror's lair. It is not a trip we take lightly. It takes months of planning and preparation. If you must go now, you go alone.*"

"Wonderful." Danica stated.

The Elder tried to raise her spirits. "*Know this. During their sleep, our tribe frequently visits the island and observes the Horror. During its rest period, we have wandered the caves without their interruption. And once, a young member even struck one and it did not awaken from its deep slumber.*"

Carlos finally smiled. "I like that."

"*But make no mistake...*" The Elder warned. "*They're not dead. They can be awakened. The cave walls echo sound and can make even the drop of a fruit that much louder than when first made.*"

Carlos started to understand now why the whispering seemed so loud to him so long ago. The question remained what the source was.

The Elder crossed his hands over one another and glowered. "*Also be forewarned. Two of the Horror do not sleep during this period. They are the caretakers of the island and the guardians who watch over the others. They move about the island like soldiers, setting traps, protecting its sleeping brethren. We call them the Sentinels.*"

Hayden gestured for the Elder to draw the *Horror,* clearing a sandy spot before him on the ground until it was smooth.

Everyone around the fire looked stricken at the request, chanting and muttering loudly to one another, some visibly upset.

The Elder seemed angry, brushing the sand back into a random mess. He fired back with some fear in his voice. "*Recreating its picture could give it power. We refuse to take the risk.*"

"There goes a hope we'll know what we're up against." Danica sighed.

Hayden decided to change the topic seeing the anger and fear he had instilled with his request, unaware how truly terrified they were of re-creating the *Horror*, in any form. He asked the Elder. "How deep is this lake around the island?"

The Elder offered his hands up in an expression of surrender. *"We have no idea. Deeper than our longest ropes I can tell you. Plus the water is not like a riverbed. It is not a gradual descent into the depths. It drops off the edge like a cliff. Dry land to water's edge dropping to incalculable depths immediately."*

"Amazing." Danica noted. "Not unlike the Marianas Trench off the coast of Australia."

"Sure." Hayden noted with sarcasm.

The Elder said something else and Hayden had to pause to confirm it.

Hayden turned to Danica. "He says the lake water burns, both hot and cold."

Danica offered a quizzical expression. "How is that possible?"

"Until a week ago, we were trying to figure out how there could be an island without a sun, so whatever it is, it's obviously possible." Hayden responded.

"We call it Fire Water." The Elder explained.

"I've never heard of it." Danica replied.

"Our God created it as their prison." The Elder offered.

"So let's go with they have no flipping clue." Hayden winked as he turned to Danica. "See, no colourful metaphors."

Danica was not satisfied with the answer, but she also smiled at the fact Hayden was trying to change. In fact, as she thought about it, the only reason he was doing it was for her. It made her feel a little good inside.

In those seconds, the Elder turned his wrist over and held up his inner forearm. The skin was smooth, almost like glass, and hard, scarred along the edges.

Hayden gestured to the arm as he listened to the Elder. "He says this is what the water did to him."

Danica examined it. "It looks like he put his hand into a campfire."

Hayden reviewed it as well. "I guess *'Fire water'* is accurate then."

Danica resigned herself to stop her speculation, at least until she could see the lake for herself. "So how do we get across it then?"

The Elder held up his two hands and moved them like he was using an oar in a canoe. *"There are three boats. Each are crafted to protect the occupants from the water. Each boat can carry six. Under no circumstance do we leave a boat on the island. All come back or you will be forced to return for it."*

The trio nodded their understanding.

The Elder took on a most unpleasant look. *"Please understand my words. I hold to my oath, while in this village and amongst my people, you will come to no harm..."*

Hayden could feel it. "I sense a 'but' coming here."

The Elder continued. *"But like your crew, we will never stop those who wish to go to the island. If you seek out its power, you must seek out its Horror."* The Elder's smile stiffened as he spoke. *"But if you or your friends try to leave the island with the Horror, know our vow still holds firm..."*

Danica dreaded what was about to be said.

"Thus for such a crime, you will all share the fate of those who tried before you." The Elder said it so calmly, so matter-of-factly, it was utterly frightening, clearly communicating, the price would be their lives.

The Elder then smiled anew and clapped his hands. *"But if all you have is curiosity, though we feel it is foolish, go as you will."*

Hayden leaned back and finished his beer, giving the bottle to an excited young teenager who wanted to have it. "Not the warmest sendoff I've ever had."

The Elder seemed to be considering something. He spoke to one of the warriors to his left.

The warrior seemed shocked at the suggestion, arguing back.

The Elder repeated his remark, more firmly, cutting off the warrior with a look.

The warrior bowed his head and departed.

"What was that all about?" Danica asked Hayden.

Hayden looked on with some confusion. "I'm unsure. But he told the warrior to bring us something."

"What?" Carlos asked.

"We'll find out shortly I suspect." Hayden replied.

The warrior returned, still sporting a dissatisfied look on his face, carrying a small leather canteen, approximately the size of a hardcover novel. It had a small cap on the top, sealed by some form of dried sap and looped by a long leather strap which allowed it to be carried over the shoulder.

The Elder took it gingerly and extended it to the trio.

Hayden gestured for Danica to take it.

Danica did, giving it a small shake, feeling the liquid inside splash about. She turned to Hayden. "About half a litre of whatever it is."

The Elder gestured to the cask in Danica's hands.

"This will protect you from the Horror." The Elder explained. *"In the event one attacks. It will repel them. But please know to use it sparingly as this small quantity took us two years to procure and create."*

Carlos and Hayden motioned for Danica to keep it.

Hayden noted to Danica to consider this a very great gift as the tribe are entrusting us to our mission and giving their only defense to virtual strangers, when they could be saving it for themselves.

Danica offered a genuine thank you to which the audience all bowed their heads.

"*And know this.*" The Elder lectured. "*Though potent, it does not last long, so if utilized, retreat should be your only option.*"

Hayden gave a thumbs up. "Run away... Consider that our number one plan."

The Elder finally commented as he rose, readying himself for bed. "*But make no mistake, do not underestimate the Horror. If they awaken, all is lost.*"

The trio took the warning to heart.

Within seconds, one of the warriors came out of the woods. He sidled up to the standing Elder and whispered to him.

Hayden frowned as he listened. "It appears four giants are approaching from the west. According to the scouts, they will reach the cave entrance by tomorrow afternoon. They are mired in the deep woods and marsh."

Danica looked shocked. "You mean the Thornes?"

"Know any other giants?" Hayden queried.

The Elder spoke again.

"The Elder has advised us to get some sleep." Hayden translated. "He claims a better rest before facing the island is vital to our success."

Carlos nodded. "Then we'd better get some sleep. So we can rise early."

They all, the trio, the Elder and the audience exchanged messages of good night and many turned, stumbling back to their camps and tents of ramshackle huts.

The Elder took Hayden aside and whispered something. After a few seconds, the Elder pulled back, his face an expression of dismay. He shook his head and departed for his bed into the night as the remaining fire was dying out.

As they departed, Danica came up to Hayden's side. "What happened?"

Hayden nodded. "He was warning me of the cave system going down and its vast complexness. He was going to explain to me how to find my way down until I showed him the map on your Smartphone."

Danica patted her back pocket in dismay realizing it was gone. "Did you steal my phone?'

Hayden gave her a sour look. "Steal is such as harsh word. I prefer borrow."

Danica snatched it back and pocketed it in the front of her pants this time.

Hayden continued. "When I informed him of the chamber and the cave map, he was shocked. But he was pleased to hear it was destroyed. All he could say was 'I knew that son of mine would do something foolish like this. If he had only stayed at home with his family.' And then he left to bed."

Danica found her left eyebrow rising. "Son? But the chamber is over four hundreds years old."

At this Hayden could only smile and shrug. "I'm only repeating what I was told."

The trio shared a look of quick understanding, some things were never meant to be found.

Danica stood, motioning her departure for sleep. "Then come tomorrow, we'll find our Lost Island, followed by a way to take the prize from the Thornes for our very own, without inciting the tribe into killing us."

"Nice Danica." Hayden threw in. "Just what I needed to hear before bed."

Carlos laughed as they all went their separate ways to crash for the night.

33

The next morning, after a healthy breakfast of forest greens, corn flapjacks cooked in peanut oil and slathered with thick syrup made from a local plant resin, added to that a side of lemon ants, which tasted surprisingly like lemons to Hayden, the trio was almost ready to depart.

Danica gestured kindly to the serving girls she would pocket the ants for later in case she became '*snacky*' on the way up to the cave.

Carlos laughed softly to himself as he overheard.

Each of the trio was dressed in comparable hiking shoes, denim shorts and long-sleeved light cotton shirts with wide brimmed caps for sun protection. They spent a good five minutes spreading bug repellent and sunscreen on in thick coats.

While Danica slept in the sleeping bag beside him, Hayden had spent the morning cleaning his weapon and spraying on gun oil. He knew a clean gun could be the difference between life and death.

Carlos had thrown their equipment pack over his back, adjusting his coat collar to avoid being dragged down on his throat, shifting the handles high to his right shoulder to support the large amount of weight.

The trio gave themselves one quick look over and moved towards the tree line.

The Elder was waiting for them at the camp's border, two warriors at his side, one holding a spear while the other was carrying a wooden stump, likely the same one from the night before and ready to be placed at a moment's notice.

The trio nodded a greeting to their host as he and his men returned the gesture.

A third warrior slipped suddenly from the trees, brushing remnants of dirt and mud off his lower legs. He came up alongside the stationary Elder and whispered something in confidence.

The Elder upon hearing looked up and gestured for Hayden to approach.

The Elder explained. *"It appears we underestimated the giants. They've already reached the cavern entrance. Based on the time it took my warrior to reach us to relay this news, they have an hour head start."*

"I can't believe it." Danica noted, her shoulders drooping at the news. "All of this for nothing."

The Elder seeing Danica's displeasure waved his hand dismissively. *"Fear not. They have already taken the first wrong turn. As indicated, the cave system is vast. By the time they figure out they have gone the wrong way, it will be late afternoon. And presuming they take all the correct routes in their back tracking to find the entrance, they still will be behind your party by at least a day. And with the...."* At this the Elder scowled. *"Map from the chamber... You should be at the island before sundown. Trust me when I tell you, your night's rest will be the difference between success and failure."*

"Half way by late afternoon?" Danica turned to Hayden in dismay. "It didn't look that big on the model to...."

Hayden cut her off. "Unlike our current maps of today, the chamber did not come with a scale. I presumed the possibility existed the cave could be much larger or smaller than the map portrayed, but we couldn't be sure until we were actually within it. Remember, whoever crafted the map did so from memory. In such cases, design tends to take precedence over size."

"It doesn't matter." Carlos interjected. "We already planned to descend it and we, well more me, knew it would be a long way down. But I should point out; the longer we sit here debating its size, the smaller the lead we'll have, so it's best if we get going."

The trio nodded their understanding amongst one another.

The Elder bowed one final time, followed by his warriors, all of them sharing a wish of good fortune.

Within a few minutes, the trio was on their way, their goal line getting closer and closer, the camp shrinking behind them.

Over the next hour, the trio walked, sometimes jogged, over a weather beaten path pressed hard by time and exposure through the trees and shrubbery. The route before them was somewhat hidden by plants and leaf-filled branches so unless you were looking for it specifically, the trail would seem only a commonly used animal track.

Eventually, by the bottom of the next hour, the trio reached their destination.

The stone wall housing the cave to the lost island.

As they approached, the jungle arbour formed a large canopy over their heads, with thick heavy branches from decades of growth, recently trimmed for maximum development. The greenery shielded them both from the heat and rays of the rising sun, but also curious eyes in the skies such as low flying helicopters or planes.

Nature took good care to cover this cave and the tribe did their best to maintain it.

It was a massive stone wall. It consisted of one single boulder, fifteen feet in height and a good thirty feet long. It was pushed back into a large dirt mound which buried the rock completely from the rear. Trails of dirt framed the rock structure to all sides with long tendrils of plant life and foliage which had proliferated all over the front forming a beautiful tapestry of coloured flora, individual vines and flattened leaves which further hid the surface beneath it.

Hayden could not see a single etching, design, painting or picture drawn on this rough layered rock. "It appears the tribe does not decorate this particular location."

Danica was confused. "Why's that? If this island is so sacred to their tribe, you'd think this wall would be covered with ornamental paintings and decorative pictorials."

Carlos turned to them both. "Unless they don't want the cave entrance to be found."

Hayden agreed. "If someone came along looking for something, anything, the lack of symbols here would deter a more thorough search. Even a single pattern not natural to its environment would have any archeologist, such as me, stopping for a better look, if only to examine it to dismiss it. And one picture, no matter how minuscule, could quickly lead to finding the cave entrance."

"Something the tribe would very much like to avoid." Carlos noted.

Danica stared at the rock wall. "So where's the entrance? On the other side?"

Carlos stepped forward and seemed to sink into the stone, the wall appearing to close around him like the grey rock had melted and poured in and around his body. Amazingly, the cave entrance was hidden at an angle to the rock itself, making it seem like it was a solid structure with no opening or deviation. A natural optical illusion if you will.

Danica's mouth dropped slightly open, which she closed immediately to prevent it being intruded upon by insects.

Hayden whistled. "Now that's impressive. If I'd not been looking for it, I'd never have found it."

Carlos looked downtrodden for a second at Hayden's remark. "I was equally as impressed with it too when I first saw it. So much so, I detailed the specifics of it in my journal."

Hayden and Danica understood Carlos' displeasure. His description would have allowed the Thornes to find the invisible cave portal along the rock face much easier as a direct result of his personal and written historic walk through memory lane in his diary.

Carlos lowered the equipment bag from his back and placed it upon the ground. In seconds, he had unzipped it from top to bottom and laid everything out for the taking.

In minutes, the trio were each wearing a solid helmet, leather work gloves, pads for both knees and elbows and a wool jacket. Cave walls could be sharp and unpredictable so any protection would be important.

They all took a selection of rock climbing rope, two coils at a hundred feet and one at fifty. Hayden and Carlos carried the longer rolls while Danica attended to the shorter one.

Each of the trio carried a small fanny pack on their waists, equipped with screw link carabineers, two long frame descenders and matching ascenders, anchor rigging and a small hammer with claw.

For vision, each of the trio was sporting a pair of the double flashlight headbands, not unlike the ones Hayden had used in the chamber with Danica. As she found them far preferable to flashlights or lanterns, since both were hands free and they could be quickly hooked onto the helmets, she had specified the devices to her father. Based on their brightness and focused directional beams, she felt they were perfect for cave exploring. All three of them packed replacement bulbs and lithium batteries.

Carlos found the double lights amusing as he fastened them to his helmet. Looking forward, he felt like an automobile with headlights.

Hayden suggested night vision goggles on the plane, but Danica declined the idea indicating if the Thornes did come upon them unaware, the last thing they needed was the disadvantage of having their eyes blinded at the Thorne's arrival by the backlash of light into the goggles, turning them into easy targets.

Hayden acquiesced as he had no desire to be trapped in a cave system blind with the Thornes and the *Horror*.

Finally, they each strapped on a small backpack which included protein snacks, trail mix, bottled water, vitamin supplements and extra ammunition. In each of these packs, they individually carried their own selection of personal accruements, with Hayden having archeological picks and brushes, including a digital camera and Danica sporting her medical kit which included research and sample recovery cases, glass slides and a selection of scalpels, syringes and surgical gloves.

Carlos was happy with his shotgun, nothing more and all his ammunition. "This time, I shoot first and ask questions later."

Hayden and Danica were okay with that, especially with the unknown *Horror* awaiting them below.

Hayden posed the question. "Since we can't take this *Horror* off the island, how do we expect to get the miracle to the world before the Thornes?"

"Simple." Danica said, sounding more confident than she believed. "We know for a fact the tribe has confirmed that whatever it is on the island that provides for the miracle of rapid healing and long life can be stolen from the *Horror*. So we need only to find out what it is and take the miracle for our own, leaving the *Horror* behind."

"Logical assumption." Hayden accepted, but thinking, *'Easier said than done as the tribe refused to divulge how they take the Horror's precious gift in the first place.'*

"Plus," Danica smiled as she considered this. "The Thorne's still think the treasure is the Fountain of Youth. Though they know the *Horror* guards the prize, and are intrinsic to the power, they don't know the *Horror* in fact carries it."

Hayden fastened and clipped the last of his gear around his waist. "Then let's get this little wagon train on the road."

With that, the trio entered the cave.

34

Hayden reached the first junction almost immediately. His dual beams caught the carved cube before them inset into the wall, etched with a black painted symbol. He quickly deciphered it, but as he did so, he paused, perplexed at what he was reading.

"What is it?" Danica asked.

Hayden looked down at Danica's Smartphone and reexamined the symbol. "The map tells us to turn left, while the symbol tells us to turn right."

Carlos interrupted. "Go with the map. Remember, the tribe who guards the island doesn't want people on it. So they will use any trickery to deceive the searchers. The tribe's chamber you found were not concerned with the original mission, only the story, so I will assume theirs to be correct."

"That and you're not giving the tribe many points for intelligence." Danica pointed out.

"How so?" Hayden replied, shocked at her assumption.

"Ever hear of reverse psychology." Danica retorted. "Show someone something with the intention they do the other. Deception One Oh One."

Hayden had to chastise himself as she was right. *'I won't tell her that though.'*

Carlos directed Hayden and Danica to the recent scuff marks on the ground. "Plus it appears the Thornes went right as the tribe noted, so they trusted the symbol before us."

Hayden smiled. "Then left it is."

Over the next three hours, the group descended downward, slow at first, but getting steadily faster at certain points.

Danica caught her hand on a rock as she climbed down over an outcropping of jagged stones, which Hayden leapt over with some ease.

Carlos followed suit.

So far, the trio had not used any of the ropes or rock penetration equipment. Obviously the tribe over the centuries had smoothed out the path for easier traversing. This was evidenced by the fact a large pile of boulders had been brought down to fill a small chasm before them.

Danica imagined it would have taken months, if not longer, to carry that much stone down here, but then again, the tribe, if anything, had time on their hands.

Danica's Smartphone chirped from the front.

"What's that?" Danica queried.

Hayden held the device aloft. "We just lost our cell phone service."

Danica continued her forward motion. "Did the bars at the top of the screen vanish?"

"No." Hayden replied. "My call with Mistress Kitten was cut off mid-sentence. She was about to tell me I deserved a spanking. By the way, are there roaming charges on 9-7-6 numbers for your phone?"

Carlos suppressed a grin.

Danica on the other hand was thinking. *'More like deserving a good punch.'*

The trio maintained their pace for another three hours, making their way down through the maze of caves, descending two more sets of natural stairs, ignoring carved signs depicting certain directions which were in direct opposition to the three dimensional map they carried with them, past hidden corridors, dead ends and the occasional pitfall on their course into the depths of the earth.

Twice they shimmied along rock ledges and once had to jump over a small crevice with thin rivulets of steam rising out, laced by a foul scent of dead animals.

"I'm surprised there are no bats." Hayden commented.

"For God's Sake...." Danica snapped. "The last thing I need to be worried about is bats. Let's try to avoid talking about other monsters down here besides the *Horror*."

"I highly doubt bats qualify as monsters." Hayden rebutted. "Most don't even drink blood."

"But they love hair." Danica noted, pushing the strands of her hair up and under her cap.

The trio continued on.

Surprisingly, the deeper they got, the easier the trail became to transverse, with the exception of being extremely long. The paths got much smoother with less gaps, cracks or openings to fall into. But they were making good time.

Hayden had to admit, now in the cave system, had they not had the map, it could have taken weeks to make their way down and they'd have probably given up long before succeeding.

Hayden reached the next junction and stared at the new symbol inset into the wall with dismay. He double checked Danica's Smartphone screen. "This is odd."

"What's odd?" Danica asked stepping to the front.

Hayden gestured to the symbol. "The past dozen or so we passed directed us in the wrong direction. This one is telling us the correct one?"

"Reverse, reverse psychology." Carlos inserted. "Once you pass some signs and follow them blindly and then you realize each time, you were going the wrong way, what would you do next?" He pointed to the signs direction. "More likely than not, you would ignore the direction on the signs going forward and do the opposite. But at this point, with the signs now being accurate, you would eventually have to assume none of the signs can be trusted, and of course, even more time wasted."

Hayden grinned. "I'm starting to like this tribe more and more."

The trio resumed their course, this time, in the direction the sign pointed.

Four more hours and they had to stop for food, drink and more importantly rest to recharge their reserves. At least Hayden and Danica did.

Carlos was standing as Danica and Hayden munched away on bags of nuts, raisins and dried fruit. "I find one thing curious Doctor Lattimer." Carlos posed the question as the trio rested.

"And what is that?" Hayden replied.

"Your skill set. Based on your tribal knowledge and interpreting skills, you would think you would be more suited to the study of anthropology as opposed to archeology." Carlos stated it as more of a fact than a question.

Danica turned to listen, chewing on a mouthful of granola.

"I studied both facets." Hayden responded, not thinking anything of it. "But I found the ancient study of tribes and their ancestors to be more intriguing from a structural perspective. The physical discoveries of their civilizations were more attractive than the evolutionary growth of their cultures. So I focused more on the archeology side in that regard."

"I see." Carlos responded.

"Don't get me wrong." Hayden defended. "I still studied anthropology. As I needed it to understand the foundations of the culture and more importantly, their language. I can't use a map if I can't read it. Archeology taught me how to locate the physical history first and use that to delve into the anthropology second."

Carlos nodded, satisfied with the answer.

After a good half hour of rest, the trio resumed their course.

The last leg of their journey was only an additional forty-five minutes as they reached the base of the seventh set of stairs.

Hayden was impressed they actually appeared like stairs, many of which seemed to have been smoothed down by wear, tear and hard work.

At the bottom, they could see a large opening in the rock face before them. It was a gaping yaw shaped like a giant upside down "U", a rounded point at the top and widening to ten feet at the ground. The entire portal was carved with numerous etchings, symbols and drawings.

"What do they mean?" Danica asked, already suspecting it as they approached.

Hayden barely paused as he glanced up and resumed his course. "Several statements, written in numerous ways, but basically all saying the same thing. 'Turn back now or forever forfeit your life.'"

"Or at least thirty years of it." Carlos softly added.

Hayden and Danica decided not to comment on that.

The trio walked under and through the upside down 'U' and found themselves frozen in their tracks, staring up and around in absolute astonishment.

Even Carlos who had been there before was mesmerized as the last time he was here was well over a hundred years ago.

The cavern was enormous in size. The gloom and darkness vanishing in every direction. Even the trio's powerful lights were sucked into the blackness like luminesce consuming parasites filled the air. The grey sand and rock covered ground ran in every direction for miles. Dozens of large stone pilasters, naturally formed, some several feet in circumference and in immediate proximity, grew from floor to ceiling, creating a base of support for the roof far above. More could be seen in the distance. So many more, Hayden lost count.

As the trio continued forward, they could hear the gentle bubbling of cooking water. They cautiously advanced, unsure of the source until the lights of their combined headgear converged and revealed the lake before them.

The lake was equally as large as the cave, completely filling the space in front of them, circling off and into the night. The water was yellow in colour, exactly as depicted in the chamber model, with a somewhat mucous appearance to its tint, milky and cloudy beneath, with pockets of bubbles bursting up at dozens of individual points along the surface, filling the room with hot air and the stench of rotten eggs.

"It's awesome." Was all Danica could state with stunned shock.

Even Hayden found himself hard pressed not to whistle. "You can say that again."

Carlos stepped to his friends' side. "This cavern is over five miles wide. It took my men over five days to scout the area. The lake is approximately four miles across in almost every direction, but not a complete circle" He took a breath as the memories trickled back. He actually found himself shaking with nervousness. "I swear the memory just came back to me and for some unknown reason, I know it to be right."

Danica smiled to Carlos, gently touching his forearm. "I believe you."

"And our island?" Hayden asked, interrupting their moment.

Carlos pointed across the lake, into the nothingness. "It's out there. Half a mile and like everything else, it's big. It's about a mile and a half wide and equally as tall."

Hayden stared into the blackness. "Lovely."

"Not the word I would have chosen." Carlos replied with precision, offering nothing more, as his memories were thinning now.

The trio turned in the island's direction. Even with the combined luminesce of their six optical beams; the light was quickly absorbed, revealing nothing of the mysterious island.

Danica looked skyward at the dozen or so rock columns close to her as their tops were sucked into the twilight of the ceiling above. Several more columns in their visual range grew up from the lake itself, all tasked to hold up the gigantic structure. Though not a structural engineer, she found the creation of a cavern this size and being supported for this long inspiring. She pivoted her gaze downward to Hayden and Carlos. "So how do we get across? I recall the Elder making mention of some boats."

Carlos turned, his lights lowering to the water's edge, near to the left.

Positioned comfortably were three watercraft.

Each boat was seven feet in length, two feet wide and well built. All three boats appeared to be crudely carved canoes, each sporting two oars and a stick, the purpose of the stick was unknown. They had drag marks running from the water's edge, in numerous deep rooted grooves following up to the rims, clearly denoting the boats were used recently.

Carlos casually walked over and lifted one with ease. "It's very lightweight." He ran his hand over the bottom. "The base is soaked with a thin crystal medium, embedded into the wood to make it more durable and resistant to the heat of the lake."

Coming to the lip of the water's edge, Danica smelled the heated liquid. Her nose scrunched up. *'Sulfur?'*

Hayden knelt down beside her and stared into the bubbling yellow froth. "I can barely see through it. It looks like chicken soup."

"Don't scoop up yourself a bowl." Danica commented. She reached for a handful of gravel off the ground and tossed it forward onto the top of the water. It landed and for several seconds, it seemed to float, followed by it slowly sinking into the broth and vanishing beneath the yellow depths. "It has a small amount of viscosity, meaning it is somewhat thicker than water, but not by much." She stood. "Technically speaking, a living thing could tread in it, but not for long. The prolonged heat would drain the swimmer of energy pretty fast. That and combined with its mild density, it would make swimming more laborious than in natural water." Danica had one positive point to add. "The advantage of the water's consistency is a boat would be less likely to sink in it."

"Whoopee." Hayden raised his thumbs with a sarcastic twist.

Carlos remained standing. "How does a lake turn into…?" He paused to frown. "..into this?" He gestured to the steaming water, small condensations of fog running over the top and escaping into the distance.

Danica waved her hand and swept it up and around the lake within her view. "Most likely, due to the depth of the earth we're at, I'd suspect a strong magma flow underneath us."

Hayden's eyes widened as he stood up quickly. "Are you referring to a volcano?"

"Absolutely not." Danica replied countering the argument before it could begin. "Magma is always flowing beneath the crust of the earth. Just in this case, probably a little closer than most. And with the flushing heat, it probably causes large amounts of natural geothermal power to be excreted. Most of the energy and heat would be absorbed by the rock and displaced, but energy always seeks out the path of least resistance and with a water based medium nearby such as this lake, it would be a perfect target."

Carlos found himself impressed with Danica's scientific knowledge.

Danica drew from her pocket a thin strip of blue paper, no bigger than a matchstick.

"What's that?" Hayden asked, moving around to watch what Danica was doing.

"Litmus paper." Danica replied.

"You carry that everywhere?" Hayden queried curiously.

"Of course I do." Danica answered confidently. "I'm a scientist."

Hayden whispered to Carlos. "If I haven't told you yet, she's a bit of a nerd."

"I heard that." Danica shot back. She dipped the paper in and quickly drew it back out. The portion that had been submerged had turned light red, closer to pink.

"What does that mean?" Carlos asked, genuinely interested.

Danica rose and tossed the paper aside. "It means this entire lake is some type of natural occurring acid. Unsure what kind. Not a very strong PH level, but I still wouldn't swim in it."

"An acid lake?" Hayden mocked. "You've got to be kidding me."

Danica moved toward the boats, motioning for Carlos to help her drag it toward the water. "It's not all that uncommon. In fact, in Indonesia, there is the Kawah Ijen Lake. The water has a turquoise color with emerald tints. According to documentaries, the lake consists of hydrogen chloride, sulfuric acid, aluminum sulphate and iron sulphate. A rather nasty mix if you ask me."

Hayden stepped in beside her and took a sniff. His nose wrinkled up. "Well this only smells like sulfur."

Danica lifted the rear end of the boat, Carlos still holding the front as they moved toward the water's edge, Hayden taking up the middle.

Danica continued. "That's good. The milder the better. The last thing we need is sulfur dioxide in here. Even with a five mile open expanse and likely lots of crevices, cracks and fissures in the rock to dissipate the air, it would be irritating on our respiratory system."

Carlos looked down at the water as he approached it. "Is it deadly?"

Danica shook her head. "It's nowhere near the strength of sulfuric acid, but again, no dipping our feet in."

The trio set the boat in the water.

Danica hopped in first and took to the front.

Hayden held back. "The cool kids are always at the rear."

Danica thought to herself. *'So are the assholes.'*

Carlos on the other hand, stood at the back of the boat, on the beach. He was breathing deeply and carefully, but not yet getting in. He could feel flitters of memories coming back to him, dancing across his brain, some with flashes and others, he was sure were warnings. He declared, "I'm not sure what I fear most. What is actually there or what I can't remember and think is there."

Danica stared forward to the darkness. "Well we know one thing for certain."

"And what's that?" Hayden queried.

"Whatever is on that island, this *Horror*, it must be a living thing." Danica surmised.

"And how do you come to that assumption?" Hayden looked surprised.

"If it were a ghost, a demon or *Legion* as you implied, a lake of acid would not be able to contain it." Danica pointed to the open expanse of the cave with only rock pilasters impeding flying traffic.

Hayden mocked. "I assume you got this from your '*Encyclopedia of natural weapons to use against Biblical enemies.*'"

Danica glared in Hayden's direction. "You know, you can be really asinine sometimes."

"You don't need to remind me of my strengths." Hayden retorted.

Carlos smiled, stepping into the boat, his companions' arguments amusing him, letting his confidence return knowing who he was with and how safe he felt in their company.

Danica turned back to the blackness ahead of them and replied to Hayden. "I may not know what is on the island, but I do know natural selection. And in my mind, this prison, and that's what I'd call it, is nature's way of declaring whatever is on that island is meant to stay there."

Hayden pushed the boat off the shore and into the water. "Unless it's an island of vampires? According to myths, they cannot cross water which is constantly running."

Danica stared at Hayden, her eyes slowly rolling, thinking to herself, sometimes, she felt she picked the wrong ally.

Within minutes, the trio was sailing across the bubbling hot waters toward the island, their boat, oars and lights vanishing into the blackness of the Eternal Night as they approached.

All hoping for the best, but fearing the worst.

35

The trio drifted toward the island, their paddles gently grazing the top of the water as they stroked and creating small ripples in the bubbling basin. They kept pace with enough force to keep them floating forward, even if slowly, all the while trying to prevent the hot liquid from splashing into the boat.

Hayden could feel the heat of the hot springs beneath the soles of his boots, regardless of how thick they seemed. But then again, since his feet weren't moist with sweat, he suspected it might be psychological.

The trio stared at the ceiling of the massive cave in awe.

The double beams of their optic lights shooting up into the darkness all around like a Hollywood movie premiere. Each of the shafts of luminesce accentuated dozens more cylindrical columns of stone, some much wider than the ones nearer to the shore, but this time, they ran from the walls off to the sides of the cavern and riding at forty-five degrees, some more acute, others obtuse, creating a superior support system for the ceiling above like natural shelving wedges.

Other equally massive pillars spewed forth from the bubbling yellow lake in abundance as they neared the dark island, like the architect who built it was more concerned with the roof collapsing than esthetics.

Several times the trio had to alter the boat's course to paddle around the rock formations for fear of crashing into one of them, sending them and their small craft into the burning yellow depths, ending their quest with a slow pain-filled dunk.

What amazed them the most was not a single one of these roof supporting pilasters, regardless of the angle or position, were within a hundred metres of the island silhouette, above, to the sides or through it. The island was completely column free, from their vantage point, as though even the stone dreaded touching the shore for fear of disintegration.

Danica found this unprecedented formation unbelievable.

The beauty of nature was she could always surprise you.

As deduced by the tribe, nothing could reach the island except by boat or air, and equally, nothing could escape. Even with a grappling line, the heavy stone of the pilasters appeared to be granite, thus likely unable to be pierced by even the sharpest arrow or hook, presuming one had enough rope to get it across without grazing the water.

It truly was a prison.

And the *Horror* were its inmates.

"How is this even possible?" Hayden asked gesturing to the cave and the way it was constructed.

"Anything is possible." Danica replied with trepidation. "Obviously such is the case. My suspicion is that over years... scratch that, millennia, there was a slow and gradual buildup of stone, rocks and dirt. Due to the extreme heat and geothermal vents, it created what we see here. It's possible the air pockets generated by the hot springs cracked or destroyed the less sturdy rocks to form this cave expanse. The remaining formations, not unlike huge stalactites, untouched by man's brutal hands, grew as time when on and reached up in the only direction it could go, the celling." She offered a wink.

"And voila. I'm sure there are many more untold wonders around the world and beneath the Earth if mankind ever started digging deep enough to find them."

Carlos on the other hand had seen it before and it still gave him the shivers. "And like the tribe said, the *Horror* remains."

"Well, since this *Horror* has never escaped, we can presume it has no wings." Danica theorized. "Or it would have flown out of here long ago."

Hayden agreed with that conclusion. "Or gills for that matter."

Danica accepted it; doubtful even if it had gills it could swim in that toxic pool for very long.

Hayden and Carlos settled into a steady stride, moving together in tandem for maximum speed, until they could see the island start to take real shape. It materialized out of the nothingness.

It seemed to grow out of the darkness like a black mold being revealed by the opening of the fridge door after a big party, the light giving life and existence to the growth within by the mere extension it had been seen.

Like the cave they traversed to get down here, the island was as gloomy and dire as they expected. There was no light anywhere to be seen. It was a mountainous structure of black stone, surrounded by a large flat beach of grey and dark brown sand. Amidst it all, trails and scuffs in the dirt from constant foot traffic, but as for the prints, they were oddly shaped and ran close together.

The trio continued forward, Carlos paddling on the left and Hayden on the right, slower now as the island closed in.

Once they reached the shore, Hayden directed aloud before anyone could disembark. "Once we set foot on the island, there's no turning back."

"Technically..." Danica pointed out. "We can just step back in and paddle away."

Hayden sighed. "Once we set foot on the island, there's no THINKING about turning back!"

Carlos prepared to rise.

Danica stated with conviction. "We came this far. I for one intend to see it through."

Carlos nodded his agreement.

The trio got out, checked all their gear and felt they were ready to invade the island, as they felt in their hearts, this was an invasion.

Carlos lifted the boat up out of the water, careful not to get any acid on his clothes and dragged it onto the beach so it would be waiting for them upon their return. He left a part of the tip dipped at the water's edge, just in case they needed to make a fast departure. He threw the two oars inside, one atop the other.

The trio formed a small triangle as they walked forward, the purpose was so they could see in every direction as they moved.

"Is it me or is it hotter on the island than on the exterior shore?" Hayden queried, wiping the top of his brow with the back of shirt sleeve.

"We're in the centre of a hot springs lake, so I suspect it's not just you." Danica pivoted around slowly, looking over the terrain. "But our bodies are natural adaptors. It will adjust."

"Well even mine is having some trouble with the heat as well." Carlos stated, as he too was feeling hot moisture building up in his loose fitting shirt and pants. "But from what I remember, at least it doesn't get any hotter."

"You could have told me to bring an air conditioner." Hayden pointed out.

Carlos raised an eyebrow. "And how pray tell would you have carried it?"

Hayden gestured to his right. "Director Swift would have been up to the challenge."

"And where would we plug it in?" Danica replied. She knew Hayden was simply trying to boost their spirits up, especially with the heavy balm of the sauna-like heat of the island and the ensuing *Horror* they were encroaching upon.

At this Hayden shrugged. "I guess solar power is out huh."

Carlos and Danica laughed.

The trio spotted a carved opening at the base of the mountain, heading inward.

As they all approached, they came together as a group and looked skyward.

The height of the mountain was unprecedented for an underground peak; its top vanished into the blackness above. Up close, it was dark and dreaded, absolutely no vegetation whatsoever along the sides, edges or cliffs. It was as lifeless as a barren planet.

"Not as scary as I imagined it." Hayden commented right away, more for himself than the others, his eyes moving up and along the mountain sides and to the shadow shrouded top. "Dreary, creepy and damn hot, but not as scary."

Danica hesitated before speaking. "Take into consideration, we're not inside yet."

Hayden dropped his gaze to Danica and scowled. "Hello rain. Welcome to my parade."

Danica returned the glare.

Carlos stepped between them both, having drawn his shotgun, carrying it before him with his finger on the trigger. "Looks can be deceiving. From his point on, I recommend extreme caution."

Around the cave entrance, about twenty meters before the mountain portal, were two individual single foot high wooden posts, driven hard into the dirt, each outfitted with ropes, many ripped and shredded.

Hayden was the first to speak before the others could ask. "They're for sacrifices. The tribe obviously brings down animals they capture to present to the *Horror*. Either to pay tribute or at least, draw them out for whatever nefarious purpose they need them for. My guess, likely for its miracle *juice* as the Elder called it.

Danica offered a disgusted look, not expecting to see animals intentionally presented as food to another predator, regardless of the reasoning. "Barbaric."

"And mandatory." Hayden replied. "Like the tribe said, if they keep the *Horror* happy and sedated, they won't even attempt an escape."

The trio continued forward.

Carlos maintained their flank for a surprise assault, watching for the Sentinels they were warned about. "Hard to keep your eyes peeled for an enemy when you don't know what it looks like."

"In a place this barren and dead, anything moving is likely it." Danica stated.

Right in front of the entrance, Hayden came before a large stone pedestal, a foot high, composed of clay and rocks, and tightly bound with rope, almost haphazardly built, more for need than endurance. In the centre, on a five foot bamboo-like shaft, at the top, wrapped several times around was a moist material, smelling of something sweet, coated in dark charcoal stained streaks.

Hayden leaned forward and took a sniff. "Oil?" He drew a lighter from his pocket. He snapped the flint and placed the flame to the oil drenched cloth.

Within seconds, a warm glow illuminated the dark expanse around them as it lit up.

A bright glow filled the empty space for a good twenty metres in every direction, including the first few feet into the cave, which revealed nothing,

Danica watched the flickering light for several seconds. "Is it wise to light the torch? Is that not what usually attracts the *Horror*?"

"The Elder did indicate the *Horror* sleeps at this time. Plus, as far as I'm concerned, anything to enhance our seeing an attack coming at us from out of this gloom outweighs the prospect of attracting them." Hayden offered her an offhanded look. "And since we need to find one of these things, if a little light brings one our way, so much the better."

"Presuming they're not sentient." Danica commented. "And they can figure out what we're doing and outsmart us."

"Had they any semblance of problem solving skills, I'm sure they could have found a way off this island by now, which leads me to believe the *Horror* acts on instinct, not intelligence." Hayden argued.

Carlos listened intently to both Danica and Hayden. He joined them at the entrance. "I would have to agree with Doctor Lattimer. I would prefer some light to find our transport as opposed to wasting any time searching." He gestured to the water's edge, the boat visible under the glow of the torch.

Danica acquiesced.

Hayden pointed up to the mountain side. "Well, will you look at that?" Now that they had the light of the torch to bring some well-deserved sight to their vantage point, things looked a lot clearer. "The entire structure is pockmarked with holes. Either that or dozens of cave openings. It's like a giant sponge."

Danica stared up at it with a quizzical look. "I honestly have no explanation. Some rocks form holes due to air pockets, but a whole mountain?"

"Unless they were dug?" Carlos threw in, thinking this would be a welcome tidbit to the conversation.

Hayden ran his hand along the mountain base. "Well the stone is pretty hard, so if it was dug, the *Horror* either has sturdy digging hands or…."

Danica cut Hayden off. "Or claws." She patted her front pocket. "Not unlike the one Carlos gave me on the plane."

Hayden turned to her. "But it would take a long time to dig a whole mountain."

"Based on how long this tribe has been guarding this place." Danica replied. "They had all the time they needed."

The trio dropped their examination and returned their gaze to the cave opening into the island mountain.

Danica felt her body twitch as she tightened for action. "I guess this means we're going in."

Hayden commented. "You know, in the movies, when I see the brave and ruggedly handsome archeologist heading into the dark temple in search of ancient horrors that a tribe has dedicated their lives to protect, I find myself thinking… 'What the Hell is wrong with you?'"

Carlos laughed. "Well, as I've been here before, I can tell you, I'm thinking the same thing."

"So…." Hayden posed it. "This is our last chance to turn and run people."

Danica looked to Carlos, then to Hayden and back to Carlos. She took a deep breath and declared. "We came this far. We need to see it through. And more importantly, we need to beat Maximus and his cohorts to the secret of this lost island."

"Even if it kills us?" Hayden joked.

Danica smiled confidently. "I have no plans to die today." She drew her weapon and held it at her side, lifting the safety.

Carlos held his shotgun aloft. "I can't say the same for the *Horror* though.'

Hayden grinned from ear to ear. "Then I guess its 'Tally Ho!" He declared, being the last to pull his weapon from the holster, ready and willing to fight.

And with that, the trio entered the island cave.

****

Unaware to the trio, high above, on the mountain side, observing from a small cliff ledge, something had watched them enter.

That same something later crept back inside to find them and stop them before they found the others.

36

Hayden stopped five feet into the cave entrance and held his hand up to Danica and Carlos in the rear, signaling for them to stop.

They halted in their tracks, pausing to listen, straining to hear anything.

When no sound followed, Danica asked with a whisper, "Why did you stop us?"

Hayden pointed to the wall before them, which seemed to divide their route into two equal paths, one left and one right. And because Hayden could see around the wall on both sides, both paths led to an equally large room behind.

But that was not what had attracted Hayden's attention.

Directly before him was a large stone tablet with inscriptions deeply engraved and painted or repainted recently. The first thing he noticed was unlike all the previous inscriptions he had come in contact with by the tribe or its predecessors, this one was not done as a part of the structure itself. Nor was it bolted, attached or engraved into the wall, but it was done as a separate and individual slab leaned up against the outcropping of solid rock in which it rested, a few feet into this particular cave. It was composed of a lighter coloured mineral, with speckles of crystal, which stood out significantly as not having originated here.

Hayden cautiously approached, knelt down on one knee and began to examine it. He ran his fingers over the edges, around the sides and brushed away bits of dried sulfur powder and salt from inside grooves and where it had dried onto the previous wet paint.

Carlos and Danica stood back and waited patiently, as much as they could, but due to where they were standing, even fully armed, it was a tall order.

After a good two minutes, Danica was feeling a slight tremor of annoyance, laced lightly by fear, so she asked Hayden, impatience in her tone. "Does this thing have any significance or what? I mean, I'd really like to get this show on the road? Don't you?"

Hayden, without turning, held two fingers up, gesturing to give him a few seconds. After a good minute, he replied. "Unlike the carvings above, this message was carved first and brought over here."

"So?" Danica queried curiously. "Is it important?"

"Well, it says a lot to me." Hayden stated, rising from his kneeling position. "It means whoever placed this here had no desire to be sitting here for any length of time doing the carving. They wanted to have it finished *before* coming to the island. This way, they could drop it off and leave it… and likely, very quickly."

"Another good reason we shouldn't be dilly dallying." Carlos threw in, still tempering his fear, keeping the barrel of his shotgun high, unsure why. "Let's get what we came for and get the Hell out of here."

Danica turned to Carlos, trying to sound sympathetic, but knowing she had to state a fact. "We still have to go deeper you know?"

"I'm aware of that Doctor Swift." Carlos bristled. "And that we came here to prevent your employers from getting the prize, and I plan to see it through. But standing here at the entrance and reading an ancient warning will not help us in the least."

Danica turned back to Hayden. "Is that what it says?"

Hayden shrugged. "Pretty much. Same standard warning that the fluid of life comes at a high cost." He gestured to the lower text. "But it also makes a special mention, which to me, almost reads like a fortune cookie."

"What do you mean by that?" Danica asked.

Hayden repeated what he translated. "It reads, 'Ask yourself the value of an extra year or an extra lifetime and weigh it against what you find. You may discover, death offers a sweeter release than survival.'"

Danica's face scrunched up with surprise. "If I ever got a fortune cookie with that message, I'd probably shove it up the waiter's butt."

Carlos nodded. "I second that. Not a future I would look forward to."

"It ends with, 'Let this Fountain of Life forever be forgotten.'" Hayden finished.

Danica curled her left eyebrow. "It almost sounds like they are referring to the Fountain of Youth again?"

"I assure you, it's not." Carlos said emphatically.

"I agree. But I think the message is supposed to denote a different meaning." Hayden responded.

"And that is?" Danica asked as she turned to Hayden.

Hayden hesitated and then offered his translation. "Paraphrased, I think it aims to say, 'Some things were never meant to be found.'"

At that, Carlos turned to stare at Hayden's face, realizing he was speaking seriously. He turned to the tablet. "It appears, even over the centuries, all who visit seem to voice the same thing."

"And here we are, looking for it." Hayden pointed out.

The trio remained quiet, none saying anything else.

What could they say.

They resumed their course into the cave.

As they moved, the trio changed up their positions. They maintained their triangular formation; now with Carlos at the front, Danica in the middle and Hayden at the rear as they delved deeper into the second cave system.

The flickering of the torch outside and orange glow on the stone walls started to pull back and fade away as they vanished deeper into the dark rocky expanse.

The trail inside was far less worn and beaten down than the one they took to get down to the lake. It was naturally jagged at points, smooth at others, with large bubble shaped pits the size of basketballs pressed deep in the rock face, both to the sides as well as the top and bottom, as though having been dribbled continually in a unending game until the divots were left as its signature.

The cave corridors were also smaller in size as the trio had to take most of them single file. Others were more narrow, enough so as to allow easy contact with both hands as they passed. At one point, they had to turn to their sides to slip through, Carlos muttering about lowering his bread intake when he returned home.

As they pressed on, not finding anything of note, the dread started flowing through their veins, both the fear of having found nothing and the concern they will. The sensation had a warm feel in their circulatory system, which resulted in the cooling of their outer skin, causing goose bumps to form. It also slowed their pulses and agitated their nerves erratically, causing the trio to become antsy, on edge, but ready to defend themselves.

Hayden had to set his safety back to the 'on' position, fearful he might pull the trigger at a wrong sound or someone in front of him coughing.

As they dropped over the next dip in the cave, almost immediately, Hayden raised his hand to his nose, lightly pinching it closed. "Do you smell that?" He sounded like he was speaking through a tube.

Danica turned back to him. "Why, did you *express* yourself?"

Hayden cocked his head with a grin, not releasing his nostrils. "If I did, you wouldn't have to ask." He paused to give her time to check for herself.

Both Carlos and Danica took a small whiff, afraid to breathe in too deeply. Both their noses scrunched up causing them to grimace.

"Wow. That is pungent." Danica declared, putting her hand to her face. "It smells like a combination of food going bad and or moldy cheese."

Carlos frowned, having a sudden feeling of Déjà vu, but no images came with it. "I smell something too, but it does not remind me of old clothes." He took another small intake of air through his nostrils. "And not a cheese I would be serving to any guests." He took one more small breath. "I can't say for certain, but it reminds me of body odour… And not the good kind."

"Is there ever a good kind?" Hayden asked.

Danica smiled. "You'd be surprised how a hot male body can smell alluring."

Both Carlos and Hayden snapped a look in Danica's direction.

"What?!" Danica glared at them both. "You asked."

Hayden turned away, trying to force his one eyebrow down in intrigue at Danica's last remark. He took another softer breath. "Whatever it is, it's everywhere. It's coming from practically every direction." He pointed to several holes in the rock for air to pass above and beside them, too small to use for travel, but too large to ignore.

Danica suddenly felt fearful. "Like we're surrounded?"

Carlos put his hand on Danica's shoulder. "No. There's no sound with it nor is the scent shifting in a way to denote an assailant in motion. With a smell such as that, if there was movement, it would heighten and lessen with its approach and egress. So whatever it is, it's stationary and creating the off-putting stink."

The trio tried to imagine what could generate the smell so powerfully and so easily.

No ideas came to them.

The trio continued deeper, trying very hard to ignore the stench.

Once around the next bend, to the right of the fork, Carlos placed his hand in front of Hayden to prevent him from stepping forward, gesturing to the ground.

Hayden stopped mid stride and looked. He knelt down and examined what Carlos had prevented him from stepping in.

It was one of the basketball holes which littered the entrance, but this one was filled with a blob of white jelly, slivers of yellow laced within it, extended up and out of the grove forming a bubble like lip around the edges.

Hayden tilted his head. "It looks like a balloon filled with a white liquid or something. And as it was half covered in dirt, it makes me think it was set as a trap."

The trio immediately looked around for the unknown Sentinel. After thirty seconds, they determined they were alone.

"I don't think it's a liquid." Carlos pointed to the ceiling.

Hayden and Danica looked skyward. There were two more such white pools, but upside down, not pouring out, glossy and shiny under the beams of their lights.

Danica stepped forward because this was more her area of expertise than theirs. She examined both pockets of white and then returned to the closer one on the ground. She extended her open hand and asked Hayden for one of his dirt brushes he used in excavation.

Hayden paused and handed it over reluctantly, unsure what she planned to do with it.

Danica wiped away most of the dirt, carefully caressing the top with the bristles, leaving the white half globe sticking up and in the air. She looked around the entire ball and surmised, "It's gelatinous it seems on the inside, whatever it is." She ran her finger over and around the edges, being very careful not to touch it. "But it's encased in what seems like a permeable shell. Clear, soft and probably easy to break. The substance inside could be a liquid, but then again, it could be a gas. And who knows what would happen when exposed to air." Danica stood up. "And I'm not too keen to puncture it in these conditions without knowing more about it."

Hayden was not listening. He was reaching for the second one on the ceiling.

Danica grabbed his hand and pulled it down with a violent tug. "What are you doing?"

Hayden jerked his arm away a bit miffed. "I was…"

"You were going to do what I just suggested might not be wise?" Danica cut him off with authority. "Plus how do we know that's not the *Horror* itself?"

Hayden dropped his hands to his sides. "I doubt it."

"I doubt it too." Danica stated. "But since we still have no idea what IT is, let's not go poking anything we don't recognize until we're certain."

Hayden chastised himself for what he almost did. *'Good advice.'*

Danica shook her head and they got back into formation.

The trio carefully stepped over the bubbles of white and continued downward until they found a pile of old ripped and torn clothing in front of a dark cave opening. It hung haphazardly on the ground, looped over an outcropping of rock.

Danica moved to the front of the group, dropped down and examined the strange patch of material. She picked it up using the wooden pointed end of Hayden's brush.

It was a deep cherry red, not bigger than a small hand towel, with white stitching, worn down from years of wear, with several rips and holes in it. There were several small holes and with each opening, a dark stain surrounded it.

"It's old." Danica noted. She held it up to her face and sniffed lightly. "It smells like... copper."

"Copper?" Carlos asked. "From the lake?"

"Could be, but unlikely." Danica rose. "But I more suspect its blood. Not entirely fresh, but not too old either." As she stood, she took a gentle step back, unaware of the loose shale beneath her tread. A small chunk of stone collapsed beneath her heel, taking her off balance. Danica fell backwards into the cave opening, disappearing into the darkness, rolling back over shoulder, three full rolls, her shoulders taking the full brunt of each rock she passed over, until she came to a complete stop at the bottom with a muscle wrenching crash.

Carlos and Hayden were in quick pursuit, chasing her spinning light beams down the forty-five degree incline until they found themselves at her feet.

Carlos extended his hand and helped Danica up.

It was then they realized they were standing in a much larger chamber than the rock corridors they had traveled down to get here.

It was as wide as half a football field, the ground clear of debris, but smelling of animals.

Hayden noticed it right away. "Now it smells like a barn. Combined with B.O."

Carlos had not noticed, more concerned with other matters. He asked Danica. "Are you okay Doctor Swift?"

Hayden suddenly realized. "I'm sorry." Feeling genuinely remorseful at his tact. "Did you hurt anything?" Looking to Danica.

"Just my pride." Danica had picked herself up, brushing off dirt and rocks. She noticed a corner of her shirt had ripped. She put her finger through the tear, but before she could examine it, they all heard it.

Deep, slow and heavy. Very clearly, something breathing. A lot of something breathing. Laboured, tight and from all around them.

And it was easy to determine, it was not their own.

Within seconds, all three had their weapons drawn and at ready. They triangle stance formed, each staring out in a different direction, but covering off any form of frontal assault.

All three of them aimed their lights upward and around the huge cave, dimly illuminating the entire structure.

The chamber was massive as they suspected. Standing at over one hundred metres tall, dry and yet muggy, it was an odd combination of shapes and worse, smelling of animals.

The walls were filled with holes, crevices, caves and exits to both deeper into the island or higher into the mountaintop. It looked like a combed hive with the exception there were no honey or bees.

Carlos was looking for it, having heard the intake and outtake of breaths, yet holding his own. His body shivered uncontrollably. He quickly grasped at his arm to regain a semblance of control, but moreover, to prevent himself from pulling the trigger.

The trio stood back to back and waived their lights over the holes. Many of them were filled, all with large furry balls, moving up and down in a slow repetitive pattern, bodies of animals breathing, sleeping deeply, all facing inward into their natural dug homes.

Hayden let his beam settle on the closest one. "You've got to be kidding me? Bears? The *Horror* is a mountain full of bears?" He laughed quietly. "And they're not even big bears. The biggest one I see is about the size of a Labrador at best."

Carlos on the other hand was trying to remember. He had no recollection of bears being on the island. But then again, he could not remember anything. If anytime was a good time to have a flashback, he was hoping for one now.

None came.

Carlos theorized if there were enough of them, they could be a murderous pack, chomping and ripping away on his flesh, but he doubted he would have been institutionalized for decades because of bear attacks.

Combined with, how would they have anything to do with his miraculous survival? It did not make any sense.

Carlos whispered to Hayden. "Do you think it's wise to be beaming our lights into their sleeping quarters?"

Hayden replied. "You heard the tribe. They sleep for months at a time. Plus bears are extremely heavy sleepers. Most hibernating animals are not disturbed by light." He lowered his goggle lights, seeing it was disconcerting to Carlos.

Carlos shivered. "Well for the sake of decorum, let's try not to wake them up."

Danica on the other hand stared in quiet contemplation, her eyes squinting under the beams of her lights, slowing running her examination over the forms, some too high up even for the best bears to climb, the hairs on the back of her neck rising.

Something was wrong.

Terribly, terribly wrong.

37

At that precise moment, she was not Danica Swift, friend, fighter, adventurer nor seeker of lost legends.

She was Doctor Danica Swift, field microbiologist, PhD, specialist in the scheme of modern lifeforms, domiciled and wild, and the environment for which they live.

Being a field microbiologist for a large pharmaceutical firm was not a task for the faint at heart. There was no course offered in Universities with text books that started with "Encyclopedia of All Things Undiscovered."

So to be sent out into the deepest and darkest jungles of the world, where few humans dared to tread and to be able to recognize, understand and procure the unfounded and undiscovered was momunmental. Either in the form of natural miracle cures or untapped reserves of biological wonders, a field specialist had to dedicate their lives to learning all there is to know of all the things that were already found.

Everything most investigative researchers, scientist or doctors did not have the time or inclination to spend hours toiling through databases to match what they discovered to what was already documented.

So a field microbiologist's memories were their greatest tools. The ability to recognize the nuances of difference, either in flora, animal or insect life to find that what has remained hidden to mankind until they came upon it.

No doctor wants to be the one to come forth from the jungle yelling in joy. *'My God! You won't believe it. I found penicillin.'* And a few seconds later, have to ask. *'What Scotsman? Alexander Fleming who? Nobel Laureate in 1928 for discovering what? Ah Crap.'*

Such errors could destroy careers.

So Doctor Danica Swift had to be able to analyze, understand and determine in seconds, with all the life the earth had to offer, what was new and what was not, by comparison of all the fields she had studied and kept filed in her brain.

So in those seconds, as she stared around the chamber and the slumbering forms, a connection was made. And when she made it, she said the only thing that came to mind. "Holy sweet Mary mother of shit and assholes with a serious side of mother fucking fuckity-fuck-fuck-fuck and extra fuck-fuck."

Even with the heavy breathing in the chamber, everything seemed to go even more silent as Hayden and Carlos both turned and stared wide-eyed at Danica.

"Who the Hell are you?" Hayden asked "And what did you do with Danica?" Even Hayden could not hide the total shock in his face, a look shared by Carlos.

Carlos and Hayden could see Danica's face was ashen white, pale as though what blood she had in her cheeks had been drawn down to each of her lower extremities to warm her suddenly chilled looking form.

Danica did not answer right away, as her head snapped both left and right, looking high and low, checking and rechecking the cavern walls as though a second look could counter her original assessment. With each sweep of her lights, her view of what she had confirmed remained as originally derived.

Before Hayden could ask again, he remembered what Danica told them when they had been standing over the chamber door before this adventure began.

'Oh I swear. But trust me, when I do, there'll be a very good reason for doing it.'

Danica had no time for humour. She knew she had to tell her friends before it was too late. "They're not bears."

Hayden replied. "Excuse me?"

Carlos felt his blood run cold.

Danica was already at zero degrees, her teeth chattering lightly whenever she paused for a breath. "They're not bears." She took a step back, her weapon fully drawn and in her hand. "They're spiders. Big mother fucking spiders."

Whatever sarcastic remark Hayden imagined had dissolved in his mind. He stared around the cave at the large slowly pulsing forms, sound asleep in their crevices, breathing deeply and heavily. His mouth opened and closed again. He looked closer, each time, his eyes squinting that much tighter, as though he could zoom in with supervision. After a good solid minute, he turned back to Danica in utter astonishment. "That's not possible." Saying it more for himself than for her as he could not, did not want to believe it. But then turning to give another freaked out look.

Before coming to South America, Hayden read some guides on creatures to look out for as a possible deterrent, but it was rudimentary review at best. Since this was Danica's area of expertise, he would normally defer to her, but he was having serious reservations with her conclusion.

Carlos on the other hand was paralyzed by fear. He knew with all his heart and soul she was right. That and he knew damn well being trapped in a nest with these monsters, for seven days, thirty years shaved away from his mind was not impossible.

The trio had banded together, their flashlight beams piercing skyward into the upper ceiling of the chamber, their converging beams intensifying the glow to reach that much higher.

They could see it.

They could all see it.

Webbing. Sheets of it, long silky blankets of swishing silk draped over the sides, dangling from the middle with elongated white ropes running from edge to edge, crisscrossing and drooping down like tired ghosts too exhausted to scare, unaware just being there was frightening enough.

As Hayden's scope of vision continued to move from crevice to opening, his blood was getting colder, slowing down like a river freezing in winter temperatures until he finally spoke. "But there are at least a hundred of these things in here. And this is only one small chamber of probably many." Hayden was still refusing to voice Danica's assertions aloud as though giving voice to it made it true. Plus he felt he had to argue it, if for no other reason, he was terrified beyond any stretch of the imagination. "Spiders are solitary creatures. They neither live nor hunt in packs."

Danica gestured about the room. "Think about it. For one, this is obviously a species we've never seen. More importantly, remember the lake of boiling water with acidic qualities? They have nowhere to go. If they've been here for centuries, likely millennia in my estimates, possibly longer, they would have to adapt to one another. They'd have no choice. Chances are, like the tribe said, feeding on their own young when food was not readily available, but learning to live together if for no other reason than to survive." She remembered a news article she read once. "A few years back, in Pakistan, flood waters drove millions of spiders into trees where they encased entire foliage's in ten to fifteen foot balls of webbing filled with spiders. This was where they were forced to reside until the water levels dropped. Make no mistake, if they had to form a hive to exist and survive, they would do it."

Hayden pointed with his hand, trying to keep the light beams away from the eye lines of the creatures, as though now concerned it could wake or stir them from their heavy slumber. "But they're as big as dogs. Some are bigger. Spiders don't grow that big!" He was speaking with hope in his tone.

Carlos was trying not to hyperventilate, but he was remembering. It was coming back. Not a lot, but seven days of darkness, legs running all over him, something constantly stabbing at him and being pumped with something both miraculous and horrifying.

Danica interjected. "Remember the Great White Shark. Millions of years ago, there were bigger ones, the Megladon Carcharodon, which based on scientific records, could have been near twenty times the size."

"I'm not a math whiz, but these things are bigger than fucking ten to twenty times." Hayden argued, swearing resumed in his language.

Danica snapped. "And what, you have God's rule book of what can grow big and what can't?"

Hayden grimaced, not liking when his own arguments were used against him.

Carlos gestured to them both, his face ashen. "Why don't we take this away from here? I find arguing in a room full of giant sleeping spiders a bit on the nerve racking side."

At this, they all agreed.

The trio turned in the direction Danica had fallen from and the men had chased her down.

Danica flashed her beam over the wall of four different caves. She stared at the rock floor surface which showed no scuffs, piles of dirt or trail validating which one of the four they had entered through. She looked to Carlos. "I don't suppose you have a copy of the island's cave system do you?"

Carlos looked up with a hint of desperation. "Sorry. If there's a chamber for that, it hasn't been discovered yet."

Hayden spat from behind. "Great. Just great." Followed by, "Fuck!"

38

Finding their way into a small crevice outside of the main hive, the trio re-converged.

Hayden felt decidedly safer, even if only by a mere fraction. "I guess we can look at the bright side. We didn't wake any of them up."

Danica shook her head. "That chamber out there is only about one hundred feet high. This island itself is a mile in length, half a kilometer tall and God knows how deep. There have to be at least a dozen, if not more of these chambers."

Hayden glared at her. "Let's stay with the bright side shall we?"

Carlos remained completely quiet, both trying to remember what happened the last time he was here, as much as he was trying to forget.

Hayden turned to Carlos. "Carlos?"

Silence.

"Earth to Carlos." Hayden repeated. "We could really use you right now."

Carlos was shaken out of his reverie. "My apologies. I found myself..." He swallowed hard. "Trying to remember back to my previous encounter here and how I found my way out, even if I was carried." His words were mere whispers, softened by fear. "I find myself short in that regard."

Danica placed her hand on his forearm. "Right now, I'd prefer you stay with us in the present. If we found our way down, we can find our way up."

"It's a one in four pick. Three now as this one led us here." Hayden noted gesturing to the chamber they were in. "So of the three, we preferably want the one we took when we arrived, the one least occupied by you know what."

In that, the trio agreed.

Thinking of the cavern they exited, the size of the island and likely how many more such caverns existed based on Danica's estimations, Hayden stated aloud. "I wish we brought more bullets."

Carlos turned to him with a frown and spoke with a depressed tone. "Not to rain on your parade Doctor Lattimer, but I don't think we have enough boats to carry what we needed."

Hayden knew Carlos was right.

Danica interrupted them both after listening to their ideas. "Before we plan our all-out assault on this little nightmare army, why don't we keep with the original premise of trying very hard not to wake them and escape. Remember what the Elder said, the *Horror...*" For several seconds, she paused, finally understanding and most certainly agreeing with their deemed name. "... Sleep sound and heavy. Likely due to the lack of food. Early risers would tend to starve faster. So as long as we keep to ourselves, remain quiet and get out of here, we can leave this place behind... and alive."

"What about the Sentinels?" Hayden asked. "There are two awake at this very moment according to the Elder and prancing about the place." He looked at his watch. "Based on the time we've been in here, one or both have to be aware of our presence."

Carlos was hoping that was not true. "How do we deal with them?"

"Avoidance at all costs." Danica ordered with firmness in her tone.

Hayden gently placed his hand on Danica's shoulder. "Carlos and I find ourselves a tad bit ill prepared." He spoke kindly. "Knowledge is power and you're our resident expert. Anything you can offer us about our enemy might make us feel like we have a greater chance for survival. Even if only in our minds."

Danica completely understood. Confidence bred strength. She knelt to one knee and drew a picture of one of the *Horror* in the grainy sand on the floor, not worried as the Elders did of creating its likeness. She pointed to the shape as she etched, depicting what she had observed. "Technically speaking, by their large bulb shaped abdomen and the segmented legs, of what I could see anyway, as one was half in and out of its crevice, they appear to be of the *Theraphosidae* family of spiders. Or in common language, a typical tarantula."

Hayden chuffed with sarcasm. "Your and my definition of *typical* wildly differs sweetheart."

"Size notwithstanding Dumbass." Danica sniped back, rolling her eyes. "Fact one. They're very fast, completely predatory and have a remarkably advanced sense of smell."

"Good start." Hayden chided. "Let us know how much better they are than us."

Carlos gritted his teeth imagining their speed and being chased through the caves.

"If you don't know what they can do, you can't hope to avoid it." Danica pointed out.

Hayden nodded. "Understood. Keep going."

"Try to avoid physical contact with the *Horror*, even the sleeping ones." Danica explained.

"No issue there." Hayden replied. "Our sleeping…"

Danica cut him off. "Not because you could wake them, but because of those." She pointed to a thin layer of dried hairs on the ground.

Carlos and Hayden's eyes shot downward.

Hayden's beams outlined a small pile of thin hairs around the edges of the cave. "And what are they?"

Danica waved her hand over them, careful not to touch them. "They're called *urticating* hairs. It's a defense mechanism." Without making contact, she ran her finger along a few of their lengths. "They're barbed, not unlike a thorn and penetrate quickly. Based on their size and length, they would be very painful if they get under your skin." Danica made a motion of throwing. "Tarantulas tend to kick them off from behind or when they graze up against you. But if they're that close, you have bigger issues to contend with."

Hayden grimaced. "Great. Even their hair is dangerous."

Carlos had no memory of the hairs, but could recall itching a great deal.

Danica stood and was about to describe another feature when she froze.

Carlos saw this and his ears perked up. After a minute, he whispered. "There's something in here with us."

In seconds, all weapons were drawn and the trio were back to back, each facing out in triangular formation, able to shoot in any direction of an attack.

The trio all went quiet and listened.

It was breathing. Labored, slow, but not as heavy as in the chamber they had exited. Their fears rose at the thought one of the two Sentinels were in there with them, making all their blood run cold.

When nothing launched itself at them from the darkness, Danica turned around, her lights moving up and along the rear wall. She could see what appeared like dozens of cubby holes and almost half of them were filled with webbed sacks. Only one was dragged out and in the middle of the floor at the rear corner. It's white bag moving up and down near the middle, slow and erratic.

Hayden asked, his concern rising. "Is it an egg sack?"

Danica shook her head. "No. They are more rounded, usually sealed up against a wall or in a hole for security. Considering the cannibalistic nature of spiders and the lack of food here, most mothers would never leave their sack alone."

Carlos gave another peer around, his shotgun aimed and ready to fire, searching just in case Mama was still in residence.

Danica moved in.

It was not a Sentinel, but it was equally disturbing.

As the trio approached the corner, they found the sack was laid out on an elevated flat rock tableau. It was a white cocoon, six foot five in length, with a pair of leather boots, long faded, turned up and ripped at the edges. Some points seemed chewed with cowhide slivers dangling out of the base. The rest of the body was encased in the webbing.

Hayden found himself cringing. "My God. It's a person isn't it? Please don't tell me it's still alive?"

Danica, without speaking, drew a thin scalpel from her medical research pack, it having been placed within a folded leather wallet for such purposes. She donned a pair of surgical gloves and ran the thin razor sharp blade carefully from head to chest at the middle of the webbing, only millimeters deep to prevent harming the person inside. She made another incision at the top, forming a "T" pattern, so she could pull the white mesh open and outward to both sides at a forty-five degree angle, revealing the face within.

A bearded face stared up her, face pale, eyes wild and laced with bloodshot. His mouth opened to scream, but all that came out was a dry rasp.

Before anyone could speak, Carlos pushed Danica out of the way and dropped to one knee, his eyes welling with tears. "My God." He did the sign of the cross, both over his body and the one before him. "You poor bastard."

Hayden was silent, as was Danica.

After several seconds, Hayden posed the question. "Do you know him?"

Carlos sadly replied. "I do."

More silence.

"He's my savior." Carlos mumbled.

Hayden turned to Danica and mouthed the words, *'Jesus?'*

Danica silently responded back that Hayden should count himself very lucky he was not within punching range.

Carlos continued. "He's the man who saved my life and later became my friend. A friendship which ended when he went in search of this dreaded island over a hundred years ago." He paused caressing his brow. "It's Captain Estefan Rios."

Hayden and Danica looked on in total amazement and pure empathy, unable to imagine over one hundred years trapped in this manner.

The trio found themselves all gesturing the cross on their chests, unsure if anything else would do.

As Carlos bent over him, he lightly kissed Rios on the forehead, a tear tricking down his cheek to his fallen friend. "You damn fool."

Before anything else could be said, Hayden put his hand to his nose. He gestured to the wet patch at the midpoint under Rios' wrapped form, the webbing soaked brown and pink. "What is that?"

Danica and Carlos looked to the origin of the pool, following it via a thin wet trail leading behind the rocks. It ended at a much larger puddle, long dried with remnants of dark matter and moisture. It all lead down from the occupied cubbyholes, flowing away and smelling lightly of ammonia. The trail ended at hundreds of small cracks where it seemed to trickle down into and vanish.

Danica looked on with compassion. "It's waste. It appears the victims excrete their waste as a liquid."

"Lovely." Hayden shook his head. "I swear with each new discovery, it only makes this place more and more disgusting."

In that, they were all in agreement.

Danica knew, without solid food, the human body would have no other choice but to vacate its bowels in this manner. Again, remorse hardly met the level of feelings she had for this victim and likely many more.

Before anyone could move, Carlos reached behind to take the scalpel from Danica's open grip. With one swooping move, he ran the already made slit to Rios' waist.

"We need to save him." Carlos declared.

Hayden and Danica looked to one another, wondering how they were expected to carry him, let alone boat him across in this condition when Carlos suddenly reached inside the lower part of the cocoon and withdrew a huge Navy Cutlass.

Carlos stood and stared down at his friend. The man, who saved him from the oceans, madness and certain death and by his actions, was here today because of him.

Hayden looked at Carlos. "What are you going to do?" Figuring he was going to cut the rest of the webbing away.

In a quick gesture, Carlos pulled the sword over his head, its leather handle with an iron forged basket hilt slightly rusted from use held tight in his grip and he slammed it down into the upper chest of Captain Rios, twisting savagely when he hit the heart, ending his life.

Danica stared at Carlos horrified. She looked at him in utter shock and sputtered. "I thought you said you were planning to save him?"

Carlos released the sword, leaving it extended out of Rios' body. He turned to lock eyes with Danica, stoic and direct. "I did."

Danica remembered what the Elder told them the night before. *'No blood flow, no healing, no life.'*

Danica watched as the remaining light in Rios eyes flickered out. For a solid few seconds, she could almost see in those pools, him thanking them. She admitted to herself, Carlos probably did save Rios.

Hayden had turned away. Unlike Danica, he was not used to such bloodletting.

Danica turned to Carlos and asked him something Hayden did not hear.

Carlos leaned back. "He's an empty shell now. Learn what you can."

Danica knelt down. Ignoring the sword, she carved with her scalpel downwards to the stomach, pulling the ripped and torn clothing aside, filled with holes and likely fang tears.

Hayden had looked back and turned away again, this time totally aghast. "Seriously. Is this absolutely necessary?"

Danica shot back. "Yes it is. We'll never have an opportunity to do this again. Something is bothering me. Yes, I suspect the venom is obviously the key to the rapid healing trigger and prolonged aging, but it does not explain an important factor."

"What is that?" Hayden asked with incredulity, staring at the wall and seeing the remaining bodies, equally horrified.

Danica continued. "No matter how fast your body heals or how long you live, venom can't sustain a human body. I need to know how that is happening. Somehow, they're getting sustenance. I have a theory, but I need to be sure."

Hayden turned back, his eyes getting some curiosity now, but not looking down at Danica working. "What do you mean by sustenance?"

Danica was carefully carving around the inner chest and into the abdomen. "The symbols on the chamber stated the *Horror* feeds upon you, while you in turn feed upon it." She reached the stomach lining and sliced it open delicately. Inside was a dark gel, pasty and moist, filled with bits of hair and remnants of sedimentary solids. She scooped up a finger full, bringing the mass up to her nose. She smelled it.

Carlos watched with some reservation.

Hayden on the hand was pulling further back. "If I'm next, I'll pass."

Danica snapped her fingers and let it drop back into the corpse. She double checked and saw the same dark matter trickled from the veins, through the circulatory system into the lower cavity. Her eyes widened. "They're being fed intravenously."

Carlos looked down at the dark pools in the body of blood. "How is that possible?"

Danica stood up, reached into her pack and withdrew the silk wrapped claw Carlos had given her on the plane.

The one Rios found on the Leviathan embedded into the railing.

Danica looked down at the corpse again and reexamined the double tubules in the claw. Her eyes expanded even more, starting to comprehend. She looked to Hayden and Carlos. "My God. I think I understand now." Leaning against the wall, Danica felt a fleck of gravel run down her back, giving her the '*heebie-jeebies*' for a second. She brushed it off quickly. "It's the only factor that would explain everything." Her whole body shivered uncontrollably.

"What?" Hayden asked again. He watched Danica with fascination, her scientific mind at work.

"It's not a claw. It's chelicerae." Danica held it up for them to see it as she did...

Hayden and Carlos looked at her with bafflement.

Hayden casually smiled. "Duh... Want to dumb it down a bit for us 'non-field microbiologists?'"

Danica turned it over, letting her lights beam down the thin holes. "Chelicerae are the pointed appendages spiders use to grasp their food. Like mandibles. Some are hollow like this and contain venom glands to inject venom into their prey."

Carlos shook deeply imaging how many times one of those fangs was pushed into his body.

Hayden on the other hand raised his eyebrow. "So their life sustaining venom is injected through their fangs. I figured that already because they're spiders and all when you first mentioned it, but how does that explain them being fed intravenously."

Danica looked at him, realizing neither of them understood what she was comprehending, but she was thinking how best to explain it. "It's a form of symbiosis." She paused changing her train of thought. "Scratch that. Though both the *Horror* and the prey benefit in some way, this is more an ecto-parasitic relationship as the prey's longevity is more a punishment than a gift."

Carlos was listening with both rapt and horrified interest, but having no idea what he was being told.

"With ecto-parasitic bonds, the *Horror* need to keep their victims alive though exterior invasion..." Danica sounded fascinated. "So it's more biotrophic than necrotrophic."

Hayden repeated himself louder this time. "DUH! Come on Danica. Help a few cavemen out."

It had been a long time since Danica had to lecture someone and being scared did not help the matter. "Necrotrophic relationships involve the parasite eventually killing their host. Biotrophic on the other hand rely on their host surviving. And with the miracle venom healing all wounds and injuries, they can keep victims alive for unknown amounts of time."

Carlos felt the terror of his ordeal becoming more real. "But how do they keep their victims alive? You just said with the vaunted high speed healing they need to be sustained. How do all these victims..." He pointed to the breathing sacks. "...survive for years in here without dying of starvation or dehydration?"

Danica gestured to the ground. "Notice there is no waste or feces from the spiders? Either on the ground or in the passages?"

Hayden was still lost. "Lack of shit?! We're looking for shit now? I still don't see how that is relevant."

Danica scowled and then explained. "Spiders are still living things. So it has to dispose of its waste somehow."

Hayden knew he was going to regret asking it. "So where is the shit?"

"The second tubule in the chelicerae." Danica's whole body shook from core to skin as she pointed. "When you're in its grip, after it delivers its venom, while it's drinking you up, it's delivering its waste back into your body through the other tubule. It's evolutionarily perfect. It's not unlike an IV drip, just working in two ways, one to drain the fluid while the other replaces it by providing the proteins its victims need and the spiders don't, sustaining their lives."

Hayden completely understanding now, his face curled up in abject dismay. "Are you kidding me?"

Danica pointed to the fang. "One is intake and one is outtake."

"Let me get this straight." Hayden was more scared than he was arrogant, but he was keeping it under wraps. "These things encase you in its webbing until you expire, trapped in the dark, their venom giving you super life and in return, they pump you full of their shit as food."

"You have an amazing way to turn a miracle into something crude." Danica replied. "But that pretty much sums it up."

Hayden declared. "You know, if we combine arachnophobia, fear of spiders, claustrophobia, fear of being trapped in small places and finally, Phagophobia, fear of being eaten into a one word disorder, we could rename this evil little island."

Carlos was looking down at Rios' body. "Doctor Swift. I should mention something."

Danica turned to him. "What?"

Carlos gestured. "Since I saw him last, I have physically aged thirty to forty years."

"Yes?" Danica asked, wondering where this was leading.

Carlos frowned. "By my estimates and from my recollection of having seen him last, Rios has barely aged a day."

Danica looked down at Rios and understanding. "It appears as long as you have a fresh dose of the venom, your life expectancy is greater than for example ones like Carlos who escape."

Hayden asked the question. "Then how long would you live alive in here with a constant dose of this venom?"

Danica did not have an answer.

All three of them fell silent, their blood running ice cold, imagining the life expectancy of the poor souls trapped down here to be kept as food.

Danica finally turned to Hayden. "I take back what I said on the plane."

"Take back what?" Hayden asked. "That you thought I was immature? That I can be an idiot? That I drink too much?"

Danica shook her head. "No. I still stand behind those."

Carlos laughed quietly, thoroughly amused they could still have humour at a time like this.

"I said I disagreed with you." Danica commented with conviction. "But I now stand corrected. This is *Hell*."

39

Danica removed her surgical gloves and tossed them to the side of the cave making a wet smack at they landed. Littering was the least of her worries. "That's likely the real reason for the Sentinels. They don't simply guard the nest while the rest hibernates; they are delegated to the duty of crawling through the cave chambers during the rest period to keep their prey pumped up with their protein filled waste for when the others do awaken." She shivered. "That and I suspect they probably freshen the web cocoons every couple of months."

Hayden looked to Rios' corpse and the remaining white mesh strands encompassing his legs. "What makes you say that?"

"For one, a hundred years of being cooped up in one of those sacks and it should stink a lot more. Humans if anything smell, especially over time. That and the mess from the release of the body fluids…" Danica pointed to the moist area on the ground where all the pools converged and trailed to the cracks on the floor. "Our vacating bowels would have saturated the entire cocoon by now if not cleaned or changed."

Hayden moved forward and spotted long flecks of hard white and yellowed chips. "And what are those?"

Danica picked them up, examined them and tossed them back down. "Fingernails. They probably break off when the webbing is redressed. I would not be surprised if hair growth diminished over time and fell off like the nails."

Carlos stared as his fallen friend. "When the Sentinels remove the webbing, why don't their victims try to escape? I mean, if it's just the Sentinels awake at the time, aren't they outrunning only the one, two at most?"

Danica gestured to the dark coloured sinew-like layers of muscle beneath the skin on Rios' arms and chest. "Atrophy. Regardless of how fast you heal, lack of use will deaden muscle tissue to the point of uselessness. After a certain period, your mind is basically living in a body that cannot do anything more than breathe." She shuddered uncontrollably as such a life sentence.

Hayden, not being an arachnologist, asked the question, "Why don't they just rip out of the webbing at the start? It's just spider webs isn't it?"

At this Danica seemed to stiffen. "Spider silk is stronger than you would think. Weight for weight, silk is stronger than steel and as many scientific studies have shown, spider silk has a tensile strength comparable to that of most high-grade alloy metals. So no, once you find yourself in this quantity of it, created by things of this size, there's no simply '*ripping*' free."

After listening to Danica's lecture, Hayden had only one thing to left say. "Up and until a few minutes ago, since I was a little boy, my greatest fear was being eaten alive by a Great White Shark. I always found the prospect of having been caught defenseless in the water, it coming up underneath me, snatching me up and chewing on my flailing body, even if only for a few seconds, unimaginably the worst fate that could befall my precious self. But based on what I've learned today, the price of immortality is having to spend the rest of your life as a webbed up drinking box for an island of these monsters, it makes my dark little shark fantasy my number two."

Danica grimaced as she shared the assessment. "Mine too."

Carlos on the other hand. "Mine already."

Silence.

Hayden looked to Carlos. "Let me tell you this, even twenty-four hours as a meal for one of those things my friend..." Hayden exhaled slowly. "I can tell you, I'd need a lot more than thirty years to recover."

Danica felt in her mind, far longer.

Hayden paused and added, speaking to Carlos with sympathy. "You're a better man than me."

Carlos felt somewhat uplifted by Hayden's words. "Thank you Doctor Lattimer, but I think you underestimate yourself."

Danica admitted Hayden was a lot stronger than he was giving himself credit for.

"What about weaknesses?" Hayden turned back to Danica resuming his focus. "Is there something we could exploit?"

Danica turned to them both and spoke like she was lecturing a class. "When I was studying for my doctorate, part of my studies required me to focus my area of expertise, to allow for greater career specialization. I chose plants and horticultural life. I did minor with insects, but I very specifically avoided spiders. Not because of their ability to find secrets within them, as one of my colleagues was doing some fantastic research with black widows and the anti-coagulating properties of their venom for use with heart attack patients, but I found spiders far too unpredictable. They are, in my estimate, the ultimate survivor. They're the most aggressive, vicious and cannibalistic carnivores on the planet. They kill without remorse and they're infinitely patient. Anything that can sit in a web and wait for hours for prey is truly terrifying to me." She took a quick breath. "Only humans are as close to them when it comes to waiting for food. Personally, I found any creatures such as this were too evil to be studied."

"So...." Hayden jibed. "No weaknesses then?"

Danica offered an almost sad look. She had no answer.

Carlos was taking slow and gentle breaths. At one point he was near hyperventilating at having imagined how different his life might have been had the tribe not had a debt to pay. He quickly changed his thought direction or he would end up a quivering mass on the floor. "Based on the tribe's stories, they've only been guarding this island for a few centuries, a thousand years tops. How could these things have lasted this long?"

Danica pursed her lips. "With this species, anything is possible. Spiders have been on the earth for millions of years. Some records show even as far back as sixteen million years. Remember, without food, they will eat each other."

Hayden quickly decided his learning lesson was at an end. "We came, we saw and we discovered the island's secret. And like Carlos said, it's not the Fountain of Youth. As far as I'm concerned, this little island of giant spiders and their miracle shit venom can all belong to Maximum Pharmaceuticals for all I care."

At this suggestion, Danica's eyes widened. She turned and stepped into the path of Carlos and Hayden ready to depart for the surface, her face pale and sullen. "We can't."

Carlos stared at her.

Hayden spoke instead. "What do you mean, we can't?"

"I mean. We can't let them have it." Danica looked like someone had walked over her grave. "I've worked for Maximus and Maxima for over a decade. They speak to religion a lot, but they're not zealots. They are money hungry and ruthless. In my mind, they're utterly insane, especially when it comes to miracles. They believe, truly believe, in the survival of the fittest."

At this Hayden shook his head. "So what's the worst that could happen? They find one of these things, steal its venom and come back with an army to kill the rest for their venom sacks."

Danica immediately recognized this would not be the route Maximus and Maxima would take. "There's no way they'll allow these things to die. If it truly extends life by an incalculable amount as I suspect, they will, to paraphrase a point, want to keep the well full. They'll do everything they can to keep the *Horror* alive."

Carlos, not a business man of the medical world felt compelled to ask. "To what end."

"Trust me. With this, they could make billions, if not more. As long as someone wants to live a little longer, they'll have customers." Danica replied..

Hayden raised an eyebrow. "But how could they possibly expect to control these conditions? It's not entirely ideal."

"They won't think that way." Danica surmised. "First, they'll never run the operation out of South America. Were the government here to discover what these things can do, regardless of the countless victims, the politicians will seize the creatures for themselves. Maximum Pharmaceuticals would never take the risk of allowing a billion dollar asset to be removed from their complete control." She was still ashen. "Whoever holds the key to eternal life, or even a very long life, can control the world. Which means only one thing, they'll want to take these things off the island."

"The tribe will never allow it." Hayden pointed out.

"Regardless of the tribe's healing abilities, unlike the warriors of yesteryear..." Danica referring to Carlos' old crew. "Maximus would come back with weapons that would kill so fast, the tribe would have no time to heal."

Carlos admitted, with today's weaponry, the tribe would be easy prey.

"Second, they would need to get these things locked up and out of sight fast." Danica pointed out. "One bleeding heart, reporter or animal rights activist could halt any action they would take. I mean, regardless of the *Horror*'s modus operandi, Maximum Pharmaceuticals keeping these things for the purposes of draining their fluids forever for corporate gain would be alarming to any consumer group or country."

Hayden and Carlos could offer nothing to this argument.

Danica was starting to warm again, red flowing into her once pale cheeks. "Be it God, Evolution or plain old bad luck for these things, this lake of acid is here for a reason, if only to keep them away from the world. And I, for one, think it should stay that way."

Hayden looked to the exit. "So if one escaped, would the army not quickly find it and kill it?"

"Eventually, possibly. But what if that one escapee was a pregnant female?" Danica asked with a dark suggestion to her words. "One tarantula can release over three thousand eggs in a single cycle. God knows how many these things lay. One pregnant adult female, in the world, would have an army of these things in under a year. My God, humanity would be destroyed in less than two or three generations."

Carlos and Hayden started to envision what terrified Danica so.

Danica continued. "Have you ever heard the quote from Capri, "If spiders were the size of cats, there would be no mankind. Well these monsters are a Hell of a lot bigger than cats and that's only the ones we've seen so far. There could be thousands of these spiders below and a lot bigger than the ones up here."

Hayden pointed out the obvious. "Problem is... Maximus and his brood are already in the cave system above us. Do you really think they'll give up after a few days?" He asked. "They're going to find this island eventually."

Danica winced. "This is a nightmare of epic proportions."

Hayden added. "Plus we have no idea how many other people they told."

At that Danica seemed to brighten. "I can guarantee, they've told no one. Trust me. When I spoke to Mr. Darby the other day, he was furious. His was doing his best to protect the company stock from hemorrhaging with the disappearance of the top two executives with no means of contact. For the Thornes, this is a family mission. Until they secure the find, which they still think is the Fountain of Youth; they aren't sharing this with anyone."

"What do you propose? We're not exactly cold blooded killers." Hayden offered. "We can't just wait at the bottom and shoot them as they enter."

Carlos interjected. "Speak for yourself. I'll do it and we can drop their corpses into the acid lake for all eternity."

Hayden and Danica turned in Carlos' direction with deep scowls.

"Let's call that plan 'B.'" Hayden quickly retorted. "We'll just put 'B' in the bank for now."

Carlos shrugged. "I'm simply saying."

Danica tried a different tact, thinking as a scientist. "There must be a way to destroy all these things."

Hayden offered a shake of his head. "The tribe claim they've tried for years. Like you said, these things adapt and survive. And I can assure you, something that has been around for sixteen million years, won't go easily."

Danica had a wild idea. "This lake is obviously deep right? And this is an island... And I'm damn sure something this big doesn't float. So that stands to reason something beneath it is holding it up. What if we put enough explosives under it to destroy the foundation and sink the entire thing into the boiling water? Once the island was submerged, it would pour down each and every hole, cave and crevice turning this entire place into a massive lobster pot, killing the *Horror* and all their trapped victims."

Hayden was wide eyed, impressed but still stunned. "That's a huge operation. Months of planning, mining, digging and placing the explosives. And how are we supposed to swim to the bottom of a lake of boiling water with an acidic quality to plant explosives?"

Danica looked at Hayden. "I only come up with the ideas, not implement them."

Carlos smiled gently. "My resources are vast and be assured, over a hundred years of investing notwithstanding, there are two things of bigger concern. One, I doubt we could pull it off before the Thornes either found this place or discovered its secret." He looked to her with genuine sympathy. "Plus none of us are structural engineers. We would need specialists to assist. And if you start moving that much machinery or explosives into South America, the bigger problem surfaces, the government would find out. And as horrible as these monsters are, someone will dedicate themselves to protecting them. Or worse, they would want to exploit them."

Danica felt the wind drift from her sails. "It was just an idea."

Carlos consoled her. "And a very creative one. But the most important factor here, the force and the quantity of explosives required to sink the island, even if it could be done, would likely bring down the roof above before it sunk. Many of the ancient columns and pilasters, even tipped over, could reach the upper cave structure. Be assured, if these things have a choice between drowning in boiling acid or getting to the top and out into the world, they'll climb. Spiders if anything are damn good climbers."

Danica could suddenly picture a giant crack in the Earth falling inward and creating a mile wide crater in the middle of the deepest part of the Amazon Jungle and it suddenly filling with hundreds if not thousands of hungry giant spiders in search of new homes and food.

It would make their believed destruction of the ancient chamber nothing more than a small fleck on the South American government's radar when the entire country's populace would be at war with a newly discovered prehistoric arachnid species fighting for dominion whose venom kept their citizens alive for centuries as food.

And that would only prelude the chaos once they expanded to rest of the world.

Hayden lowered his gaze to Rios' expired form. "Well that leaves us with a pickle. How do we stop your employers from stealing a spider community that can grant immortality by its venom? Or by the same token, convince them to leave for fear once broken free could lead to the demise of all of mankind?"

"They're no longer my employer." Danica snapped.

"That is entirely regrettable Doctor Swift." Resonated the voice of Maximus from the darkness of the entrance they originally came through, causing the trio to turn at his unexpected arrival. He entered, carefully activating the light on his headpiece, a single bulb spotlight affixed to a metal construction helmet not unlike those used in mining, a light he had obviously extinguished to eavesdrop on their conversation. "You will be entirely missed at the company Christmas party."

Standing behind him was Maxima and their two sons, also turning on their helmet lamps, filling the chamber with a spotlight luminance in every direction.

Maximus raised his right hand. In it was a high powered semi-automatic rifle which looked small in his massive palm. "Now if you please, lower your weapons before I decide to let you join your friend behind you." Motioning to Rios.

The trio suddenly felt their universe close in on them.

Out of the frying pan and into the fire.

40

The trio stared down the foursome before them, the family Thorne.

Maximus was front and centre, Maxima to his immediate left, and in behind, their two sons. They were all dressed from head to toe in black; heavy wool sweaters, matching denim pants, finger cut leather gloves with open and exposed phalanges for easier motion with mid-calf military boots laced to the top. All of their clothes were pulled and stretched taut around each of their powerfully built frames. Atop their heads, unlike the trio, metal hard hat helmets with a single illuminated bulb set high, front and middle atop the cap, with the light beaming forward. All were equally armed with semi-automatic hand held weaponry with long clips.

At this range, none could miss.

Only the second son in the rear wore something different, a metal T-brace across the bridge of his nose supported by his forehead. It had white foam pressed loosely under the metal frame exposing the fresh black and blue bruising beneath, protecting an obvious fractured nose.

Hayden was dumbstruck. "How the Hell did you find the way down here?"

Maximus grinned, his gun still leveled on the trio. "Down here? I admit, we were well lost... But then..." Maximus held his Smartphone up and pointed to Danica. "YOU showed me the way."

Hayden turned to Danica, eyes scrunched in disbelief, shocked that she could have sold them out.

Maximus smiled viciously when he saw Hayden's reaction. "As much as I would love to sew the seed of discord between my two doctors...." He was far too proud of having outwitted them. "Doctor Swift's cell phone is the paid property of Maximum Pharmaceuticals. The moment you all entered the caverns, your phone networked with ours and the map was shared with one download." He nodded to Danica. "Thank you by the way."

Danica glared, more annoyed at herself for not knowing that nor turning the feature off in the first place.

Carlos on the other hand had his attention on the two sons. He could tell by the way they moved, they were the two who had attacked him in London and stolen his journal pages. That and the one's nose clearly showed the signature of Doctor Swift's recently delivered perfect front kick.

Hayden turned to the two men in behind with a grin. "I preferred the ski masks by the way. In fact..." He started patting down his khaki side pockets. "I may even have one with me..." He paused and then sighed. "Wait a minute. I only have one. I guess there's no point really since covering one of your ugly mugs will still leave the other." Hayden turned to Danica. "Did I mention I hate identical twins?"

Danica snickered to herself, amazed at Hayden's bravado.

"I hate all twins." Carlos threw in as he glared in the direction of Maximus and Maxima, appalled at the abomination of their relationship.

The sons, though genuinely angry at the insult, remained stationary, letting their father hold the stage.

Maximus proudly spoke, keeping control. "I guess formal introductions are in order. Meet our two sons, Max and Maxwell."

Hayden let out a suppressed burst of laughter. "Seriously? Max and Maxwell? So it wasn't just the Leviathan's Logbook and the survivor's journal missing pages, your baby naming book was shy a few as well."

Maxima face scrunched up in annoyance. "A Legacy is born in a name."

"So are assholes." Hayden retorted. "As my father would say, it's simply a matter of who's writing the history books. But for the sake of distinction, you don't mind if I call them Fuck and You." He looked to them again. "Doesn't really matter which one is which does it?"

Max and Maxwell oozed fury from their eyes.

Maxwell, the one without the face shield, took a step forward.

Maximus raised his hand, gesturing for him to hold his position. "For a man who can eloquently speak and translate dozens of ancient languages, you seem to utilize a great deal of abusive slang."

"It's a form of expression." Danica defended.

Hayden shrugged, pointing to Max and Maxwell and then letting out a slew of jumbled sounds and phrases, not unlike the tribal Elder from the night before, but oddly different.

Maxwell asked with a snarl. "What the Hell was that supposed to mean?"

Hayden smiled. "If you thought my slang was abusive, what I just called you in ancient Aramaic is far worse."

Maxwell, nostrils flaring beneath the metal brace, pointed at Hayden, still standing behind Max. "I told you this wasn't over."

"Is that what you said? I don't remember it that way." Hayden remarked. "Why don't you turn around, put your tail between your legs and run away. Then as you do it, repeat what you just said. I might remember it better if it happened the same way."

Maxwell glowered and skulked in with his fists clenched, stopped again in his tracks by a look from Maximus.

Hayden watched in amusement.

Maxwell slunk back to his position sufficiently chastened.

Maximus spoke to his sons. "Doctor Lattimer has some use... for now." He then turned to Carlos, but speaking to Hayden and Danica. "The two of you I had expected to have to deal with at some point, but what possessed you both to bring along Mr. Santiago?"

Hayden shrugged in a non-committing manner. "He had something we needed."

Carlos casually looked in Hayden's direction.

Maximus appeared curious. "And pray tell, what was that?"

"A senior's discount for air travel back to South America." Hayden replied smoothly. "Doctor Swift and I were very grateful to get the orthopedic seats and all the prune juice we could drink. I might have an extra bottle if you need to clear some blockages you may have."

For a good minute, Maximus considered pulling the trigger, his hand tightening on the grip and his teeth clenched. But for the moment, he needed Doctor Lattimer. For his understanding of the tribal symbols on the cavern walls on the opposite of the lake seemed important. And the less people he brought into the equation, the better. He could always kill him later.

Max pointed his finger at Hayden and then traced it across the exposed area of his neck, noting a clear indication of his attention to slice it.

Hayden smiled and blew him a kiss.

Danica watched the entire exchange with fond amusement. She was not surprised at Hayden's persona, simply the fact he could be so cavalier while he was trapped on a subterranean island with a family of killers and a mountain of giant spiders sleeping feet from their position was fascinating.

Maximus kept his weapon locked on the trio. He made a nod with his head and Maxwell threw a large empty duffle bag to the floor in front of them. "Now if you please, if we could have all your weapons placed in the bag. Including any extra ammunition and clips you may have. You'll no longer have any need for them."

Realizing the position they were in, the trio dropped their weapons into the bag without an argument. Once filled, Maxwell strut forward, zipped it shut and handed it to his father. Maximus threw it over his shoulder like a packsack.

Maxima stepped forward to be beside her husband when suddenly Maximus' eyes went wide with astonishment.

Maximus signaled for Maxima to keep her weapon on the three prisoners. He pushed past the trio and knelt down to the sword skewered corpse. "It cannot be. But....My precious Lord... It's unbelievable."

"What is it?" Maxima asked, genuinely interested.

Maximus was staring at the face. "It's Captain Rios. He looks just like the old paintings before he disappeared over a hundred years ago." He was breathing heavy. "This is an amazing discovery..." He suddenly cut his words short as he realized what had been done. He sneered and turned to the trio. "And what possessed you to kill him?"

Coming from a sociopath, Carlos found this comical. "He tried to attack us Mr. Thorne."

Danica raised her eyebrow. The fact Carlos was not offering Maximus the respect of his title, doctor, was not lost upon her.

Carlos continued. "Once we freed him from the webs, he lunged at Doctor Swift. Both Doctors Lattimer and Swift were able to secure his arms. When I saw his sword, I knew he could not be controlled, so I used it to dispatch him."

Maximus looked to both Danica and Hayden with renewed confidence. "I knew you both had some darkness within you." He shook his head with a small '*tsk-tsk*' sound. "Regrettably, killing him could put us back several steps in ascertaining the miracle."

Danica interjected, preventing Carlos from doing so and revealing who he really was. "I assumed there would be more victims alive in these caves. I needed to see the insides of the body to confirm my diagnosis of his hyper-active healing."

Maximus rose, his face filled with disappointment. "Though I applaud the intent, your impatience leaves a great deal to be desired. We could have found this out back at the lab after we transported the body... alive."

"Over four hundred crew went missing Doctor Thorne." Danica responded, not mentioning the fact the tribe took out most of them."

"And how do you know that?" Maxima asked with surprise.

Hayden interrupted Danica. "It was on the chamber wall. The tribe spoke of a great battle with water riding warriors and them claiming victory, leaving many of the enemy to fend for themselves on this island."

Maxima was impressed, not having seen that, but then again, she did not translate ancient texts as a hobby as Hayden did.

Danica turned back to Maximus. "From the Logbook estimates, I figured we'd have no shortage of sources for living tissue, even if we killed the one."

Maximus accepted that. "That is a logical conclusion." He rose from his position. "And as I overheard, it's the spider's venom that is the source of the miracle. Truly amazing. Not exactly what I imagined, but how can I complain?" He turned and found himself admiring the sword in the body.

"We did it." Maxima declared.

Maximus on the other hand was focused on the Cutlass. He quickly gripped the hilt and pulled Rios' sword from his corpse. Maximus then wiped the blood on Rios' clothes to Carlos' dismay. "What a fine weapon." Maximus held it aloft. "Befitting a CEO."

"Or a pirate." Hayden snidely offered under his breath.

Maximus ignored the remark. He moved past the trio and took his spot beside Maxima.

Maximus and Maxima shared a deep kiss.

Each of the trio turned away in revulsion.

Max and Maxwell held their side arms, two nasty AK-47's on the trio. "What's with you three?"

"You mean them kissing or the fact they're brother and sister?" Hayden commented.

At this Max and Maxwell's faces seemed to go stiff.

"Oh?" Hayden looked amused. "You mean you two didn't know? Bet it explains a lot of your failings huh? Either one of you have fourteen toes or something?"

Maxima stepped forward quickly and swung the butt of her gun across Hayden's jaw.

Danica let out a quiet wail into her shirt sleeve as the blow connected.

Hayden on the other hand dropped back a step. He regained his composure and moved back into line, wiping some blood from his lips. "Well I guess that means you don't like me anymore?" Referring to the comment she made when they first met in the boardroom back at the company headquarters.

Maxima almost struck him again when Maximus grabbed her arm and held it firm.

Maximus spoke to his boys. "Your bloodline is pure. Something most of the masses can never dream of. As I have told you before, your mother and I were born to be together. And that alone ensured your creation as one of a kind."

Both sons smiled, pleased with the prospect of being unique.

Maxima pulled her arm away, but held her weapon on the trio, closer to Hayden if she needed to shoot someone first.

Maximus turned to his family. "Well, we need to get this party moving. I want..."

Danica stepped forward, about to speak when Maxima turned and locked her weapon on Danica's chest.

Before anyone could do anything, Carlos had stepped between the muzzle and Danica and smiled. "You're not going to fire that weapon in here."

Max and Maxwell turned to Carlos with vicious smiles.

"And why's that?" Maxima asked.

Carlos pointed to the entrance the Thornes had come through, pointing specifically to the sleeping forms. "Your guns will sound like explosions in here, not to mention echoing down all the neighboring halls and chambers in this one mile long island. And I wouldn't want to be trying to outrun hundreds, if not thousands of these things in winding caves and corridors if you didn't already know the exact way out."

At this Maxima froze, a genuine face of terror, imagining such a happenstance. She motioned to her sons to lower their weapons.

The sons did, but in doing so, drew out two foot long combat blades, almost swords by their razor's edge and wickedly curved grooves on the reverse designed for the sole purpose of tearing flesh when withdrawn from a stabbed victim. "We don't need guns." Max and Maxwell spoke in unison. "I told you these would come in handy."

Maxima smiled at their ingenuity. She then looked to Danica. "You're surprisingly comfortable in here knowing what's living in these caves."

"They're in deep hibernation." Danica replied. "They cannot be awakened until the end of their cycle except by extraordinary means."

Maxwell asked for the first time in the conversation, under the darkened eyes of Maximus. "How do you know that?"

"By how long they've lived trapped here, it'd be a natural mechanism to survive. Otherwise they would starve. So they need to remain comatose, much deeper than sleep, as this would be the only way to slow their digestive process." Danica guessed.

"Plus it was written on the chamber wall." Hayden offered up, lying, keeping the existence of the tribe secret.

Maximus turned to him. "I did not see that."

"Remember the symbols I could not identify at first?" Hayden asked.

Maximus nodded *'Yes?'* He replied with trepidation.

Hayden continued. "One referred to the *Horror*'s rest. A sleep so deep, the trembling of the earth cannot awaken it." He fabricated. "It was a warning to those who sought the mystical properties of the '*juice*', or in other words, the spider's venom. Obviously the tribe did not want innocents to fall prey to the *Horror* when encroaching upon the island."

Maximus' head bobbed up and down in understanding. "I would agree. It would not be logical to bait people into a trap here for the power of immortality." He turned to his family. "But be careful none the less. We do not need to create an extraordinary circumstance."

Danica gave Hayden a quizzical look of, *'What are you doing?'*

Hayden gave her a wink, communicating subtly. *'An easier enemy to defeat is one who is not on guard.'*

It was like Danica and Hayden were born on the same day, as she understood by his facial expressions his plan completely.

Carlos on the other hand, stood by his friends, trusting in their intelligence to save them all.

Maxwell was not so easily persuaded. "I saw the same pictorials printed in my book from your pictures, but I never concluded that."

"Why am I not surprised you find picture books more up your alley?" Hayden asked. "But unlike your standard reading, the chamber walls did not include 'Dick found his way to the island. Jane saw a boat….'"

Maxwell stormed forward, again halted by Maximus' look informing them to gain control. They did not have time for this.

For now.

Max snapped at Hayden, speaking in his brother's defense. "You think you're better than us?"

"Of course not." Hayden seemed offended at the remark.

Danica and Carlos turned in Hayden's direction, surprised at his answer.

But Hayden wasn't finished. "*Thinking* presumes a prospect of doubt. No matter how miniscule. So be assured, I don't *think* I'm better than you" He winked. "I know it."

Maximus decided this little debate was over. He gestured to his sons. "We need one of these specimens to take with us... Preferably alive." He pointed the spider chamber. "Try to find a small one without waking the others."

Both sons looked horrified at the prospect, but feared their father's wrath more.

Danica pleaded the moment the order was given. She looked to Maximus. "You can't. If you bring these things off the island, it could unleash upon the world a plague of monsters that cannot be stopped."

Maxima laughed. "Ridiculous."

Danica being a scientist challenged the argument. "Think about it. Spiders are the most dangerous, vicious and cannibalistic creatures in existence. You'll find they have no equal. If they were released into the world, even accidently, they could decimate the human population in two or three generations."

Maximus nodded. "We can secure them, I assure you."

"By trying to keep prehistoric monsters like this in line?" Danica was thunderstruck Maximus was not thinking this through. She had worked so hard for these people to find this out now was unsettling. "You're pure evil."

Maxima kissed Maximus on the lips again. "Our parents said the same thing."

"Before we killed them." Maximus interjected. "What's the world after that?"

Hayden was equally astonished. "You can't be an evil megalomaniacal mad couple lusting for the world's destruction." He sounded shocked. "You're Canadian."

Maximus was visibly amused at that. "Who says other countries have the exclusive rights to world killing villains? Canada is due a few in my estimate."

Hayden retorted. "Well as an archeologist, I think you're the first. But down here, maybe we can stop you and keep our pristine reputation intact."

"I doubt you're in such a position." Maximus challenged. "Plus, sometimes man needs to learn. We've become complacent in our years. According to the Bible, men fought for far lesser goals. So if God has deemed this world to end in such a manner, it will. With or without our help."

Danica stood firm. "But God isn't here. We are. Using your own analogy, man has free will and YOU and only YOU are choosing to risk the release of these things upon the world."

Maximus' eyes tightened, his voice tempered by anger at having the Word used against him in what he perceived was an ill-conceived manner. "Be assured, Maximum Pharmaceuticals will take great care to recover these things without incident. I find myself highly offended you doubt my company's capabilities."

"I think it's more the leader she doubts." Hayden threw in.

Max moved in and within seconds, shoved his fist directly into Hayden's gut, doubling him over and to the ground with a gasp.

Maxwell smiled viciously.

Danica had ignored this, keeping her focus on Maximus. "These things have survived for centuries, maybe longer. They'll continue to survive. We simply cannot take that chance."

"Like I told you in the boardroom Doctor Swift." Maximus reminded her. "Some people were meant to take these risks. We are such people." He shared another deep kiss with his sister.

Hayden shuddered.

Maximus leaned back, wiped his lips and resumed his command. "Max and Maxwell. As I ordered, I need you both to search the caves …" Gesturing to the sleeping spiders. "And see if you can find one in a lone chamber, preferably small in size, we can capture and take with us."

Both Max and Maxwell provided a displeased look.

Maximus ignored them. "Immortality has its price gentlemen, so buck up."

Max and Maxwell, holding their combat knives at ready, turned and exited the chamber reluctantly.

Maxima smiled. "And myself?"

"You take Doctor Swift deeper into the caves to find more living victims. I don't trust the ones in proximity to here being viable as our saboteurs could have tainted the source." Maximus glared at them all. "Since I doubt we'll be able to carry any bodies out, get us as many vials of blood, tissue and skin samples as you can procure." He smiled. "And don't worry too much about hurting them. I'm sure they'll heal."

Danica grimaced at Maximus' mocking of the possible victims and their condition at having been trapped on the island with the *Horror*.

"As for myself and our two men here, nice sturdy boys, they can help me carry the last of our supplies in to set up a station." Maximus ordered. "We'll then crate up our specimen for transport, but not before drawing out the venom. And with you down here with Doctor Swift, knowing their potential rebellion will lead to her harm, I'm sure they will stay nicely managed."

Both Hayden and Carlos' eyes blazed with fury.

Maxima grinned and departed, Danica in front of her, a knife at her neck.

Once the women were gone, Maximus thrust the point of the sword he had procured from Captain Rios' body forward, jabbing Carlos at the nape of his spine and gesturing to Hayden. "Now let's move gentlemen. We have a lot of work to do."

41

Fifteen minutes after the groups had split up, Maximus had escorted Hayden and Carlos through the second of the four cave corridors leading from the main chamber they had all first entered occupied by the first of the sleeping *Horror.*

Maximus took the rear position, his Cutlass held steadily before him with Hayden at the front and Carlos in the middle.

Maximus' hope was he was taking them in the direction of topside. Their goal, to return to the boiling lake to retrieve the remaining gear of the Thornes. He had no intention of leaving this island empty handed.

Hayden knew immediately it was not the same route they had taken when they first arrived. But he kept that to himself.

Once Maximus felt they had covered sufficient distance, safe from his voice carrying back into the main cavern, he had activated his cell to call back to Canada.

After several long minutes of arguing, Hayden and Carlos could tell Maximus was trying to keep control.

"You're breaking up, Mr. Darby." Maximus shook the phone and put it back to his ear. "No I don't care how many times you say, 'I advise against this.' I'm not prepared to tell you where we are until we secure the find." He listened for fifteen additional seconds. "I'm the CEO, not you. All I want you to do is guard the helm until I and Maxima return."

As Maximus was focussed on his call, Hayden silently communicated to Carlos with mouthed words. *'We need to distract him and take him out.'* He winked. *'I'll try to put him off his game.'*

Carlos nodded his understanding, suppressing a smile knowing Hayden was planning to aggravate Maximus as he loved to do.

Maximus raised his voice. "I could care less what shareholders think. Maxima and I hold the majority stake between us anyway. Once we bring back our discovery, a few million dollars in stock drops will be pennies in the bucket. Trust me. If the public thinks we're out gallivanting on their dollars, they'll forever choke on those words."

Hayden was suddenly glad he had not taken stock options instead of cash.

Maximus hissed. "By adding the adjective 'seriously' before 'you advise against' hasn't changed my position." He replied snidely into the phone. "Be assured, when we return, the world will bow before us on their knees."

Hayden rolled his eyes.

Maximus disconnected the phone and tossed it into his jacket pocket as they cleared the next cave corner.

"How do you get reception this deep in the earth?" Carlos queried.

Maximus waved the sword, but aimed the tip down. He pulled it back a few inches as he walked. He seemed pleased to have a question he could answer without fighting with someone. "As Maxima and I descended into this God forbidden rock fortress, we dropped a few cellular beacons at corners and bends, all which lead to a large satellite antenna we planted topside."

Hayden found that difficult to believe considering how deep they were. "A few cell beacons can bypass nearly two miles of sedimentary rock? I find that a little far-fetched."

Maximus offered a satisfied smile. "Our phones are also powered with neutrinos to enhance the signals."

"I beg your pardon?" Carlos stated with confusion, never having heard of it.

"Neutrinos." Maximus replied, a little excitement leaking into his voice. It was obviously something Maximum Pharmaceuticals had either discovered or achieved recently. "They're a weak negative charge with essentially no mass, which allows them to travel through almost anything. By allowing the cell signal to travel using the neutrino, solid rock and matter is no longer a hindrance. A university in the states pioneered the idea. We simply capitalized on it."

Hayden interjected. "I remember hearing about neutrinos in the university. It was the talk of the radiology labs as they did a lot of my carbon dating." He thought about it. "Neutrinos are supposed to be very difficult to generate. The simplest way is using decaying radioactive matter?" He spoke over his shoulder with a bit of dismay. "You don't actually have radioactive material in your phone decaying do you?"

Maximus shook his head. "Don't be a fool. It's in the beacons I placed."

"What about the environmental damage that could cause?" Hayden asked.

Maximus shrugged. "A few dead animals or cancer ridden birds at most. A call that never drops is worth far more."

"Sounds like a million dollar idea." Hayden threw out sarcastically. "Why not go with that and leave this evil little island to itself."

"Why not have both?" Maximus smiled. "In my world, there are no limits."

"Or morals." Hayden replied.

Maximus growled. He would have jabbed Hayden with the Cutlass, but Carlos stood between them, so Maximus pushed it forward into the bease of Carlos' spine.

Carlos sensed it coming and hopped forward before the skin could be pierced. He was biding his time and knowing, soon, very soon they had to make their move or they would have no moves to make.

42

With Max and Maxwell having taken a left from the main *Horror* cave they first found, now carefully creeping inward in hopes of locating one of the smaller specimens to capture; Maxima had led Danica right and deeper into the dreary superstructure in search of entombed victims from which to acquire biological samples.

The slow and heavy breathing of the spiders was fading into a low level background noise, but was still loud enough to keep the two women on edge.

Twice Maxima had to wipe moisture from her brow and upper lip with the sleeve of her shirt, likely due to the humidity, as the enduring heat was both exhausting her mentally and having dire effects on her water retention. She was wishing she had brought more water bottles with her, that or a hydrating fluid.

Danica remained in front, Maxima behind her with the combat blade in her grips.

Their footsteps sounded hollow on the rocky ground, giving way to the fear of causing echoes. Once or twice, they both found themselves unconsciously lifting their feet when they tried to soften their steps.

Danica had her hands at her side, facing forward, fists clenched, carefully waiting like a cat ready to pounce. She knew with the two sons out of earshot, and her being one on one with Maxima, her best opportunity to escape was a matter of opportunity. But she needed to wait for the perfect chance as otherwise, it would be back to square one, or worse, dead.

The two women found and passed through both a second and a third cavern, each equally as large as the first, all filled with the unconscious *Horror,* many in smaller cubbyholes, one stationary and asleep in the middle of the floor, looking like it had suffered a bout of sleepwalking.

Both Danica and Maxima slipped past it with looks of absolute panic as they moved.

As they exited the third one, it was followed by two smaller chambers filled from floor to ceiling with webbed cocoons, some smaller and rounder in shape, appearing to be either animals or some form of large lizard, maybe even a Kimono Dragon.

Danica was thankful she had found no children. But she suspected the tribe would have saved them by now during these hibernation periods as the Elder spoke of the many times they came down here while they slept

In the second chamber, Maxima looked satisfied. Under the light of her bulb, she placed her medical sack on the floor from off her shoulder. She held the knife tight in her other hand and she began pulling out numerous small airtight glass travel cases, a box of unused hypodermic needles and collection of stainless steel tools for cutting and digging to procure medical fluid from cadavers, or in this case, the living dead.

Over the next ten minutes, Maxima took a selection of samples, watching Danica with the corner of her eyes. At one point, she used a catheter to drain the urine from one victim, filling seven one ounce acrylic test tubes. This was followed by capping them with rubber stoppers.

Danica, while collecting her samples, under supreme duress, took a few careful opportunities to use her hypodermic to inject air bubbles into the bloodstreams of some of the victims she could tell were on the cusp of death. Some were so far gone, she felt they had suffered long enough. She knew in her heart, she could not in good conscience leave them here alive any longer in this island's inhabitants clutches.

A good air bubble would stop the blood flow quickly.

Danica could never have imagined in her lifetime taking another's life, in any circumstance, but today, she learned, some things were far worse than death.

Imaginging being trapped here as one of them, she understood the entrance's warning now.

Once or twice Maxima turned around when a cocoon bucked suddenly as the heart stopped, but Danica would hold the collected sample aloft and indicate she must have hit a bone, noting to Maxima plants were her area of expertise, not human beings.

As they sealed up the case in search of a new area, Maxima finally spoke. "Who would have imagined it?"

Danica was almost afraid to ask, but knowing conversation could lull an enemy into a false position of friendship, making them vulnerable to attack, so she attempted to be sociable. "Imagined what?"

"Seriously, Doctor Swift?" Maxima snapped. "You have to ask that?"

"Oh... I understand." Danica replied, some distain in her voice. "And you're right. I certainly couldn't have imagined it. Being stabbed in the back from the very start by my own employers."

Maxima sighed. "Don't be such a child. I meant the prehistoric spiders of an unnatural size holding the key to human immortality."

"Or the end of the human race." Danica retorted.

Maxima zipped the bag closed. "You can't be this naïve Doctor Swift." She snorted. "Don't tell me you weren't even a bit curious when we first told you what we were after. Otherwise, you wouldn't have jumped aboard this little expedition. Now that you've discovered the secret, I can't believe your interest ends there."

"We were interested all right. But for different reasons."

"Really?" Maxima inserted a stray hypodermic into one of the white sacks. The body inside struggled, a muffled cry emanating from deep within the strands causing Danica to wince. The body went still as Maxima drew the needle out and capped the holder. "I wouldn't be all that surprised if you'd found the prize and in a few short months, Swift Pharmaceuticals would have joined the scene with your new miracle cures."

"Then you don't know me at all Maxima." Danica sneered. "Now that I and Doctor Lattimer know the truth behind the *Horror,* we've chosen to leave nature to its decision to keep these monstrous things where they belong, trapped on this Godforsaken island."

"Then you're bigger fools than I ever derived. How you got hired by our company escapes my sensibilities."

"That presumes you had any."

Maxima glared in Danica's direction. "And what's that supposed to mean?"

"If you think you and Maximum Pharmaceuticals can contain these things, you're the fools." Danica lectured. "Unlike mankind, nature is absolute. It establishes a course and very little can force it to deviate from it. And like this island, sometimes even for a millennia. The only exception being the malevolent involvement or destructive intrusion of man." She looked in Maxima's direction. "Or woman."

Maxima's tone tightened, becoming more serious. "We've every intention of securing these creatures with the best facilities within the means of our company."

"And you think I'm naïve. You saw the movie about the dinosaurs being brought back to life in Costa Rica." Danica pointed out. "They thought by altering the DNA, they could control them. They failed. Some things cannot be contained by man-made constructs. There are so many factors you can't control. Greed, laziness, technology failure and so much more. The more it takes to do something, the more complicated it becomes, and with it, possibility for human error. And with these things, that's one too many. One escape could lead to the end of us all." She shook her head, saying it with such deep reservation; it pained Danica to envision it. "At least here, it's simple. The island is devoid of escape with nothing else to intervene. You should leave things they are."

"Too bad I'm not burdened by human emotioins and weaknesses." Maxima remarked. "Conscience is for the inferior and I'll never be softened by such things." Maxima gestured for Danica to take the lead again, both because Danica's lights were brighter and to use her as a human shield in case they were attacked from the front.

After ten more minutes, they could both sense a quiet before them, no breathing could be heard, nothing.

The source being a cave entrance a good thirty feet away.

In there, a few feet felt likes miles.

Maxima asked. "And had it not been these giant arachnids you found, tell me Doctor Swift, what would you have done then? "

"Honestly?" Danica answered. "We had every intention of finding it and giving it to the world... For free."

Maxima chuckled in disbelief. "Then you and Doctor Lattimer deserve the fate coming to you."

Danica could sense the threat in those words.

Maxima continued. "I'd have preferred corporate thievery to ignorant benevolence. Had you two revealed to the world the secret in the manner you had chosen, you could have led our planet into a population explosion of an unprecedented order. With no one dying and all disease wiped away, overcrowding would have led to civil war. And let me tell you, man has lost more lives to wars than giant spiders."

Danica rolled her eyes thinking, *'Yet.'*

Maxima was talking loudly to Danica, impassioned by her argument. "So who do you think would have been the harbinger of the world's end? Us or your and *'generosity?'* I think you know the answer."

Danica was amazed at Maxima's arrogance. *'Like husband like wife... Or for them, like brother like sister.'*

"And if the *Horror* were to escape, which in my mind is only an eventuality, regardless of your planned zoo to hold them, what then?" Danica asked honestly.

"Some things were simply meant to be." Maxima recited, sounding like she was a pastor at her pulpit reading a sermon. "At least with our plan, we can filter out and control the future. Only those worthy to survive will be able to afford it. Some genetic lines were not meant to extend. We're basically God's gardener, weeding out the weak." She looked to Danica. "And the worthless."

"Like inbreeding sociopaths?" Danica replied quickly.

Maxima's eyes widened. She took a deep breath, trying to regain her control. After a few seconds, she snarled in a whispered tone. "I think you've been spending far too much time with Doctor Lattimer."

Danica grinned without turning. "I prefer his company to yours any day."

Maxima hesitated before answering and then whispered, loud enough for Danica to hear. "You'll regret the day you turned on us."

Danica spat out. "Technically speaking, you turned on me first by attacking and then abandoning me in London. But for the sake of decorum, I'd have turned on you eventually, especially after discovering your plans."

Maxima was quiet for a good twenty seconds. "So you know, I disagreed with Maximus when he first arrived here." She stated. "You won't be missed at our company functions."

Danica knew right away by her use of the past tense, Maxima had no intention of letting her leave this island alive.

Maxima's boot caught an outcropping of rock and she staggered forward, her helmet light bounced up and down quickly with the jostle.

Danica knew fate had given her the chance and she took the opportunity. She leapt up onto a small rock edge, her foot catching it for leverage, spinning herself around and delivering a double knife-hand strike, the upper hand leveling across the exposed open neck of Maxima, the lower one the back of her wrist sending the knife clattering away into the darkness.

Maxima almost screamed, but knowing what could be awakened, grunted instead as she found herself and her bodyweight being shoved face first into the cave wall. She felt a wad of cave dirt fill her mouth as she slammed into the wall and slid down. Her face scratched along the edges with a hot deep gouging roughness. But in that same motion, she rolled forward, pushing herself back up and returning a thundering charge in Danica's direction.

Danica pivoted, using a *too sul* maneuver, diverting Maxima's momentum against her and sending Maxima past and into the opposite side of the cave, back to the ground. Danica could see the thin blood trails running down from Maxima's fingertips as she had used her palms and hands to lessen the impact.

Maxima was already in motion, as she was still a woman who exercised daily for hours at a time. Stamina and strength she had in abundance, so a few hits and pushes were not draining her as fast as Danica hoped.

Maxima thrust her leg back and used her two hands to push herself off the wall. Her foot fired like a ball out of the cannon straight at Danica. The combined force of the shove gave it both speed and power.

Danica twisted to avoid it, but Maxima was too fast. She was able to lessen the blow Maxima delivered by her motion, but the strike still sent an explosion of pain up her upper torso and down her limbs.

Maxima shifted around and charged again.

Danica dropped to one knee and did a smooth upper punch, not unlike an uppercut, using the ground for support. Her fist slid perfectly under Maxima's front arms to connect into the lower jaw with a resounding crack.

Maxima's head snapped back and she toppled over a pile of rocks on the ground dropping into the dark. Had her helmet not been attached by a strap, she would have lost it, rendering her defenseless.

Danica moved in again, this time with her open palms in front of her to strike.

Maxima rolled over twice and then used her full lower calves to boost her body forward at Danica, her arms open wide.

Danica may have a black belt on her side, but Maxima was a force of physical nature.

Within seconds, Danica found herself in between the open arms of Maxima. With the intent to strike, she parried, but missed her chance to hit the eyes.

 Maxima closed both limbs around Danica's back and formed a powerful bear hug, her arms like a garbage compactor.

Danica felt her chest and lungs compressing under the power of Maxima's squeeze. She was starting to black out. Her vision went blurry and her muscles went lax.

Maxima opened her arms to let Danica land directly in front of her.

Danica raised both her arms to block, but her world teetered before her.

Without realizing, Danica in one of her moves had sent Maxima to where she had lost her knife.

With one quick motion, Maxima drew up her combat knife, having held it the entire time during the bear hug and thrust it into Danica's abdomen and twisted.

Danica felt like her body was on fire. She contained her scream, but the pain was excruciating.

Maxima used the bottom of her boot to shove Danica back through the silent cave opening.

Within seconds, Danica felt a breeze behind her. She turned and looked down to the darkness below and where the cave floor ended.

It was a cliff within the island. As to how deep, it could not seen with the lights they carried, nor with focus to determine the bottom. The darkness absorbed the light like a sponge.

Danica dropped to a crouch at the cliff's edge to prevent from going over, holding her bleeding side as Maxima sauntered towards her.

Maxima was grinning, holding the blade and wiping the blood on her pant leg. "Nice try Doctor Swift. This is what happens when you face superior foes."

Danica was not listening. She felt woozy, like she had been drinking heavily, but knowing there was no alcohol in her system. She had her hand over the tear in her abdomen. She felt warm fluid cascading out into her palms, soaking her shirt and upper pants. She was a doctor and she knew she was mortally wounded. She never pictured her life ending like this.

Maxima watched with satisfaction.

'*I never even had a chance to ask Hayden to...*' Danica stopped her thought, not wanting to be sad as she died. Her legs buckled and she collapsed completely to the ground. She felt nothing when she impacted with the exception of cold, a chill that oozed into her extremities even with the heavy balm of the caves.

Maxima leaned forward and down, close to Danica's face, like she was going to give her a kiss, but within inches to whisper. "You could've been a part of history. Instead now, you simply *are* history."

Danica was in a world all her own.

Maxima placed her boot to the lower hip of Danica who lay bleeding, holding her stomach on the inner cave's edge. She sneered. "Some people were meant for greatness, while others are simply meant to fall." And with that, Maxima used her foot to push Danica, side over side, rolling her backwards over the precipice into the darkness.

As Danica fell, her light spun with her deep tumble, her lights dancing on the walls away like a vertical top on a midnight coloured backdrop curtain drawn closed on the stage.

Twice Maxima observed as Danica seemed to hit the cliff side and at one point, for several seconds, seemed to almost float, obviously landing on a rock edifice or cliff before falling further. At that brief airbourne point, Danica hissed, obviously puncturing a lung in Maxima's eyes. She resumed her plunge

Maxima heard Danica hit the sides of the wall followed by her body coming to a dead halt at the bottom with a bone crushing wet smack.

Then only silence, eerie and foreboding.

Maxima smiled as she listened. She squinted her eyes, unable to see much, but she could see in the dim glow of the lights on the cave floor, the unnatural angle of Danica's rlight leg and a dark pool forming beneath her, all around her body.

Maxima smiled, offering a sarcastic salute and laughed quietly. "Good riddance bitch."

Maxima turned and resumed her mission, to get the specimens as Maximus sought.

She thought to herself. *'One down, two to go.'*

43

As Maximus stalked forward, he swung the cutlass back and forth through the air, cutting the wind and making a swishing sound with each pass.

"Must you do that?" Carlos asked from in front of him, twice nearly being sliced by the tip of the blade which had been not so delicately grazing his shoulders.

"You've obviously never brandished a sword before Mr. Santiago." Maximus chided, sounding pleased with himself at maintaining the upper hand.

"You'd be surprised." Carlos replied.

"A sword is an extension of one's arm." Maximus explained. "A true man, make that a warrior, knows how to hold it, wield it and more importantly, kill with it." He stopped the motion and held it pointed forward again in Carlos' direction, directly behind Carlos' shoulder blades. "Using it to dispatch an unarmed man lying on the ground too weak to fight back is not a manly thing to do."

"I guess coming from a *man* ..." Carlos remarked with disdain the term 'man', "Who plans to unleash upon this world this island's inhabitants with total disregard for the repercussions, letting man, woman and yes, child fend for themselves, then I find myself in good company."

Maximus offered no response, only a low hiss. He causally mimicked the gesture of using the sword to separate Carlos' head from his shoulders without Carlos seeing it.

As the three men reached the next cave junction, there were two more caves leading off in opposing directions, one downward and further into more caves, the other skyward with equally dire prospects.

Hayden yelled from the front. "It took us only fifteen minutes to get down to where we were and so far, you're at fifty and I don't see an exit."

"I know where I'm going Doctor Lattimer." Maximus replied, venom lacing his voice, the sword moving a tad faster in the air. "If you recall, the exterior of the cave was littered with entrances and exits."

"So we're going with *Keep going and eventually* we should reach the outside." Hayden mocked. "You might want to keep your career aspirations as a tour guide under wraps."

"I find taking advice from the ones at the business end of my sword rather amusing. If one is trying to advertise which one of us is the fool, look in the mirror?" Maximus retorted, jabbing the blade forward to poke Carlos' lower spine, not enough to penetrate, simply to reveal who was in charge.

Carlos jerked forward, his fists clenching and unclenching.

Hayden dodged under an edge of rock too low to walk under without crouching. "Ever go to the zoo?" He asked aloud, directly to Maximus.

Maximus found himself confused. "What does that have to do with anything?"

Hayden continued, ignoring Maximus' question. "Personally I love the zoo. My favourite is to go down to the gorilla pen and check out the apes. I always find them entertaining to watch. They'd lumber around, beat on their chests and throw feces at one another. That and grunting back and forth as all apes do."

"And this is important how?" Maximus asked.

"Well, some even know sign language." Hayden mentioned. "And as a purveyor of ancient languages, I found this uniquely fascinating."

"And why is that relevant?" Maximus shot back.

Hayden shrugged. "One time, one of these apes actually gestured to me I was a fool."

Maximus chuckled. "I guess even the primates must have known you like I do. You're telling me this why?"

"Well my friend said to me at the time, 'Hey, Are you going to do something? That ape just called you a fool.'" Hayden ducked again under some more rocks. "You know what I said?"

Carlos asked, knowing Maximus would not. "What?"

"I said to my friend." Replying to Carlos. "Who Gives a Fuck? It's just a big dumb ape."

Carlos choked a laugh into his sleeve.

Maximus snarled from the back. "Your value is losing traction very fast Doctor Lattimer."

"Like you have any intention of letting us live Maximus." Hayden fired back sarcastically. "If my last words will be anything, it will be mocking you and your incestuous little clan."

Maximus held firm on his temper, planning how many words Doctor Lattimer would get out as he sunk his struggling prospective corpse beneath the bubbling yellow waters of the underwater lake, his mouth filling with burning fluid as his lungs were crushed with the last vestiges of his final breaths.

Carlos kept walking, slowly moving, keeping to himself, but extremely pleased Hayden was doing his best to force Maximus to lose his cool and succeeding.

Angry people make foolish decisions and often before considering the results.

Maximus directed them to turn right.

After walking another ten minutes in an uphill manner, ducking under more low ceilings and sharp rocks, this cave not meant for human travels, Carlos saw the exit before him.

Even in the darkness, the flickering glow from the beach where Hayden lit the tribe's ceremonial torch was shining like a lighthouse beacon in the fog off a Newfoundland stormy shore.

As the men proceeded, Carlos could see the opening they had chosen exited far higher than the one they originally entered, with a cliff ledge almost twenty-five feet from the rocky floor below.

Maximus prodded Carlos and Hayden forward with the sword, thrusting them on, not seeing their higher location.

Carlos intentionally tripped, his knee hitting a chunk of rock, keeping Maximus focused on his hostages, not the view.

Maximus stopped and used his boot to shove Carlos forward.

Carlos wobbled and resumed his forward pace smiling.

"Shame on you Doctor Lattimer." Maximus stated. "You and Doctor Swift."

"And why's that?" Hayden replied, knowing as long as they were talking, Maximus was not hurting anyone.

"Bringing him into this." Gesturing to Carlos. "Some old British collector who couldn't figure out the journal when he had it. Then you come along and give him his chance for adventure and here he is, barely able to continue." Maximus spoke loudly, directing the question to Hayden, but with equal opportunity for Carlos to answer. "What did he expect to receive, a chance for a few extra years from the Fountain of Youth?"

Hayden grinned as he faced forward. "I don't know. I got the distinct impression Carlos would be an asset. If for no other reason than age brings experience. I sort of thought he had a lot."

Carlos chuckled as well, amused Maximus had no idea who he really was, suspecting he would be far more amazed and treating him very differently had he had such insight.

Time was of the essence, with Danica stuck down in the deeper regions of the island with the remaining three Thornes trying to capture one of the sleeping *Horror*, Carlos sensed, as the cave entrance widened with proximity, the time for action was now.

With a gentle kick, out of Maximus' eye line, Carlos sent a rock into the back of Hayden's calf, clearly indicating he was about to do something.

Hayden slowed his pace, preparing himself.

Carlos spun around and with one smooth move, walked directly towards Maximus and his long sword.

Maximus grinned maliciously for several seconds, extending the blade forward. "Keep moving hero."

Then to both Hayden and Maximus' utter shock, Carlos thrust forward, reaching the blade and continuing.

Carlos walked into the blade, it positioned at stomach level and used his full body weight to take the sword deep into his abdomen.

Maximus' eyes widened in total incredulity and astonishment as Carlos advanced upon him like some sort of clay golem seeking vengeance, the blade sinking into his stomach with each step, until the full blade was embedded in Carlos' body up to the hilt.

Maximus mouth was open with dumbstruck revulsion, mostly in total disbelief any human being would intentionally sacrifice themselves in such a manner.

Carlos caught Maximus' eyes and he lashed out with a powerful haymaker, using his right arm and spinning his upper body to level Maximus across the lower jaw with a thunderous blow, closing Maximus' exposed mouth with a teeth cracking crunch.

Maximus was totally unprepared in how to react as his head, chin and face snapped back, his body remaining stationary.

Carlos dropped, transforming his body into dead weight and taking the sword with him to the ground, and out of Maximus' grip, which had loosened completely with the surprising action Carlos had taken.

Not needing a second cue, Hayden leapt up, turned and pivoted on his foot, using his legs to shove his full body upwards and back in midair. He connected with a devastating elbow directly into Maximus' already struck cheek.

Maximus coughed and arced back, staggering several steps trying to regain his position, still not falling as his massive form was used to punishment.

Hayden landed on his two feet, his elbow and forearm feeling like it was on fire, having hit his funny bone and thinking. '*Totally wrong name for a bone.*'

Maximus shook his head back and forth, clearing his vision of the stars and started forward, fists formed and ready to hit, looking like two bowling balls on tree branches, ready to crush some pins.

Hayden dropped and rolled around Maximus, thus having himself deeper in the cave and keeping Maximus' back to the gaping opening and high ledge behind him.

Shaking the pins and needles out of his arm, Hayden sprang into a runner's crouch and bolted forward, using his shoulders like a battering ram as he walloped into Maximus' abdomen.

Maximus let out a burst of air as his body bent forward with the blow.

Hayden pulled back and away with the utmost haste, to keep out of Maximus' massive arms, ensuring he was not ensnared into a bear hug which would most assuredly crush his spine.

Maximus shuddered and took another half step back, his face red with exhaled air and spittle on his chin. He shook his head again, inhaling deeply, pumping his chest up and out like a primate, twice even slamming his forearm over his upper body, to trigger more fury and push his adrenaline to start flowing.

Hayden knew letting Maximus tap his reserves was not the optimal thing to let happen, thus he was back in motion, this time, pivoting his body up and using the full force of his legs to raise both feet up, hitting Maximus mid chest with a full frontal drop kick.

Maximus tightened up, taking a half step back, his eyes filling with sweat as it trickled down his brow and into his eyes, his helmet still tightly fastened. Combined with the intense heat and anger, Maximus was losing his control, wiping the tears and sweat with his shirt sleeve.

Carlos was still on the ground in a fetal position, probably never having done what he did before, depending on his healing abilities to cure the stabbing.

Hayden could see Maximus was still a good few metres from the cliff's edge. He had to keep Maximus off his guard, especially to ensure Maximus was unable to draw his sidearm or reach for the pack of weapons he had relieved the trio of in the lower chamber, which he still had strapped tightly to his back. He knew if Maximus could draw even one and fire, in these close quarters, they would be dead.

Amazingly, most likely based on Maximus' solidly built form and lumbering strength, he was still standing.

Hayden knew if Maximus was able to get focused, his chance for survival would be equally grim.

Hayden resumed his attack, knowing he could not stop with a man like Maximus.

Maximus stepped forward, his eyes open wide and gritting his teeth, now filled with blood.

Hayden and Maximus moved around one another like two lions in the jungle until Maximus had the cave exit behind him again.

Hayden bolted forward and launched a second powerful drop kick, hitting Maximus higher this time, his feet connecting with his full weight into his lower jaw.

Maximus had tightened his chest muscles, leveraging his legs like a foundation and he barely budged.

Hayden bounced off and dropped to the cave corridor's rock covered ground, feeling like he had hit a dump truck. He spun as he landed, getting himself back up for another attack. With the twenty five foot ledge behind Maximus, he only needed to shove him a few more feet, which right now felt like a mile. He launched another devastating drop kick maneuver.

Except this time, Maximus was prepared. Sensing Hayden was going for a third, he caught Hayden's two feet moments before impact. Using his massive upper body strength, and Hayden's forward momentum, Maximus spun left, his chest heaving, Hayden's legs in tow. Like a catapult, he slammed Hayden's full body, back first, with bone crunching force into the side of the cave wall.

Like Maximus, Hayden let a burst of air.

Hayden dropped to the ground, gasping and wheezing, having the wind knocked out of him. He was effectively down.

Maximus stalked forward to the now kneeling Carlos.

Maximus raised both hands over his head, grabbed both fists and came down like a sledgehammer, cracking across Carlos' side.

Carlos let out a tightened moan.

Maximus had the advantage of superior strength.

Even combined with Carlos' healing abilities and energy reserves, the blow felt like he was being hit by man that could probably bench-press cars.

Maximus lifted Carlos' limp form from the ground, amazed that Carlos was still alive. He shoved his fist into Carlos' side forcing him to wince as he had no means to dodge.

With the compressed quarters in the caverns, Hayden and Carlos' mobility was limited immensely, making Maximus' connections that much more devastating.

With Hayden down, Maximus held the fallen form of Carlos up with one arm. In one swift pull, Maximus drew the sword from Carlos' body. He let Carlos crumple back to the cave floor. "What a waste...." His words were cut short as his eyes caught the edges of the sword.

The blood was coagulating, far too quickly by normal means.

Maximus peered down and could see the wound where he drew the sword out.

The torn skin was knitting slowly together.

Maximus looked up into Carlos' pain filled face. "It seems Mr. Santiago, there's far more to you than I was originally told." He glared in Hayden's direction, still collapsed on the cave floor. "I should not be surprised."

Carlos groaned, still too weak to move.

Maximus slipped the cutlass into the gap between his khakis and his leather belt. He bent down and lifted Carlos over his head with both hands with no more difficulty than hefting a sack of dry sand. "We've far more to talk about Mr. Santiago, but not here. On my operating table for sure. But for now, I need you out of my way." With a running fireman's carry, Maximus charged down the cave to the precipice of the ledge and with a double handed toss, threw Carlos twenty five feet to the beach floor below.

Carlos spun in the air and was able to twist to land on the ground using his legs and knees first, preventing bone breakage, but still crashing hard, effectively disabling him for the time being.

But worse, leaving Hayden alone at the mercy of Maximus, out of reach, with no way for Carlos to help him.

Carlos was trying to rise after having been tossed over, but as he looked up, he knew Hayden was on his own.

'God help him.' Carlos prayed as he rolled onto his stomach to heal.

Maximus had already returned to Hayden's fallen form and struck with a gut crunching punch.

Any remaining wind spewed forth from Hayden's lungs.

"Not so mouthy now are you Doctor Lattimer?" Maximus mocked, kicking Hayden while he was down.

Hayden pushed back, away from the ledge and hopefully, the brutal beating. He slid his body along the dirty ground, with Maximus smiling and following behind.

"Oh I don't know." Hayden commented. "You kick like a girl."

Maximus drew out the Cutlass.

Hayden pushed further until he found himself back under the rock ceiling that was too low to walk under fully erect. Hayden rolled over onto his stomach to try and crawl away, but Maximus kicked Hayden hard, forcing him face up, arms splayed.

Maximus crouched and placed his massive foot in the middle of Hayden's chest and held him down.

Hayden was powerless.

Maximus arched his body back, both hands gripping the hilt of the sword. He raised his fists for the maximum momentum to bring it down with deadly velocity.

Hayden closed his eyes, preparing for the death blow, knowing life's release would be coming. All he could think was, 'And I still haven't kissed Danica yet.'

That and he was still worried about her in the caves alone with those animals...

And the spiders.

'What a useless archeologist I turned out to be.' He thought. "I didn't save anybody.' He waited for the blade to strike through his chest.

Nothing came.

After another few seconds, Hayden heard Maximus struggling. He opened his eyes to see Maximus, still towering over him, but no longer staring down at him.

Maximus was staring upward and seemed to be fighting something out of sight, his feet and body trying to drag him down with no success.

Hayden rolled out from under Maximus' twisting legs. He rose, gasping, but he could suddenly see what had occurred.

Maximus' double fisted grip on the sword had penetrated one of the white gelatin pools, one of the ones Danica had warned them about when they first entered the cave.

Like the one Hayden nearly dipped his hand into. They seemed to be everywhere.

It was some form of web ball, placed out of sight behind the upper side of the rock on the ceiling.

Maximus was entangled in it, drying strands and globs of silk oozing down his forearms.

Liquefied balls of webbing for catching prey as they struggle getting thicker and tighter with each pull.

The Elder had warned them the *Sentinels* would likely set traps.

With Maximus' attempted angle, using both hands to increase the force of his downward thrust with the sword, they were deeply caught when he penetrated the trap. That and the handle of the sword was also stuck between his palms, glued between his intertwined fingers and useless to cut him free.

In those powerful pulls, Hayden saw something else at the corner of his eye.

A thin thread originally hidden by the cave dust and dirt, running from the web pool along the interior wall, shaking violently with Maximus' twisting and turning.

'*Poetic.*' Hayden thought. He padded Maximus on the back and said. "See you sport." He turned to leave.

Maximus screamed to him. "This isn't over!"

Hayden stopped, turned his head around and smiled wickedly. "Actually it is. Do you not see what it's attached to?"

Maximus looked up in confusion and his helmet light caught the shaking thread vanishing into the darkness below.

"You ring a dinner bell, someone's coming to eat." Hayden smiled. "Personally, I wasn't invited, so you can be dine upon solo."

"You can't leave me like this!" Maximus declared with authority.

Hayden turned to him. "Oh yes I can. When you left Danica… Doctor Swift with your darling wife… oh sorry… sister," He shivered unconsciously "And your disgusting boys, to fend for herself, be assured, I can leave you like this and I will."

The web started to shake, this time without Maximus' help.

The landlord was coming.

And very fast.

Maximus started to panic. "You better..."

Hayden turned and with one swift motion, using his pocketknife, sliced the strap on the duffle bag holding their weapons, pulling it free from Maximus.

Maximus eyes went wide with comprehension.

Hayden turned and walked to the cliff's edge, deftly tossing it over the side to Carlos below and giving Carlos a salute.

Maximus was pulling and tearing, the web getting stronger and stronger.

Before Hayden leapt over the side to the beach below, he turned to Maximus. "One more thing, Maximus."

Maximus turned to Hayden, his eyes softening, expecting him to change his mind.

"Maybe this is Destiny." Hayden winked.

Maximus swore something unintelligible with clenched eyes in Hayden's direction followed by, "You better hope I die."

"Actually, I hope you live. A very long time." Hayden smiled maliciously.

Maximus screamed. "No. No. NOOOOOOOO!"

But as the last 'No' escaped his lips, Hayden was gone.

Maximus heard it, a furry patter of large legs moving along the cave toward him.

He started to scream.

And scream and scream.

44

Maxima carefully placed the last of the filled test tubes and pressed glass slides into the insulated leather pouch located on her waist. After having collected the final selection of samples from the cocoons she found in the lower caves, left and off from the cliff she passed, she was feeling excited, almost to the point of giddy.

As Maxima twisted the clasps tight, engaging the brass lock and releasing the liquid nitrogen cartridge inside to keep the contents cool, she giggled to herself, which echoed around her softly.

'Maximus will never believe me.' She thought. *'Not in a million years.'*

Maxima was sure one of the cocoons housed a *Homo Erectus,* an extinct species of hominid that lived from the end of the Pleistocene period or so evolutionists claimed.

It seemed impossible, yet, there it was, gift wrapped in white silk paper.

Even more fantastic, she suspected it could also mean a far longer life expectancy than originally assumed for humans when introduced or maintained with the spider's venom.

'We'll be the new Messiahs.' She thought energetically. 'A new religion where Maximum Pharmaceuticals will decide who shall live and who shall die."

Maxima stared skyward, not seeing the cave but an open sky and a beam of light shining down upon her like a beacon from parted clouds. 'Like Kings and Queens.' She paused and corrected herself. 'Queens and Kings.' She smiled at the idea.

On her way back up to the main entrance, she passed back through the two hive chambers she had traversed earlier, warily stepping around the sleeping beast in the one.

Maxima could swear each chamber seemed to be filled with more sleeping monsters, even though she knew in her heart it was just nervousness.

As Maxima rounded the next bend, stepping over a large pile of rocks, she heard a small whoosh.

Maxima peered up, her light leveling forward and she walked right into the rubber treads of a foot pivoting out of the darkness, striking her right at the centre of her jaw, sending her snapping back face first into the rock wall, her teeth making a resounding crack, resulting with her dropping to the ground with her helmet falling between her knees.

Maxima twisted up and back onto her feet in an instant, grabbing her helmet and fearing the worst, one of the spiders were awake, not considering the fact most monsters don't wear hiking boots.

Within seconds, Maxima slammed the helmet back on, raised her fists in preparation to defend herself when a second equally devastating punch leveled across her cheek. She tasted warm copper in her mouth as she staggered backwards again, not falling this time, but using the cave wall for support.

Maxima spun around, anger in her eyes, fury in her heart, but within those moments, the cooling shock of disbelief seeped into her veins as she found herself awestruck, her eyes widening, causing her to drop back a step in total astonishment.

'Impossible.' Maxima thought. *'Fucking impossible.'*

A slim shadowy female figure materialized out of the darkness, stepping into the glow of Maxima's bulb.

With a flick of the switch on her head, the upper double lights flashed and Maxima found herself face to face with the smiling form of Doctor Danica Swift.

Danica stood before Maxima, her head tilting ever so slightly with a small little grin. "You know, I found standing in the dark, stepping out and putting the lights on at just the right moment very melodramatic."

All Maxima could do was mutter, her fists lowering. "But you're... you're dead..."

Danica cut her off. "Then you can call me Lazarus." She pressed back into a *ready stance*. Her shirt and pants were torn, dirty from the drop down the cliff. Her hair was askew, yet she still exuded attractiveness.

"I...I'..." Maxima repeated her words. "I stabbed you. I threw you over the side of the cliff. I watched you fall. I heard you land. I saw all the blood....." She gasped. "You were dead."

"Not quite dead really." Danica smiled. "I was hurt, yes. Broken, also yes, but the blood pool you saw forming was not mine." She turned, revealing her back which was soaked with a dark blue fluid. Danica gestured to two large holes just below her shoulder blades, rimmed with yellow.

Maxima knew immediately, Danica had been bitten by one of the spiders. *'But how?'*

Danica had turned back around. She lifted the bottom edge of her blouse where she had been stabbed. The blood was still moist as the material was partially stuck to the skin underneath, but the stab wound itself had vanished.

Maxima's mouth was open wide. She snapped it shut fearing if Danica lashed out too quickly, she could lose her tongue.

"Marvelous stuff this venom is." Danica added. "Not exactly how I envisioned the Fountain of Youth, but it's not the only disappointment I've had to contend with recently."

Maxima was too stunned to reply.

Danica added. "But I have to thank you."

"Thank me?" Maxima sputtered.

"Yes." Danica replied. "You see, while I was lying on the cliff's edge bleeding to death, a few feet under the outcropping of rock was one of the Sentinels, making its way up to us to attack."

"What the Hell is a Sentinel?" Maxima asked.

"Oh yeah." Danica pivoted around to a better striking position. "A Sentinel is one of the spiders who stay conscious during the hibernation period to protect the others and keep the prey fed. It was stalking up the cliff towards us. In fact, had you not rolled me off when you did, chances are, we'd both be its food."

Maxima was steadily regaining her composure.

Danica continued. "When I rolled off, I landed right onto it and my weight and our momentum crushed it on the rocks below. It actually softened my landing. And amazingly enough, as I fell, it bit me as its final act. Probably just instinct, but who's complaining." She flexed her energized body. "Though I feel fantastic, it's still not worth the risk of letting these things into the world, but hey, all I'm happy for is being here for round two with you." With that, Danica lowered to a crouch and launched her fist forward.

This time Maxima was better prepared, spinning out of the way, only getting an off swipe of Danica's palm, which still sent rivulets of pain up her shoulder and down her lower back.

Danica came to rest behind Maxima.

Maxima quickly rectified the situation by turning to come face to face with Danica again.

"The kick was for stabbing me. The punch was for throwing me over the side of a cliff. The rest..." Danica was smiling. "The rest will be because I can."

In those seconds, Maxima drew out her combat knife, still stained with Danica's semi-drying blood, streaks following the blade as she pulled it free from her sheath. "We'll see just how fast you heal a second time then."

Danica spun and leveled another spinning back kick which hit Maxima mid-chest. She was focusing on using her legs this time to strike instead of the close quarters fistfight she had made the mistake of engaging in before. Never bring your hands to a knife fight.

Maxima fell back a few steps, taking the brunt of the blow, letting out a huge grunt as the foot impacted.

Danica pushed herself back and resumed her position.

The immovable object that is Maxima up against the unyielding force that is Danica.

Maxima turned and backed up, giving Danica less room to move, which she needed to deliver her energetic leg strikes.

Unlike the last time, Danica knew now that she needed lots of space to maneuver, to increase the momentum of her blows if she was to win.

Maxima stood back, gesturing Danica forward.

Danica turned and raced down the corridor, back into the main chamber to get more room. She froze in mid stride as she found her path blocked by the huge two sons still looking over the cubbies for a small *Horror* to capture.

They both turned, smiling and pumping their fists at Danica's arrival.

Maxima raced in from behind, coming to a halt when she realized her boys had Danica cornered. She smiled. "Welcome to my web said the spider to the fly."

Both boys chuckled, moving toward the surrounded Danica, each drawing their combat blades, licking their lips in tandem like lizards lapping for an insect, forming a triangular formation, blocking all of Danica's means of egress.

Danica suspected that unlike Carlos, she only received one dose of venom, thus though she may heal for a short while, the effect would not be long term. That and as the Elder had made clear, *'If the blood stops pumping, so stops the life.'*

Maxima signaled to her two boys to hold their positions.

Max and Maxwell did, each waiting for their opportunity.

Maxima stalked forward with a grin which vanished as she stopped in her tracks.

Danica was standing steadfast, legs apart and in those seconds had drawn from behind the back of her shirt, inside her waistband and out of sight, an 1805 Harper Ferry Flintlock pistol. Within those same seconds, Danica pulled back and cocked the trigger with the barrel locked on Maxima's forehead.

"Where the Hell did you get that antique?" Maxima asked, more surprised than frightened, genuinely impressed at Danica's resourcefulness.

Danica replied. "I pulled it from Rios' corpse. After I climbed back up from where you threw me, I snuck back here and retrieved it. Took me a while to ensure I avoided *Fric* and *Frac* here…"

Max and Maxwell growled at Hayden's nickname for them.

"Amazingly enough, it had not been fired." Danica had her finger inside and under the trigger guard.

Maxima laughed. "Do you honestly believe that weapon will still work after all these years?"

"The devil is in the details Maxima." Danica mocked. "You obviously didn't read the Serenade's logbook in its entirety." Without taking the barrel off Maxima, Danica rolled it enough for them all to see the holes lightly layered with an unbroken seal. "Rios put a dab of paraffin on the muzzle and the firing pin of his weapon to keep the elements away." Danica remained focused. "And as I showed you, it's still intact. So I'm willing to gamble it will fire. Are you?"

At this Maxima's smile waivered and leveled out.

Danica grinned.

Maxima raised her left hand, letting the long silvery blade she held reflect the light of Danica's eyepieces around the cave. "Go ahead. Pull the trigger. You have one shot at best, and whoever you get, you have two left to contend with. If it's me you shoot, I'm instructing my boys to rape you until you're so torn open, no miracle venom will close the wounds."

Max and Maxwell could be heard snickering behind her.

Danica turned and saw Max rubbing his crotch area with his open hand, his eyes bloodshot and glittering with hope in his face, sporting an equally vicious erection under his pants.

Maxima offered a malevolent smile, hinting to her boys. "Of course Doctor Swift, if you happen to kill one of my boys, I'll personally use my fist to invade your body far deeper than their genitals could ever reach."

Danica found herself a bit shocked at Maxima's crudeness. But then again, she was sleeping with her own twin brother.

Both men offered leering glares and sneers almost hoping if she killed one, the other would get to see their mother do it. It clearly implied the Thorne's idea of entertainment was not the same as Danica's.

Maxima dropped the gauntlet. "So you best make your shot count, because when we're through with you, you'll have wished you used it on yourself."

Danica shivered inside, but holding the gun steady. As long as she had it on locked on Maxima, her finger on the trigger, Max and Maxwell were not prepared to advance and cause the killing of their own mother. But sand was slipping from the hour glass.

Maxima signaled and the three Thornes each took a step forward, readying their assault.

For a long moment, Danica wished Hayden was there. Besides evening the odds, his presence made her feel genuinely better, even safer. At least when he was not annoying the Hell out of her anyway. Even when they argued it did not feel that it originated out of anger. More out of a core disagreement between comrades, the kind only shared between two connected people. She hated to think she would never see him again. That and imagining these three faces would be the last she was forced to envision was heartwrenching.

Maxima, Max and Maxwell circled around her counter clockwise, the boys licking their lips, Maxima raising her eyebrow and exerting a feral smirk.

Danica for the first time ever felt true fear. Her self-defense was at best, good for one-on-one combat, and not with people of this size working as a team. She hated herself for getting caught in this position and worse, with these three predators having her trapped. All it would take was one wrong move and she would be at their mercy.

Without Hayden and Carlos, she was alone and outnumbered.

She needed to even the odds.

As the three Thornes closed in around her, Danica thought to herself. *'What would Hayden do?'* She let her mind drift, imagining, thinking like an immature, if not intelligent child. *'What would he do right now? Something crazy for certain.'* Then it came to her in a flash. *"Yep. Right up his alley for insane ideas.'*

The Thornes gave one another nonverbal cues of actions to take. They were about to attack.

Danica saw it and closed her eyes for a second, a full second, and prayed. *'God? Allah? Flying Spaghetti Monster? I don't much less care who is listening right now, but if it's one of you, please don't let this be my final stand.'*

Max pointed to Danica's feet for Maxwell to grab them so she could not use them to strike.

But Danica was already in action. She opened her eyes, stepped sideways and with one smooth gesture, thrust her hand down the front of her open shirt and pulled out the tribe's cask from the night before and cracked off the seal with her teeth. Within seconds of that, she dumped the entire contents over her head, face, chest and body, to the quizzical stares of the three assailants. The thick oily goop, slightly warm, oozed down her body and into the openings of her clothes, skin and hair.

Maxima grimaced and pulled away, covering her face as the retched odour overwhelmed her nostrils.

Max and Maxwell looked at Danica like she was insane.

Maxima cackled as she held her nostrils tightly closed. "My God, did you plan to stink us to death in here? I think my boys can hold their noses long enough to finish with you, regardless of how fucking vile that stuff is."

But Danica was not listening. She was in the moment. She was riding the wave of no return to its ultimate destination. Upon tossing the empty cask to the ground, she raised the Flintlock skyward and pulled the trigger.

The explosion sounded like a thunderbolt unleashed, like the skies had opened up and Zeus was yelling down for attention, rocking the entire chamber.

After several seconds, the two sons cleared their ears of the ringing. They laughed as they prowled closer, ready to start raping their prize.

Maxima shook her head as the echo vanished. "You stupid bitch! You wasted your shot!"

Danica tossed the Flintlock, now spent, to the ground. She lowered her gaze, locked on Maxima's face and grinned maliciously, a look so cold, so malevolent, Maxima was momentarily frozen for words. "No." Danica replied with superiority in her tone. "I didn't…. BITCH!"

As Maxima and her sons were about to pounce, they suddenly heard it.

Groans, hisses, scratching, clicking, grunting, scurrying hair covered appendages on dozens of rock walls and caverns.

Hundreds of giant spiders awakening, moving and coming forth from their peaceful holes.

Maxima and sons stared up and outward, their lights sending beams in every direction, illuminating large portions of the cave.

The walls themselves looked like they were breathing, undulating with motion with all the moving forms.

Crowds of slumbering *Horror*, followed by the skittering feet and claws, coming forth along rocks, cracks and ledges, fast and furious, sounding like thousands of unintelligible voices.

Low voices.

Whispers.

Danica thought of how Carlos had described it in London. *'My God. Carlos, you poor bastard.'*

Like mankind, this was also a species who did not like being awoken early, especially in such a manner, thus they were extremely pissed.

The *Horror* had awakened.

Only one thought came to Danica's mind.

'If the Horror awaken, all is lost.'

45

Dropping from the cave entrance above, Hayden went limp to allow for an easier impact.

Carlos saw this. In those seconds, he moved underneath and caught Hayden under the shoulders with his forearms, seconds before Hayden hit the beach with the full force of his weight and added kinetic energy, in hopes of slowing the descent.

It was not by much as Carlos was still reeling from the fall he himself took when Maximus threw him from the cliff, combined with the rapidly still sealing wound on the inside of his stomach.

Hayden groaned as he landed, his two feet finding purchase but sending him forward face first in to the dirt, dragging Carlos with him.

They both landed with a solid whump, Carlos on the top and Hayden on the bottom.

After a good minute of them lying on the ground, Hayden blew some dirt out from under his face. "As far as Doctor Swift is concerned, this didn't happen."

"Agreed." And Carlos got back to his feet, brushing himself off.

Carlos' attention was quickly drawn upward as he heard Maximus' wail. He turned to Hayden with confusion.

Hayden looked up from his seated position. "Maximus lost a contact. I recommended he stay up there and look for it. He's probably getting frustrated."

Carlos looked back up and after several long seconds, no more sounds followed.

Hayden rose slowly, stretching his back and lower thighs to clear the burning from his muscles. He took a step forward which almost resulted with him toppling over. He had earned an unexpected limp on his left side. He took a second step on it and moaned, this time with serious pain, biting his lips to suppress it. "I think it's sprained."

Carlos looked down at the throbbing muscle. "I would agree."

"Think if you bite me it would heal?" Hayden asked.

"I'm afraid you need it from the source." Carlos laughed, referring to the *Horror*. "Plus I find biting my friends most distasteful."

Hayden placed his foot firmly on the ground with a tight-faced wince. "Then I guess I'll have to suffer through it. I don't need it healed that badly."

Carlos moved in to let Hayden lean on him.

"You're going to have to take that sword stabbing trick on the road you know." Hayden declared. "I saw a sword swallower once at the circus and I think you have him beat."

Carlos slapped Hayden on the back. "If we survive this, you can sell the tickets."

Hayden's face went ashen as he suddenly thought of the giant eight legged monsters they had left behind, and Danica still in the caves with them. "We need to get back down there and save Danic..." He paused and corrected himself. "Doctor Swift."

"An admirable cause." Carlos interjected. "And one we should get right onto. After we ascertain your injury."

Hayden took a slow but solid step, screwing his face tight and absorbing the angry nerve endings as they ripped at his tendons. He ignored the raging pulses in his muscles knowing, as far as he was concerned, Danica's life was more important than this own.

'Fuck the pain.' Hayden thought. "Wait... I promised. Screw the pain!'

Before they could plan their next move...

BOOM!

Both their heads snapped in the direction of the closest cave entrance as the sound resonated outward.

Hayden turned toward Carlos, his eyes filled with fear. "Was that a gunshot?"

Carlos stood firm, his face filled with bafflement. "I believe it was."

"Danica is still in there." Hayden spoke, panic lacing his voice. He lodged his foot into the ground to race toward the island, no longer worried about his sprain. But before Hayden could run, he felt Carlos' two hands grab his shoulders firmly and pull him back.

"No." Carlos declared. "You won't stand a chance in there if the *Horror* has been awakened."

Hayden glared at the dark island mountain. "But what about Danica?" His voice cracked.

Carlos turned to Hayden with genuine sympathy, but his eyes lighting up. "In all my years, and I've had many, I've never met a woman as capable as our Doctor Swift. And I believe if anyone can get out of there alive in the next few minutes, it would be her."

Hayden turned back to the island and for the first time in a long time, he prayed.

'I hope so.' Hayden thought. *'I mean to ask her on a date.'*

46

In those seconds after the weapon discharged, the smell of gunpowder permeated the air, tickling Maxwell's nose. He hardly noticed with the already thin trace remnants of sulfur from the boiling lake outside.

Both Max and Maxell had looked up and down the walls after the shot, taking less than five seconds, but seeing all they needed to see. Upon dropping their gaze to floor level, they immediately realized Doctor Swift had escaped.

They could not be faulted too much, considering their attention was drawn to more dire concerns, that which was stalking towards them.

It was then they noticed who was also gone, their mother.

Both Max and Maxwell turned to one another and mouthed the words. *'Time to get out of here.'*

But before they could, one of the *Horror* dropped from the ceiling above, either launching itself from the wall or dislodging its limbs from the webbed centre. In the darkness, neither could be sure.

It landed square on Maxwell and sent him face first into the cave floor, the metal brace on his nose taking the brunt of the impact.

Maxwell tried to rise, but the spider's momentum and sheer size, which was equal to that of a Great Dane, kept him effectively pinned.

The spider started shaking and moving in a circular pattern, spinning almost on its own axis, using its legs as push poles to generate its momentum.

Maxwell tried to grab a leg to pull or trip it, but there were seven more to contend with, making his efforts impossible.

He was getting frantic. He tried to roll, but failed as a dozen more spiders were upon him, their weight compressing his chest and forcing the wind from his lungs.

Then he felt it. The biting, stinging and grasping as they worked as a team, keeping him contained. This was followed by the sensation of a warm moist cloth being thrown over his body as he was wrapped in webs.

He looked to his brother, his vision going cloudy with the silk, but like him, Max was already covered by an equal amount of *Horror*, also soaked in moist white threads.

Maxwell tried to scream, only to find his mouth filled with wet fluff, sticky and strong, yet aerated enough to breath. His screams sounded like muffled wails in a wind tunnel.

Maxwell's last thought. *'Who's going to feed Fluffy?'*

47

Maxima was in motion, her legs and arms pumping like a train engine as she barreled forward with one goal.

'To get the Hell out of there.'

Her first thought as she exited the first chamber, looking over her right shoulder as she ran, watching the gigantic brown spiders dropping and pouncing on her two boys from above was not, *'My God, I have to save my sons.'* It was, *'I'm still young. I can have more kids.'*

She had no desire whatsoever to go back into the nest after hearing how Doctor Swift described the spiders kept their prey and seeing the illustrious Captain Rios. She knew she could always come back later with a platoon of reinforcements to save her boys and of course provide them whatever psychiatric counseling they needed.

The bonus was, they would all have a long, long time to recover combined with being stinking rich to top it off.

Maxima turned left at the first rock formation she saw and ducked down, but not fast enough, as her helmet and light scratched the hardened edges of a sharp stalactite.

At that moment, she was envisioning her brutal revenge upon Doctor Swift when she found her, maybe even drowning her in the lake slowly, her screams bubbling away into nothingness.

In those seconds of distraction, Maxima felt her legs taken out from under her. She fell, catching in a sideways glance, Doctor Swift near to the ground, using a forward leg sweep maneuver to send her off her feet.

Maxima dropped, hit the ground, spun, adrenaline pumping and found herself standing, coming face to face with Doctor Swift again. "This is getting tiresome Doctor Swift."

"In that I would agree." Danica glared at her. "The leg sweep, that's for thinking of having me raped."

Maxima smiled with a vicious sneer. "The night's not over yet." She lunged forward.

Danica jumped straight up from the ground, using both her legs for increased power, catching the upper lip of the cave ceiling with her hands, pulling with her arms with all her might, adding speed and power to her motion. Once her feet left the ground, she snapped her right leg up, accelerating upwards like a lightning strike, in a perfectly executed front kick, delivering a devastating blow directly under Maxima's extended chin.

Never in Maxima's life had she been hit so hard. Her whole body lifted a full inch off the ground as her head shot back, taking her shoulders and chest with her, her body following suit as she landed flat on her back with a dust rising smack.

Danica landed, fists at her side, knees bent, taking on a *ready stance*.

Maxima saw stars, sparkles and she was sure, a few bursts of colour. She shook the stars from her vision away and stumbled back to her feet, inhaling deeply to regain her oxygen levels, anger filling her every available pore. She spat a glob of blood to the ground and snarled.

Maxima was about tolunge again when she saw Danica's eyes widen in fear as she peered upward.

Danica turned and in seconds, was gone.

Maxima already sensing it, tried to run, but her last vision before her helmet was knocked from her head were two large furry legs of a massive spider reaching around from both sides, grabbing her around the waist and pulling her up in the crevasses of the cave.

All that Danica heard as she ran were Maxima's bloodcurdling screams.

48

Danica cleared the next vault of caves and continued running.

Suddenly, a giant spider, bigger than a Shetland pony, raced toward Danica from the shadows.

It reared back, four legs on the ground to provide stability, the other four up like a horse bucking, but reaching to grasp her. Its belly moved in and out erratically, acting excited with thin rivulets of webbing spitting out the rear.

Danica, on pure instinct, spun, pivoting all her weight onto her right leg, using her backward spin to build momentum and lashed out with a brutal combination roundhouse side kick, letting her hiking boot hit the dead centre sternum of the spider.

It snapped back and hit the wall with a crunch, unprepared for the brutal strike.

It hissed and was back on its feet in seconds.

The targets Danica was trained to hit in Tae Kwon Do only had two legs. Most didn't have an extra set of legs to land back on, least of all, six to catch their fall, reposition and resume an attack.

The spider lunged forward, grasping for her with its body arced back, its upper two legs moving back and forth, its *chelicera* fangs rising up and down.

Danica dropped to use another kick as her legs had the most strength against these things.

But before the spider could snag her, it instead got a face full of the tribe's fluid stench.

Spiders absorb smells with scent detecting hairs located on their legs, feeling their prey and confirming if it is consumable.

Whatever this scent was, it did not like it.

It screeched, it's body twisting away in disgust, dropping to all eight legs and running away down a dark corridor.

Danica did not need another signal.

She had no idea how long this deterrent would last.

She bolted again, thinking. *'When I see the tribal Elder, I owe him a big kiss.'*

She was not tired in the least, amazed at how energized she felt.

Shivering in her mind, knowing its source.

49

Hayden and Carlos stood on the beach, staring at the caves, hoping and counting the seconds, each one dragging on like an individual eternity, unsure of what to do, relying on Danica's skill, knowledge and luck to get out of there.

Carlos had removed the shotgun from Maximus' duffle bag and cocked the barrel.

Hayden kept thinking to himself. *'If I only solved those clues faster. If I had only done something in the caves. If only....'*

Hayden knew he had to stop blaming himself, but it was hard. Instead, he focused on revenge. *'If I've lost her... By God I'll come back here with a nuclear device and turn this accursed island into Chernobyl.'*

Hayden looked to his watch and spoke to Carlos. "I'll give her two more minutes and then I'm going in after her."

"After two minutes, I'm coming with you Doctor Lattimer." Carlos replied, handing Hayden back his weapon, safety turned to off. Then he added. "But she's coming. I can feel it."

Hayden looked to the island with desperation. *'Please be right Carlos. Please.'*

50

Danica ran hard, her muscles fueled by adrenaline and powered by fear, weaving in and around corridors, knowing from memory she was nearing the final exit. She could hear another *Horror* scurrying behind her, still a good ways back, far down in the tunnels, but it was closing fast.

Its multiple legs racing, its claws finding purchase in the cracks and rivets of rock as it tore along the walls, using the sides for momentum knowing a possible dinner was escaping.

Danica pivoted around the last corner and skidded to a stop.

Directly before her was another giant spider, bigger than the rest she had seen thus far, having a leg span of at least ten feet. It was poised, legs spread, not having noticed her yet, spinning in a circle in search of prey.

One coming from behind and one in the front.

A terrible game of monkey in the middle if she ever imagined.

The one in front turned, spotting her now. It seemed to know it was blocking Danica's last exit from the cursed island cave system. It hissed and rose up with two legs extended forward, its jaws moving open and closed in a vicious manner.

Danica did the only thing she could think of. She turned her head with a quick flick, her hair spinning with a hard twist, the still moist tribal oil laced ends snapping. A thick wet globule of the oil splashed forward and with a light wet slapping sound, splattered directly into the spider's *pedipalp* feelers.

The spider instantly freaked. Its highly sensitive sense of smell now overwhelmed by the vile fluid. It started to shudder violently, slamming its body into the ground over and over, up and down, vibrating its entire exoskeleton like it had suddenly been hit with a stun gun. Legs twitched and fluttered, all the while, trying to get out of the cave to find some means to clear it off. But due to its massive size and upset state, the small creviced area prevented it from escaping. It dropped to the ground and started scraping the source of the horrific smell off its skin with its front two appendages, the entire time, quivering uncontrollably.

Danica, not being a veterinarian, had no idea if this was some sort of spider epileptic seizure as a result of the oil, but then again, she did not really care.

The spider was doing something other than coming for her and that was all the mattered.

Danica turned as she heard the second spider closing in from behind.

'God help me.' She thought one last time. *'And fuck their urticating hairs hairs.'*

She raced forward, using her left leg like a thrusting board, launching herself forward directly at the spider. She rolled and tucked her body in a frontal direction, spinning and turning almost in midair, doing something she had not done since kindergarten, somersaulting in a frontward motion, head over heels across the top of the giant spider's open *Cephalothorax* centre body, to which all the legs are attached. Her head and back coasted over the bubble shaped abdomen at the rear of the beast until she landed on her both feet with double planted perfection, wishing she had a video camera for what she had just accomplished.

In one final gesture, she rocked forward and lashed out with a powerful reverse back kick directly into the web spinnerets at the back core of the monster's abdomen, sending the beast face first and into the path of the second chasing spider, slamming them into one another.

Within seconds, both squealed in fury and started fighting for dominance, the one trying to get past, the other in even more hysterics to get the new selection of vile fluid now running from head to tail when Danica rolled over it as a gymnastics mat, off its skin and body.

No longer interested in her, the two giant spiders engaged in battle in the darkness of the cave.

Not that Danica turned to look.

She was long gone, out the entrance and onto the beach.

Her feet pounding, her fists pumping, racing for the boat.

Running for dear life.

Praying Hayden and Carlos were all right.

Thinking again, *'If we awaken them, all is lost.*

51

Hayden saw it in the distance.

A glow emanated from deep in the cave edifice, a soft white puff of energy which blossomed from the darkness. This was followed by two bright beams firing forth from the opening, dancing frantically from the mouth of the cave, jumping up and down like a jeep gone off-roading.

A second later, Danica dived out of the opening, running toward them.

Hayden's eyes lit up and for the first time in a long time, he was truly excited. For a moment, his breath hesitated in his lungs, almost causing him to gasp. He turned to Carlos and nearly shouted, *'You brilliant predicting bastard you.'* But it came out. "She's alive!"

Carlos smiled from ear to ear, not doubting Doctor Swift for a minute.

Well, maybe thirty seconds.

As Danica approached, Hayden wanted to scoop her up and carry her in his arms to safety, until he saw the giant blood stain on her shirt at the base of her stomach. His heart sank with a thud and he almost ran to her, but he quickly realized, based on her pace, fiery and furious, she would reach him first.

From his immediate observation, combined with her speed and perseverance, the gore on her clothes must have been from someone else.

'Hopefully Fric or Frac,' Hayden thought.

Danica raced on, her arms pumping back and forth like she was an oncoming locomotive. In seconds, she reached them, looked at them and continued running, the gust as she passed causing Hayden's hair to bristle. As she blazed between them, she screamed one word. "RUN!"

Hayden and Carlos both turned back in the direction of the dark mountain, their double beams illuminating the massive island peak above and they saw it.

It looked like black lava flows bubbling up and pouring out of hundreds of openings, flowing forth like a river of dark mud.

Except it was not steaming hot magma oozing down towards them but thousands of the *Horror*, legs moving in tandem, attached to giant tarantulas and coming fast.

Hayden did not even have time to swear as he turned and ran for the boats. *'No need to translate this!'*

Carlos was right on his tail.

The trio blazed down the beach.

As they neared the water, Danica leapt first, up and over the boat's stern, hitting the pointed front end with a small dip and a splash, sliding the boat toward the water like a surfboard on sand.

Hayden followed suit, thrusting his body like a football tackler, catching the oar of the boat, which had been upended at the back and he shoved with all his might, the water welcoming the mighty boat as Hayden dropped in the middle.

Carlos, last but not least, catching his foot on the rear end with both a push and a jump, threw the rest of the boat forward, his body landing at the base as they coasted inches away from the beach's edge.

Within seconds, Carlos had the second oar and was ready to paddle.

The trio ignored the second boat adjacent to theirs, barely inches away, half in and half out of the water, filled with bladed tools, steel cables and large metal canisters with scoops, likely for the Fountain of Youth waters the Thornes had expected to find and carry with them, totally unaware at the time of the terrible truth.

Before they could all breathe a sigh of relief, the trio heard it.

A primal blood wrenching scream of untold fury, curdling the nerves and chilling the flesh.

Hayden turned back and scowled in the direction it originated from. "Now there's something you don't see every day."

Carlos and Danica followed Hayden's gaze.

Maximus was charging down the beach toward them like a champion bull, rage in his eyes, his face covered in blue spider blood, his hair slicked back with it and slightly askew, his shirt and pants torn and shredded in areas. He was obviously infused with spider's venom as he must have manhandled the Sentinel into submission.

Hayden yelled in Maximus' direction. "Sorry Maximus. The next ferry is scheduled for later tonight. Hope you brought a magazine."

Maximus growled with a beast-like fury, his mouth filled with spittle as he yelled something unintelligible, too far to be heard clearly.

Hayden turned to Danica. "I'm not well versed in that language, but I would suspect based on his tone and body positioning, he's not happy about something. Did you say something to offend him perchance?"

Danica almost laughed, had it not seemed so horrible to do so.

Maximus was running, pointing, screaming, waving the blue blood covered cutlass in the air like a fiery torch at the Olympics, white webbing still encasing his fists. "I told you that you'd better pray I died. Now I'll kill you all with my bare hands!"

Hayden put the first oar into the water and pushed further away from the beach, the bubbling water slowing the thrust.

"I'll watch your bleeding corpses tear apart in my hands!" Maximus bellowed again, maintaining his ruthless tirade in his mad rush towards them; totally oblivious to the danger fast approaching from the rear.

"Not a very hospitable fellow if you ask me." Hayden commented as he turned to Carlos. "I think he never found that contact."

Carlos shook his head with a bit of a smirk.

Danica was amazed Hayden could joke at a time like this.

Maximus was almost within one hundred metres of them when with one final gesture; Carlos drew his shotgun from behind his back and aimed it at the charging Maximus.

Maximus offered a malignant grin, like a boogeyman reaching into a child's bedroom at night to terrorize and pull them from their beds in tears, appearing to invite the shot. "Shoot you spineless coward." He screamed, bits of blood flecking from his lips. "Fucking shoot. I bet I'll heal and still be able to rip each of your legs off like I did that fucking spider."

Carlos winked, followed by a curled grin, in a way that even Maximus found confusing, slowing his forward momentum for a brief second.

Carlos dropped his aim and pulled the trigger. The blast shook and echoed through the interior lake cavern like a thunderclap causing ripples in the boiling lake to flutter in circles away from their boat with the sound the explosion.

Maximus froze in his tracks, eyes wide and stunned, watching as the second boat tipped beneath the yellow bubbling waters, now adorned with a giant watermelon sized hole punched through the bottom by Carlos' shotgun.

Carlos quickly slammed his boot down on the front tip of the second boat, sending the other end into the air like a seesaw, the empty metal canisters firing past him like they had been shot out of a catapult, splashing into the bubbling water behind him.

The ones with the open lids quickly filled and sunk beneath the surface, the remainder floating away. Within those few seconds, the second unoccupied boat torpedoed downward into the water and with a burst of steam, vanished beneath the frothy surface.

Carlos glared in Maximus' direction and shouted. "Heal that."

Maximus offered a look of utter hatred, contempt and insanity, all fueled by his fury. "Whoever the Hell you are, do you think a single boat sinking would stop ME!? MAXIMUS THORNE!"

"No!" Carlos replied, returning the smile equally as malicious, all the while nodding his head upward in a way for Maximus to turn around. "I suspect they will."

Maximus spun around and for several seconds, his clenched fists loosened as he saw the onrushing mountain of the ancient *Horror* scurrying toward him, his one hand unable to fully expand with the sword webbed up in it.

Hayden would have paid a million dollars to see the expression on Maximus' face at that second. *'Well, I did pay twenty five thousand to see the back of his head. I guess that's a deal.'*

Maximus turned again and raced for the shore, panic in his eyes, like a gazelle being chased by a lion born from the depths of Hell. He pushed his arms together, preparing to dive in and swim across the boiling waters, hoping his new healing factor would protect him. He almost made it as the first spider ran under his legs, scrambling up his stride and forward momentum.

Maximus dropped like a giant oak tree having had its base severed out from under it by an enthusiastic lumberjack. His legs, chest and face crashed into the ground with a smack, narrowly missing the spider that tripped him.

Within the seconds it took him to look up one last time, he was overwhelmed by an avalanche of fur, fangs and legs. His muffled screams were lost beneath the squeals and hissing of the armada of giant spiders now engulfing the beach.

As the boat pulled away from the island, Danica pivoted her light along the full length of the island shore.

The entire rocky beach was covered in writhing spiders, some the size of collies, some the size of cats, while a few in the background, seemed to be the size of automobiles.

Maybe it was simply the light.

Danica turned away. She had no interest in finding out. It was too awesome and frightening to imagine.

A small spider, young in experience, no bigger than a poodle, lept forward towards their boat, hoping for one bite.

Carlos brought the oar up and slammed it like a tennis ball with the wide end, sending it up and into the water.

The small spider screamed as it sank in the bubbling and burning waters, trails of steam coming out as it vanished beneath the dark surface.

Danica had stepped on spiders before, swatted them with books, but she had never heard one scream.

Its sound was so terrible, she would remember it for a while, as it drowned beneath the milky depths.

The rest of the *Horror* hissed and snapped, more angry than disappointed, but unable to do anything more than remember the trio's faces with millions of eyes.

Carlos dropped down and leaned forward, facing the front of the boat, not looking back.

After several seconds, as the island vanished behind them, Hayden put his hand on Carlos' shoulders, Danica looking on. "Are you okay?"

Carlos replied deadpanned. "Too bad my former institution has closed down"

"Why is that?" Danica asked.

"I think I might need some more therapy." Carlos answered.

It took a few seconds, but then all three of them burst into laughter. Deeply exhausted, adrenaline filled blasts of hilarity.

Still shaken, frightened, but having escaped both the Island of Eternal Night and the *Horror*, the trio had won.

Danica suddenly grabbed Hayden by the scruff of his shirt and pulled him close, kissing him hard.

Hayden's arms went limp. Once he regained his senses, his arms filled with energy and he embraced her.

They kissed for a good minute.

After the boat drifted fifty more metres, Carlos cleared his throat.

Both Danica and Hayden stopped and turned to look at him.

"And what about me?" Carlos asked.

Hayden grinned. "You're rich, handsome and a hundred and eighty seven years old. I'm sure you're way ahead of me on the "Get the Girl" score."

Carlos smiled back. "Touché my friend." And he started to paddle away from the island.

"Score?" Danica noted with annoyance, staring at them both in disgust. "I'm not a notch in a bedpost."

"Of course not." Hayden responded with some surprise. "I would never gouge precious wood in such a way." He held up his Smartphone. "They have an App for that now. I can keep track of all my conquests, load their profiles online and make trading cards out of them to exchange with virtual friends. Technically speaking, they're the actual *score* cards."

Danica put her finger under Hayden's chin, raising it to her hers, locking eyes on him. "If I ever hear of a 'Danica Swift' trading card..."

Hayden cut her off. "Trust me, considering where you just came from and likely what you did to get out, I'd want more than a trading card, I'd demand an action figure."

Carlos burst aloud with amusement.

For several seconds, Danica stared at Hayden. She felt actually complimented and kissed him one more time.

Hayden suddenly scrunched up his nose and pulled away. "Mother of God. You stink." He turned to Carlos who also had his finger under his nose. "You know, when we were in London, I would've gone with you to Duty Free to pick out a scent. Next time, try the tester."

Danica, remembering the giant spiders coming at her full tilt and then watching them turn tail and scurry away after having gotten a good snoot full of the tribe's potent brew, grinned. "Had you been in the cavern with me, you'd think it's the greatest perfume on Earth."

The trio turned back as the darkness had enveloped the island once again, hiding it from the light.

Hayden turned to Danica. "Should we tell someone? The army? Once the Canadian military finds out what monsters live down here, I'm sure they could get international support to come down here and wipe the population of these things out."

Danica stared back forlorn. "The problem is, the South American government and world animal rights group would never support the total eradication of a species, regardless of how horrible they are. And, if one soldier or one world leader found out the life extending properties of the spider's venom, all it would take is discovering a single century old living victim in the caves, then we'd have the same problem, saving the species to give mankind a new lease on life. Even if only one spider escaped, all of mankind would be in a war for its survival." She stared back. "As a human, this is the greatest discovery to ever have been found. As a scientist, it's the most terrible to imagine."

Carlos placed his hand on Danica's forearm. "Though I thank the Lord for my gift of long life, I can tell you, I'd probably have given it all back during those seven days to die."

The trio turned away from the island, still able to hear the loud whispering from the shores, deciding, this island may get discovered one day, but this will not be this day.

As they coasted back to the other side, Danica looked at Hayden. "Do you think there really is a Fountain of Youth out there?"

Hayden shrugged. "Personally, you make me feel younger than any well of water could ever achieve."

Danica smiled. "You know, after having been bitten by one of those spiders, I might outlive you and stay as pretty as I am today."

Hayden offered an offhanded comment. "That's perfect. This way I won't have to dump you later for a younger chick when I reach old age."

Danica punched him hard in the his arm, followed by kissing him again.

Carlos simply laughed.

In the distance, they saw a flickering flame.

As they closed in, standing on the beach, beneath two halogen lights, likely mounted by Maximus and his crew, several feet from the water was the Elder of the tribe with his two warriors from the camp. Like before, one sported the spear while the second looked to be carrying the tree stump, except this time, it was at his feet, the warrior's brow laced with sweat.

Once ashore with the boat, the trio moved forward, brushing themselves off as they approached the Elder and his men.

Hayden quickly whispered. "If any of you have any of the *Horror* with you, now is the time to confess."

This time Danica gave Hayden a shot to the back of the arm, all watched by the amused eyes of the Elder.

Once the trio reached the Elder, they let out a quick breath.

The Elder spoke to Hayden.

Hayden replied, noting to the others he would translate their responses and the Elder's conversation. "He wants to know what became of the other boat."

Carlos answered. "I sunk it."

The Elder nodded. *"We can build more boats."* He then tilted his head and stared at the trio. *"What of the others?"*

Carlos replied matter-of-factly. "They opted to stay behind."

The Elder nodded again, not asking further questions on the matter sensing the trio knew what had befallen their enemies. The Elder turned to them all. *"Have you found what you were looking for?"*

"And then some." Hayden replied.

"And what are your plans with what you've discovered?" The Elder asked.

Carlos answered right away. "Some things were never meant to be found."

At this the Elder smiled widely. *"Then follow me my friends. Before you go, I will see our camp sends you off with a fine meal."*

The trio nodded their thanks.

"I promise no jaguar on the menu tonight." The Elder turned to Danica and winked.

Danica smiled sheepishly, realizing the Elder had known she had not been fond of their menu and that Hayden had cleared her portion off the plate.

The Elder turned away, not letting her remain embarrassed, opening his arms and gesturing for the trio to follow.

Danica then called the Elder's attention.

The Elder turned as Danica moved in towards him with a smile. His face scrunched up as she neared.

The two warriors almost stepped in between them, but the Elder waived them off.

Danica reached forward, leaned in close and kissed the Elder on the cheek gently and delicately. She whispered. "That's for the tribal *Horror* repellent."

The Elder blushed, bright red and muttered. *"What about your husband?"* Turning to a now smiling Hayden.

Danica frowned.

"I told you they married us didn't I?" Hayden chuckled.

"You inform them that at tonight's dinner, I expect the dancers to come back and reverse that little dance of theirs into a divorce ceremony." Danica replied.

Hayden laughed. "I'll do no such thing. Plus in this culture, that decision is up to the husband."

Seconds later, Hayden found himself flat on his back, unable to prevent Danica's quickly moving low leg sweep from sending him into the dirt.

Even the Elder and the warriors were staring at her in impressed astonishment.

Danica smiled down at him. "Just so you know, becoming a widow and getting a divorce is the same to me."

Hayden quickly rose, brushing grime from his clothes.

Carlos slapped Hayden on the shoulder. "Hey. It was a good marriage while it lasted."

Hayden glared him. "Speak for yourself. First, I can think of better islands to spend a honeymoon. Second and more importantly, I didn't get *any*…" Clearly denoting what *'any'* was referring to.

Danica looked over her shoulder as she walked behind the Elder. "No divorce and it will stay that way."

Hayden caught the insinuation in that statement and snapped back with authority. "One divorce coming our way honey."

Carlos bellowed a deep laugh, and in doing so, spotted a small crate on the ground in front of the water. He almost missed it.

Atop it, the logbook of the Leviathan, his journal and the eight pages folded neatly.

While the others all waited, Carlos casually walked over to it and with one push, tipped it over, sending everything into the lake, sinking forever out of sight. "This island will be discovered one day, but it will not be my past that will lead the way."

Hayden applauded, followed by

Danica.

Hayden then called to the Elder.

The Elder turned, the warriors peering around him, both Danica and Carlos looking at Hayden curiously.

Hayden asked. "Wait a good God darn minute. You had no idea if we'd survive or not. Least of all if we'd be coming back. Or if we would have still tried to take the *Horror* off with us. What were you planning to celebrate had this not all happened?"

"Your funeral of course." The Elder smiled. *"And had you taken the Horror off with you, you'd have been on the menu."* He smiled, turned and resumed his course.

Hayden was cut silent.

At that, the trio, the Elder, and even the two warriors laughed as they vanished through the exit of the cave, heading to the surface, leaving the island to remain as it had been for a very long time...

LOST.

Epilogue

An indeterminate number of years later...

The Island of Eternal Night remains just that, shrouded in darkness, and lost.

Deep within the depths in the main cavern hang two figures from thin filaments of web, dangling upside down, but angled to prevent flooding the brain with blood and drowning the body, were Maximus and Maxima.

Below them, a few feet down on a ledge, were the webbed forms of two more, Max and Maxwell, also encased in webbing. One with his hands trussed up behind his back like a Christmas turkey.

Maximus and Maxima were facing one another, their eyes locked, but all sense of their humanity lost. Their minds, their souls and their sanity vanishing years ago in the daily stabs, pricks and fangs puncturing, drinking, absorbing, feeding, nourishing, healing and leaving them to restore for a later meal.

The air was dry and the hibernation period was ending again this year.

Even without their sanity, they could hear the waking beasts, the creeping legs, the furry appendages moving and the claws scratching.

Followed by the rise of thousands of *whispers.*

It was instinctual, they started to scream.

Loud and empty, shrill and horrifying, yet worst of all, penetrating.

Echoing down the other caves and crevices where those hoping to sleep late this period are forced awake.

And not happy about it.

OTHER TITLES WRITTEN BY DAVID CHARLES FILAX

THE NEFARIOUS MR. X

A once famous actor, brain damaged by a horrible accident, using his once famous skills of deception, mimicry and illusion to enter into innocent lives, commit crimes in their names and vanish. Until one detective finds one frame too perfect and in his investigation, draws this elusive nemesis from the shadows, who can become anyone he wants to, making the detective suspect everyone around him. And in one final play, the detective baits the enemy out, in hopes of ending his reign of destruction and prove to the world, there really is a Mr. X.

450

Copyright © 2012 by David Charles Filax
Website: www.davidfilax.com
All rights reserved.
ISBN: 1477559671
ISBN-13: 978-1477559673
Cover Photography by www.808photography.ca

Made in the USA
Charleston, SC
02 November 2016